STORMS

STORMS

MARIA FERNANDEZ SNITZER

Author Reputation Press ®
Creativity & Branding

Author Reputation Press LLC
45 Dan Road Suite 5
Canton MA 02021
www.authorreputationpress.com
Hotline: 1(888) 821-0229
Fax: 1(508) 545-7580

Ordering Information:
Quantity sales. Special discounts are available on quantity purchases by corporations, associations, and others. For details, contact the publisher at the address above.

Printed in the United States of America.

ISBN-13:   Softcover   979-8-88514-826-9
            eBook   979-8-88514-827-6
            Hardcover   979-8-88514-859-7

Library of Congress Control Number: 2022905036

CONTENTS

FOR JEFF

In every human life, there is a storm,

by which time is measured...

A storm through which the past is

reexamined, and the future unfolds.

M. F. S.

WEDNESDAY

Elise sat on the back steps with her grandmother LaLa and watched the elderly lady peel potatoes, which would soon be added to the big pot of soup, already simmering on the stove. The aroma of the rich broth flowed through the screen door, mixed in with the heavy, humid air, and was soon overtaken by smells from the packing sheds and the wharves.

LaLa was fixing what she called her "ice box" soup. That meant she was cleaning out her refrigerator and putting just about everything she found into the soup pot. LaLa never did get used to saying "refrigerator" instead of "ice box." She would laugh and say that she was too old for all of those newfangled words. Anyway, just about everyone was cleaning out refrigerators and freezers. There was no doubt that the electricity would be shut off even if the storm didn't hit Bayou Chouteau directly. So rather than lose all of the food or come home to the rancid odors of fermented and rotten meat, seafood, and vegetables, they cooked everything.

Some of the prepared food and baked goods ended up with the families in hurricane shelters, a friend's or relative's home, or a hotel—wherever their evacuation plan would take them. The rest of the food would be eaten during the day or two before evacuating—somewhat of a pre-disaster feast. Friends and relatives got together for dinners and suppers to make plans, compare preparation strategies, and oftentimes bemoan the fact that out of the very sea that nourished and nurtured their bodies and souls could come the ruin of their homes, businesses, and livelihoods.

The storm would begin as a mere wave in the eastern Atlantic, near shores that their eyes would never behold. Along its westward course, it would slowly grow into a monstrous predator, slipping through narrow passages into the Gulf of Mexico. There the warm, tropical waters would become its adrenaline, giving it more strength, more power, and more vengeance before striking its prey somewhere along the Gulf Coast. Where? When? Those were questions that would only be answered when the monster decided to strike.

The minutes, hours, and days of watching and waiting brought the grown-ups of Bayou Chouteau together in a cohesive group, concentrating and focusing on a common concern. This created a certain freedom for the children, who also were brought together in their own cohesive group, concentrating instead on taking advantage of their days off from school. Elise had noticed that LaLa handled the anxiety of watching and waiting very differently than her parents. She was more relaxed. While doing her part, LaLa seemed to watch the others move restlessly from place to place, their eyes glued to the television so as not to miss a second of any recent updates. And as she watched, her expressions and movements seemed to suggest an omniscient air about her. It was as though she were watching a horror movie with a roomful of people who jumped and shrieked at every scene, but she already knew the script. She knew what to expect. She knew that she couldn't change the script either—so she just sat and watched each scene play out, unmoved, unshaken. Her reticent manner and her silent reserve were calming reminders to Elise that, in the end, after the storm, everything would be all right. After all, LaLa had survived many storms in her long life.

As Elise watched the wrinkled fingers of her grandmother diligently shear the last potato of its last strip of peel, her eyes were drawn to the sky by the plaintive calling of a flock of seagulls, circling above the packing sheds. LaLa, too, looked up in their direction.

"Um, hmm. There they are," LaLa said. "That storm is two days away at the most."

"How can you tell?" Elise asked. The weather seemed so still and calm.

"They came to tell us—to warn us."

"Who? Who are you talking about?"

"Stormbirds. See those gulls up there with the black rings around their necks? My daddy called them stormbirds—Mother Nature's messengers. They live way out in the open sea, but when their territory is invaded by the high winds and rains of a hurricane, they are driven inland. That's when we knew to get ready. Pack up and batten down the hatches."

"Didn't you know before that? Didn't the weathermen let you know?"

"Oh no, child," she laughed, but not in the patronizing way that adults sometimes do when children say things that are not meant to be funny. LaLa never did this to Elise. She explained, "We didn't have television when I was a child. No weathermen with radars or airplanes flying into the eyes of storms. Just Mother Nature. Just them stormbirds. That's all we needed. That's all I need now, too. Why, I see everybody rushin' to the TV sets, waitin' for the reports on the storm—for what? Nobody can predict where those storms are gonna land."

"Mama says that's why they name them after ladies—'cause they are fickle. That means they can change their minds as many times as they want to."

"Hmph." LaLa gave that little defiant breath that inevitably preceded a profound, disagreeable statement. "I've heard all that nonsense. But don't believe a word of it, ya hear. Why they say women are fickle, I don't know. It's the menfolk who are fickle. All the women I know are too busy to be fickle. Start working when they put their feet on the floor in the morning and don't stop till they pick 'em up and put 'em back in bed at night. Who has time to be fickle, I ask you?"

"Well then, why do you think they name hurricanes after ladies, LaLa?" Elise trusted her grandmother's ideas more than any other's.

"You know, Lissy, I'm not quite sure," she answered to Elise's dismay. But then she added, as though she were thinking out loud, talking into space, as if Elise weren't there, "My daddy told me once that the old people used to name them after the saint's day that the storm hit shore on. Somehow, I can't imagine that though, naming something so bad after a blessed soul in heaven—unless, of course, they thought that by doing that, the saint may pray extra hard to the Lord for his mercy." LaLa proclaimed herself to be a devout Catholic even though she never went to mass. She hated the priests, she said, because they got all the glory while the poor nuns did all the important work and didn't get any credit. She still gave money to St. Michael's, though, and kept her faith in God and "all the angels and saints" until the day she died. She went on pondering Elise's question. "We never gave the storms names," she said. "Just called them by the year they hit. Like 'the 1918 storm.' That was a bad one." Elise saw LaLa take a deep breath, close her eyes, and briefly lift her head toward the sky as she said this. Then, as if waking to the present moment, she continued to explain, "To tell you the truth, Lissy, I'm not sure when they started giving storms ladies' names. I think it was in the '50s. As a matter of fact, it might have been the year you were born, 'cause your mama loved the name Frances. She had said that if she had a baby girl, she would name her Frances and call her Franny. But Hurricane Frances hit in September of that year and flooded the whole area. By December, when you were born, we had just gotten things back to normal, and your mama said that she didn't have the heart to give you that name. So, she name you Elise, instead. Pretty name, but I sort of wish she'd named you Frances. Shoot, I wouldn't mind being named after someone so forceful and powerful with a mind of her own. A lotta good can come from qualities like that."

Elise felt something drop inside of her. She had to agree with LaLa. She knew that she could never be forceful or powerful. It just wasn't in her. But maybe, she thought, she could work on the "mind of her own" part. She looked up at LaLa inconspicuously so that the old woman wouldn't feel her stare and break the silence of the moment—a moment that she wanted to suck into her body and keep with her forever. At nine years old, she knew that LaLa would not live forever, in fact would not be with her much longer. She had heard her parents talking about LaLa's "condition" when they didn't think she was listening. She felt her eyes swelling and knew that she was only seconds away from crying, so she struggled to get words out in order to start the conversation again.

"LaLa, how'd you get to be so smart? You always know the answers to my questions." The old worn face that revealed to Elise all of the wisdom and love that God had created, looked upon the young, adoring face, and Elise saw that she, too, was holding back tears. She saw her grandmother's lips tighten a bit as she struggled to both respond to the question and hide the barely controllable emotions that Elise's precious innocence had touched.

"I'm an old lady, Lissy. I've been in this world a long time— too long, I think. And through all those years, I've listened and paid attention to everything that was said and went on around me. And over those years, I learned to sort out the nonsense from the truth. I know that when you're an old lady like me, you'll be just as smart as you think I am. Just remember to be patient—always be patient. You're not going to learn everything by the time you're a teenager—although you will think that you have. You won't even learn everything when you're your mama's age. Let it happen in its time. I only hope that when you're an old lady like me, you have someone special to share all those wonderful things you'll learn about, someone who cares what an old lady has to say—just like I have you, my angel."

LaLa put her colander of peeled potatoes on the step below them and wrapped her thin, frail arms around Elise. In a silence that bespoke all the love, joy, fears, and sorrow that filled their hearts, they let their tears flow freely—with no need for explanations. With their bodies held so closely that their hearts seemed to touch, Elise felt a quiver pass through her body, some sort of inexplicable current of energy, something one might call spiritual. It comforted her. It gave her peace. She knew then that LaLa's spirit would be with her forever.

Then, suddenly, everything around Elise turned to complete darkness. She saw nothing; she felt nothing. She was only aware of her own existence, her own sense of being, surrounded by what seemed to be a vast, black, empty space. And she was alone. It was the only thing she was sure of—she was totally alone. The first sound she heard was the sound of her own breathing, becoming quicker and shallower as her desperation grew. And then the strange, breathy voices, resonating whispers, were coming from all directions. "Delilah Charleville is dead; Delilah Charleville is dead…" And then she thought she heard her mother's voice. Yes, she was sure it was her mother's voice, "Your grandmother died, Elise."

"No! No, she's not dead, I was just talking to her. She was right here, right beside me," and though she reached out into the darkness to feel the old woman's body, she felt nothing. Just empty space. "She can't be dead, she…" The strangers' voices were whispering again, and she began to feel their voices touching her skin, but, when she passed her hands up and down her arms, she felt nothing but her own prickly skin. They repeated, this time more loudly, "Delilah Charleville is dead."

"Who's saying that? Who are you? Where's my grandmother? Where's LaLa?" There were groups of voices now, mocking her growing fear with a variety of exclamations. "She's dead. Poor Elise, poor, poor Elise! Delilah Charleville is dead." Painful words attacking her from all directions, pounding inside her brain with the same rhythmic throbbing of her breaking heart. "Stop it! Stop saying those horrible things. Just stop it! LaLa! LaLa!" Her arms, once again were stretched out, reaching out, into the empty space, only to find the nothingness that continued to surround her.

Then her mother's voice returned, and, although her voice was comforting in the presence of all of the cruel, invisible strangers, it brought little relief from their tormenting message. "I know you're upset, honey, but everything will be OK." Elise shrieked, hoping her voice would reach her grandmother, wherever she was out there in the darkness. "LaLa! LaLa!" But the only response she got from her attempt was laughter from the hideous strangers' voices. The laughter grew and grew, as though more and more voices were arriving and surrounding her. And then the thickness of the voices and the darkness began to close in on her, ever so slowly, steadily, and methodically, smothering her, to where she felt her life flowing from her. She had to breathe…she just had to breathe…

Elise awakened with a start and sat up quickly, gasping for air. "It was so real," she mumbled, awakening her husband who reached out to pull her closer. Her skin still felt prickly, as though each nerve ending in her body were screaming for attention, and she felt pins and needles everywhere Brad's body was touching hers.

"What's wrong, Lissy? Had a bad dream?"

Tears were streaming down her face, and she was glad they were in the darkness of their bedroom. "Yeah," she answered, her voice quivering. "It was that same dream. You know, the one about LaLa."

"Mmmm. You must be worried about something. Come here. I'll rub your back, and you just try to get some sleep."

"That sounds nice, but I don't think I can get back to sleep very easily now. All I'll do is toss and turn and keep you awake, and you have to get up early in the morning. I think I'll go downstairs and fix a cup of warm milk. That always relaxes the restless soul." As she kissed him lightly on the forehead, she heard the steady, slightly heavier breathing that was a sure sign he had already drifted back to sleep. "Good thing I opted for the warm milk, instead of the back rub," she thought, with her spirits lifted by his good intentions.

She slipped her arms through the big, baggy sleeves of her terry cloth robe, which felt especially cozy as she tightened the belt snuggly around her waist for an added sense of security. Walking in her thick winter socks, which were an absolute necessity for her slumber, she tiptoed down the hall, pausing in the doorway of each child's bedroom.

Lilah's room was first. Delilah Charleville Steiner was Elise and Brad's firstborn and only daughter. Next in line was Joseph Paul, better known as J. P., and then Casey, whose given name was William Bradley Steiner. On the day that Elise found out she was pregnant with her third child, she had informed Brad by telling him that their caboose was on the way. When the doctor surmised from an ultrasound that the caboose was a boy, Brad started referring to the baby as Casey Jr., after the fictitious train engineer, he had read about as a child. The name caught on, and after months of referring to the unborn child as Casey, it was difficult to call him by any other name after he entered the world. So, Casey it was.

The children were all sleeping soundly, snug in their beds. In spite of the possibility of waking up the sleeping tigers, Elise went in each room and gave each child a kiss and a blessing on the forehead. It was a little family tradition to trace a cross on their foreheads each night, giving a little blessing and asking the angels to keep good thoughts in their heads and guard against nightmares. But at this particular time and at this hour of the night, the kisses and blessings were more for Elise's state of mind. It always amazed her and touched her heart to see her three bundles of energy, lying so still, so peaceful, as though they were resting in the tender caresses of the angels who were watching over them.

She left their rooms and quietly made her way down the kitchen stairs. Once she arrived in the kitchen, her "sacred space," she felt sure that she could move about freely without waking anyone upstairs. She took a deep breath, as if exhaling would rid her body of the tension left behind from her nightmare, and fixed herself a cup of hot, steaming milk. She sprinkled it with a tiny bit of sugar and nutmeg, just like LaLa used to do. Then she walked into the family room and plopped down on the fluffy, overstuffed chair that she claimed as her own. It was the only seat in the room that didn't face the large-screen TV that unfortunately seemed to be the glue that held her clan together most evenings. She hated the television, but if she wanted to be with her family, she had to find a compromising corner. On such a sleepless night, though, a little television might help to relax her, so she turned her comfy chair around to face the big, black obnoxious screen. She pulled her old quilt down over her bent legs and sipped her hot milk. She wasn't sure if she wanted to go back to sleep, because she couldn't bear the dream again.

Brad was right. She was worried about something. Earlier that evening, the ten o'clock news was blaring while she busied herself making sure the two boys were tucked in, kissed, blessed, and asleep. Lilah, her habitual procrastinator, was still awake finishing her mountain of homework when Elise heard her daughter shout from the kitchen. "Look, Mom, it's Key West. That's the restaurant we ate in that night Casey got sick from the conch chowder and threw up. Remember?"

"It sure is. Nice place, bad soup, huh Sweetie?" They both laughed. The family had spent Easter break in Key West just months before. It had been a great trip, and the whole gang had loved the place in spite of Casey's delicate stomach.

"Everyone is leaving the Keys because of a hurricane. I'll bet it takes forever for all those people to leave on that little road. Don't you think, Mom?"

"Yes, I do, because it took us at least four-and-a-half hours to drive there from Miami on a beautiful Friday afternoon. Of course, the drive wouldn't have seemed half as long if the car rental company had rented us the minivan we requested, instead of a Chevy Cavalier we had to settle for."

The highway that had led the Steiners to their tropical vacation and was now leading Key residents and tourists to safety had been constructed on the remains of the railroad track that had been built in the early 1900s by Henry Flagler. He was the entrepreneur who turned the Florida swampland into a vacation paradise. His railway connected the chain of tiny islands with the mainland and allowed passengers to board a train in New York and travel to the southernmost point of the United States—Key West, Florida. The famous train and its track were destroyed in the 1935 hurricane that swept across the Matecumbe Key in Islamorada, leaving hundreds of unsuspecting and ill- prepared people dead and even more injured and homeless. Elise remembered seeing the statue erected in Islamorada in memory of those who lost their lives and livelihoods in that devastating hurricane. The storm struck the tiny landmass at night, and she shuddered to think what it was like for those passengers on Flagler's train when they saw the wall of water—the enormous storm surge heading for their vulnerable steel coaches, riding on the bridge of tracks that ran about 30 feet above ground level. The terror of that night was beyond Elise's comprehension, and she tried to clear her mind of these thoughts by concentrating on Lilah's detailed version of her swim with the dolphins in Key West.

At that point, however, the reporter, standing in the drizzling rain in Key West, turned the broadcast over to a colleague reporting from the devastation in the Dominican Republic. Like the people of Islamorada, residents of the Dominican Republic had been taken by surprise by the wrath of Hurricane Georgette. Weather bulletins had predicted that Georgette would pass through the less inhabited areas of the island. Residents of Santo Domingo and other northern regions had gone to bed that night assured that they were going to be spared. But in the middle of the night their whole world was ripped apart by 150 mph winds, tornadoes, and flash floods. Hundreds of people died, hundreds were missing, and most were homeless. Just like 1935, Elise thought.

It was no wonder, Elise thought, that watching the ten o'clock newscast, just before going to bed, had stirred memories in her subconscious. LaLa always appeared in her dreams when she was troubled, and it used to be that the dreams would soothe and comfort her. But in the last few years, the dreams began to change. They would begin in the same manner, with her grandmother at her side speaking softly in her calm, knowing voice, and Elise would be happy and carefree. Then suddenly, as if the beginning were meant to set a wicked trap for her, the scene would change, and LaLa would be taken away. She was gone, and Elise was left alone in the darkness with strangers and strange voices, enveloped by a penetrating threat of the unknown terrors around her. Why had her happy dreams deserted her, she wondered. She longed for them. She missed them. They allowed her to revisit her past on the bayou with LaLa at her side. She wondered if LaLa was upset with her about something, or maybe she was sending her a warning.

The warm milk was doing little to calm the restlessness that the darkness and the silence of the night seemed to intensify. Elise decided to turn on the television and catch the latest on the tropics update. She turned it on just in time to see a young weather correspondent wearing a bright yellow L.L. Bean rain slicker and an expression of absolute shock standing on a heap of rubble in Port-au-Prince, Haiti. His quick, excited delivery of information exemplified his novice position in hurricane coverage. The more experienced reporters would be covering the major landfall areas in the United States.

Nevertheless, the apprentice managed to spell out the graphic details of Haiti's encounter with the infamous Georgette. The death toll was at two hundred and fifty and expected to climb. Thousands of homes were swept away or covered, along with their inhabitants, by mudslides. Farms and livestock were destroyed by high winds and flash floods, obliterating the already struggling economic backbone of the island.

The reporter ended his report by giving a follow-up on the conditions in Puerto Rico, where the hurricane had paid a visit just a couple of days before. Although Georgette spared the island the horrific scene she had left behind in Haiti and the Dominican Republic, the loss of electrical power and the contamination of the water supply kept more than thirty thousand people in poorly constructed shelters around the island. Cuba and Key West were next in line for Georgette's attention. And although the mountainous terrain of the other islands had knocked a lot of power from her punch, she was still considered a formidable category 2 hurricane with winds of 110 miles per hour and a storm surge expected to raise already high tides to ten feet above normal levels.

"Enough of this," Elise muttered to herself, flipping through the channels in search of something to entertain her during her fear-induced insomnia. An old star-studded, black-and-white movie, she thought. That's what she needed. Glamour, glitz, and a good love story. She stopped clicking when a close-up of a very youthful Barbara Stanwyck filled the screen. "This will do." She dropped the remote, pulled her quilt up to her neck, wiggled her toes, and situated her tired, restless body for a romantic get-away. Just when her mind and body were perfectly prepared for the escape, the station went to a commercial break and a deep voice announced, "We'll return to Stella Dallas in just a moment."

"Stella Dallas?! Geez. Not exactly what I need right now." Elise began checking her satellite options again until she found a channel displaying a beautiful waterfall with Pachelbel's Canon in D playing in the background. "Pachelbel, yes!" She sighed and closed her eyes, listening to the music that was played as she walked down the aisle toward Brad on the night of their wedding. "Good thoughts. Think good thoughts," she told herself, as though Martha, her therapist, was sitting next to her advising her. She breathed in deeply, counting to five, held her breath, counting to five, exhaled slowly, counting to five, and then held her breath again, counting to five. She repeated the cycle envisioning her wedding, which seemed like yesterday, and allowed the warm milk to settle in her now thoroughly exhausted body. Finally, she drifted off to sleep.

THURSDAY

Elise was awakened by a variety of suppliant calls from upstairs and down, ranging in pitch from Brad's bass to Casey's soprano. Elise! Mom! Mama! Mommy! Where are you? I need my clothes! I'm hungry! Can I have French toast? Do I have to go to school today? The cacophony of pleas, inquiries, and commands clashed in her head like the discordant sounds of Saturday mornings when the stereo, computer, and Nintendo could be heard at full volume in the family room.

She jumped up quickly and clutched the back of her neck, which ached from behind her ear down to her shoulder. Elise wasn't sure if she had pulled a muscle when she was so suddenly awakened from her deep slumber or if she had a crick in her neck from sleeping with her head in an awkward position in her chair. What difference did it make, she thought. She felt like she had been hit by an eighteen-wheeler and dragged across the state of Louisiana. Stress, bad dream, very little sleep. Not a good combination. Of course, she had very little time to think about her present state of fatigue, because it was a school day for her three children and a workday for her husband. She was needed. So, seconds after her unpleasant awakening, Elise pulled herself together and began her morning routine in a semi-military fashion.

She had definitely overslept, and she hated to start her mornings behind schedule, because for Elise, every minute of the morning routine was accounted for, with its own purpose and meaning. As tired as she was, she sprang into action. After taking care of the immediate needs of her imploring loved ones, she pulled on her comfy jeans and her favorite, and very old, oversized sweatshirt. Even though it was only the second day of September and still extremely hot and humid in New Orleans, Brad kept the climate inside their house at near-blizzard temperatures.

There would be no shower for her before taking the kids to school. But Jacqui was coming for a little brunch at around 10:30, and if Elise knew her cousin—and she did—Jacqui would be dressed in the latest fall fashions, color coordinated from head to toe, perfect hair, perfect nails, perfect makeup. And Elise did not want to hear any comments about her frumpy attire and ponytail. She brushed her hair back and twisted it up into a big tortoise-shell clip, brushed her teeth, washed her face, skipped the makeup, slipped on her backless topsiders and ran downstairs to start school lunches.

With the help of a second cup of very strong coffee with chicory, she energetically put the morning assembly line into high gear, talking to herself as she moved along. "Mustard only, mayo and mustard, mayo only…add the turkey, cheese, cheese, no cheese…crust, no crust, no crust…cut in halves, halves, quarters…now wrap them up…" Each morning, she would brew an extra cup of coffee for Brad, and each morning he declined her offer. She just knew that the one morning she decided not to make enough for him would be the morning he would decide to partake in her morning vice. He had left a little earlier than usual, kissing her good-bye and mumbling something about spending his day pleading a case before a crooked, corrupt politician of a judge, and what was the use. She ignored his whining and only responded sarcastically when he reached the door, "I love you, too, honey." And then added, "Call me if you get a chance!" With the sound of the car backing out of the garage, Elise's attention became entirely directed toward the children.

"Casey, did you potty?" The little guy sat on the bottom step. His thick, dusty, brown hair was still tousled from his tossing and turning during the night. He moved his tiny rigid fingers very deliberately and methodically in an effort to tie the laces of his little black school shoes.

"No, I don't have to."

"Casey, at least try. If not, you'll be panicking to get to the bathroom while we're in the car line." Elise could see by the determined look on his face that nothing was going to deter him from his task. Casey mentioned earlier in the week that his teacher had decorated a bulletin board with cut-out construction paper shoes—a pair for each student in the class. As each child learned to tie his or her shoes, a pair of colorful, sparkling laces would be attached to that child's paper shoes. She felt badly for Casey, because it bothered him that he was the last boy to master the challenge. He was the youngest boy in his class, and he was her baby, so it bothered her, too, that he was made to feel so incompetent. She made a mental note to talk to his teacher about the matter.

"I don't have to potty, Mama."

"Fine, fine, fine…Lilah, make sure you've gathered all of your books, homework sheets, signed papers, and whatever else you need to turn in today. I don't want to make any other trips to school today."

"I will, Mom. Anyway, remember, I'm in the middle grades now, and they don't allow parents to bring anything their kids forget—except lunch."

"That's right, I forgot. You're in the fifth grade now, so they expect you to act like an adult. Umhmm, I'm sure the teachers never forget anything."

"What did you say, Mom?"

"Oh, nothing, sweetie, just voicing a little difference of opinion. That's all."

"Are you upset with us, Mom?"

"No, Lilah. Why would you think I'm upset?"

"I don't know. Your face looks like it does when we've aggravated you all day."

"No, no. Come here old lady—my little worrier. Give me a hug. Your mama's just a little concerned about the weather. That's all. I've got a lot to do, a lot to think about. I'm sorry if I've made you feel that I'm angry with you."

"It's OK. But look outside, Mom. The weather is fine. I don't think you have to worry."

"I think you're right. I should talk to you more often, Miss Lilah. Now, go get your things together, Love. By the way, where is J. P.?"

"Don't know. Haven't seen him."

"Casey, go find your big brother for me, please."

"I can't." Casey was still sitting on the bottom step, shoes untied, and his big, sad, blue eyes and pouty frown were all Elise needed to see to know that in the next few seconds, tears would be flowing.

"What do you mean, you can't."

"Just can't."

"Casey, Mommy needs a little help here. C'mon, I'll help you with your shoes. That's what mommies are for. Please go find your brother."

"I can't."

"For Pete's sake, Casey, why not?"

"Cause I think I might have wee-weed in my pants."

"What! Oh, Casey. Why didn't you go to the potty when I asked you to go? Now I have to clean you up and pray that you have another pair of uniform shorts. Camella is coming today to do some washing, and I think all of your shorts are dirty. Come on upstairs. Let's go to my bathroom." She picked him up and flew up the stairs. When she walked into her bedroom, she was so focused on getting to the bathroom that she barely saw the movement under her comforter.

"J. P.! Why aren't you ready for school? We have to leave in five minutes, and you're still in your pajamas. Did you brush your teeth, yet?"

"Nope."

"Then, come on, get out of my bed, and get moving, or you're all going to be late for school."

"School? Lilah told me that today was Saturday, and we didn't have school."

"What are you talking about? Why would she say that?"

"I don't know. Ask her."

"Lilah, come here. Lilah! Come here right now!" Immediately, quick footsteps could be heard ascending the kitchen stairs. Then, the innocent face, with the look of an angel appeared right before Elise's eyes.

"What's wrong, Mom? I was getting my stuff together, just like you told me to do."

"Did you tell J. P. that today was Saturday and there was no school?" The angelic expression melted like an ice cube on the sidewalk on the Fourth of July.

"Mom, I was just joking. I can't help it if he doesn't know the days of the week."

"I heard that. I do, too, know my days of the week. I just forgot. You're just a witch, Lilah! A mean, evil witch."

"All right, all right, that's enough. You'll be punished enough, Lilah, by being tardy, now that we have to wait for J. P. Now, go into Casey's room and get a clean pair of shorts. Pleeeease!"

"I can't believe that he actually believed me. I swear."

"Don't swear. The Bible says, don't swear. Now, go!"

Somehow, Elise managed to get everyone dressed, fed, packed up, and in the minivan. She was grateful that St. Michael's was not too far away. Most of her neighbors had opted for schools in New Orleans, which meant an hour of commuting in the morning and afternoon. How do they do it, she wondered, especially on mornings like this?

"Mom, J. P. is not wearing his seat belt right."

"Stop tattling, Lilah. J. P. how many times have I told you not to put the shoulder strap under your arm?"

"It feels weird, Mom."

"You're going to feel weird, all right, if we get in an accident, and you're not wearing your seat belt correctly." Good Lord, I sound like my mother, she sighed under her breath.

"Abbey Carriere's mom never makes her wear her seat belt. She says that if they go in the bayou wearing seat belts, they would surely drownd."

"Drown, not drownd. And remind me never to let you ride with Abbey Carriere's mother."

"She's got a tattoo, too," Lilah added boldly, ignoring her mother's correction.

"Who? Abbey?"

"No. Her mom. It's a snake or something."

"How do you know this? Have you actually seen it?" Elise asked, now wondering if maybe she should have her kids in a school in New Orleans.

"No. Abbey told us about it in class. She said that she got it after she divorced Abbey's dad. It was supposed to remind her of him. Something like that."

"OK. That's enough. I really don't need to hear any more. And why did Mrs. Garrison let Abbey tell the class something like this anyway?"

"Oh, she wasn't listening. It was during art group, and we were allowed to conversate."

"Lilah, conversate is not a word."

"It isn't?" This time she addressed the correction, but not without a challenge.

"No. It isn't."

"Well, it should be. Don't you think it sounds like a real word?"

"It doesn't matter what I think, Lilah, or what you think. It's not a word."

"Well, Abbey's getting one, too, you know."

"Getting what?"

"A tattoo. She says she's getting one for her 13th birthday."

"Oh, please, Lilah. Let's change the subject." She looked in the rearview mirror, to make sure J. P. had adjusted his seat belt.

"J. P., see if you can straighten your hair a little, will you? You look like you just rolled out of bed. I know that you did, but the rest of the world doesn't have to know it. Here, use my brush."

"But Mom, I hate brushing my hair. It makes my hair hurt."

"You dork. Your hair can't hurt. Your scalp hurts." Lilah's laugh carried with it the unmistakable condescending quality typically found in words of wisdom received from older siblings.

"Shut up, you witch. How would you know if my hair hurts or not?"

"All right, all right. Enough of that. No name calling and no saying 'shut up.' If you don't want to use my brush, at least use your fingers, J. P. Just try to do something with your hair."

"Mom, can you turn on some music?"

"Sure, but we're going to listen to the radio. I am not going to listen to you three argue over which CD to put in."

"Aw, come on, Mom."

"Sorry." Luckily, Lilah's latest song of the week came blaring out of the minivan speakers.

"Yes! That's exactly what I wanted to hear!" Lilah shrieked.

"Good. I'm glad that you're happy. Casey, why are you so quiet this morning?"

"I'm sad."

"You're sad? But why are you sad?"

"Because I'm going to miss you today. And you might not come and pick me up."

"Now, Casey, when haven't I picked you up at the end of the day? You know that I am always there, usually the first mom in the car line. Why would you think that I won't pick you up?"

"Because I wee-weed in my pants, and you said you had to pray that I have more pants...and I..."

"You are so stupid, Casey." This time it was J. P. who added the older sibling commentary.

"J. P.! That's not nice, and it's not acceptable. Now apologize."

"Sorry, Case."

"Casey, I miss you very much when you go to school. I miss all of you goobers. But when you go to school, you stay very busy with your work, and I stay very busy with mine. And today while you're in school Camella and I will wash all of your uniforms to make sure you'll be ready for another day of school. Wow. Here we are troops. Feeling better, my love?"

"Yup."

After the kisses and blessings, the minivan doors flew open, slammed shut, and they were off. Elise turned off the radio, slowly pulled out of the carpool drive, and allowed the peace and quiet to soak into her overwrought mind and body. No matter how hard she tried, mornings never went smoothly. It always seemed that it should be such a simple feat. Have all uniforms washed, folded, sorted, and ready to wear. All book bags packed and placed at the door. School shoes lined up, ready to be filled by the feet of each respective owner. Lunches prepared for, quickly assembled, packed according to varying specifications, and off to school. But somehow, things always seemed to be muddled in the last minutes of the morning rush, usually by some unforeseen chaos.

Her friends and Brad knew not to call her during the morning routine, unless, of course, it was an emergency. But her mom, in spite of Elise's many requests for her to wait until after the kids were dropped off at eight thirty, still called every now and again when she was in the midst of organizing the crew. And to Elise's mounting impatience, she would ask, "So, what are you doing?" or "How are the kids?" or "Are the kids going to school today?" In fact, Elise did not need the convenience of caller ID to know that the ringing of the phone as she entered the house was the announcement of Peggy Anne Charleville's morning call. "Thank goodness, she waited this morning," Elise mumbled, as she searched for the cordless phone, which never seemed to be where it was supposed to be.

"Good morning, Peggy Anne," she said as she picked up the phone.

"How did you know it was me?" her mother asked, as though her routine call were meant to be a surprise.

"Just a good guess," Elise shook her head and wondered if her mom really didn't realize how predictable her calls had become. She knew what her mother's next response would be before the words were out of her mouth.

"So did the kids go to school today?"

Elise wanted to answer, "No, they took the car and headed for the coast, today," or something ridiculous, just to throw a little twist into the conversation. But instead, she answered, "Yes, they all got off to school," and perpetuated the morning ritual that had become as rote as a child's prayer.

"Elise, did you see the latest weather bulletin?" Peggy Anne asked with a voice at once revealing fear and foreboding as well as excitement and anticipation. It could have been the voice of a child standing in line for that first big roller-coaster ride.

"Actually, I haven't," she lied. She was already nervous about the hurricane, and she knew that her mother's heightened anxiety would not help the situation. But Peggy Anne was not ready to drop the subject.

"Your daddy says that this thing is heading right for us. He says it's going to be worse than Camille. He says there won't be anything left of Bayou Chouteau if that thing hits us. Are you going to stay at your house if it comes here?"

Again, Elise's patience level was declining as her anxiety level began to rise. She could feel her body becoming tense and her neck starting to ache again.

"To tell you the truth, Mama, I haven't given it much thought. The storm is still pretty far out in the gulf, isn't it? Anything can happen to change its course." She was trying to keep a rational mind, in spite of the internal and external pressure to overreact.

"That's not what they are saying. They said that there are no fronts close enough to stop it from heading straight to the mouth of the river. Your daddy thinks your house would be strong enough. What do you think?"

"I told you Mother; I haven't given it much thought…" Then she was interrupted.

"Well, you better start thinking about it soon. All our friends from the mouth of the river and Grand Isle are already evacuating."

"But we don't exactly live at the mouth of the river or Grand Isle, so I have a little more time to think about it. Let's change the topic for a minute. What else is new?"

"Oh, I almost forgot to tell you. My cousin James died last night. Louise called me early this morning to tell me. It seems he had been sick for a long time. Poor fellow didn't pick a good time to go, with this hurricane coming. And they don't even know when they can wake him, because he has two children living out of town. Who knows what they are going to do with the airport. They might not be able to come in for a week. That's the trouble with kids moving away. I tell you, it's always something. I hope we can make it to the wake."

Elise was flustered. "Who are you talking about? I've never even heard of your cousin James."

"Oh, sure you have. He's my third cousin, from my mama's side. His grandma and my grandma were sisters."

"I've never even heard of this man, and in the middle of this hurricane situation, you're worried about going to his wake? When was the last time you saw this man alive?"

"I really can't remember the exact time…" and as she paused to ponder the question, Elise asked, "Well, was it twenty or thirty years ago?"

"I'm not sure, honey. He lived in Houma, but we were close when we were kids."

"Mama, why on earth would you be concerned about going to a wake for a person you've not seen or heard from in over twenty years?"

Now, Peggy Anne's feathers were ruffled, and her tone quickly became defensive. "What kind of question is that, Elise? I would go to pay my respects. That's why."

Elise was too tired to argue and too tired to try to make her mother understand her point, and she should have just dropped this topic along with the hurricane topic, but some nagging aggravation kept her going. "But you didn't bother to see him when he was alive. Those wakes are nothing but parties at the expense of grieving families. I hate that whole tradition. If something happens to me, I don't want anything like that." Now, she had done it. She had crossed the line. She had questioned age-old tradition.

"That is heathen how you talk. I cannot believe you say things like that, Elise."

"It's not heathen. You know as well as I do that everybody will be there, looking at this poor man in his coffin and will spend more time commenting on how he looked than how he lived his life. I can just hear it. 'Poor James. He didn't even look like himself.' And 'No, Cher. Did you see how skinny he looked?' or, 'I don't remember James parting his hair on that side.' It's gruesome, so don't do that for me. That's all I'm saying."

"Well, I can just see it now. You're probably going to throw me and your daddy in the ground before we're cold, without a proper good-bye. I got news for you, Elise. That's the way it's been done since long before you were born, so don't think your heathen notions are going to change the world."

"Never mind. I have to get going, anyway. Jacqui is coming over around ten thirty, and I was hoping to have time to shower." Elise looked up at the clock above the oven and realized that time would not be on her side.

"OK. Oh, by the way, I talked to Lucy this morning. I called to tell her about James, and she wants me and Daddy to go up to Memphis and spend a week with her if we have to leave for the storm."

"That's great. You should go whether the storm is coming or not. She's always begging you two to visit. It would mean so much to her." Lucy, Peggy Anne's youngest sibling, was practically raised by Elise's mother and father. They had helped her through high school, college, and graduate school. She had never married and lived alone, devoting her life to her job as a social worker in Memphis.

"Nah I told her that you would need me to help with the kids if you have to leave."

"What!? Why did you tell her that, Mom? You make it sound like I'm a child, incapable of taking care of my own family. Besides, I do have a husband who is just as responsible for the children."

"Well, if you don't want me and Daddy to stay with you, we don't have to."

"That's not what I said, Mom. You're always welcome to stay with my family, but you make it sound like…Never mind. I have to go take a shower, so I'll talk to you later."

"OK, honey. Give Jacqui a hug for me."

"OK, bye." Nothing ever changes, she thought. She could talk and explain ad nauseam, and nothing would ever change. If her heathen notions would not change the world, her independent notions would certainly never change her mother.

Jacqueline Charleville would never change either, arriving promptly at ten thirty, looking like she had stepped out of the pages of a fashion magazine. Elise was still wearing her comfy jeans and oversized sweatshirt. Not a stitch of makeup on lips, eyes, or cheeks, and her hair was still twisted up and secured in the tortoise-shell clip. But Elise was always willing to forfeit the fashion points to Jacqui's corner, because she just didn't seem to have the time or desire lately to keep up with the trends. She would readily admit that she spent most of her shopping time and clothing budget on keeping her three kids in the latest fashions. She hoped Jacqui would not try to give her "pay more attention to yourself, Elise" lecture. But Jacqui didn't. She really didn't have a chance, because Elise was eager to use her cousin's visit to relax and reminisce.

"Do you remember Hurricane Bertha, Jacqui? I was ten years old, so you must have been about five, right?"

"Yeah, but I don't remember it as well as you do, obviously. I guess I was too little to really understand what was going on. Anyway, with Billy, hell—you know how he tried to turn any occasion into a reason to party. I remember staying at the Roosevelt Hotel in New Orleans."

"That's right, I do remember that. Only your dad would manage to turn an evacuation into a luxurious vacation!"

"Well, he tried to. He said that if we had to leave our home, we might as well live it up. Of course, he and I made an effort to, but, as usual, Kitty bitched the whole time. I guess she was nervous, not being used to hurricanes and all. But nothing made Billy nervous."

"That's funny, I would have thought that your mom would have loved being at the Roosevelt while the rest of us were living like refugees moving from place to place like nomads seeking higher ground. Why, I can just see her now, having a facial at the hotel spa while the rest of the Bayou Chouteau ladies were trying to find clean water to wash their faces!"

Elise knew that she could joke about her Aunt Kitty as long as Jacqui was talking about her Uncle Billy in the same conversation. Whenever a topic of discussion allowed Jacqui to include both of her parents, she inevitably depicted her father as her kind, compassionate, happy-go-lucky soul mate, as opposed to her selfish, ever-complaining, materialistic, social climbing mother. However, if Billy Charleville was not included in a conversation, Jacqui would talk frankly about her mother and offer excuses for her less than gracious behavior. She'd say things like, "Poor Kitty, she always told me that her Aunt Penny, who raised her in Jackson, after her Mama and Daddy died, made her work for everything—her own shoes and clothes. And it was her own money, her own inheritance." Elise knew on such occasions not to joke about Aunt Kitty, for fear of offending her rather emotional cousin. On this day, however, Uncle Billy was a part of the moment, and it was quite clear to Elise that she could get by with a little humor at her Aunt Kitty's expense.

"Man, Kitty was so aggravated with Billy and me. Isn't it weird how that's what I remember most about that storm? I still hear people talk about 'Bertha' and how they remember seeing all of the destruction when they went back home. They talk about everything that was lost. And I remember my mother bitching—bitching at my dad. And what's weirdest, Lissy, is the fact that I think I enjoyed it. I did all that I could to egg her on."

"I don't think that's so weird, Jacqui. You were just so close to your dad. It happens all the time. Freudian. You were probably a little jealous of Kitty, so you enjoyed being allied with Billy during their little spats." Elise could never resist a little psychoanalysis. Brad despised this habit of hers. But it turned into a sort of defense mechanism for her—a way of understanding the negative aspects of human nature, a way of making these things a little more acceptable within the realm of so-called normal behavior. "But I am a little curious as to how you egged her on."

"Oh, it was just silly, childish stuff. It started on the drive to New Orleans. You know how Billy always called my mother Kitty Cat, and she hated it? Well, while we were driving, he and I made up a little game where he called me Jack Rabbit and I called him Billy Goat. Silly, huh? But I was only five, so I got a kick out of it. We knew it was bothering Kitty, but we kept it up for days, until I swear, she was about to pull all her platinum blond hair out of her head. And then they had an awful fight. At least she did. Billy never fought. He'd just fix himself a drink and say, 'C'mon Kitty Cat. Calm down. You don't mean what you're saying.'"

"I can just picture him now. Jacqui, you sound like him after all these years. Gosh, it must've been a big fight for you to remember it so well."

"Um-hmm. It was. One reason I remember it though is because it was a fight, they'd have all the time. Over and over."

"Let me guess. Money?" Elise thought for sure that she was right, knowing her Aunt Kitty the way that she did.

"No. Actually, it was about your mom."

"My mom? My mom? You're kidding me, right? Why would they fight about my mom? She's perfectly harmless."

"Believe me, Elise, this mint tea isn't strong enough to encourage me to revisit that episode in family history."

"Well, that's as strong as it gets around here before noon—especially when I have carpool."

"Well, I don't have carpool duties. And haven't you ever heard of mimosas? Or did living in the Midwest for so long strip you of all of your capabilities of letting the good times roll?"

"Yeeeees, I've heard of Mimosas, and you know very well that they are one of my weaknesses." She opened the refrigerator and grabbed a large carton of orange juice from a shelf on the door. "Let me check to see if I have any champagne. If I do, I'll mix a pitcher for you, as long as you allow me to stick to my mint tea."

"Aw, c'mon Elise. You've got hours before you have to pick up the kids. Camella is here cleaning the place. Brad's at work. You're all stressed about this stupid storm in the gulf…wait a minute. I've got a great idea. Let's have a coming out brunch in honor of Georgette, who is making her debut into the social scene this weekend. Huh? C'mon, it'll be fun. You whip up an omelette. I'll do the mimosas. You make a great omelette—like LaLa's. Put a lot of stuff in it—green onions, sweet peppers, a little andouille—you got any andouille sausage? And use real butter to sauté, OK. Now let's see…" By then, she was standing in front of the open refrigerator, eyes roaming up and down, in search of chilled champagne.

"I swear Jacqui, you can be just like your dad—crazy and persuasive."

"Thanks. I'll take that as a compliment. Now where can I find champagne to mix with this orange juice?"

"If I have any, it will be in the wine cooler by the bar."

"Oh, excuuuse me. I keep forgetting that I am in one of those exclusive, luxurious homes in the Manors of Mont Ste. Michel."

"Would you knock it off."

"Hey Lissy, you think any of these out-of-towners buying in this subdivision realize that the 'Mont' that their homes are sitting on is really a chain of Indian mounds. Shoot, I could never live in this neighborhood after seeing that movie…what was it called?"

Elise could hear Jacqui rattling the bottles in the cooler in her pursuit of bubbly. "Are you talking about Poltergeist?"

"Yeah, yeah, that was it. Didn't those people live on some sort of Indian burial ground or something? Damn Elise, all I can find is this rare selection of $8 Asti Spumante sitting in the middle of your private collection of Boone's Farm and Mogan David."

"Ha, ha, ha." Elise returned with a playful, sarcastic laugh. "Stop exaggerating. I know it's not up to par with your wine connoisseur's taste buds, but there are some good wines in there. But you're right, the Asti did only cost $8—good guess."

"Let me guess again, then. Has this been around since the in-laws' momentous visit."

"You got it! And as you can see, things didn't get joyous enough around here to open the bottle. God, that was two-and-a-half years ago—do you think that Asti is still good?"

"Not that I am an expert on this particular label, but I can't see where a little age can hurt."

"It's hard to believe it's been two-and-a-half years since I've seen or talked to Brad's parents. Yet my body still tenses up when I think of them. And I haven't had to deal with them in two-and-a-half years. It's so bizarre." Chopping the fresh green onions was bringing tears to her eyes, and she was relieved when she took her knife and scraped her chopping board in a downward motion, dumping a compilation of fragrant vegetables into the butter that had melted in a timely fashion in the old skillet, which once belonged to Delilah Charleville. How many omelettes had been made in this pan, she wondered, as she turned the skillet on the burner, cautiously grabbing the handle as though she were dealing with delicate China.

Jacqui awakened her from her momentary trance, caused by her precious memories and the distinctive aroma that frequently graces southern Louisiana kitchens. "Didn't you visit his sister this summer when you were in Europe?"

"Yeah, his younger sister, Tracy. She was as nice as could be, and I know Brad was really happy to spend time with her away from their folks' home. Sort of neutral ground, you know. Although Tracy has never been like the rest of the family. She always did her own thing, set her mind on what she wanted out of life, and did it. She's so different than Brad's older sister, Pam. Pam is a carbon copy of Phyllis. And she would never go against anything that Phyllis says or does for fear of being cut off from the gravy train. She's even got her husband, Marc, dancing to the Steiner family tune."

"I remember both of them from your wedding. They both seemed pretty stiff to me. All I can remember about Pam is her makeup beading on her face and hearing her complain about the humidity down here and how she hated this filthy city. All I could think was, 'Poor Elise. Is this what she's going to live with?' But the younger sister was a lot nicer. Stiff, but nice."

"What do you mean by 'stiff?'"

"Like Brad when you two first started dating. Remember how puritanical the man was? He needed some serious loosening up. And don't pretend that you don't know what I'm talking about either, because you know as well as I do that he didn't exactly fit in at the Bayou Chouteau fais deaux deaux. Ooooh girl, that is smelling good! Here, has a mimosa."

As she poured the orange juice cocktail into the crystal goblet she had found in the bar cabinet, she asked Elise, "Does she have any children?"

"Who Pam or Tracy?" Elise asked, sticking with her tea and slightly irritated by Jacqui's tempting her with the more spirited drink.

"Tracy. I don't want to talk about Pam."

"No. And it was funny to see her trying to relate to my three. She tried real hard, and the kids enjoyed her, but she was just so awkward playing the 'auntie' roll. She would tense up anytime one of the kids got too close to any of her collectables, which were placed in the most precarious places—dead giveaway that we were in a house belonging to people unaccustomed to children. She and her husband, Mike, are real corporate machines. And they're both very successful and very happy with their lives and what they've accomplished."

"Now, where are they living? Sweden?"

"No, they live in Switzerland."

"How long were you there?"

"We were there for five days, and then we took a train to Italy to visit my friend Talia, who was vacationing in her hometown outside of Genoa."

"Nice. Nice. Back to the in-laws. I'm sure you'll be hearing from them before the weekend. Maybe you'll even be invited to their home for the evacuation. Would you go?"

"Absolutely not. If Brad wanted to, I'd go to St. Louis, but I would use the opportunity to visit my friends there. But believe me, I won't have to worry about making that decision. They probably won't call."

"You're kidding, right? Even if they hated you, their son and grandchildren are living in the path of a potential Category 3 hurricane, and you don't think they'll call to see that they'll be safe?"

"We shall see. You may be right. But where they are concerned, nothing surprises me, and I guess I'm just trying to prepare myself so as not to be upset by their ignoring my husband and children."

"Man, they are weird! I mean, I know that Kitty can be weird, but they are really weird." Jacqui picked up a piece of the omelette that had broken off into the pan as Elise scooped it up with a spatula and placed it onto a platter.

"How is Kitty, by the way? What's she going to do if Georgette stays on track? Go with you to Adam's ranch?"

"I don't know. We haven't discussed it yet. I don't know if I can stay cooped with my mother for a very long time without any contact with other human beings. I'll go nuts! But if she doesn't come with me, I'll just worry about her, so what the hell, maybe we'll bond after thirty-five years. Wasn't that supposed to happen already—somewhere along the road?" She appeared to be joking, but Elise knew that Jacqui really longed for a close relationship with her mother. So, she laughed along with her, while offering a somewhat consolatory response. "Poor Kitty. I think she tries, but she just doesn't know how. How old was she when her parents died in that boating accident?"

"Well let me see. Sometimes she says ten, sometimes twelve, and sometimes I seriously wonder about the whole truth to that part of her life."

"What do you mean by that?"

"Well, just think about it, Elise. Why can't she remember exactly how old she was when something so horrible happened in her life? When Billy died, I was eight years old, in the third grade. And I remember it like it was yesterday. I couldn't forget that day if I tried, and God knows I have tried. I remember what I wore to school that day. I remember what he was wearing and what he looked like, lying on that wet road in front of our school bus. I even remember what you looked like that day, Elise. Your face so pale. Your arms wrapped around me, holding me, both of us trembling, standing at the front of the bus, waiting for someone to tell us what was going on, all the while knowing exactly what had happened. I remember it all. So it's hard for me to understand how Kitty can't get it straight about her age when both of her parents died."

"Maybe she has some sort of mental block. I've heard that can happen to people who refuse to accept traumatic events in their lives. Haven't you ever heard about that?"

"I guess so. But you will never understand how hard I've tried to get to know my mama, Elise. I mean really get to know her. And she just has this brick wall around her. I see you and your mama together. And even though you have your little disagreements every now and then, you are so close. You know each other so well. You can feel for each other. But me and Kitty. I don't know. We're like oil and vinegar."

"I know. I take my relationship with my parents for granted sometimes, and then I see you and Brad struggle to hold on to the little remnants of family ties that you have, and I can't even imagine how I'd deal with it."

"Well, I don't think Kitty is hateful. She's just distant and self-centered. She's in her own little world, and I'm always there trying to find my place in her world, but never really fitting in—never belonging or feeling wanted—sort of like a fart in a crowded elevator." She released one of her howls of laughter, which usually indicated that she was in a state of inebriation, only she wasn't. "Look at you, Lissy, blushing because I said fart. You are too much! What? Did you think I was going to get all mushy and analytical with you. Forget that! I got over the situation a long time ago. And Brad probably has, too. Take my advice, my sentimental friend; you stay out of his relationship with his folks. Let him handle it. People like me and Brad don't have the same expectations from 'family' as people like you, Elise."

Now Elise wanted to change the subject. She was enjoying this rare tête-à-tête with Jacqui and remembered the topic that had turned a simple visit into a rather pleasant brunch. "All right, Jacqueline. You've got your mimosa, so speak up. Tell me why in the world your parents were arguing about my mama during your stay at the Roosevelt Hotel during Hurricane Bertha. Come on, 'fess up."

"Oh, they argued about your mama all the time. Kitty can't stand your mama—never could. She always complained to Billy about how Delilah Charleville played favorites with her sweet little Peggy Anne. How they were both jealous of her because she had class, and they were nothing but bayou hicks. How they loved to pass judgment on how she dressed, how she kept her house, how she spent her money, and how she was as a mother. Billy would ask her when she'd heard them talk about her, and she'd snap back, 'They talk behind my back you fool, and you know it. You never defend me. For all I know you join in and have

33

a good laugh on me.' Then he'd say she was imagining it all. And she would accuse him of still being in love with Peggy Anne."

"In love with my mom? That's almost humorous considering all of the women your dad dated before he met your mom. What made her choose Peggy Anne as the woman of his dreams?"

"Didn't you know that Billy had the hots for your mama?"

"Jack, my mom is seventy-two years old. It's kind of hard for me to imagine her as someone's hot item."

"Oh, I know. But long ago—like in high school. Haven't you heard anything about that?"

"Yes, as a matter of fact, I did. From LaLa. She used to tell me the story of how my parents met—how my mom was good friends with Billy when she fell in love with my dad. She made it sound like a fairy tale. You know how she used to make up those stories. I loved them all. But the one about my mom and dad was a favorite of mine. There were nights when I'd sleep at her house, above the store, that I'd have a tough time getting to sleep. So, she'd tell me the story of my mom and dad."

"Well tell me. I want to hear it. I'm always in the mood for a good love story."

"Oh, I can't tell it like a fairy tale, and I can't talk with that French-German accent that made LaLa's stories so intriguing, like fantasies."

"Intriguing? Fantasies? I always thought her stories were kinda boring. I mean, I loved Delilah to death, but shit, you can only hear so many stories about the old days."

"Oh, I don't know about that. I couldn't get enough of them. I'd give anything to hear one from her right now."

"All right, all right, don't get all melancholy on me. I know you loved the old lady."

"That's right, I did, Jacqui. And I still love her. Sometimes I can't believe how you talk about her. Why do you have such different memories of LaLa? She loved you so much."

"Why? Oh, come on, Elise. You…you were always her favorite. Always. She hated my mother, and no matter how hard she tried, Delilah couldn't separate her feelings for Kitty from her feelings for me."

"That's not true. She…"

"Oh, Elise, grow up! I mean, listen to yourself. Listen to how you describe her stories like fairy tales. She told you fairy tales about your mom and dad. Do you think she ever told me stories like that? No! She couldn't. If she did, she would have to call it 'Billy Boy Knocked Up Kitty.'"

"Jacqui Charleville, why would you say that? I have never heard that. Why would you say such a thing?"

"Because, little girl, it's the truth. Kitty was guilty of entrapment, and Delilah knew it. That's why, no matter how hard she tried, she looked at us like outcasts. Kitty saw Billy as her ticket out. After all, the Charlevilles were wealthy according to Bayou Chouteau standards. My dad was a real catch. Confirmed bachelor, playboy even. But he did have enough morals to feel obliged to marry my mom after he put her in family way. But it backfired on my mom, in a way. Billy poured all his love out on me. Delilah never really accepted Kitty into the family. My mom and dad would fight like cats and dogs. Why do you think I don't have any brothers or sisters? So, you see, Elise, that's the love story I grew up with. My mom's plan backfired so badly that I think that's why she insisted on that abortion instead of allowing me to marry Marsh. She probably thought I was like her, looking to move up by trapping the rich boy."

Elise still got chills through her body when Jacqui brought up her abortion. How could her reference to it roll off her tongue so easily, and with so little emotion—especially when the prospects of Jacqui ever having children were so slim? "But Jacqui, she had to know that it was different. Anyone could see that it was different. You and Marsh loved each other so much."

"Obviously, only one of us did, Elise. If you really think about it honestly, Kitty probably saved me from the same kind of marriage she had. I suppose I should be grateful."

"Hmm. Sounds like you're moving on, Jack. Things must be going well with Adam, huh?" The "conversation game" had begun, and after all of their years together, Elise knew how to play the "conversation game." The rules of the game were simple. Rule Number 1 dictated that Jacqui set the boundaries of the conversation. For the game to continue, Elise must stay within the boundaries. Venture beyond, and the game was over—not to be played again for days, sometimes weeks. Rule Number 2 allowed Jacqui to choose the character roles. She could choose to be either the free-spirited, daring woman of the world, with Elise playing the bored, mundane housewife who is amused, shocked, and entertained by her flamboyant cousin. Or Jacqui could play the victim—the victim of the world's greatest heartbreak, the victim of the world's most emotionally abusive mother, the victim of a fatherless childhood, the victim of loneliness, of being childless, husbandless— the list could go on and on. In this case, Elise would play the role of one who had everything desirable in the world. The lucky one. Rule Number 3 warned that each player had to be prepared to change characters in the middle of the game, depending on how much alcohol Jacqui consumed during the game.

In all honesty, Elise hated playing the conversation game, but she loved being with Jacqui, even if it meant that she sometimes had to bite her tongue, so to speak, and abide by the childish, unspoken rules, just in order to spend time with her. Because rule Number 4 of the conversation game deemed that Jacqui was never wrong.

And so, on this particular day, at this particular hour, the game began and continued with the free-spirited character telling Elise that she had heard the latest news about her old beau Marsh Delacroix. "The latest news? And what exactly might that be?" Elise asked inquisitively as she watched her brunch guest suddenly playing nervously with her short tight auburn curls. "Lissy, you don't have to pretend on my account. I know you were at that garden club luncheon the other day when Felicia Delacroix told the world that her precious Marsh was marrying a luuuuvly girl from a perfectly maaaarvelous family, whom he met in the chaaarming little town in Connecticut, where he practices law in a moooost successful firm started by her most distiiiiiinguished father."

Elise was in the middle of a mouthful of omelette and had to cover her mouth as she giggled at Jacqui's comical imitation of Marsh's mother. After she swallowed the last morsel without choking, she politely wiped the corners of her mouth with her napkin and looked up to notice the pained expression in Jacqui's eyes, which could not be overwhelmed by the smile on her face and jocularity in her voice. Elise wondered if anyone else could see through to Jacqui's heart the way that she could. She stopped laughing, her voice taking a more serious, if not apologetic tone, "Yes, Jack. I was there. I heard the announcement, and it went through me like a knife. So, I can only imagine how you felt when you heard about it. I'm sorry. I'm so sorry."

Elise reached across the table in order to take hold of Jacqui's hand, but when Jacqui sensed this expression of consolation approaching, she quickly slid her hand off of the table and placed in on her lap, out of Elise's sentimental reach. "Why are you sorry? You don't have to feel sorry for me. I'm happy. He's happy. I've got Adam. He's got…what's her name…Margaret, his suitable social butterfly. Like I said, Kitty probably saved me from a miserable life. Life goes on, Elise. I'm happy. He's happy." She took a long drink, finished the mimosa she had in front of her and poured another.

The tension was building, and Elise knew she had broken Rule Number 1, so she quickly changed the subject in order to keep playing the "conversation game" with Jacqui. "Oh, wait a minute. Shhhhh, let's listen." She drew Jacqui's attention to the Weather Channel's hourly tropical update on Hurricane Georgette, which they watched on the small television sitting on the kitchen island. Elise had muted the sound all morning but stayed tuned in to the station, just in case there were any changes to report. She jumped up and tripped over her chair, nearly falling in her attempt to reach the remote which she had placed on top of the set.

"God, you are obsessed with this, aren't you?" Jacqui remarked, surprised by both the abrupt change in the conversation and her cousin's panicked haste in responding to the familiar graphics on the television screen—the little circular object, moving in a counterclockwise direction across a background of tropical scenery—which typically preceded storm updates.

"Shhhhh," Elise repeated, giving Jacqui an agitated look, which she frequently gave her children when they failed to heed her initial requests or warnings.

Hurricane Georgette has made its way into the Gulf of Mexico… Category 2 hurricane by tomorrow…strike probabilities, based on latest advisories, range from Morgan City, Louisiana, to Biloxi, Mississippi… city of New Orleans in greatest danger at this time…

"Elise, look at that thing. It's still so far out there anything can happen. Geez, I can't remember seeing you this worried in a long time."

"I know. I know. It's easy for you to say. You don't have three small kids, a new house, and a husband who has never before had his hearth and home threatened by a hurricane."

"Aaah. So, this is all about Brad. Is he pouting or something? Making you feel responsible for his impending doom? What is it? C'mon."

"No, no, and no. I'm not sure why I'm reacting this way. I guess I've lived away so long that I'm just not used to the annual threats anymore—like we were when we were kids. It was exciting then. Now I'm scared. I don't know. I just have a bad feeling about it. That's all." The truth is, she thought to herself, nothing seemed like when they were kids anymore. Back then, life meant moving on from one adventure to the next. Now life meant moving from one worry to the next, dealing with one stressful situation and moving on to another. Sometimes even running away from them, if that were possible.

"Jacqui, remember how we used to love summer squalls? We'd run upstairs to LaLa's attic, with that big front window overlooking the bayou. There were all of those old trunks and chifforobes that belonged to LaLa's parents and brothers and the Charlevilles. They were all filled with those old books and things. Old clothes that smelled of cedar and mothballs. Remember how we'd try on the old hats and gloves? We'd sit there while the lightning cracked and the rain pelted on that tin roof, and I'd make up scary stories. You'd hold my hand so tightly. But you never wanted me to stop. Sometimes we'd fall asleep up there and wake up to find the sun shining through the window, as though there never had been a squall at all."

"And what exactly does this trip down Memory Lane have to do with anything we were talking about?"

"Well, you were talking about my worrying about this storm. Heck, it seems that I live in this constant state of anxiety lately. It's sad, it really is. I used to love summer squalls when we were kids. Then, as I grew older, I found them to be so romantic. Now that I'm a mother, well, I dread them. I listen and watch for signs of approaching tornadoes. I keep my kids with me for the duration of the storm and make sure that they do nothing to attract the lightning. I…"

"Oooooh girl, you really need to lighten up. Here, throw away that mint shit and drink a mimosa with me."

"Naaah, I'll be OK. It's just all of this disaster preparation."

"You know what, Lissy? My whole childhood can be looked at as disaster preparation. I mean, you have all of these happy little stories of our idyllic little childhood, and I'm sitting here thinking, 'Was I really there with her???' I sure don't remember the fantasies like you and LaLa. And while part of me is jealous because you can remember your happy little childhood on the bayou, there's another part of me that is glad that I remember my confused and twisted childhood because…

hell…I'm not scared of this hurricane like you are! I learned to roll with the punches a long time ago."

A brief silent pause for thought and nourishment was interrupted by a cell phone playing a very annoying, shrill rendition of the first few bars of "The Ode to Joy." Jacqui jumped up and retrieved the mini symphony as urgently as Elise had rushed for her TV remote moments earlier. "Hello-o-o," Elise was always amused by the "cute and sexy" voice that Jacqui used to greet her phone callers. She listened to the one side of the conversation as it unfolded at her table. "Oh, hi babe." It was Adam. Babe. Brad would barf if she called him babe. "Commander's Palace! What's the occasion?" She watched Jacqui's persona change right before her eyes. Superficial, she thought, in an uncharacteristically spiteful manner. "You are too sweet." Oh God, I think I'm going to be sick, Elise thought, as she heard Jacqui's Southern drawl intensify to impress her Midwestern honey. "Oh no! I'm starved. I haven't had a bite to eat all day." Jacqui looked at Elise and puffed out her cheeks, giving the impression that she was really stuffed from the half an omelette and mimosas she had just consumed. "Okay, babe, I'll see you in about twenty minutes. Depending on the traffic. I love you." Elise could tell by the expression on her cousin's face that Adam had not returned the sentiment at the end of the conversation. Jacqui put the cell phone back in her purse, stood up straight, stamping her feet on the floor, in order to get her silky pants to fall gracefully over her shoes, while she straightened the waistband that had likely gotten a wee bit tighter from the hearty brunch she had downed with no restraint. "Oh well, I'm off to lunch. Never turn down a free meal, especially at Commander's." Her voice had returned to its normal "conversational" tone, which she felt free to use around ordinary people.

"And what exactly do you call this, if not 'free?'" Elise jokingly asked pointing to the empty plates and glasses on the table, not knowing if she was feeling disappointed by Jacqui's sudden departure or jealous because of her freedom to do so.

"This, I call 'gone.'" And she gobbled down the last morsel of omelette remaining on her plate. "This way, I'll have a delicate appetite when I'm with Adam. Kitty would be proud, right?" She kissed Elise on both cheeks, in her new continental style of greeting, and added in a rather ingenuous flair, "Sorry to leave you with such a mess, Lissy, but I gotta run. Isn't he just so sweet?" Elise decided to pass on responding to any laudatory praise for a man she knew to be a womanizing rat—a rich rat—but still a rat. Jacqui stopped at the mirror next to the front door and passed ten perfectly manicured fingers through her hair, which seemed to be more attractive because of its wild, unmanageable state. She applied color to her faded lips, puckered them into a practiced smile, and satisfied with the reflection in the mirror, placed her sunglasses on the bridge of her nose and proceeded out of the door.

Elise followed her and watched from the front porch as Jacqui hurried to her car, turning only to yell back, "Call me later! And don't look so worried. It'll give you a wrinkled brow!!!" Elise was glad the conversation game had ended. But it seemed, as always, that Jacqui had won. Elise was burning inside, thinking about Jacqui's self-righteous commentary on how she survived her piteous past. Who was she trying to kid? She'll probably tell Adam everything we talked about and make me sound like some poor, neurotic housewife on the edge of a nervous breakdown, while painting herself as my unwavering pillar of strength. What does it matter, anyway, what Adam Blum thinks of me? Why should I care? She watched Jacqui back out of the driveway, returned her coquettish wave, and felt a sense of relief as she saw the little red BMW convertible disappear around the brick wall that stood between Manors of Mont Ste. Michel and the rest of the world. I wonder if Adam bought that car for her, Elise thought. And then out loud, as if to reprimand herself for thinking like the old gossips at the club, she added, "So what if he did? That's her business. It's hardly any business of mine." Satisfied with her ability to tell herself exactly what she would have told her mom or one of her friends if they had questioned any aspect of Jacqui's personal life, she closed the front door and made her way into the kitchen which still smelled inviting from the impromptu brunch.

"Look at this mess," Elise grumbled, although she wasn't really surprised that Jacqui had left her with the cleanup duties. *It's just like her to leave me with all of the work, as though I have nothing better to do with my time.* If it hadn't been for Adam's call, she would have thought of some other reason to rush off and avoid getting her hands dirty. "I swear, she's more irresponsible than Lilah. Maybe that's why she's foolish enough to be in a relationship that has no potential beyond casual sex." Elise was angry, but why? Jacqui's visits had the ability to raise her spirits to the highest level and then moments later drop them into the deepest of doldrums, and she wondered if Jacqui was aware of this power that she had over her. Then a bothersome thought occurred to her—a thought that popped into her mind occasionally, only to be swept away by a voice of reason that she had trained over the years to rescue her from her moments of doubt.

This thought always suggested the possibility that she was actually jealous of Jacqui. After all, Jacqui was going to Commander's Palace for lunch with her lover. Brad had not even called all morning. He and Adam worked in the same law firm. Why didn't Brad ever think about spending a little quality time with her in the middle of his workday? And Jacqui was driving there in a little sports car, hardly suitable for kids' car seats and the consumption of Happy Meals in the back seat. Maybe Jacqui didn't want marriage, children, and homestead. And Elise silently admitted to herself that such a lifestyle was not for everyone. Not everyone is cut out to handle the type of stress involved. In fact, Elise wondered if maybe she only thought that she was cut out for the job. Maybe, Jacqui was wiser for her choices. "Oh my God, here I go again," she thought. She clenched her teeth and said, "Voice of reason you can step in at any time now." She didn't realize she had said this out loud until she heard Camella coming down the kitchen stairs.

"Did you say somethin' to me, Miz Elise?"

"No, no, Camella," she answered the middle-aged Creole woman, who was carrying a basket of dirty clothes into the laundry room. "I guess I was just thinking out loud. It's almost noon. Can I fix you something to eat or something to drink? How about a little mimosa to give you a little lift, huh?" She held up the pitcher, which contained only a quarter of its original batch of bubbly, knowing that Camella would not likely take her up on her offer. "Lord, no, Miz Elise. If I drink dat mimosa, ri' now, I would fall asleep ri' here."

"OK, OK. Then come sit down, and I'll get you a nice tall glass of iced tea. I know you can handle that!"

Camella sat down, taking a rare time out from her chores, and allowed Elise to pamper her with an iced tea break. Elise had just about put the last dish in the dishwasher when Camella asked, "Yo' cousin lef' awready?"

"Yes, she left about fifteen minutes ago. Why do you ask?"

"No reason. I like yo' cousin, Miz Elise, but she not like you. She different."

"Oh? In what way?" She was curious to hear this comment from Camella, who never really joined in on personal conversations going on in Elise's home and always seemed hesitant to become involved in family matters for fear of being a busybody. Busybodies didn't last very long as housekeepers in the Manors of Mont Ste. Michel.

"She just like my sister Jasmine, or 'Jazzie'—dat's wha' she calls herself. Jasmine is my baby sister. Befo' my mama died, she made me promise to take care of Jasmine. But dat's a tough promise to keep, Miz Elise. I work to make a better life for my kids, and Jasmine, she thinks I'm crazy. She works to have fun, eh. She tells me, 'I ain't never gonna tie myself down wi' no husband and house full of kids. I'm gonna take care of myself first.' And I think to myself, mmm-hmmm, you gonna be a lonely person one day, Jasmine. And when you realize it, you gonna be too old to do anything about it. I worry about her so much, Miz Elise. But der ain't nothin' I can do."

"Maybe she's happy, Camella. She may not be cut out for being a mother and taking care of a family and home."

"Now, come on, Miz Elise, can you imagine yo' life without yo' babies running around dis big house? What would dis house be like without lil' Lilah and J. P. and Casey. Empty, das all. Just empty. And das what Jasmine's life will be. I know. My mama use to say, 'Don't waste any time chasin' rainbows, child, cuz you gonna fin' dat it's been right under yo' nose da whole time.' See what I mean, Miz Elise? See dat it's right under dey nose all da time, eh?"

Elise walked over to Camella, bent over, gave her a little hug, and tried to give her a little reassurance, "Don't worry Camella, Jasmine will be fine. She's got you on her side, and you are a very wise woman, my friend." Only Elise knew that the hug was a sign of thanks, not consolation.

"Miz Elise, you look really tired. Why don't you go take a rest? You know I can take care of da house."

"Thank you, Camella. I think I just might do that. I really didn't get very much sleep last night. And I do have a little time before I have to leave to go pick up the kids." She sat down in the overstuffed chair that had served as her bed just hours before and closed her weary eyes. But try as she may, she could not get to sleep. She could not get Jacqui off of her mind.

What was it about that day fifteen years ago that made her remember it so vividly? Was it the perfectly pleasing way that it started or the pitiful, heart-wrenching manner in which it ended? She had slept late that Saturday morning, making up for a long week of finishing three research papers, marking an end to her last fall semester of graduate school. Reading, writing, editing, deadlines—and yet, the first thing she did on her first morning of freedom was grab a book—*For Whom the Bell Tolls4*—her all-time favorite. She had read it so many times for pleasure, for research papers, and sometimes just browsing through favorite parts, that she knew that it would require very little concentration to enjoy it once again.

It was a perfect morning for it, too. A steady rain-the sort of rainfall that lasts all day. An overcast sky—no dark clouds—just one vast background of the palest of gray, peaking through the trunks of the oak and pecan trees that had stood in those same places long before her parents decided to plant her roots on this very spot of the Earth. So often, throughout her early childhood, adolescence, and even more so her college years, Elise would lie down on the big, old, reupholstered couch in the family room and look at those tall trees through the picture window that formed a frame around her view and on very still days gave her the illusion of gazing at a Van Gogh landscape painting. She could lose her thoughts in her intense gazes and only be brought back to the present when her dog or cats would run across the back yard, giving motion to the framed masterpiece, breaking the silence and stillness of the moment. And hard as she might try, she could rarely retrieve her previous drifting thoughts and return to the calmness that settled over her in her mental escape.

She put a fresh cup of hot coffee and chicory on the end table—just the way she liked it, strong, with a little sugar and a little cream. She curled up on the couch, wrapped herself in the old, worn quilt that she'd had since she was ten years old, opened her book, and once more followed Ernest Hemingway to the romance and turmoil of war-torn Spain. She would catch herself dozing periodically and would close her book, marking the spot where she left off, and allowing her tired mind, body, and soul to catch up after a fatiguing week.

She pulled her quilt closer to her body and felt its therapeutic power reaching out to every stressed nerve ending of her body. That quilt had gone everywhere with Elise—family vacations, sleepovers, and, of course, her college dorm. Her grandmother LaLa had hand-stitched a quilt for her and one for Jacqui and given them to them for Christmas just a few months before she died. The quilt was made from the scraps of fabric she had saved from all of the dresses she had sewn for the girls from the day they were born. Elise recognized some of the dresses represented in the quilt, especially those she wore in early family pictures. She remembered how her mom had cried when she opened the package on Christmas Day. Although she couldn't quite comprehend her mother's emotional reaction on that day, the eventual death of her grandmother shortly thereafter opened her eyes and heart to the symbolic value that the quilt would provide—the earthly connection with the plain, wise woman, whose strength, Elise prayed, would be passed on to her.

The old quilt would always remind her, also, of the summer day, just a few months after LaLa's death, when Jacqui came over to watch the Saturday morning cartoons with her. They had their usual hot biscuits, dripping with butter—real butter—and settled down on the floor, each with her favorite stuffed animal, directly in front of the television. Elise pulled the quilt off of the couch and rolled into what she felt was her grandmother's arms.

"Aren't you hot?" Jacqui asked, looking rather quizzically at her cousin wrapped up like a colorful burrito.

"Nope," Elise answered, without taking her eyes off of Mighty Mouse. "It's just soft and cuddly. You should bring yours next time." Jacqui didn't reply and since Elise was expecting some sort of a response, she looked up at Jacqui as if to ask, "Well, are you, or aren't you?" She could see that Jacqui was suddenly uncomfortable, so she asked her what was the matter. Jacqui began stammering and stuttering like a person might do when the priest slides the window of the confessional open and you know that you have to say something, but you're really not sure where to start.

Then she just blurted out, "My mom gave my quilt to the 'poor people.' She said that it was bad enough that LaLa made those old-fashioned homemade dresses for me, and that there was no way we were going to keep a quilt that reminded us of them."

Elise's mother walked into the room just in time to hear the "confession" and could only manage a gasp of disgust. Even the innocence of childhood could not shield Elise from the heartbreaking sentiment Jacqui shared at that moment. But she loved Jacqui, and deep down, she knew that Jacqui was sad because she didn't have her own quilt with her. So, Elise broke what seemed to be a three-hour silence. "I got a great idea, Jack. Let's both roll up in my quilt." And as soon as their two little bodies were snuggled together, and once again focused on the Saturday cartoons, the sadness that had moments before engulfed the three people like a thick heavy cloud of smoke was replaced with the happy sounds of girly chit-chat and giggles.

Elise drifted off to sleep that Saturday, with memories of that morning with Jacqui, of her grandmother, of her long week of finals, and thoughts of her next semester all intermingling and intertwining to the point where all thoughts become inseparable and indescribable— that strange point where the body gives in to fatigue, but the mind refuses to rest and ventures into the realm of nonsense and confusion. She was in this dream state when she heard the phone ringing. She could hear the ringing clearly and felt as though she were getting up to answer it, but her body would not respond. It was a most peculiar and frightening feeling, and a wave a panic swept through her somewhat paralytic body, awakening all of her sleeping nerve endings and arousing her from her stupor. Happy to be back in the world of the conscious, she answered the phone in a rather exaggerated, cheery voice.

Met with silence on the other end, Elise thought, perhaps, that she had taken too long to get to the phone. The other party may have hung up. But when she repeated her greeting, she was able to hear someone on the other end, barely audible, definitely not comprehensible. Her next "hello" sounded more like a question, in her puzzled attempt to connect with the caller, and it prompted a response in a voice that she barely recognized as Jacqui's. "Jack, is that you? What's wrong?" Mumbling and sobbing followed on the other end. "Jacqui, answer me! What's wrong? Where are you?"

Then, finally, she heard, "I'm home, Lissy. Can you please come over? I need to see you." Then, click. She had hung up.

Elise dropped the phone and without a second thought ran through her kitchen and out the back door. The rain continued to fall, as she ran across her yard and the driveway between her house and Jacqui's. She felt drops streaming down her face and couldn't tell if they were raindrops or if she were actually crying. Something was desperately wrong with Jacqui, and she was afraid to find out what that something was. She might have held her breath all the way to Jacqui's house, if not for the cold chill that traveled from her feet to her chest every time her bare feet ran through a puddle of water, causing her to take large breaths of moist air.

She noticed that Aunt Kitty's car and Jacqui's were both parked in the carport. In a frenzy, she opened the back door without knocking, and, to her surprise, discovered her aunt standing calmly at the kitchen sink, rinsing a couple of cups and saucers. With her back to Elise, Kitty held the phone up to her ear by bending her neck toward her shoulder and seemed to be in the middle of making a lunch date with a friend. It was only when she started to laugh uncontrollably and accidentally dropped the phone that she turned around and noticed Elise standing in the kitchen, drenched from head to foot with a rather crazed look in her eyes.

"Let me go, sugar," she said after she picked up the phone and returned it to her ear. "My little niece just came by to pay me a visit. Umhmm. OK, well, I'll see you at the club, at noon. Umhmmm— (a little more cackling laughter)—bye now." She hung up the phone and looked at Elise as her cajoling little voice switched to a tone of both bewilderment and concern. "For heaven's sake, Elise, look at you. What on earth are you doing out in this weather, dressed like that and soaking wet? Why, you don't even have shoes on. Sit down and I'll fix you some hot tea, or would you rather have hot chocolate?"

Elise just stood there, out of breath, when a terribly unsettling and embarrassing thought crossed her mind. Maybe Jacqui's phone call was part of a dream, part of that frightening, semiconscious experience that awakened her from her slumber. After all, Aunt Kitty seemed perfectly fine, showing no signs of disaster, as far as she could see. It had to be a dream, she decided. Rather self-consciously, she closed her eyes, brought her hands to her face, and rubbed her forehead in disbelief. "Hot chocolate sounds nice, thank you. I'm so sorry I barged in on you like this, Aunt Kitty. I was sound asleep on the couch, and I could've sworn that Jacqui called. Upset, really upset." She pulled a chair away from the kitchen table and let herself fall onto the seat. "God, I must have been dreaming, but it seemed so real. Where is Jacqui, anyway? I saw her car parked outside."

"Oh, she's here, in her bedroom. In fact, honey, she just might have called you, cause she's on some heavy painkillers right now. I didn't want to worry anyone—the doctor assured me that it was a nothing procedure—but I had to take her to the hospital day before yesterday. She had terrible pains in her side. Course, I thought right away it could be her appendix, but they said she had a big cyst on her ovary. So, they did emergency surgery, right then and there, and sent her home last night. Really nothing to it. She has a little discomfort, of course, but no more than the doctor expected. And believe me, he gave her some little pills that have her in another world. Here's your chocolate. Why don't you go on in and see her?"

Jacqui was home recuperating, just as Aunt Kitty had said. But that was the only truth in the story Elise had been told in the kitchen. There was no ovarian cyst. There was, in fact, a baby—Marsh Delacroix's baby. And Jacqui was recovering from an abortion. She made Elise promise over and over again that she wouldn't tell anyone. Jacqui told her that she had to talk to someone, and that she, Elise, was the only person she could trust. Kitty would die if she knew she was telling anyone. And Elise could envision her aunt telling the story of Jacqui's ovarian cyst to all her friends at lunch that day, lying so well that she actually believed herself. Elise also knew that the lie was important to Kitty, because the truth might jeopardize her membership in her little social circle—a membership that was about as secure as a pig hanging from a spider's web.

"Jacqui, I'm really not concerned about your mother, right now. I'm worried about you. I have to ask you, did you really want this abortion or were you forced into it? You seem so upset. Is this what you wanted?" What a stupid thing to say, Elise thought, as soon as the words came out of her mouth. Of course, she's upset. Of course, she didn't want this to happen. But it was Marsh's baby, and everyone assumed that Jacqui and Marsh were going to be married eventually, and Elise couldn't help wondering if Aunt Kitty had more to do with the decision than Jacqui and Marsh.

"Jack, did Marsh know about the baby?"

"Oh, yeah, he did. He felt that this was the right choice, too." And then, in her groggy, drug-induced stammer, Jacqui went on and on, telling Elise how supportive Marsh was throughout the whole ordeal, how he kept assuring her that going through the experience together would make their love for each other stronger, how his heart ached for her, how he wished he could bear the pain instead of her, because he knew she was only going through with it because of his future—their future. "Don't worry about the cost," he said. "My father will take care of everything."

Sure, he would, Elise thought. But not to alleviate Jacqui's worries. Only to alleviate his own. His own worries about Marsh going to the best law school, getting in the best law firm after graduation, following in his own footsteps from district attorney, to judge, to the state senate. Raising an illegitimate child might alter the plans he had made for Marsh from the second the doctor had slapped his baby boy's behind. Elise liked Marsh, but the thought of Jacqui dealing with Lamar and Felicia Delacroix for in-laws was sometimes more than she could bear in silence. She knew that she could never say anything to Jacqui, anyway, because Marsh Delacroix was the only person that Jacqui had ever loved as much as she loved Uncle Billy. And, in all fairness, Marsh seemed mutually crazy about Jacqui. Their fifth-grade crush had only matured and grown stronger over the years, and the miles that separated them when Marsh started law school seemed to increase their need to be with each other. Much to the Delacroix's chagrin, of course. They had higher expectations for a daughter-in-law than the daughter of Billy and Kitty Charleville. Even though, Marsh's father had been practically best friends with Billy, Felicia Delacroix barely spared a glance toward Kitty when they found themselves in the same circle, which, of course, would be a rare moment.

Kitty did little to encourage the relationship between her daughter and the senator's son, which always surprised Elise, knowing what a social climber her aunt tended to be. Sometimes she thought her aunt was actually jealous of Jacqui, marrying into an automatic social position, while she had to work so hard to secure one of her own. Kitty was just the type of mother who could be jealous of her daughter, she thought.

Jacqui dozed off to sleep, still murmuring praises for Marsh, with a smile on her lips as though she were imagining him, not Elise, sitting on her bed, holding her hand. The disturbing feeling that Elise felt throughout Jacqui's emotional rendition of what had occurred was not unwarranted and could have been what her grandmother used to call a premonition. Jacqui never heard from Marsh Delacroix again. No calls, no letters. And her own were never answered. His phone number was changed and unlisted, and her letters were returned with a stamp across the envelope informing her that no one by that name lived at the address anymore. His parents, of course, were of no help, and Kitty did little more than tell her daughter that it was time to move on—forget about Marsh Delacroix. But Jacqui never did.

FRIDAY

Mr. Henry Marchand was up on a scaffold hammering and nailing plywood over the windows of the second story of the house. Elise had called Mr. Henry the day before to make sure that he would be available to help her with her hurricane preparations. Inevitably, the closer Hurricane Georgette got to the coastline, the harder it would be to find a good, reliable carpenter. She knew, though, that Mr. Henry would put her at the top of the list, no matter what time or day she called. He, like his father and grandfather before him, had worked many times for the Charlevilles, who kept them fairly busy with the needs of the docks, packing sheds, and general store.

For decades, the Marchand men were the only local carpenters amidst a population of fishermen. But, like Elise's father, Mr. Henry had no sons. He would be the last of the Marchand woodworkers, and Elise could tell by his slowing pace that the end of another bayou tradition was coming to an end very soon. She had been surprised to hear Mr. Henry, himself, speak so eagerly of retiring, though. It used to be that the men on the bayou worked until their hearts stopped beating. Times were just changing, she guessed. Anyway, the Marchand men were also known for their duck-carving skills. In the old days, the ducks served as decoys for the hunters, but lately the utilitarian trade of carving decoys had become a highly recognized art. Mr. Henry traveled all over the country entering his carved ducks in contests and showing them in art exhibits. Elise imagined that he would devote all of his time to carving when he hung up the hammer.

Except for the sheets of plywood completely covering the large windows of the house, it seemed like a normal afternoon to Elise. Brad was shooting hoops with Delilah, praising her for being able to use the regulation goal that Santa brought last Christmas. Brad had set the basket at its lowest position, still quite a challenge for a nine-year-old. Lilah practiced every afternoon, all spring and summer, determined to reach the basket.

Finally, one day in August, right before the new school year began, Delilah succeeded. It was perfect, because Brad was home at the time, working patiently with her, encouraging her, and occasionally giving his expert pointers, as though he were a retired NBA player. Elise was in the kitchen, at the stove, making a roux, which requires constant stirring of the flour and oil, until the resulting paste-like mixture turns the desired shade of brown.

As she stood there stirring, she looked over the school supply list for Casey, who was starting preschool this year. Jumbo crayons, blunt scissors, wide-rule paper…and then she heard Brad's screaming, coming from the direction of the driveway.

"Oh my God, oh my God, oh my God," she repeated as if to wake up her higher power in case she needed some attention. She just knew something terrible had happened to one of the kids. She dropped everything she was doing, ran through the laundry room tripping over a pile of dirty clothes on the floor, opened the garage door, and made her way through the garage, stumbling over roller blades, tennis rackets, and tricycles carelessly left in the walking path.

Before she even reached the driveway, she started shouting, "What's happened, what's wrong?" Then she saw Brad, swinging Delilah up in the air, her long spindly legs stretching outward, and her thick, wavy, unmanageable auburn hair flying in the wind. The tragic scene Elise had anticipated was instead one of total jubilation. "Thank you, God, thank you God, thank you God," she said to herself as Brad shouted, "Hey, Lissy, she did it!! She did it! I knew she could if she kept practicing!!" He put Delilah back on the ground, and she ran toward Elise grabbing her mom around the waist.

"Watch, Mom. Watch me." Elise tried to look thrilled for the determined child, but she could hardly catch her breath, her heart still pounding from the horrific images she had in her mind only seconds before.

Elise stood there, with her arms bent, her right elbow resting in the palm of her left hand, while she gently rubbed her neck with her right hand—a sure sign to Brad that Elise was upset. "What's wrong, Lissy?" Little Lilah, stood there, holding her basketball, looking up with her curious eyes.

"Nothing. Really. I'm fine. I was just a little startled when I heard the screaming." She didn't dare tell Brad what she imagined she'd find outside. She knew that she worried way too much and overreacted to the point that she and Brad often had discussions about her being too overprotective of the children.

"C'mon Miss Lilah Lou, let's see you go for two." Elise broke the brief tension with a homemade cheer. Delilah grinned, showing her new teeth, which at this point were out of proportion with her petite features. When she raised the big ball over her head, in order to aim and shoot, she looked as if she'd topple over. But in spite of her awkward style, the ball bounced off of the backboard and dropped through the net.

Before the supportive spectators had a chance to cheer properly, a loud, blaring, intermittent beeping noise sounded outside and from within the house. "Is that the burglar alarm or the fire alarm?" Brad asked as he turned to go inside and check out the situation.

"My roux! It's my roux!" Elise pushed her husband aside as she ran back through the laundry room and into her smoke-filled kitchen. She made her way to the cook-top, turned off the burner, and with the help of her mitts, picked up the pot and carried it to the back porch. She came in coughing, eyes burning, opened all the windows and doors, and turned on the ceiling fan.

Brad had turned off the alarm, but not in time to prevent the fire department from sending a truck, siren sounding, loaded with enough men and equipment to put out the Chicago fire. When the smoke had settled and it was determined that no damage had been done, they all had a laugh and agreed that they would never forget the day that Lilah made her first basket.

That happened less than a month ago, and now Lilah was shooting baskets as though she'd been doing so for years. She and Brad were playing a game of h-o-r-s-e, and she was giving her dad a pretty tough time. The little Fisher-Price goal was set up near the garage doors, and Elise was helping J. P. and Casey take turns at their own version of h-o-r-s-e. For Elise, these were perfect moments. Brad and the children, all home, all healthy, all happy. She looked at the four of them—playing together, laughing, teasing, and chasing each other—and imagined herself, as she too often did, separated from them, as though she were looking at them from a distance. As though she were no longer a part of their lives. It was such a spooky feeling. Was this a premonition? Was this a vision or a warning that something was going to happen to her?

She reached out for three-year-old Casey and pulled him close to her. This was the best way to make those awful feelings go away. Feeling his little body close to hers, smelling the outdoors in the dust and sweat in his curly black locks. "I love you," she said as she squeezed him tightly, pretending to "squeeze the sugar out of him." This brought her back. It always did.

She was sure it was the stress, but maybe she should talk to Martha about it when all of this hurricane mess is over, she thought. Although, she already knew what Martha would say. "Guilt, guilt, guilt. You never allow yourself a moment of happiness without compensating with a moment of worry, fear, and anxiety. You're afraid that if you're too happy with your life, God will surely send you torment and sadness to even the score."

This wrathful God was the topic of many of her discussions with Martha, and at eighty dollars an hour, one would think that these nightmarish illusions would go away.

A shiny, black Mercedes-Benz pulled into the driveway behind Elise's Suburban. The three children, out of habit and training, gravitated toward Elise and watched eagerly to see who the visitor was. Elise recognized the car immediately and knew that her best friend Talia, as planned, was there to drop off GianCarlo for the afternoon. Elise's children loved Talia's younger son, who was Delilah's age and was in her homeroom at St. Michael's this year. She hadn't mentioned that GianCarlo would be spending the afternoon with them, because she had learned from experience that people very often change their plans at a moment's notice, and she didn't want the children to be disappointed. Talia was going out to pick up some needed groceries and emergency supplies, and the two moms agreed that it would be fun for the kids to get together and not have to be in the middle of all of the hustle and bustle that might needlessly frighten them.

It had been discussed and agreed upon earlier in the day that Talia and her two sons, Dominick and GianCarlo, would stay with Elise and her family, if the hurricane became a serious threat to their area. Talia's husband, Nicky, was attending a conference, in London, and, in all likelihood, would not be able to return before Georgette's expected landfall.

Elise was very surprised at Talia's ease in dealing with her husband's absence in the face of a crisis situation. She seemed more distressed by the fact that her father had plans to visit with his new, young wife, whom Talia had never met. They were supposed to fly into New Orleans on Sunday, of all times. Elise suggested to her that they would more than likely change their plans. But Talia was not convinced.

"Surely, they must be aware of the fact that people are leaving because of a hurricane, Talia. Your father is the Italian ambassador to the United Nations. He's not a foolish man"

"He's not a foolish man?! How can you say this is not a foolish man? He marries a woman as young as his daughter, less than a year after his wife, my mother, dies. And you say he's not a foolish man? This, I tell you, is a man who would fly into the middle of a hurricane!"

Elise hugged Talia and spoke softly, like a mother quieting her crying baby. "My poor little friend," she said, in a somewhat teasing tone. "I can just about promise you that the evil Georgette will keep away the evil step-mother." They both laughed as Elise walked her friend to her car. "Now, go on. GianCarlo will be fine, and you can spend the rest of the day doing what you do best—shopping!"

"Yes, yes, yes. You are right about that. I'm off. Ciao!"

People were getting out of town already, giving Elise an uneasy feeling about Brad's unilateral decision to stay in their home. Jacqui had called in the morning to let her know that Adam was sending her and her mother up to Casa Victoria, his horse farm and party house just north of Baton Rouge. She begged Elise to join them; they were leaving that afternoon. When Elise suggested that it was a little soon to evacuate, Jacqui reminded her that Adam was so sweet to be so concerned about her safety. He insisted that she leave as soon as possible. He would be leaving on Sunday to join her and Kitty. "Are your parents staying with you? You know that they are more than welcome to come, too. Adam loves your parents."

"Thanks, Jack, but Brad really wants to stay here."

"Is he nuts? Never mind, you don't have to answer that. He's not nuts—he just thinks he can control the weather like he can control everything else."

"Jacqui, that's not fair…"

"I know, I know. But he has no experience with these storms, so I think you should be making the decision to stay or leave. Good Lord, what are you going to do with your three kids, your dad, your mama, and Brad, locked up and boarded in that big house with no electricity, no phone. I'd go nuts, too. Your mama's going to be a nervous wreck before she even gets there. You know that. She always is." Then she laughed. "I'll bet she rubs the shine off her rosary beads!" Elise had to smile, even though she felt uncomfortable when Jacqui joked about her mother's religious habits and hang-ups. But Jacqui didn't mind making Elise feel uncomfortable. In fact, she sometimes enjoyed it. "So, tell me, does your mama still nag you to get your marriage blessed by the Catholic Church?" Jacqui asked, knowing that it would strike a nerve in her cousin's conscience. She loved Elise more than any other woman in the world, yet she still derived mischievous pleasure in disturbing Elise's "perfect" little world.

"Actually, she hasn't bugged me about it in a long time. I guess she's finally realized that I'm not interested in dragging Brad through any religious ceremonial pomp and circumstance when it means absolutely nothing to him. If anything, he disdains anything having to do with organized religion. Is it any wonder? And as far as I'm concerned, it would be totally hypocritical for me to tell a priest that it's really important to us, as a couple, when God knows it's not. And in the end, who is more important, the priest or God?" Her defensive response seemed tense and rehearsed, as though she were trying to convince herself, as well as Jacqui, that she really believed in what she was saying. But Jacqui was not interested in delving that deeply into Elise's state of mind and abruptly replied, "OK, Lissy. I really didn't intend to have a religious, philosophical discussion today. It was just a nosy question. A simple yes or no would have sufficed, honey."

"I know, I know. It's just that even though my mom has stopped bothering me about it, I know that it's killing her to think that I'm 'living in sin.' In fact, I think that she may be talking to Father Thomas about it without involving me. But I can't see how he could bless my marriage for my mother's sake if Brad and I don't go through the proper procedures."

"What? Proper procedures?"

"Yeah. There are strict procedures for these things, Jacqui. Classes, meetings with the clergy, all sorts of red tape."

"I swear, sometimes I wonder how you made it to adulthood being so naïve, Elise!"

"What's that supposed to mean?"

"It means that if Peggy Anne offered a substantial amount of that Charleville inheritance to His Most Holiness at St. Michael's Church... what's his name...Father Thomas...hell, he'd go to the Pope, himself, to get your marriage blessed, with or without Brad's request. That's what I mean."

"Jacqui, I hardly think it's that simple, or that crooked, for that matter."

"Oh really? Do you remember Debra Holden? She graduated two years behind you. Curly, curly red hair. She moved to Bayou Chouteau from Alabama. You know who I'm talking about?"

"Yeah. She still lives in Bayou Chouteau. I see her in church every now and then. But I never really knew her well. Her family sort of kept to themselves."

"Well, I did. And she has a baby now. No husband, but a baby, mind you. Well, Kitty was telling me the other day that Father Thomas christened that baby at St. Michael's—private ceremony, I guess. Now you tell me, since when can a Catholic priest christen an illegitimate child? Huh?"

"I don't know. Maybe there's certain red tape for that situation, too. And maybe Debra was willing to do what was necessary, with a sincere heart."

"Oh right! Do you really believe that crap spewing from your mouth, Elise? I'll tell you what she willingly and sincerely did. She either flashed two benjies and/or two new, store-bought fits in front of the good padre's face, and he willingly and sincerely accepted and complied."

"Jacqui! Don't talk like that! You may not like the man—I'm not crazy about him myself—but don't you think you should show him a little respect?"

"Elise, I show respect for people who earn respect. The only reason you respect him is because he's a priest. That's all. You would feel 'sinful' if you didn't. Well, I have no remorse for my disrespect, because I don't see him as being anybody special, when he clearly uses his position to live high on the hog, never having to worry about a roof over his head or where his next hot meal is coming from. And he uses the pulpit every Sunday, and I mean every Sunday, to beg those poor fishermen for more and more money. That man is in the business to save money, not souls." Elise silently agreed with every word Jacqui had said, but she would never let Jacqui know, or anyone else for that matter. Jacqui wasn't finished, either. "Poor Peggy Anne, praying and begging for the blessings from that womanizing money monger."

"All right, Jacqui, you don't have any proof of what you're saying, so let's change the subject, before you lead me to breaking more commandments than I already have."

"That's right, you harlot." Jacqui laughed until she realized that Elise was not enjoying the humor. "Come on, Lissy, I'm just teasing you. I didn't mean to upset you. Is something wrong that you're not telling me? I know there is, I can always tell."

"Nah nothing more than the usual. It's just the whole religion thing. You wouldn't understand. You always seem to live your life for the moment, never dwelling on the past, never worrying about the future." Elise remembered her own daddy using the same words to describe his brother Billy. "You live your life so freely. You have a way of concentrating on the good things in your life and setting aside the imperfections."

"And you, Elise? Now that we know how I live my life, tell me how you live yours." She was so uncharacteristically serious that without seeing the smirk on her face, Elise couldn't tell if she was mocking her or being sincere. But she jumped at the chance to answer the question.

"Torn. I am forever torn. I will make a decision after dwelling upon what is right, what is wrong, doing what's best, doing what's fair. And yet, look at my life."

"Yeah, I've looked at your life. What's so bad about it? I mean, whenever I describe you to a friend, I always say, 'Well, she's somewhat of combination of Martha Stewart and Mother Theresa.' So, what am I not seeing in your life?"

"Think about it, Jacqui. We were taught to live by the Ten Commandments from the day we were born. And for most of my life, it seemed a pretty easy task. Now, with Brad's situation with his parents—there goes 'honor thy father and mother.' And our marriage not blessed—there goes the adultery law. I can't even remember the exact words anymore. Do you ever think about your life in terms of what is expected of you?"

"Let's see, the last time I gave serious thought to the Ten Commandments was in the sixth grade, Sister Dominick's class. For the life of me, I couldn't put those things in order. Flunked, outright. It must have been a sign, huh?"

They both laughed. "You are hopeless, you know that?"

"No really, Elise. You live by the rules your parents bore into your brain, and I live by the 'rules of Billy.'"

"And what exactly are the 'rules of Billy,' I'm afraid to ask?"

"Billy would always use that old saying, 'I'm just playing the cards I was dealt, baby.' "

"And how does that help you make the right choices?"

"Well, you know, if nothing else, Billy knew his cards. He showed me real early in life how to get rid of the shitty cards early in the game, so as to give yourself a better hand to play."

"I admit that's good advice if you're playing booray, but how…?"

"Just face it, Elise. Your in-law situation is a shitty card—get rid of it. This whole business about Father Thomas not blessing your marriage—another shitty card—get rid of it. Listen, I promise you, if you get to the gates of Heaven and you can't get in, it'll be because Father Thomas and I died before you, and we're stuck outside blocking the door!"

She couldn't help but laugh at Jackie's scenario. And it did feel good to laugh about the problems in one's life every now and again, even if laughter never made the problems go away forever. "Thanks, Jacqui."

"You should thank me. I've used up my whole lunch break talking to you about this nonsense. On my cell phone, too. They say you can get brain cancer from that. I just thought I'd throw that tidbit of information in so that you can worry and feel guilty for the rest of the day."

"Oh, you are so funny. But seriously, I can't believe you're showing houses today. I would think everyone would be more concerned about evacuating for this hurricane than they would about moving or buying a new home."

"Oh, there's this real young couple from Minnesota—Missouri—Montana—somewhere up there. They're so excited, because they're going to be here to experience their first hurricane. Can you believe that? Stupid Yankees!"

Elise was about to admonish Jacqui, in her maternal fashion, for her "stupid Yankees" comment and remind her that the Civil War ended well over a hundred years ago, but she just let it go and wished her luck with the showing. And before hanging up added, "Hey, don't forget to call me before you leave town."

"Will do—love ya!" Click.

Elise hung up and took a deep breathe. What a character! She had never really talked to Jacqui about religion before, and she just assumed that they were equally engrained in their Judeo-Christian traditions. But how could she be, with Kitty and Billy for parents? Joseph and Peggy Anne had certainly taken their duties as Catholic parents seriously. And Delilah, even though she had her qualms with the clergy, she had remained respectful until the end of her life. But Jacqui, for the most part, was raised by Kitty, alone. Kitty wasn't raised Catholic and never made a secret of it. She hated everything about the church and being Catholic. She did convert to marry Billy, though, and now, Elise wondered if LaLa had to flash any Charleville money before Father Frederick's eyes. She hated the thought. She just couldn't imagine her highly principled grandmother doing such a thing. But maybe she did, because it was even harder to imagine Aunt Kitty going to those adult catechism classes just to please Delilah Charleville.

Elise walked into the laundry room with the intention of organizing the emergency supplies and groceries, which had been gradually piled upon the dryer. The many lists she had made since the likelihood of Hurricane Georgette hitting had become more and more of a probability, were strewn all over the house. So, she opted to rely on the mental notes she had created during her relentless attempt to be perfectly prepared and in total control of any situation that might arise with the storm. After all, that was her job; that was what was expected of her. At least that was what she expected of herself.

At that particular moment, however, her mental notes were not coming in very clearly. Jacqui's conversation had aroused her memory of a little engagement celebration that her cousin had planned when she and Brad decided to get married. It was to be really special, Jacqui had promised. Just the four Charleville ladies—Jacqui and Kitty, Elise and Peggy Anne. They met at The Court of Two Sisters, in the French Quarter, each mother and her daughter, at eleven o'clock, on an absolutely perfect Sunday morning.

Although Jacqui had requested a special table in a private setting, they were seated in the courtyard where the usual Sunday jazz brunch was already in full swing. Jacqui was noticeably upset with the arrangement, but Elise was quite pleased with the table, because it was such a perfect day. In addition to the mountain of traditional New Orleans food set out for their partaking, a fountain set on a round table near them overflowed and trickled with cool, pink champagne.

It was a well-known fact to all who knew Kitty Charleville, that when it came to most alcoholic beverages, she could drink any man under the table. But it was also a well-known fact that only a few small glasses of the bubbly could turn her into a drunken sot. She was aware of this weakness and usually stayed clear of the champagne tables, but on this particular day, the champagne demons took control of her, unmercifully so. With each sip, her voice got louder and louder, so that by the time the foursome had finished their appetizers, Kitty was easily attracting the attention of the diners in their vicinity. From Elise's vantage point, she could see the stares and the heads quickly turning in their direction—some to show their disdain, others just to get a better idea of the topic of conversation at the very lively table, just in case it was more interesting than the ones at their own quiet, reserved gatherings.

Aunt Kitty did not mind causing a stir. In fact, it often seemed that she would devise ways to become the center of attention. But Jacqui had planned the brunch to honor Elise and was determined to do her best to prevent her mother from upstaging her cousin. Kitty, however, had her own plans. At first, her loud exhortations were harmless—embarrassing because they captured the attention of others—but harmless. Several times, she raised her glass, as if it were the first time, to "toast the bride-to-be." Elise's face blushed so that she could feel her nerve endings prickling from beneath her skin. Neighboring diners raised their glasses politely each time a toast was announced, probably to comfort the bride-to-be, who was visibly uncomfortable with the attention.

As the meal progressed, however, Kitty's remarks became intentionally sarcastic, laced in her bitter, angry tone. "I find it so ironic,

Peggy Anne, that your daughter, of all people, will be the first person from Bayou Chouteau to marry a Jew—with you being so Catholic and all. Aren't you the tiniest bit upset?"

Instinctively, Peggy Anne's hand moved to find her daughter's hand just a few inches from her own. Always protecting me, Elise thought, as she heard her mother's response come out almost as a whisper, in an attempt to get Kitty to lower her voice. "I'd be lying if I said it didn't worry me, Kitty. Marriage these days is tough enough without differences in faith. But Brad seems to be a good man. And if he makes Elise happy, well then, Joseph and I are happy."

Peggy Anne's quiet, diplomatic answer seemed to calm the wired setting only for a moment before Kitty answered boisterously, "Oh, I'm with you there! I've always heard that Jewish husbands treat their wives like queens—put them on pedestals, they say. Whether they love them or not!" And she laughed loudly at her comment as though she had created the world's first comic moment.

"Aunt Kitty, I hardly think that Jewish men are categorically different than all other men in the role of husband. I think it has more to do with the nature of the individual, no matter what his religious background may be."

"Ha!" It seemed as though the whole courtyard jumped in response to her sarcastic burst of laughter. "Don't you ever believe that, little girl. Those Jewish men are taught to respect women. It comes from their mothers. But the Catholic men…they think God created man during a moment of inspiration, and then created woman during a bowel movement. Therefore, they can treat women like shit!"

"Mother! Lower your voice! Please. And stop drinking. Everyone is staring at us." Elise had been wondering just how long it would take Jacqui to say something to Kitty. Jacqui was always very careful not to take attention from her mother. She knew Kitty couldn't stand that. But even Jacqui was at the point of embarrassment.

Kitty glared at her daughter in a way that sent chills down Elise's spine. Then she slurred, in Jacqui's direction, "You're just afraid I'm gonna say something bad about your precious daddy. But I won't," she said, turning away from Jacqui, in order to get another little sip. "I'll be nice."

"Kitty, you know that was a terrible thing to say." Peggy Anne spoke in uncharacteristic fashion. "Joseph has been a fine, loving husband and father to me and Elise, and I won't have you saying things like that to the girls."

"The girls?" Kitty mockingly looked around. "I don't see any girls. These two are grown women. I'm only giving them some advice. Good advice, too. Besides, I always told Billy that, in my opinion, his brother Joseph's real loyalty was to his mother—not you, Peggy Anne. Lucky for you, I guess, he was never put in a position to choose between his mother and his wife. I think you would have been sorely disappointed."

"Mother, please. You are ruining this day and I wanted it to be so special for Elise. Now lower your voice and apologize to Aunt Peg."

"That's not necessary, Jacqui." Peggy Anne was once again appeasing for peace. This time it was Elise who reached for her mother's hand. And as she did, she wondered if what Kitty said was true. She had never thought of that aspect of her parents' marriage. Would her father have put Delilah Charleville ahead of his wife? And now that it was brought to her attention, she could see by the troubled expression on her mother's face that it wasn't the first time Peggy Anne had considered it. "Joseph was a teenager when his father died, Kitty. Billy was merely a child. I think both boys admired their mother for holding the family, as well as the family businesses, together. She was a strong woman and a kind-hearted mother. I would never deny her Joseph's loyalty. I never saw it the way that you did. She was kind to me, too." It was hard for Elise to determine if she heard anger or apology in her mother's voice. It didn't matter, though. It was exactly what she needed to hear at that moment.

"She may have been kind to you, Peggy Anne, but I swear I thought they'd find vinegar in her veins when they did her autopsy." Again, Kitty laughed harshly, while her three companions sat in silence, digesting her last remark.

"I think I'm going to have a cup of coffee. I feel a chill in the air. Aunt Kitty, would you like some coffee?" Elise asked.

"Nah, honey. I have my two cups in the morning and that's it. Anyway, I'm enjoying this champagne. Why aren't y'all having some?"

"We've each had a couple of glasses, Mother. And I think you've had enough for all of us," said Jacqui in an attempt to get her mother to stop drinking.

"Jesus H. Christ, Jacqueline. Who are you to tell me when I've had enough? I hardly think I need you to be my mommy." She lit a cigarette and smiled as though she had really put her daughter in her place.

"Kitty, you know that I tolerate just about anything that comes out of your mouth, but Elise will tell you that I do not tolerate anyone using the Lord's name in that manner."

Now she's mad, Elise feared. And when Kitty saw that she had upset Peggy Anne, she started to laugh her loud, raspy, uncontrollable laugh. She was so loud, that the maître d' walked over to the table and politely asked if she could lower her voice a bit. In his timid approach, he looked as though her were attempting to tame a wild lion. It was by far one of the most humiliating moments in Elise's life. Jacqui's face had turned a sickly pale shade, and Peggy Anne was noticeably fighting back tears.

The waiter asked if he could bring them anything else, and with the exception of Kitty, they each ordered coffee and dessert. "I'm sorry, Peggy Anne. I guess I sometimes forget how seriously you take those rules of the church. After all, I'm just a convert, hee, hee. Maybe I'll have to say a couple of Our Fathers and few Hail Delilahs, hee, hee. I mean Hail Marys. It was always so hard for me to remember which one was the Holy Mother. Ha, ha." This time her laughter was accompanied by her knocking over two water goblets. And as she jumped up to protect herself from the stream of water flowing from the table, directly onto her lap, she inadvertently hit the arm of the waiter who happened to be delivering their three cups of coffee. Jacqui immediately got up from the table and grabbed Kitty's arm, as though she were a policeman catching a thief at the end of a chase. Kitty's laugh had reached the point of uncontrollable hysterical cackling. Fortunately, for the two women left at the table, and the poor stunned waiter covered in hot, freshly brewed coffee and chicory, all eyes followed Kitty as Jacqui led her away. And somehow, the inebriated woman's laughter was contagious. Laughter filled the courtyard and Elise, and Peggy Anne were spared any judgmental, scrutinizing stares that could have followed Kitty's obnoxious behavior. After a breathless moment of silence, Elise and Peggy Anne both blurted out, "Poor Jacqui."

"Mama, you'll have to take care of her when I move away. You know, LaLa used to tell me all the time, 'Take care of your little cousin. She'll need you as she grows up.' I haven't been able to help her very much, except to listen to her when she needs to talk."

"I doubt that I can take your place in her life, baby. I know that no one will ever take your place in mine." For a few moments, the rest of the world around them seemed to have disappeared, and silent, reluctant tears streamed down the faces of mother and daughter, who both hated to cry in public. But neither woman cared. And while some tears were tears of sorrow at the thought of Elise moving away, most of the tears were tears of joy and tears of gratitude toward each other. With all of their differences, all of their disagreements, they were not, and never would be like the mother and daughter who had just left the table.

PEGGY ANNE MOREAU
CHARLEVILLE
1940s

The deep bellow of the horn of the drawbridge still resonated over children's slumber as the fishing boats passed under the old, lifted structure on their way to the surrounding lakes and bays, where the catch of the day awaited. The steady hum and chugging of the boats' engines still could be heard over the chirping of birds, dedicating their little arias to the dawn of a new day. The sun would soon be rising, and the children would soon be waking up to a new day, getting ready for school and eating their breakfast in the familiar surroundings of their cozy homes, their whole morning routines orchestrated by their mothers while their fathers were well on their way to the open waters and a long, hard day, or possibly a few days of making a living.

Slowly and patiently, the captains piloted their boats through the brown, rippling water, not merely to avoid waking their neighbors, but rather to avoid making large wakes behind the boats, which could rock the other boats docked along the bayou, bashing them into the wharves and causing careless and unnecessary damage to their neighbors' property. There were no signs posted to remind the local captains to coast slowly down the bayou—it was a very well-respected, unwritten rule. And on weekends, when the commercial fishermen were all back from their weekly trips, the "sport fishermen" from the city would flock to the local boat launches, and "take over," racing down the bayou, full throttle. If they were unaware of the local law when they arrived in Bayou Chouteau, they would soon find themselves subject to a little bayou education, as the fishermen working on their boats and their children playing along the banks of the bayou yelled loudly, "Slow down, you city morons, or you won't make it back to the cement!" The cement, of course, was a reference to the city, a place where real bayou men found it hard to breathe.

There was another unwritten rule on the bayou that seemed to prevail without any explanation or enforcement. The women of the family—mothers, wives, and daughters—rarely ventured onto the wharves and boats in front of their homes. There was a very clear, respected distinction between the man's working domain and that of the woman's. Hearth, home, and health of the children naturally fell under the jurisdiction of the wife, and the financial support of the family was the unquestionable responsibility of the husband. The vegetable garden was the one area where husband and wife could be seen working together side by side. There were very few exceptions to this traditional way of life. But, in Bayou Chouteau, Delilah Charleville was one of the exceptions.

In a similar manner, there was an unwritten rule, which dictated that the women on the bayou were not to concern themselves with things happening around the world. After all, Bayou Chouteau was their entire world, and they were kept busy enough keeping their own piece of the world in order. The men, on the other hand, kept abreast of current events, and on December 7, 1941, they were shocked and outraged as the news spread about the surprise attack on Pearl Harbor. It was as though the bombing had occurred in nearby Moss Point, rather than that far-away island in the middle of the Pacific Ocean. And it was Delilah Charleville who opened her home to the concerned men on the following day, so they could gather around her big, fancy radio and listen to President Franklin Roosevelt declare war on Germany and Japan. And filled with anger and glimpses of youthful invincibility, they cheered in support of their leader, giving very little thought to the probability that some of their unwritten rules would soon become vague memories of a precious time gone by.

Shortly, thereafter, the young men of Bayou Chouteaux left their homes in the little fishing village and set off for destinations with names they had never before heard, to places they never knew existed, and to futures that only God could foretell. Their farewells usually took place at the train station or the Port of Embarkation in New Orleans. And though every family member wept at the thought of the separation and uncertainty of their loved one's safe return, the young men parted with the enthusiasm of eager patriots and the anxious anticipation of travelers setting off on an expense-paid trip around the world. For most of these men, if not all, had never been out of the Bayou Chouteau area, with the exception of an occasional trip to "town," as the locals referred to New Orleans. The war raging in Europe and the Pacific Ocean was so far removed from their peaceful, predictable lives that they could not imagine in their worst nightmares the horrific world into which their new journeys would take them.

With her elder son, Joseph, off to the war, and her younger son, Billy, at home attempting to maintain as much normalcy as possible in his few remaining carefree years of high school, Delilah Charleville found it necessary to take on some extra help to keep both of her business enterprises running smoothly. Production at the general store and the packing sheds had been virtually unaffected by the war, but the manpower had been reduced drastically. Although most of the fishermen were able to stay with their boats and nets, because they were heads of the households, just about every family had sent their sons off to fight. It became extremely difficult to find deckhands to replace the sons, who had grown up on their fathers' boats, learning the fishing business and taking their permanent positions alongside their fathers as soon as they felt they had attained enough formal schooling to get them through a fisherman's life. In unprecedented fashion, wives began joining their spouses on the boats, filling in for their sons, and living a life their own mothers had never experienced and could never imagine.

Delilah, too, had to find help from unconventional sources. She hired the older women and young girls of Bayou Chouteau, as well as those of the "colored" village a few miles away, to pick and peel the seafood and pack it up to be sold to the city markets. Ordinarily, these women would have considered it shameful to find work outside their homes, especially with "colored folk" and "white folk" working side by side. But the war had put those old notions to rest, at least temporarily. And it was Delilah Charleville's contention, that if the truth be known, it was the happiest she had seen the women of Bayou Chouteau. Their daily routines of housework had been broken up by their outside obligations. For the first time in their lives, they were getting paid for their hard work, making money to contribute to the family income. And it was a social outlet as well. When the women gathered around the long tables stacked high with the fresh seafood Delilah had bought off of the boats of their family members, pile after pile to be processed by their own hands, they found comfort and enjoyment in the conversations and camaraderie they shared with their neighbors and friends, as their fingers moved with rapid precision, peeling, sorting, and packaging.

It was during these uncharacteristic times in Bayou Chouteau's history that Peggy Anne Moreau entered the everyday lives of the Charleville family. Peggy Anne was one of eleven children born to Alfred and Clothilde Moreau. Her rank in the brood was middle child, which, in this particular family, was synonymous with unnoticed, overlooked, used, and, quite often, left to fend for oneself. The Moreaus were unquestionably the neediest family in the small village, due largely to the fact that Alfred rarely worked and spent most of his time, instead, at T-Boo's Tavern, where he could be found almost any time, any day, sitting on the stool at the end of the bar, his body leaning forward on his folded arms as they protected the tall glass of beer that he seemed to be smelling when he wasn't sipping.

There were always excuses—the boat needed repairs that he couldn't afford, the engine burned up, his back hurt, his deckhand quit without notice—the list of misfortunes was endless. Behind Alfred's back, the other fishermen would banter about how ol' Alfred just didn't have time to make a living 'cause he was just too damn busy making babies. And then they'd all complain when their wives took up collections through the women's auxiliary at St. Michael's to raise money for the Moreau family. "Why don't Alfred put those lazy-ass boys of his to work? My boys work. Ya never walk in that house when ya don't see 'em layin' around on those couches in a middle of the day, while poor Clothilde is trying to clean aroun' em. Alfred ain't taught those boys nothin' but how to make excuses."

But it was because of "poor Clothilde" that their wives offered the little help that they could. She had started having babies when she was fourteen, and her hard life, added to pregnancy after pregnancy, had resulted in the now middle-aged woman looking more like a grandmother than a mother to her eleven offspring. In spite of her rather substandard living conditions, though, Clothilde managed to keep her children clean, well-fed, and healthy. So, while Alfred Moreau was little more than a laughing matter amongst the men in the community, Clothilde Moreau was rather revered, almost sanctified, by their wives. She was seen as the image of their spiritual belief that the more burden you bear on earth, the more rewards you will receive in heaven. And perhaps, they hoped that by making such a woman the recipient of their alms, they, too, would receive favorable nods when they reached their final destinations.

In the beginning, the charitable donations were given in the form of cash, but it didn't take long for the ever-watchful eyes of the St. Michael's Altar Society to see that there was a strong correlation between the amount of cash given to Clothilde and the duration of Alfred Moreau's inability to work. At some point, they realized that the charitable donations did little to improve Clothilde's life. Thereafter, money would be collected for "the charitable needs of St. Michael's parishioners" by means of raffles, bake sales, and bingos. Then the money would be used to purchase specific items that the "poor Moreaus might need"—like clothes for the children or little gifts at Christmas.

Clothilde's cloistered life and Alfred's wonted state of intoxication spared them the humiliation of the cruel jokes and comments, which followed the mere mention of their family name amidst a group or gathering of local fishermen. But their children were constantly plagued by disparaging remarks made by their schoolmates each day. Although Clothilde was adamant about her children's cleanliness and tidiness, they continually faced name calling, demeaning little poems, and contrived rumors, which reflected and befitted the lazy, slovenly manners and appearance of their father. Peggy Anne would cringe each time the teachers decided to have "lice checks," at school, because even though the Moreau children were always declared "nit free," the other students would call them the lice heads of the school. They'd say that no one would have lice if it weren't for the dirty Moreau kids spreading them to everybody else. And there probably wouldn't even be lice checks if it weren't for them. Peggy Anne knew, of course, that this was not the case. She was a bright girl and understood that you can't spread something you aren't carrying. But the comments always made her feel like what they were saying was true. Even though she knew it couldn't be.

Although lice check only occurred a couple of times during the school year, the hurtful comments directed toward Peggy Anne's family had become a part of her and her siblings' daily routine. And somewhere around second grade, it became very clear to Peggy Anne that things would never change. Even back then, she was rarely included in the group games or activities at recess. And if she were asked to join in the play, it was only because someone was needed for the role of the villain, the crazy person, or some "untouchable" character. One of their favorite games was a version of tag, where all the children would have to run away from Peggy Anne, who during the entire game was referred to as the plague. And if Peggy Anne touched one of the little darlings, he or she was "infected" and would be sent to sit under the huge oak tree in the middle of the playground, which was designated the location of the plague hospital.

She participated in these little games in order to feel like a part of her class, to feel like she was accepted by her classmates, but she soon realized how cruel their actions were and just how horrible she felt when she submitted herself to their cruelty. As soon as she was able to read, Peggy Anne spent her recesses alone with a book, seated on the bench located near the school entrance. As soon as the bell rang, she quickly retreated to the somewhat safe haven of the classroom, where even the meanest kids would have to admit she was the brightest of all.

The Moreau children never discussed their disheartening experiences at home. Perhaps talking about their problems at home would have only extended the agony of their day and ignoring them helped to alleviate the pain, if only until they returned to school the next day. Peggy Anne tried, once or twice, to bring up the topic at the dinner table, hoping that together her mother and siblings could come up with some solution to make their lives a little more tolerable. But her attempts to change their lives were futile. She didn't bother complaining to Alfred, because, if she could catch him at home and if he were awake and if he were sober, he simply wouldn't be concerned. And, as for Clothilde, the few times Peggy Anne cried and told her of their emotional hardships, she just sighed and told her heartbroken daughter to "pray on it."

"Praying on it" was Clothilde's solution to all of life's problems. Praying on it, lighting candles, making promises and donations to the saints—these were the only methods that her poor tired body and uneducated mind could afford. Because when her body and mind failed her, she always had the spirit and the faith to carry her on. And her method worked—for her, that is. Peggy Anne had her doubts. Be that as it may, every Sunday, Clothilde could be seen walking from her home to St. Michael's Catholic Church with her brood following, like a mother duck leading her ducklings to a pond. They would fill the back pew—the first to arrive, the last to leave.

Clothilde and her children would sit in the same order each week—Clothilde on the aisle, her eyes shut in reverence throughout most of the mass. She was not to be disturbed during the only hour of the week that she could sit in peace and quiet. The children sat remarkably still, respectful, in the house of God, and to the many regulars who spent their most holy time of the week staring at their neighbors and friends, it was difficult to discern if the children's shared facial expressions depicted a look of sullen despair or one of absolute spiritual tranquility. In this manner, they sat each week, wearing the same clothes they had donned the week before, unless of course, there was a family growth spurt, in which case the same clothes were handed down to the next in line. Poor Father Fredericks. How often he must have thought he was experiencing déjà vu, when his glance took him to the back row of St. Michael's, during his recitations of the mass, which after forty years of repeated performances required very little concentration and conscious effort.

Peggy Anne cringed every Sunday and Holy Day of Obligation as she walked through the doorway of St. Michael's behind her mother in the line of eleven Moreau kids on parade, on display, feeling the piercing stares of pity from the adults and hearing the whispers and snickering of the children as they settled into their usual pew. At least she thought that was what she was feeling and hearing. She could never be real sure, because she hardly ever held her head up upon entering the church. She kept her head lowered, as though she were praying, even as she genuflected in the aisle next to the pew. She tried her best not to look around the church, avoiding eye contact with any other parishioners. She knew that her mother thought that she was praying, but how could anyone pray in the midst of a mean spirit. That's what she felt around her—a mean spirit—not a holy spirit. Didn't her mother feel it, too? How could she not feel it? It surrounded them. She could almost feel it, resting heavily on her shoulders, preventing her from sitting up straight in her seat. And yet her mother just sat, stood, and knelt, with eyes closed and a sweet, peaceful smile of contentment on her kind face. It was the same sort of expression that Peggy Anne had seen on pictures and statues of the Holy Mother. Maybe that was it. Maybe her mother had some sort of special calling, too. Maybe that's why her mother couldn't feel the mean spirit.

Little Lucy, Peggy Anne's youngest sibling, couldn't feel it either. Little Lucy, as everyone referred to the frail, freckle-faced, redhead, was the only ray of sunshine in Peggy Anne's life and holding her tiny hand during mass was about the only part of the ceremonial morning that resembled anything close to godliness. Little Lucy was the only sibling to whom Peggy Anne felt any real attachment, and that attachment seemed to give the older sister a real purpose and meaning for the life that her creator chose for her.

Little Lucy's given name was Lucille Agnes Moreau, named after two of Clothilde's aunts, who lived on the bayou near Houma. Peggy Anne had never met the two aunts who were given the honor of a namesake, so she always figured that the reason the names were chosen was not that the aunts were so special to Clothilde, but that her parents were simply running out of names. No one called the little girl Lucille, not even Lucy, always Little Lucy. On the little girl's first day of school, Peggy Anne went directly to the first-grade teacher, Sister Lawrence, and asked her to please call her sister Lucille. She did for a while, until one day, out on the playground, Peggy Anne heard the shrill voice of the nun calling "Little Lucy Moreau" to be the line leader as she led her marching students back to class. It bothered Peggy Anne to think that her beautiful little sister would grow up to be a beautiful woman and be stuck with a name like Little Lucy. It sounded like a hand-me-down name.

Other thoughts bothered Peggy Anne, when it came to pondering Little Lucy's future. She hated the idea of the little girl being teased at school, finding out that Santa Claus was really the charitable donations of the St. Michael's Altar Society, and having nothing but hand-me-down shoes, clothes, and toys. One Sunday, as the children left their house and started on their walk to St. Michael's, Clothilde looked at Peggy Anne and informed her that her dress was getting too tight, and that she was going to take it in and hem it for Little Lucy to wear. All during mass, Peggy Anne stared down at the faded print of what she thought was surely the ugliest dress in the whole world. It had little stick people, girls in pink, boys in blue, standing side-by-side, upside down, right side up, all over a graying white background. She made a promise to herself that morning, while everyone was listening to Father Frederick's homily, that Little Lucy would never wear that dress. She spent the remainder of mass praying for a plan to destroy the dress without getting into trouble, but the divine inspiration did not come to her until she reached home. Just before the family reached the front door of their house, Clothilde told Peggy Anne to go to the back yard and pull a few shallots for her to use in preparing their Sunday dinner. Reluctantly, but without complaint, Peggy Anne obeyed. And as she made her way around the corner of the house and on to the backyard, her eyes fell upon the answer to her prayer.

Alfred and the boys had spent the day before dipping a new trawl, the net used for catching shrimp, into a barrel of tar. The thick, black, smelly liquid had dripped down the side of the barrel and still looked wet from the hot, midday sun. The barrel just happened to be sitting near the side of the garden where the bright green stalks of Clothilde's shallots sprouted from the ground, looking more like spring bulbs that had already lost their flowers than a vegetable used to season an étouffée. In one of her very rare devious moments, Peggy Anne walked past the barrel making sure to get several streaks of black goo down the side of her dress. She would just tell her mama that she tripped on the shovel that her careless brothers had left near the garden and fell against the barrel as she gathered the shallots. And so it was that Little Lucy never had to wear the ugliest dress in the whole world. That night, as Peggy Anne lay in bed with her arm around Little Lucy's body, like a child holding on to a favorite stuffed teddy bear, she whispered a prayer of thanks to the Holy Mother for intervening on her behalf and asked forgiveness for the little white lie that slipped through her lips to save her rear end.

Peggy Anne was sure that the Holy Mother intervened once again on her behalf the day that Billy Charleville announced to their class that his mama was looking for some kids to help out around the packing sheds after school and on weekends. This was her calling; she was sure of it. Of course, it wasn't the packing sheds she was interested in, it was the general store. And if Mrs. Charleville needed help at the packing sheds, she probably could use some help at the store. Besides, if she got a job at the packing sheds, she would never escape the crowd she spent her entire life avoiding. Peggy Anne had given very little thought to any plans for her future, because it seemed to her that being one of the Moreau kids was her past, present, and future. It was a lifetime sentence.

But seconds after Billy Charleville's announcement, Peggy Anne found herself thinking about her graduation in two years and the possibilities of moving to New Orleans, finding a job, and working in the city, which she had only heard about, even though it was only about thirty miles away. A high school diploma and two years of experience working with Delilah Charleville could possibly make what seemed to be unimaginable a minute before Billy's announcement become a reality. A life away from Bayou Chouteau. A life of her own and on her own. A life in a place where no one even knew there was such a person as Alfred Moreau, where no one knew that she was one of eleven. It was this final thought that made her think of Little Lucy, and she quickly decided that she would take Lucille with her when she left the bayou. Yes, somehow, she would take her away from it all.

It took two weeks, for fourteen-year-old Peggy Anne Moreau to muster up the courage and self-confidence that she needed to approach Delilah Charleville for a job. She never mentioned the opportunity to anyone at home, not even her mother, Clothilde. She never even mentioned it to Little Lucy. And as she walked toward the Charleville General Store, a variety of thoughts popped in and out of her head. She giggled when she thought about how every girl in her school would be blind with jealousy when they heard that she would be spending every day after school and weekends working in the presence of Billy

Charleville. After all, he was, by far, the most popular guy in school. Quarterback of the football team, captain of the basketball team, pitcher on the baseball team. He and his buddy Lamar Delacroix could have just about any girl they wanted in Bayou Chouteau. They were both rich and good looking. But Billy was the nicer of the two, as far as Peggy Anne was concerned. Lamar had never bothered to say a kind word to her for as long as she'd known him, and that was a long time. Billy, on the other hand, talked to her every day. Sometimes it was just to say hello or good-bye, but it was always something. Just enough to let her know he wasn't ashamed to be her friend.

Peggy Anne was sure that Billy knew how the girls idolized him, and she was sure, too, that he realized that they each looked at him as a marriage prospect. Because, in Bayou Chouteau, most girls got married right after high school. So, they had to have a good prospect nibbling at the bait, if not completely hooked, by the time graduation came along. That's how things were for girls on the bayou.

The few who weren't lucky enough to hook their catch would usually find jobs as secretaries at the parish courthouse or with the parish newspaper over in Moss Point, the next town up the bayou. Very few families had cars during the war, and those girls who ventured up the bayou for employment would all put money together to pay Maurice Chauvin's son, Claude, to transport them, by boat, to Moss Point each morning before he went to school. Then, at the end of their workday, he'd transport them home. Maurice's boat would otherwise be idle, since Delilah Charleville hired its owner to manage and oversee the packing sheds in the absence of her son older son, Joseph. Peggy Anne was certain that she did not want to be a part of that group of chatty women who gathered each morning on the Chauvins' dock, gossiping and carrying on, while they could just about hear their "old maid clock" ticking away over the steady hum of their chatter.

Peggy Anne had chosen her going-to-church dress for her unscheduled meeting with the most important woman in Bayou Chouteau. Her thick, straight chestnut hair was pulled back tightly into a ponytail that fell down to the middle of her back. The green ribbon, which she had tied into a perfect bow around her rubber band, had come from the Christmas packages given to the Moreaus by the altar society just two months before. She was glad Clothilde had saved it. She was thinking about removing her tiny, gold, wire-framed glasses, since she was constantly teased for wearing them, but she couldn't see a thing without them.

Staring at the ground, arms folded just above her waist, Peggy Anne walked in a metronomic pace, as though she were consciously thinking about the timing and precision of each step. Confidence and determination seemed to set the course for this otherwise timid teenager on her mission. But suddenly, her eyes beheld the shabby, black and white saddle oxfords that she had tried to cobble and polish the night before—to no avail, she thought. The realization of her futile efforts automatically triggered the dreaded recurring thoughts, which had, for as long as she could remember, tormented her lonely days and sleepless nights. The harder she tried to ignore the thoughts, the louder and more persistently they echoed in her mind. "Why did I have to be a Moreau, God? Why did you have to give so many children to one set of parents? And then, to a father who is so lazy, who doesn't care about his wife, much less his eleven children. It's not fair! Mama is always saying how sad it is that poor Mrs. Dubos always wanted a baby and couldn't have one. So why couldn't you have given me to her? I'm sick of being poor and pitied, teased and ashamed. I hate my life!"

Such horrible thoughts could only come from the power of Satan. That's what her mama would say if she knew Peggy Anne had these awful thoughts. Therefore, only the power of God could bring her back to her senses. And Peggy Anne could always tell when God decided to step in and unleash his mighty, unlimited power, because at that very moment the resentment and self-pity that literally made her heart ache, just seconds before, would be replaced with an overwhelming wave of shame and guilt. That's how God spoke to Peggy Anne. No matter what she prayed for or what she wondered, her answer always came, she thought, in the form of shame and guilt. Clothilde always told Peggy Anne that God loved each person he created with the same joy and passion. But Peggy Anne had her doubts. Because the only way she felt the presence of God was in the form of shame and guilt. And on this particular day, as she stood all alone on the narrow bayou road that led to the Charleville General Store, shame and guilt traveled like a lightning bolt through her tall, thin body. The shame and guilt of her selfish thoughts rendered a momentary paralytic shock to every nerve ending and muscle in her body.

She stopped walking and wrapped her arms around her trembling body, as though she were hugging herself, and with her head still hanging, she shut her eyes tightly, trying to stop the barrage of tears flowing uncontrollably down her cheeks.

"Stop it, stop it, stop it," Peggy Anne commanded her emotions. But, at that particular moment, there were just too many emotions to control. In addition to her recurring feelings of anger and self-pity, which always led to shame and guilt, she was also dealing with the fear and anxiety surrounding the mission at hand—asking Delilah Charleville for a job at the general store. Unable to pull herself together, she backtracked about a quarter of a mile, running as fast as her wobbly legs could take her, to the only place she could ever find relief for her wrecked body and spirit—St. Michael's Catholic Church.

Peggy Anne pulled on the heavy brass rings that opened the massive oak doors and slipped her limp body into the sanctuary. Out of breath, she gasped for air, and as she did, she took in the fragrance of the burning incense and candles. She could feel and almost envision the combination of cool, moist air and the aroma of the scented oils entering her body and flowing through, slowly, methodically, from her head down to the tips of her toes, like a stream of water, flowing down a mountainside, following its natural course and providing comfort, healing, and life-giving powers all along its path.

The familiar thick, fragrant air of St. Michael's comforted Peggy Anne healed her pain, and gave her life, as she steadily walked toward the altar, genuflected, and turned right, as though she were guided unconsciously toward the statue of the Holy Mother. She knelt upon the hard kneeler with no consideration given to the discomfort this brought to her youthful, bony knees. She lowered her head in reverence, and yes, in shame, and started to say a Rosary. Although she did not have her blessed prayer beads with her, she resorted to the method she had invented herself, for moments such as this, using her fingers and hands to represent each prayer that she murmured in sincere repentance, and while her lips fled through her penance, by rote memory, she managed to pray to God in her mind, "Please God, forgive me for my selfish thoughts and know that I am forever grateful for the blessings you have bestowed upon me. Please do not punish me or anyone in my family for what I was thinking. I know that I have no right to question your plan. Mama always tells me that. I know that my problems are so small, and that if I am ungrateful, you can punish me by sending pain and sorrow to me and my family. Mama always tells me that. All the time. I beg of you heavenly Father, take away my sinful thoughts and have mercy on me..."

Peggy Anne had long stopped crying, but she realized that she had been rocking back and forth during her prayer and recitation, when her body's rhythmic motion was stopped abruptly by a hand on her right shoulder. Startled for an instant, aroused from her somewhat mesmerized trance, she quickly turned, expecting and dreading to see Father Fredericks. Instead, she found herself looking into the eyes of Delilah Charleville.

The older woman had entered the church through the side door, without Peggy Anne's notice. Delilah was not a church-going Catholic, in the sense that she didn't attend mass on Sundays and Holy Days of Obligation. And, as for the priests, well, they put their pants on one leg at a time, just like every other man, she would say. Yet, she loved her church and had a very strong belief in the power of prayer. Delilah contended, however, that she didn't pray like an ordinary Catholic. She didn't go for the poetic and pedantic "dribble drabble" that most people offered to God, in an attempt to impress him while they offered him his rightful praise. She used to laugh when she admitted that most of the prayers she was taught to memorize as a child had so many strange words, arranged in so many concocted ways, that she didn't even understand what she was saying until it was time for her to teach the same prayers to her own children. Delilah would say that she preferred to "talk to Gott." "Gott" was the only word that she pronounced like her German mother. And the word sounded so foreign amongst the French descendants who lived on the banks of Bayou Chouteau.

Delilah Charleville visited her church every weekday morning. She would walk in and find a comfortable place to rest her body. She found that the discomfort she felt when she knelt on those hard kneelers only served as a distraction by making her concentrate more on her pain than on what she had to say. After she was seated comfortably, she would let her thoughts go to the subject of most importance. For instance, she had made a promise to Gott, when her older son, Joseph, went off to war, that she would walk to church each morning at nine o'clock, and dedicate an hour of prayer to the safe keeping of her son. And every day, rain or shine, she was there, sitting comfortably in the front pew. And every day, she spoke to Gott expressing her deepest, most honest thoughts about her son. She didn't beg for his safe return. She didn't cry the tears of a fearful mother. She merely thought about Joseph. Some days, she spent the whole hour thinking of him as a baby—how she always joked that he was born with the mind of a grown man. Serious. Responsible. Fastidious. Joseph. What would she have done without him after her husband, William died? Never a day of reminding him of his duties in the family. Never a complaint about all that he sacrificed in order to help her keep the two-family businesses afloat. On and on, her thoughts would flow during her hour with Gott and Joseph. And she didn't have to ask Gott for the favor of his protection, because she believed that through her loving meditations, He knew how important her son was to her. He knew that it was a war that had taken this woman's two older brothers away from her, at the hands of their own mother's countrymen. And the pain that still remained in her heart did not have to be explained in her morning conversation with Gott. He knew all that she wished and felt about each and every matter. Of this, she was certain.

Each day, upon finishing her visit with Gott, she would genuflect before the altar, make the Sign of the Cross, and leave with the same feeling one would have upon leaving a friend's home after spending an hour sharing coffee, biscuits, and homemade preserves. And this ritual made her feel so close to Joseph that on her way back home she would sometimes make comments, out loud, as though he could hear her thoughts across the globe. She would say things like, "Be happy, my son. Try not to feel the weight of the whole world on your shoulders." But then, from the other side of her mouth, she would say, "Don't worry, Gott will send you home safely, because he knows that Billy needs you. He can't lose you, too."

So it was, on such an occasion as this, that Delilah Charleville happened to walk into St. Michael's that day and find Peggy Anne Moreau rocking back and forth on the kneeler in front of the statue of the Holy Mother. She knew right away that the girl was one of Clothilde's girls, because of the long, beautiful ponytail that was in her view. But she wasn't sure which of the girls she was until she caught a glimpse of the little gold- rimmed glasses, which sparkled a little in the flickering light of the candles. Peggy Anne, she thought. She's the girl in Billy's class. He mentions her name quite often, in fact. Talks about how she's so shy—how mean the other girls are to her, even though she's so smart and pretty, in her own way. Why is she here, Delilah wondered, all dressed up, in her going-to-church dress on a school day. She's obviously quite upset. I hope no one's sick at Clothilde's… All of this ruminating was going on in her mind as she approached the girl from behind and gently put her hand on her shoulder. "Peggy Anne is that you?" she asked, knowing the answer before posing the question.

"Oh! Mrs. Charleville. I…I didn't…"

"I'm sorry, honey. I didn't mean to startle you," Delilah broke in, realizing that her presence, being unexpected, and unanticipated, was more than likely, unwanted. But the child is a wreck, she thought, and so, she persisted, at the risk of seeming like a nosy, old busybody. "Are you OK, Peggy Anne? I mean, today's a school day, and—I know your mama's pretty strict with you kids about missing school and all…" The girl just looked off into the distance, past Delilah, focused on nothing in particular, just staring. "Peggy Anne, look at me, child. Are you all, right?" And then, when there was no answer and no change in the young girl's crazed facial expression, Delilah Charleville leaned toward her, pulled her close to her body and rested Peggy Anne's head on her nurturing breasts. She began to rock back and forth, in the same manner in which she had discovered the girl just minutes before, stroking her soft hair and humming some lullaby she had long ago put to rest.

Blessed Almighty, Delilah thought, this child is hurtin' down to her bones! And as her practical side began to ponder what to do for the child, she heard tiny whimpering sounds, like the first sounds a new-born puppy or kitten would make, and then, the child's body began to shake involuntarily as the tiny whimpering turned into uncontrollable weeping. The girl didn't try to resist this warm, genuine act of comforting from this woman who was really no more than a stranger beyond the occasional common courtesies exchanged between the two of them when she went into the Charleville General Store. Peggy Anne felt as though she had been running for hours from something that she feared and had finally found a place to rest. In that embrace, she felt so safe, so secure, so much—dare she say—affection. For, if the truth be known, Peggy Anne could not remember anyone ever holding her, hugging her, loving her. Her own mother hardly had time to speak to her. She would see other women holding their infants and think to herself that her mama must have held her, too, at that age. What a tragedy that she couldn't remember it. How she longed to remember.

Time just slipped away, unnoticed by either woman or child, and when Peggy Anne seemed to have calmed down, Delilah decided to put her own hour of prayer aside for the day, because she felt that there was certainly a divine reason for her finding the distraught girl at St. Michael's. She believed that nothing in life was purely coincidental, and that Gott had his hand in every twist and turn of events in life. And if, at first, she were puzzled by the morning's encounter, she would merely allow time and an open mind and heart to reveal its meaning and purpose. Her first step toward this revelation was to escort Peggy Anne to the Charleville home, behind the general store. Because both woman and child were deep in thought, they walked silently—the woman with her arm wrapped snuggly around the child's shoulder, unwilling to let go for fear that the girl would run like a frightened fawn.

Delilah could have put her fear to rest, however, because fleeing was the last thing on Peggy Anne's mind. She would have followed that gentle touch to the ends of the earth. She allowed all of her troublesome thoughts to evaporate into the cool, mid-morning air of Bayou Chouteau, and for the first time in years, felt at peace. There was something special about this lady, she felt it in her bones, and if for a moment, she felt like she were imposing on this good woman's nature, she quickly dismissed the self- reproach.

Delilah broke the pensive silence when they reached the bend in the road where Charleville's General Store first came into view. The largest oak tree in Bayou Chouteau stood at that bend, with beards of Spanish moss hanging from its old gnarled branches, which reached out to the bayou, cloaking the shell road beneath it with fascinating shadows, that moved beneath their feet as the Spring breeze passed through. "Glory be," the older woman exclaimed. "They're back!"

Peggy Anne sighted a small boat down the bayou, moving slowing toward them, and thought that Delilah was referring to the people in the boat. But instead, she found herself being led through the small, uncut field that bordered the manicured yard of the general store. There, lining the boggy edge of a drainage ditch, amongst wild grasses and vines, appeared Spring's first showing of Louisiana irises. Clumps of tall, slender, green leaves, standing straight and tall, like soldiers protecting the bright blue jewels that sat precariously above them on their thick green stalks. Delilah made the Sign of the Cross, as she did, almost unconsciously, any time she discovered something for which she was thankful. But the holy gesture did little to bridle her girlish excitement. "Look at these beautiful flowers, Peggy Anne! They are my favorite, my absolute favorite!" And then, she reached into her dress pocket and pulled out a tiny pocketknife, which she always kept handy for miscellaneous jobs at the store and got to work. As she cut each graceful stalk, she handed it to Peggy Anne, who watched in awe as Delilah proceeded, with precision and care, to strip each dense green plant of its distinctively delicate blooms. And as she cut, she talked. On and on she went about the beautiful Louisiana iris. Peggy Anne listened intently, as her morning companion explained how the flowers came up every year, each year yielding more than the preceding one. Wild, untamed, with no help from anyone but Mother Nature. Proof that there is a Gott, for no man, or woman, for that matter, could create something so beautiful.

She snipped and clipped and snipped some more, until a quick glance toward the flower bearer proved that her task was complete. Delilah closed her pocketknife, placed it back in her pocket and pulled out, in its place, a starched, white handkerchief, which had obviously been pressed and folded into the shape of a triangle. She lifted her glasses to wipe the beads of perspiration and tiny bits of leaves off of her face, folded the handkerchief, as though she had just finished ironing it again, and tucked it in her belt, so that it would be easy to reach if she needed it shortly. She took just about half of the flowers from Peggy Anne's outstretched arms and nodded in the direction of her store and home.

As they walked on, Delilah's discourse on the Louisiana iris seemed to take on a more philosophical tone. "I always say that there are two kinds of beauty in this world, Peggy Anne. There's the kind that you always have to work at—the kind that needs constant attention, you know what I mean. Like my roses, for instance. Oh, everybody thinks

I love those things, 'cause they always look so healthy and beautiful. Well, they should be! They take more of my time than my boys did when they were small. Prunin', feedin', waterin', protectin' 'em from the cold, from diseases, acht! The only reason I even grow them is because of my mama. You know, we lived in the city, above my papa's business, and there was no place for a garden, and mama always talked about the beautiful flowers in the old country and how much she missed them. Roses were her favorite. And so, I grow them for Mama to look down and see from above.

But to me, they are like these fancy women you see in the city, who take hours to get themselves primped and made up each day—a lot of work and worry for that kind of beauty, huh? Me, I appreciate the other kind of beauty—you know, the kind that you don't have to work at. Gott given. Like these irises here. Just think about it. Nobody planted them. Nobody watered them or cared for them in any, anyway. No. They just came up, out of that ugly, sloppy bog, and turned that spot of earth into a little piece of heaven. That's how I see it, anyway." She chuckled a little and said, "Listen to me, huh? Going on and on about these flowers, when I know you young people just don't see them in the same way that we old people do, huh?" She shifted her bunch of flowers to free one of her arms, which she once again placed around Peggy Anne's shoulder. The young girl only responded with a timid smile, silently agreeing with everything that came from Delilah's mouth. Never before had she noticed the wildflowers on her walks along the shell road, and she wondered how she could ever have missed their spectacular display.

Peggy Anne was mesmerized by her companion's simple wisdom. She clung to her every expression as though it were the first time she had heard the spoken word, and she longed to know more about this lady who seemed to see the world through enlightened eyes.

The Charleville home was actually a two-story extension from the rear of the general store. To enter it, one had to walk through the store, and go through the door directly behind the counter and cash register, or one could avoid the store and enter from a side door, which could only be reached by walking along a stone path through Delilah Charleville's renowned rose garden. Both of the entrances to the domicile led to the kitchen. There were three windows in the kitchen, one on each side of the door, which looked out upon her perfectly manicured garden and the packing house, just beyond, and one which was merely an opening in the wall, which separated the kitchen from the store.

These windows were strategically placed for the very adroit businesswoman and homemaker, because while she tended to her cooking and paperwork in the kitchen, she could still keep a watchful eye on the comings and goings at the packing shed, as well as the comings and goings of her patrons in the store.

Delilah loved her kitchen, and Peggy Anne could sense that the heart of the Charleville family was centered right there in that room, which she discovered to be just as she had always imagined. The beautiful white, cotton-lace curtains that hung on the windows broke the intensity and heat of the sunlight but allowed in just enough of the outdoors to give the room and everything in it an energy one could almost visualize and could certainly feel. Everything was shiny clean, from the big, white enamel stove to the white enamel tabletop, to the white ceramic tile countertop and backsplash, which was accented along the top border with an occasional blue, diamond-shaped tile. The oak floors looked worn in some areas, but still added to the general warmth that filled the room.

There were four ladderback chairs at the table, each donning a blue and white gingham cushion, and Peggy Anne chose to sit in the one closest to her, even before being invited. This would have upset Clothilde, who had taught her children better manners, but Peggy Anne followed her natural instincts, and in this room, she felt as if she were home—not at the Moreau home—but in a home like the one she always daydreamed about. Delilah put on her apron and started moving back and forth in her kitchen, as though she were on a track, and every movement was programmed ahead of time. And she talked. She didn't stop talking as she set out two cups and saucers, two plates, knives, forks, and teaspoons. When Peggy Anne admired the white, cotton napkins, with tiny pink and lavender flowers embroidered on them, Delilah explained that they had belonged to her mother. She chuckled a little and proceeded, barely stopping for a breath, to tell Peggy Anne how her father had owned a business in New Orleans. He used to make and sell fishing nets, and since he was always busy knitting the big nets in the back of the store, her mother would run the business end of it. That meant, of course, that she, being the oldest and only daughter, was responsible for the household duties in their home above the store and for taking care of her three brothers. She told Peggy Anne that one day her mother had come upstairs just as she had finished setting the table for supper. "Where are the napkins?" she had asked her daughter. Delilah told her that she hadn't ironed the napkins yet and thought they could eat one meal without them. "This family will not eat like barbarians," she told her young daughter. "And ever since that day," Delilah told Peggy Anne, "I make sure that my napkins are ironed, and I never serve a cup of coffee without one. Isn't it funny how we carry these habits throughout our lives? Aach! What would you know about that? You are still a young girl, with time to form your own habits." As she chatted, the aroma of frying bacon and baking biscuits began to fill the air.

Delilah poured hot boiling water from a stainless-steel kettle into a delicate china teapot, which she placed in the center of the table, and Peggy Anne realized that she was going to have hot tea for the first time in her life. "Coffee's good to wake you up and keep you going," Delilah chimed, "but there's nothing like a cup of tea to calm you down and soothe your soul." The young girl watched what the older woman did and followed suit as she put a teaspoon of sugar and just a bit of cream into her cup of tea. She loved the exotic aroma that rose up to her face with the steam from the cup.

Then, lunch was ready. Bacon and biscuits. Not a big heavy dinner, which was customary at the Moreau house for noon meals. Just bacon and biscuits. Delilah sat down across from Peggy Anne, and after a little sigh that signaled her intention to sit and relax, she gently asked, "Would you like to talk about what just went on in the church, child?" Just like that. Ordinarily, Peggy Anne would have clammed up at this sudden direct approach to delving into her private, personal feelings, but this was no ordinary day and certainly no ordinary lady. She was more comfortable with this woman than with anyone she had ever met. And as she opened up her tired and broken little heart to Delilah, she found herself talking about school, about the teasing and tormenting. It surprised her to find out that Delilah already knew about this. It seemed that Billy talked about it a lot and told his mother that he felt so bad about it, even though he never took part in it. It was true. Peggy Anne told Delilah that Billy was the nicest boy in school, and the proud mother just beamed. Delilah would be the first to admit that her younger son was no brain, and was a little irresponsible, but he was a good boy.

Words continued to flow from Peggy Anne's mouth, as she explained to Delilah that she intended to ask for a job at the store, how she was heading for the store when evil thoughts entered her mind, how she tries so hard to follow her mama's advice, but sometimes praying on it just didn't seem to make the evil thoughts go away. How all she could do to shake the evil thoughts and guilty feelings was go straight to the Holy Mother and that's how she ended up at St. Michael's, because she didn't want anyone in her family to be punished for what she was thinking. As Peggy Anne's words spilled out of her mouth in the manner of an eager confession, rather than a simple explanation, Delilah's eyebrows crept closer and closer together. She began clenching her teeth a little, causing her facial muscles to pulsate and her lips to purse. And with her elbow resting on the table, she lowered her head to rest her forehead on her middle finger and thumb.

Upon seeing this reaction, Peggy Anne stopped in mid-sentence, afraid that she had revealed too much of her evil nature to this attentive listener, who started shaking her head from side to side, in what seemed to the trusting girl to be signs of disgust and disapproval. But when the abrupt silence prompted Delilah to lift her head and look across the table at her troubled guest, she did so with such tender regard, that Peggy Anne was once again reminded that she was in a safe place. "Miz Charleville, I don't mean to have these ungrateful thoughts, really I don't. I try real hard not to, but they just come. And then, I try real hard to send them away— but I can't. I don't know how my Mama does it. She would hate me if she knew how I really feel. I mean, wouldn't you? I feel so guilty sometimes, I could just throw up! Sometimes, I do. It's just the devil's work, I guess…"

"Now that's enough! Now I want you to know that I like your mama a lot, and Gott knows I have no idea how she manages her household the way she does, and what I am going to say to you is in no way meant to sound disrespectful to that good woman." She paused a moment, took a short breath, straightened up in the chair, and placed both hands, palms down, on the table, as if she were preparing herself for a jolt. And with just a slight hesitancy, she proceeded to offer Peggy Anne her fiery opinion of Clothilde Moreau's sanctioned religious philosophy. "I don't know what Gott people like your mama pray to, child, but it certainly isn't my Gott. No, ma'am. I hear that foolishness all the time. 'Don't question what Gott sends your way. Don't feel bad about your problems, 'cause things can always be worse.' And then, the priests, like that arrogant German at St. Michael's, would have us believing that suffering is our only road to heaven."

Did she just refer to Father Fredericks as an arrogant German? Peggy Anne was shocked, self-consciously looking around to see if anyone else had heard this, even though she knew that Delilah Charleville was the only person in the room. Then, Delilah's bold voice brought Peggy Anne to attention, "Is that how you think about Gott, child? That he likes for you to suffer? That he never wants you to question things in your life? That you should always accept your life always just the way it is?"

Again, the girl looked around the room to see if they were alone. She suddenly felt naked, as though she were exposing her most private parts, and was embarrassed at what was revealed. And so, it was merely an apologetic mumble that responded to Delilah's penetrating questions. "Well, yes ma'am, I guess so."

"Um-hmm. That's what I thought." Delilah's face softened a bit as she considered whether or not she was trespassing on someone else's territory. After all, Peggy Anne was not her daughter, and didn't Clothilde and Alfred have the right to teach their daughter however they saw fit? But her second thoughts were fleeting, for although she hardly knew the teenage girl sitting across the table from her, she felt something special for her. She felt an unusual closeness to her. Peggy Anne watched as Delilah refilled the cups with hot tea. She watched the melodic movements of her hands, as she prepared her own cup with sugar and cream, and she decided that although one would not consider Delilah Charleville a beautiful woman, her classic features gave her an air of elegance and grace, a bit of refinement born of an older culture, a different world, one far beyond Bayou Chouteau.

Delilah felt the girl's tentative, yet inquisitive eyes upon her and decided to take a more congenial approach to this topic, which could ordinarily ignite a spark of heated debate between herself and one of her contemporaries. But Peggy Anne was merely a child and someone else's at that. "How old are you, Peggy Anne?" she asked, all the while knowing she was probably the same age as her Billy.

"I'm fifteen," the girl said in a confident voice, relieved to have a question that she could answer with self-assurance.

"That's what I thought. Same age as my Billy. And you're the same age I was when my mama died. She used to tell me the same things your mama tells you about Gott, about life. And I took it in—every last bit of it. I was an obedient child, like you—a trusting child. And above everyone else in the world, I trusted my mama. So, when she told me I should never question Gott's will, that I should accept all that life hands me with no complaints, and that someday I would be rewarded by the amount of suffering I endured on earth, I believed her. Just like you believe your mama. But then, my mama died. She left four children behind—I was the oldest and only girl. With Papa busy with his business, it was up to me to take Mama's place in caring for the house and my younger brothers. For that part, I was well prepared, since I had always helped Mama when she was working with Papa. As I told you before, she really ran the business. But what my mama was spared and what my mama did not prepare me for was watching my baby brother die, a month after her, of the same illness. Joseph was his name, my little angel boy. I sat at his bedside and watched his feverish body tremble from the high temperatures. He would drift in and out of consciousness, and when he had the energy to speak, he would look at me and call me 'Mama.' But I soon realized that he was so sick that he was just talking out of his head—calling for mama out of habit, not remembering that she was gone. And then, he was gone, too. I questioned Gott. Why? Why? Why? He was just a baby. I knew Mama had taught me to accept, not question. But, you know, Peggy Anne, my mama had been spared the real pain. She never experienced it. The kind of pain that feels like somebody poked a hand right through your chest and twisted your heart around and around and back and forth, until finally ripping it out. I felt that pain when I was your age. And I remember our priest, coming to dinner, and telling me things like your mama tells you, and my mama told me. But I couldn't buy it anymore. Gott doesn't want us to suffer, Peggy Anne. And when we do, we have to turn it around and look for something good to come from it. I agree that when we go through tough times, we have to 'pray on it,' we have to turn to Gott, because he wants to hear from us. But I believe that we also have to 'think on it.' I figure that's what he gave us a brain for. He gave us the ability to think, and to make our own choices, Peggy Anne. He gave us the ability to decide right from wrong. He gave us the ability to know what it is in our lives that stands between our being an ordinary human being trudging through a life, never exploring the possibilities and an extraordinary human being who searches and finds a purpose for being here on this earth. And finding a purpose, a place in life where you can be your best, that's what Gott wants for his children, Peggy Anne. He wants us to be happy and experience this world he created for us. He wants us to celebrate life, child, not hardships."

"Are you saying that you question God?" Delilah asked, thinking that she was probably going to have to go to confession after this blasphemous conversation.

"I guess I do question Gott. But my question is never 'Why did you make this happen?' as much as it is, 'What do you want me to get from this situation, and where do I go from here?' I give him control, but I take action. I don't just accept a bad situation as my lot in life, to endure and abide by as my ticket to heaven. Oh, I can see I have talked on too long, and I have probably confused you more than anything else"

"I think I am a little confused, but that's OK, because I enjoy listening to you. Nobody else has ever talked to me about God in that way."

"Well, maybe if I give you a real-life example, you'd understand a little bit better. You see, when little Joseph died, I knew I couldn't just take care of the house and the older boys and expect my pain to go away, just because I was praying on it. And I didn't want to live the rest of my life feeling the way I was feeling, even though I had been taught that suffering was good for my eternal life. So, I told Papa that I wanted to learn the business. I wanted to take my mama's place there, as well. At first, he said no. But I just kept praying and I just kept insisting, and soon he gave in. My brothers were in school all day, and I devoted all my time to learning about running a business. I loved it. I loved it then, and I still love it today. It's what I was born to do."

"But you were also born to be a wife and a mother, right?" Peggy Anne asked, understanding now why Billy Charleville was so different than the other kids in school. She always thought that it was his being so rich that gave him the independence and self-confidence he needed to step away from his circle of friends to be kind to her, in spite of the jeers he might get from his buddies. But now she realized that it wasn't his money that strengthened him, but rather his mother.

Delilah's smile broadened when Peggy Anne brought up the subject of marriage and children, and she recalled, "Heck, I wasn't even interested in getting married. And having children frightened me, because losing Joseph had been so painful, I couldn't imagine losing another child that I loved so dearly. Then the first World War came. We kids were half German, you see, and my brothers volunteered to fight. I think it was important to them to show their loyalty to this country. I lost both of them. My heart was so broken, that it couldn't feel anything for years."

"I think I was twenty-two when I met Will Charleville, and most of my friends were wives and mothers by then. Will was quite a few years older than I was, so of course, he was real interested in marrying me and carrying me here to Bayou Chouteau, to live with his family. But I held out a couple of years. I celebrated my twenty-fifth birthday here on the bayou, and I've been here ever since. You know, we are all different, Peggy Anne—in how we handle things, how we live our lives. Your mama could be very happy in her place. And that's fine. But that's no reason for you to accept her life for yourself. I can tell you are a bright girl, and you're pretty, too. Here you are today, looking to make a change for yourself. It shows you used that brain Gott gave you—and I know he's pleased you used it. So don't be afraid of those thoughts. Be thankful you have them."

Peggy Anne sat and listened. She could have listened all day, without saying a word. It had taken just a few minutes for Delilah Charleville, in her patient, unpretentious manner, to contradict years of Clothilde's religion of guilt and shame and Father Frederick's pedantic warnings of a wrathful God. As she gazed down into her hot tea, with its combination of sweet and spicy flavors lingering in her mouth, she wondered if this whole encounter was just the devil, setting her up for temptation. This warm, comfortable kitchen, the pleasing offerings of food and drink, and this kind, charming bayou woman, espousing her bold, if not blasphemous, words of advice in a most gentle, persuasive air, befitting those who have gained and become comfortable in bearing the wisdom of God's plan. Was this how Satan presented himself? She pondered the possibility. Was she falling for his temptations, encouraging her to question God? And for a brief, spine-tingling moment, she pictured herself in the deepest, darkest corner of the universe. She lifted her head to chase away the vision and locked eyes with Delilah Charleville, hoping to see through to the heart of this liaison between herself and her higher power. And she realized, in that moment, that Satan could not possibly present himself in the peaceful, reassuring message flowing from those sympathetic, cerulean eyes. The troubled expression on Peggy Anne's face softened into a timid smile that was kindly returned by Delilah and at that moment, two trusting souls were bonded.

"So, when can you start working in my general store, Miss Peggy Anne Moreau?"

SATURDAY

"He moved with some uncertainty,
as if he didn't know, just what he was
there for, or where he ought to go…"

She heard the words melodically going through her mind and coming to life in the soft, lulling song that she unconsciously sang as she finished loading the last few breakfast dishes into the dishwasher. Brad was standing in the backyard, not far from the kitchen casement windows over the sink, which were open, allowing a gentle, tropical breeze to flow through the room, giving one the feeling of Spring rather than an early September day.

"Once he reached for something
golden, hanging from a tree,
and his hand came down empty…"

For the life of her, she could not remember where she had heard the song that she was singing to herself, and then she remembered that it was an old Carole King song that she used to play a lot when she was in high school. She hadn't heard the song for years. How weird, she thought, that the brain can just store all of that unnecessary information for so long, and then throw it back at you years later unprompted, unsolicited, for some unknown reason. Perhaps, in order to avoid one of her philosophical journeys, which her mind had no business dwelling on when there were more practical matters on hand, she took a second to stretch her back and catch a glimpse of her husband.

For a brief moment, as she looked at Brad, with his hands on his hips, his head tilted slightly back as he studied something on the second floor or the roof, Elise had an eerie feeling that she was seeing her husband as an old man. It wasn't the prematurely gray hair, for she was used to that and found it quite attractive. No. It was the grave look on his face. It was the look of a person who had grown weary of life's surprises, whose eyes were tired of witnessing the beauty of life being tarnished by the passing of years and the uninterrupted, and unstoppable cycles of nature. It was a look she had seen gradually evolve on her father's face over the last few years. A look that made her stomach feel like an empty, bottomless pit that could suck her inside out if she thought about it too long.

Her melancholy trance was broken when Brad's eyes met hers through the window, and she returned the somewhat tentative smile that he sent her. She looked, again, at his face, into his deep, dark, distant eyes, and she knew why her brain had just reminded her of the words she once belted out when she was a teenager in her bedroom with her door shutting out the fears and challenges that began lurking like shadows in her adolescent years. Today, though, the lyrics were not about her. They were describing her husband. Brad seemed so out of place, drifting from one task to another, following suggestions from neighbors about all of the endless preparations for this approaching natural force —a force that could take away so many things in his life, a force over which he had no control. He could lose things that he had worked so hard for—planned for—saved for—and unfortunately things that, to him, reflected all that he was in terms of his success, in terms of his self-worth, the sum total of his life.

No matter how often she drilled into his head that he was more than the material things he could provide, Elise knew that she would never reach him. She would never be able to bring him peace of mind and heart. He had spent too many formative years with others, whose guidelines for evaluating his and other people's happiness and success were more likely to be found in The Wall Street Journal than in any spiritual or philosophical sources.

In their nearly two years of dating, Elise had seen little evidence of this influence in his personality. In fact, the Brad she dated was unpretentious—he hated the stuffy atmosphere of the many fancy restaurants in the city and preferred the local dives. He made it a point to never wear shirts with designer logos with his faded but neatly pressed jeans. Once, for his birthday, his parents sent him seven Ralph Lauren polo shirts, which he referred to as "a different, brightly colored status symbol for each day of the week." He wrapped them neatly in the box and took them back to Macy's department store where he received enough store credit to provide a year's worth of clothing.

Naively, Elise interpreted his actions as signs of his self-confidence. "This is a man who feels he needs no conspicuous signs of wealth to impress others," she thought. She liked this, and so she didn't listen to the little voice in her head that wondered why returning that gift gave him so much pleasure. She overlooked the signs that showed rebellion rather than self-confidence or simple practicality. But people tend to ignore the brain when the heart and hormones are saying, "Mmmm, isn't he perfect!!" There were other signs, warnings perhaps, that were ignored or simply put in the "I'll worry about that later" category. For instance, the way his best friend Adam smirked when he said to her, "I just can't wait for you to meet his parents." To which she thought, "Why should I worry? I've never had problems in the past with parents disliking me. In fact, the parents usually liked me more than their sons, especially when they were eager for their sons to settle down, which usually didn't bode well for the relationship."

Then she was told about the one serious relationship Brad had left behind when he left St. Louis to attend law school at Tulane. He had sworn to Elise that there was no one back home, because she made it clear that she was not interested in dating someone who was involved with someone else. When she confronted him, he admitted that he had been dating someone for a couple of years. In fact, this someone had made a visit to New Orleans just a month before he and Elise had met. But it was a dead-end relationship, he assured her. Going nowhere. "Why is that?" Elise wanted to know. Nothing in common, he guessed… attracted to her physically…but just can't go any further. Almost without expression and obviously without imagination, he offered these most commonly used excuses in the history of dating.

"Are you in love with her?" His squirming and bitter facial expression told her that although he knew this inevitable question was coming, it still made him quite uncomfortable. And, of course, she could have predicted his response which was, "Oh, I care a lot about her, but I can't say that I'm in love with her. I wouldn't be dating you, if I were. I'm not like that."

"I see. You're a liar, but not a cheater. That's comforting, that's real comforting."

"I didn't lie to you, Elise. It's over. It's been over. We talked about it when she was in town. And since then, I've told her all about you, and the truth is, she knew all along there was no future in the relationship, so it didn't come as a big surprise to either one of us."

"So, there are women in this world who are willing to spend two years of their lives in a monogamous relationship, knowing it's going nowhere?" This conversation was going nowhere but from bad to worse, so Elise didn't even stick around to hear a response to what she believed was a rhetorical question. But just before slamming the door of his apartment on her way out, she did manage to add, rather succinctly, "I will be no one's out-of-town fling. And you have insulted me by thinking that I would!"

Her standoff only lasted about a month, and on several occasions during their brief separation, Adam felt "obligated" to share a little wine and discuss with her the trials and tribulations of Brad's romantic past. To sum it up, he told her that, "Kelly was a great girl. She was real pretty, fun to be with, liked to party. She wasn't much in the intellectual department, but hell, who cares about that in college, right?

"Believe it or not, Adam, some people do. In fact..." She hated comments like that, and Adam realized it as soon as he said it, so he didn't hesitate to interrupt her in order to prevent the conversation from turning into a "brains vs. brawn" debate.

"I know, I know, but let me finish. We were all crazy about her, and I hate to say this to you, but we all thought Brad was crazy about her, too. But Brad's parents hated her, and I mean hate to the highest degree. To them, she was an uneducated daughter of an uneducated construction worker and a mother whose favorite hobby was paint-by-number on velvet backgrounds. To put it simply, she didn't go to college, she was not wealthy, and she was not Jewish. Three strikes...she's out."

Elise didn't care for the manner in which Adam seemed to relish the facts he casually spilled out before her. She couldn't help but wonder if he were the kind of person who found pleasure in his best friend's misfortunes, or perhaps it was the cabernet, which was having an opposite effect on her. She didn't want to feel sorry for Brad or his wonderful Karen, or Kristy, or was it Kelly. She really did not want to know anything else about them. But she kept listening, as though he were telling her a fairy tale, waiting for a happy ending, even though she knew that a happy ending in this story would not leave her feeling the same way she felt, for instance, when she watched her all-time favorite, never-let-you-down movie, The Sound of Music. She made a mental note that she would have to rent it and watch it again—real soon.

Adam had stopped talking for a moment, to take a sip of his wine, and perhaps to give her a chance to respond to his rambling. She didn't like Adam very much at that moment, and she found herself staring at him, wondering if he actually thought that his thick mustache really took one's attention away from his receding hairline. When she failed to give him any reaction to his unpleasant disclosure of facts, he went on with what Elise detected as a little gleam in his eyes.

"The Steiners made it very clear to Brad that he was to stop seeing Kelly if he wanted his college tuition paid. His seeing her was an act of disloyalty to them, because he knew very well how they felt about girls like her, and after all, they never asked much of him, considering all that they had done for him. But Brad continued seeing Kelly, even though he had to sneak around town to do it, all the while telling his parents that it was over. Kelly knew that they hated her. Hell, she was never even allowed to step foot in their house.

"When the Steiners found that Brad was lying to them, well, Phyllis, his mom, went to the hospital complaining of chest pains. Even though the doctor told her it was indigestion, she told Brad that he was causing her to have heart problems. Mel, his dad, didn't do anything but get on the phone and call the family attorney to get the facts on disinheriting this disobedient, ungrateful son. Brad knew he would be leaving town soon—new town, new women, new life—so he promised his parents, once again, that he would never see Kelly again. And that's when you stepped into the picture, my little friend."

His last line had convinced her more than ever that he really didn't like her dating Brad Or maybe, because of the situation which he had just revealed, he just didn't bother caring for her one way or the other, since he felt that her relationship with Brad had no future anyway. Millions of thoughts were swimming in her head, and she couldn't think clearly enough to say anything coherently or ask questions.

She was angry, but toward whom? Brad, for lying? Mel and Phyllis Steiner for what they'd done to their son and how they'd treated some innocent woman who loved him? Or was she feeling anger toward Adam, for enjoying this whole saga and being the bearer of unsettling news? Perhaps, she was angry with herself, for being so gullible, so vulnerable to Brad, his little-boy charm packaged in the very attractive, virile body of the stable, mature man she imagined him to be.

She was hurt, too, for herself, for Brad, and for this woman she had never even met. Elise felt uneasy knowing that Brad had told Kelly about her before he had told her about Kelly. She thought about the horrible things that this woman probably thought of her, and it gave her a little chill down her spine, because Elise could never be comfortable with the thought of someone not liking her. And then, unintentionally airing her thoughts out loud, she asked Adam, her questionable confidante, "So, what is my part in all of this?"

Adam's facial expression and mood seemed to change as he shifted somewhat uncomfortably in his seat. Just minutes before, she had seen on his face the hypocritical satisfaction of a neighborhood gossip spreading rumors for the "ultimate good" of everyone involved. Now it seemed to her that he was feeling what she was feeling, for the first time. The lines formed by the somewhat sarcastic snicker he displayed during his soliloquy melted into the most sympathetic, caring look she had ever seen on Adam's face. Or was she being gullible and naïve once again? His response convinced her that she wasn't.

"You know that I can't answer that question for you, Elise, although I wish to God that I could. You'll have to talk to Brad about that. He's the only one who knows his intentions with you or Kelly or his parents. But I will tell you this. I've never seen him stand up to his parents. I've seen him lie to them, but I've never seen him stand up to them."

"So, what's that supposed to mean to me?" she asked, suddenly feeling very defensive about what she thought Adam was insinuating.

"Look, Elise. If you haven't noticed, I like you very much. You are not the average kind of girl, if you know what I mean. To me, you're the marrying kind of girl. You're special. I don't know what Brad's intentions are, but I don't want the son of a bitch to hurt you. I love the guy. He's my best friend. Nobody knows him as well as I do, and nobody knows what he's dealing with as well as I do. His parents are pretty tough—tougher than he is right now."

She nodded her head as though she understood and accepted what he was telling her, and then she just let her head hang slightly, so that he couldn't see her tightly shut eyes failing to hold back the tears brought on by the wine and the conversation. There was no way that she could see Brad at that point. There was a part of her that wanted to punch his lights out, but another part that wanted to curl up next to him, lay her head on his chest, and hold him. She missed him a lot but being with him now was out of the question. There were things she needed to know but was not ready to hear. Or maybe there were things that she didn't need to know, and she should just move on.

But she didn't move on, and that time in her and Brad's lives would forever be one of those crucial junctures that people look back on and wonder how differently their lives would have been had they opted for other choices. "I wonder if he's thinking about that now?" Elise thought. "Now that his choices have brought him to a town he never dreamed of living in, where he has to deal with uncertainties of nature for which his predictable life in the affluent suburbs of St. Louis gave him little preparation."

She saw him walking toward the porch and knew he would be inside in a few seconds, so she fixed two glasses of iced tea and dropped in a few sprigs of fresh mint from their herb garden. He walked in the back door, with beads of perspiration clinging to his forehead, wiping his wet hands on the back of his old, worn jeans that he vehemently refused to throw away. Elise tried to read the expression on his face and decided to test his sense of humor. "Gee, I had to look twice. I thought you were Anthony walking through the door." She smiled and prepared her thin skin for the saucy response her comment might encourage, and as expected, her preparation was in order.

"No. It's just me. Why? Are you in the habit of inviting the yard man in for tea?"

"Touché, Counselor. It's just that I'm not used to seeing you look so rugged. I think I like this new look." And she met him halfway around the kitchen island, wrapped her arms around his neck, and gave him a quick little smooch on his uncooperative lips.

"Well, don't get used to it. Maybe you should have married one of those fishermen from Bayou Chouteau if you wanted a husband who looks like this."

"Hey, lighten up. It was a compliment, not a complaint. And anyway, I'm starting to resent the way that you're always ready to cast me out to one of those Bayou Chouteau boys." She was still speaking in a joking manner, but what she said to him held a lot of truth. His placing doubt on her choice for marriage always made her wonder if he, in fact, were the one who had second thoughts. She did find some comfort in the fact that he had practiced this annoying, immature habit ever since their dating days. And surely, if he had second thoughts, he would've acted upon them long ago. She silently congratulated herself for warding off the fears and insecurity that his comments would have aroused within her years ago.

He killed a tall glass of tea with three vigorous gulps, and as she automatically refilled his glass without a request for more, he remembered what it was, besides his thirst, that had led him back into the house. "I think we should give Leo a call, don't you?"

"Oh my God! I forgot all about Leo, Brad."

"I know. Don't feel badly, so did I. But if we don't call him, he's not going to call us. You know how independent he wants to be."

"I think we should ask him to come here to stay with us, don't you?"

"Yeah, or go with us, whichever the case may be."

"Right. But if he comes here to stay, he'll be with us already if we decide to leave, and that will be one less issue to deal with in case we're in a hurry to get out."

"And you know it will be an issue with him. We'll have to beg him and convince him that he's not putting us out."

"Poor Leo. It must be awful to be old and alone."

"Oh, I don't know about that. Sometimes I think he likes being alone. Think about it. We're always giving him the opportunity to be with us and the kids, and he rarely takes us up on it. And I know he loves you and the kids. At least as much as he allows himself to love anyone."

"Now, why would you say such a thing, Brad? As if he would be able to control such a thing as love anyway. People can't control their feelings according to their wishes." She was very adamant in her last remark and did not expect Brad to shake his head and give her what she thought to be a patronizing hug, claiming, "My poor, little Elise. Always the hopeless romantic."

"And what's that supposed to mean?" she asked in a most defensive tone.

"Calm down, it's a compliment, not a complaint," he said, cleverly throwing her own words back at her. "It's one of the things I love most about you Elise." When he used her formal name, she always knew he was being serious. "You still believe in that innocent notion that where there is love, there is always a happy ending. And even though I don't believe in your theory, I find it refreshing to be around someone who does."

"Well, first of all, I don't think that that was what we were talking about, and second of all, you'll have to forgive me if I happen to find joy in loving the special people in my life and knowing that they love me. And I feel real sorry for you if loving me has been such a burden for you!"

"Whoa, whoa, whoa. Where did that come from? Why did you automatically take my comment as a personal attack, Elise? You know very well that loving you has made me happy. We were talking about Leo, remember? And you have to admit that a person with Leo's experiences might be a little hesitant to form any close attachments with anyone. Think about it Elise. The poor man's been to hell and back, because of losing the people he's loved most in his life. He probably keeps himself at what he feels is a safe distance, because becoming a permanent fixture in our family would make him vulnerable to more heartache. He's probably afraid to get too close. And we have to accept his position, Elise, even though I know how hard it is for you to understand. Love has always brought you happiness Lissy, and giving love brings you happiness. But that experience is not exactly shared by all of us."

He was depressing her with his profound commentary, but she knew that what he said about Leo was true. She just wished that he hadn't ended his last statement with "all of us." She put her arms around his waist, hooking her index fingers on the belt loops of his jeans, and rested her head on his shoulder. He wrapped his arms around her shoulders and kissed her neck, not seductively, but tenderly. She knew that he had to get back outside, back to his yard work, and she knew before the words came out of her mouth that she shouldn't approach the foreboding topic, but she did. She couldn't stop herself. "I guess you can understand Leo so well, because loving me meant losing your family."

The same arms that had held her tenderly just seconds before were now used to hold her at arm's length in front of him, and he looked at her with the same expression he used when scolding the children. "Elise, if you want to punish yourself in some demented way, go right ahead. But don't even compare my family situation to Leo's situation. My God. He lost his wife and three-year-old son, just five years after he was married. And he still blames himself for some ridiculous reason. What have I lost? Parents who don't even worry enough about me and my kids to make one lousy, long-distance phone call to find out what our plans are for a major hurricane?"

What could she say? She stammered a weak apology and mumbled something about it being early, and maybe they'd call that evening, and with obvious frustration in his voice, Brad walked through the back door saying, "You just don't get it."

"Damn it," she thought to herself. "Why did I ever bring it up? He's right though. I'll never understand this big mess." She looked for the kitchen phone, which was once again off of its base and had to press the pager in order to find it. She followed the beep, which led her to the back porch, next to the swing, where she had left the phone that morning. Brad was just a short distance away, and he looked up when she walked into his view.

"Hey Liss, I'm sorry."

"Me, too."

"Let's just not bring up the subject again, OK?"

"Sure." She walked up to him, and they kissed. A good kiss. The kind of kiss that would have led to much, much more had there not been so much to tend to and tie down in the yard.

With a lighter heart, Elise walked back to the kitchen, pressing the seven digits which usually connected her with the older man who had become her friend and confidante, and whom her children regarded as a grandfather. After three rings, she heard the shaky, but cheery, "Hello."

"Hey, Leo, what…"

"You have reached 467-2913. Please leave your name and number, and I will be sure to return your call. Have a nice day, my friend."

Poor, Leo, Elise thought. How many friends do you have calling? She heard the beep and began again, "Hey, Leo, what's going on? Brad and I…"

"Hello, hello." There were lots of fumbling noises in the background and then, "Elise, is that you?"

"Yes, it is. So, you were screening your calls, eh?"

"No, no, just in the john."

"Oh, OK," she cut him short, because the older Leo got, the more he tended to go into graphic detail about his health and the physical ailments and side effects associated with his growing list of geriatric problems. Elise was frequently embarrassed by the subject matters that he shared with her, sometimes for her opinion, and sometimes just because he needed a friend to talk to. So when he mentioned that he was in the bathroom when the phone rang, she didn't want to give him any time to expound upon the topic. "Have you been watching the weather reports?"

"Have I had a choice?" She shook her head and smirked, allowing the old professor to turn what could have been a simple "yes or no" answer into a sarcastic commentary on television programming.

"I'll bet this is the first time in your life that you've been under a hurricane warning. Are you a little worried?"

"Oh no. I'm not concerned. I'm all settled, and I've got everything that I need. These news people just try to scare everybody just to get the ratings up. That's their racket."

"I don't think so Leo. This is pretty serious. If this hurricane hits us head-on, you could be in a lot of danger. Brad and I want you to get some of your things together and come over here to stay with us. We're planning on staying right now. In fact, my friend Talia and her boys are planning on staying with us—and of course, my parents. We're all cooking some good food and gathering supplies to try to make the best of a bad situation. Of course, if things get bad enough, we're going to evacuate, and if we do, we want you to be with us."

"No, no, no. I'll be fine. This apartment complex is big and strong. I'll be fine."

"But Leo, I don't think you understand. Your apartment is on the first floor. The flooding alone can destroy that place, not to mention the wind. Trust me, you don't want to be around if that happens. You'll have no phone, no electricity, no gas…"

"Well, it'll be nice not to have gas for a change, heh, heh. Ever since that crazy doctor put me on that new medication…" There he goes again, she thought. As if I want to hear about an old man's gas problems. So, she interrupted his statement of comic relief.

"Leo, I'm serious. What about your car? That parking lot floods with a summer shower, much less the torrential rains of a hurricane."

"That's why I pay all of those outrageous insurance premiums, I suppose."

"You are soooo stubborn. But this time, you won't have a choice. Brad will be at your place this evening to pick you up. In fact, maybe the kids and I will go, too. Then we can all go out for a bite to eat."

"No. That won't be necessary. You don't have time to worry about me now. You have enough to deal with taking care of the kids, and Brad, your folks, the house. I don't want to be a burden on you. Believe me, I've been through tougher things than a hurricane."

"Leo, you are not a burden!" She spoke each word with frustrated emphasis, but to no avail, because he moved the conversation on to a new topic.

"Did Brad watch the baseball game last night?"

"No." She was angry with Leo for being so hardheaded and angry with herself for losing the battle.

"You're kidding! The Cards are heading for the playoffs. It was a great game…went down to the wire…"

"Leo don't change the subject on me. What can I say to get some sense through your thick skull?"

"Nothing. I'm staying right here, and you'll just have to respect my decision." Damn, she thought. He had to use the word "respect." Now the battle was definitely over. And he knew it, too. Respect you parents. Respect your teachers. Respect your elders. Lessons of childhood echoed in her mind. She had never had problems with the lessons of respect. Until, that is, she had to deal with Brad's parents. Early in her marriage, it was "respect" for her in-laws that allowed her to overlook, or rather ignore, the intentional hurtful criticism and innuendoes that were frequently and strategically slipped into everyday family conversations, sometimes in private, sometimes in public. For years, it was "respect" for Brad that allowed her to hold her tongue, rather than lash out and defend herself and her family in response to his parents' verbal abuse.

But the sounds of her childhood lessons faded with the passing of time and the help of a well-paid family counselor, and she slowly gave herself permission to respect herself, as well. In doing so, however, she had lost all respect for Brad's parents. She knew this. Brad knew this. And most of all, Brad's parents knew this. Leo knew this, too. For she had told him so, many times over the last few years of his living near her and Brad. He certainly could understand her feelings, he had said. And he hardly blamed her for feeling the way that she did. And yet his understanding nature sometimes presented itself in a tone of appeasement—as if he offered his agreement to her merely to calm her down and to settle her anxiety about the situation. And so, while he did succeed in calming her feelings, he never failed to plant a tiny seed of guilt in her heart.

Therefore, when Leo said that Elise must respect his decision, he knew that he had chosen his words wisely. "OK, you win," she said, "but please keep in touch with us. I will call you if we decide to leave here, just in case you change that stubborn mind of yours."

"If you must, dear, but please don't worry about me, because while you're worrying that pretty little head, I will be settled down with the books I picked up at the library today. Even if I have to do so by candlelight."

"Oooooh, candlelight. You almost make it sound romantic. Maybe you should find a nice lady friend to weather the storm with you." Elise decided that she might as well go along with his sardonic humor, in spite of her disagreement with him.

"Don't worry, I've thought about that, heh, heh. But the only ones who would be interested are those old women with plastic hair, velour sweatsuits, and spiked heels. You know which ones I'm referring to, don't you, heh, heh?"

"Leo, you are bad. But yes, I do know which ones you're referring to."

"By the way, Elise, has Brad heard from his folks?" That's funny, she thought. Did Leo know that a vision of Phyllis Steiner had popped in her head when he was describing the older women with plastic hair, velour sweat suits, and spiked heels?

"No," she answered, making a conscious effort to return to a serious state of mind. "Can you believe they haven't called yet? It's amazing, isn't it?" She was getting angrier by the second. Her hands started perspiring as her heartbeat faster, and she recognized the onset of the typical signs and symptoms of a discussion about the elder Steiners.

"Elise, I don't think their actions, or should I say their lack of action, should surprise you. Don't let it upset you so."

"Don't let it upset me, Leo? How can parents show so little concern for their son and grandchildren? What has Brad done to deserve this?"

"I'm sorry that I brought up the subject. I certainly didn't intend to upset you, Elise. But let me offer just a little advice, if I may. And I offer it not in defense of their behavior, but rather as your defense against being hurt by their behavior. As I've told you many times before, they will never change. Your husband realizes this. He has accepted this, and he has moved on. He may not like it, he may wish things were different, but he knows that they never will be different. Now, I think it is up to you to realize this and accept it. If not, you will be heartbroken time and time again."

"But Leo, I just don't understand…"

"Elise, there are many things in life that we will never understand, and yet we accept these things, and we go on." She wondered if he were thinking about his wife and child at that moment, and then another thought occurred to her.

"Did Brad ask you to talk to me?"

"You called me, remember."

"Yes. But it's almost as though you knew that this has been bothering me non-stop for the last couple of days."

"I didn't need Brad to tell me that, Elise."

"Well, if you know that it's bothering me so much, how can you expect me to believe that it's not bothering Brad?"

"Perhaps it's because I know that Brad's past has prepared him for what's going on in his life now, and yours didn't."

"His past has prepared him? How can his past prepare him for the possibility of being practically disowned by his family?"

"Look, Elise. I've been watching this television for the last couple of days. And I've seen interview after interview with people along the Gulf Coast, who have lived their entire lives in areas threatened by hurricanes every year. Some of these people have even lost everything they owned in these storms. And in spite of the inconvenience of evacuating, several times a year sometimes, and possibly losing everything they own, they continue to live in the same area. Now, I look at these people, and I listen to their stories, and I see film footage of these horrific disasters, and I think to myself, why in the world haven't they moved to safer ground? Why? They can't enjoy it. It must frighten them each time they're under a threat. Their insurance costs must be out of this world. So why? Why don't they think like I do? And the answer is simple. They have lived their lives with the threat. They know in advance what the consequences can be, and yet they choose to face the consequences, because they love their lives just where they are. They make the choices. Brad, too, has lived his life under threats of the consequences he now suffers. But he made his choice. And although he doesn't like his family situation any more than these people like to leave their homes in the face of danger, he accepts it as an anticipated consequence for choosing the life that makes him happy."

Elise took a few moments to digest the analogy put forth by this former history professor, who had learned firsthand how the past can influence an individual's life. And once again she realized why she loved this old man with his eccentricities and sometimes grumpy ways. His lonely life, his living apart from the rest of the world, seemed to have given him the advantage of seeing life from a clearer, uncluttered perspective. While the presence of real joy in his life had been tempered, if not eliminated entirely, so had the anxiety, the fears, and the utter frustration with the audacity of his fellow human beings. He seemed unmoved and unaffected by life, sporting his Mona Lisa expression whether he was attending a funeral or watching the children opening their gifts on Christmas morning. It wasn't as though he appeared numb to the world or sat with the blank stare of a person purposely looking past the reality of life. Instead, his eyes revealed a deeper vision, a deeper, distinct sense of knowing—of knowing more than the average individual who is just trying to make it through another day of life's trials and tribulations. The expression on his face proclaimed to the world, "There is nothing new in this world—nothing about life and the series of twists and turns that it tends to take in an individual's time on Earth that will ever surprise me anymore."

Although Elise often found Leo's role as a conscientious observer, rather than a participant in life, to be a bit unnerving, she was always grateful for his unbiased opinions and challenging words of wisdom. She hung up the phone with dueling senses of worry and relief. She had known, before calling Leo, that her offer of company and safe haven would be denied, yet she couldn't help feeling a bit of failure. She was not accustomed to having her offerings of nurturing rejected. After all, it was what she did best. In fact, it seemed to her, at times, that nurturing was just about all that she did. And for someone to refuse her offer was almost like a personal rejection. But at least she tried. She'd made the offer. Just about begged, but to no avail. So, there should be no regrets. Besides, Leo was right when he said that she would have her hands full with her children, her parents, and the house.

OK, Leo was taken care of. What's next on the list, Elise thought. But as if her higher power were trying to say, "No, Elise, your responsibility to Leo is not done," her eyes fell on a little framed, four-by-six picture of Leo and the children at the zoo. It had been taken that previous Spring at the Swamp Fest. Leo was in a wheelchair, because he had recently had surgery to remove a bone spur from his heel. Brad was determined to get him out of his apartment where he had been recuperating on his own, so he called and invited Leo to join the family on the outing. To their surprise, Leo accepted the offer with no hesitation.

The kids had a ball that day, taking turns riding on Leo's lap, while Brad pushed them around the zoo. Elise had never seen Leo smile so much. He bought lunch for everyone and experimented with his first taste of deep-fried alligator tail. Elise and Brad thought that the event might be a turning point for Leo, the point at which he might recognize his place in their family. But it wasn't to be. The walls Leo had created to keep out the world were impenetrable, even by the love and laughter that flowed so freely and unrehearsed on that pleasurable day.

She picked up the picture and wiped away the thin layer of dust that had settled on its glass, revealing a clearer picture of his kind, old face, surrounded by three little heads of happy children. The kids loved him. He was their surrogate, paternal grandfather. But he shied away from their love and admiration so much that when Elise suggested that they call him "Uncle Leo," he insisted they just stick to "Leo," avoiding even a nominal familial connection. The kids, of course, loved it, feeling that Leo considered them equals, therefore not requiring a respectful prefix as part of his name, as was expected by most adults in their lives, particularly in the Deep South. But Elise's soft, sentimental heart longed for the old man to take a more active role in her family—to adopt them as they had adopted him.

Brad, however, understood Leo so well that he didn't need any demonstrative evidence as proof of Leo's feelings for him. And, of course, there was "the box." Elise put the picture back down in its original place and thought aloud, "I'd better put the box in a safe place." As though she were taking orders from an inner voice that commanded her body into action, she set out on her mission to secure the box in one of the airtight containers she had placed in the attic to store and protect all of the photo albums, the loose pictures, the kids' art work—things that she couldn't take with her if they evacuated, but things that could never be replaced.

She knew exactly where to find the box. Brad kept it in the locked file drawer of the desk in his study, away from the six little curious hands in his household. No one was allowed to touch the box. He had made that clear the very first time she saw it in his apartment when they first started dating. Brad's apartment was decorated in Kmart blue-light special décor. Bare necessities only. Lots of twos—two living-room chairs, two kitchenette chairs at a bistro-size table with white laminate surface, two lamps, two pictures on the stark white walls, two melamine plates that he was awarded for ten fill-ups at the corner gas station, two matching bowls of the same orange and brown Aztec pattern, two sixteen-ounce, heavy-duty plastic glasses, and two coffee mugs, which were a stretch, because he didn't drink coffee or any other hot beverages. He had constructed his bookshelves in the fashion of many students before him out of cinder blocks and several two-by-eight boards, each about six feet long. There was absolutely nothing in the apartment that suggested a feeling of permanence, nothing to offer a warm, cozy atmosphere, or a feeling of "home."

On her first visit to Brad's place, Elise had hoped to derive from his belongings and the ambience of his surroundings some sort of understanding of his somewhat enigmatic personality. Instead, for the first hour or so of this visit, she felt as though she were standing on a stage or a set for a television program. Nothing seemed real to her. It was as though Brad were pretending to live there. But then, her eyes fell upon a box which had been inconspicuously placed on one of the bookshelves, assuming the arduous task of holding up eight hardback books, all pertaining to history. "Ahhh," she thought curiously, "He likes history. Funny he didn't mention his interest in my field. Maybe he thought that if we seemed too compatible at first, I would rush into things. That's silly though. Common interests can make great conversation topics during those awkward silent moments when two people are getting to know each other…" Her mind was teeming with nonsensical, hypothetical characterizations as she passed her index fingers over the spines of the books, slowly, as though she were reading each title in Braille. And then her hand dropped to the box.

From her previous position across the room, her attention was drawn primarily toward the books. But from her new vantage point, she was able to get a closer look at the beautiful, intriguing object that kept them standing straight and orderly. The box was made of red mahogany, with burled, wood-veneer inlays on the top and sides. She turned the box upside down to see if there might be a winding knob, because it had the appearance of a music box. But it didn't, and that only made her more inquisitive. Although the box was not very large, it was surprisingly heavy as Elise pulled it off of the shelf and placed it in her lap. She rubbed her hand across the top of the box and wondered what a man, seemingly unfettered by unnecessary, sentimental clutter, would store in such an exquisite case, which now took on the appearance of a tiny shrine to Elise when she considered it amongst Brad's other nondescript belongings.

Once again, Elise's curious, and yes, romantic mind poured forth suggestions of possibilities, if not probabilities, as to what might be revealed if she lifted the lid of the mahogany box. "Maybe it's just a place to keep his pens or stamps, maybe pictures or letters from his friends and family, or maybe from a girlfriend back home." Her thoughts were racing when she was startled by the crashing sound of the books falling on the shelf, having lost the support of the box.

"What was that?" Brad called out, appearing from around the wall separating the kitchen from the living room, holding two glasses of white wine.

"Oh, just these books. I didn't realize this box was doing such a great job holding them up, I guess!" She tried to make light of her snooping, but the look on Brad's face was all that she needed to realize she had mistakenly slipped into a "no trespassing" zone. His momentary speechlessness, accompanied by his uncomfortable stare prompted her to rearrange the fallen books and put the box back in its original location, thinking to herself, "That's great. He probably thinks that I've looked inside the box, like some inconsiderate busybody."

"Here's some wine. I hope it's OK. I'm not very knowledgeable on the good labels," he said, handing her the glass of chilled vintage, which she hoped would rush to the task of lightening the mood that had suddenly filled the room like heavy smoke. He sat down beside her, in front of the books and his mysterious little treasure chest. "I'm sorry I picked it up, Brad. It's just so beautiful and intriguing that I was tempted to get a closer look. And these books—where'd you find these rare copies, if you don't mind my asking? I didn't even know you were interested in history."

"I'm not," he quickly responded, and then with a boyish grin added, "No offense."

"None taken," she replied, so quickly and quietly that she wondered if he heard her, because he went on with his sentence as though she never interrupted him.

"But the person who gave the books to me is a very special person in my life, and, I don't know, I guess it's kind of corny, but having his things around makes me feel that he's close by."

Her mind, of course, started again, this time stuck on the words "his things." OK, let's see, he may be referring to his father or grandfather. Or maybe an older brother—probably not his older brother, he's only mentioned two sisters. So, who could it be—oh my God—is he going to tell me he's gay? That's all I need is a bisexual boyfriend. Stop it! Stop it right now! Look at the positive side—there's no girlfriend back home. She took a big sip of wine and decided to speak in order to drown out the messages spewing from her brain, "Did the same person give you the box?" Damn it, she thought, that was too personal, especially if it's holding love letters from the homosexual lover, she had dreamed up seconds before.

His response did not quell any of her suspicions, "Yeah. Yeah, as a matter of fact, he did. Look, it's a long story, but I met this guy in college. He's a history professor at a small college in Cape Girardeau, Missouri."

"I thought you went to the University of Missouri in Columbia."

"I did. But during my senior year, last year, in fact, there was this big flood in southern Missouri. You may have heard of it." He paused, expecting her to say yes, that she did hear about it, but instead, Elise answered him with a negative shake of the head and a look that implored him to go on with the more important facts of the story.

"Well, anyway, it was a big disaster in our state. I gather flooding is not unusual in the Bayou State, huh?

"Not really, but I can understand how devastating they can be. So, what happened?"

"Well, the Red Cross was asking people to volunteer their time in any way possible to help the victims of the flood. So, my fraternity organized a group to spend a week on site, helping to fill sandbags, placing sandbags, helping people raise furniture and appliances in case their homes or businesses became targets for the river water."

"Believe me, I am very familiar with the routine. In Bayou Chouteau, we had the process down to a science."

Brad shook his head and smiled as though he were amused by her casual familiarity with what seemed to him a disaster of a lifetime, and Elise noticed how his smile softened his face, giving a rare, tentative appearance of a boyish, carefree nature, which she knew was her main attraction to this otherwise serious, practical man.

"Well, I was not accustomed to the scene waiting for us there. We didn't know what to do or where to go. So, the first thing they did was to introduce us to Leo. He was to be our supervisor for the week. I remember, I looked at him and thought, 'Now what is this old man going to do to help us?' I had no idea how strong and wise he was, but after a week of working side by side with him, having dinners at his house, spending a couple of nights there, we became so close. I just can't explain it. I could talk to him about everything, like I'd known him all of my life. And it was the same for him, too. I didn't want to be with my friends. I preferred talking to him. He's one of those people who become a part of you, and you know, you feel that even if you never see or hear from this person again, that he will remain as dear a friend as any in your everyday life." Then Brad laughed, and Elise could tell by the look in his eyes that he was back there, with the old man again, as he recalled, "He was just disappointed at my ignorance of history. That's why he gave me these books. That's when I knew that our meeting had been special for him, as well."

"I'd say. These books are worth a fortune," Elise said, still a little uncomfortable about the relationship he was revealing. "But I've heard that people can form very meaningful relationships at a time of distress. Like war buddies, survivors of plane crashes…"

"No Elise. I know what you're talking about, but actually it was more than that. I just don't feel comfortable talking about it with you, right now. So, let's change the subject." Just like that! Her silent voice was screaming. And though her heart cried "No, no, her rational side knew that she'd better follow his lead.

It was months later before Brad brought up the subject of his friend Leo again. They had gone to see a movie about Vietnam. Afterward, when they went for a bite to eat, he commented about how lucky he was to be living his young adult years in a time of peace. "I'm not sure I could've lasted in a place like that," he confessed, as they recalled all of the gory and graphic details of the film. "I would like to think that I would do my patriotic duty, but I don't think I would be a 'ready, willing soldier.' Especially after hearing Leo talk about his experiences in Europe during World War II."

"Are you referring to your history professor friend?" she asked in a casual, unassuming tone, all the while hoping that her question would encourage further discussion of this mysterious, influential person in Brad's life.

"Yeah. One night, during my week of 'flood duty'—actually I think it was my last night there—Leo invited me over for dinner. The rest of the guys were all going out drinking that night, and they all gave me hell, because I was going to the old man's place, instead, but I went anyway. He had told me that there was something important that he wanted to discuss with me, and I couldn't imagine what it could be." Brad passed his hand over his mouth as though he were six years old and wiping off a milk moustache, and he suddenly seemed uncomfortable. He picked up his fork and began to gently tap the tines on the table. The steady, rhythmic motion, like the drum cadence of a marching band, seemed to get his thought process back in step, just in time for him to respond to Elise's bewildered expression and question. "This history professor invited you over to talk about his wartime experiences?"

"No, no, no. Not just for that. But, during the course of the evening, after a few beers—quite a few, as a matter of fact—we were talking about history, I think, and we got on the topic of World War II. And Leo just started talking, almost like he was talking to himself—like I wasn't there. He told me that he had been taken prisoner by the Germans near the end of the war. Like a fool, I mumbled something like, 'I'm so sorry.' And he turned to me and said, 'Don't be. I was one of the lucky ones.' Apparently, his platoon had stopped for a while to rest in a deserted barn, somewhere in the Belgian countryside. It was freezing cold, and so foggy that they could hardly see where they were going. They were in some forest. I can't remember the name now."

"Was it Ardennes?"

"Yeah, I think so. How'd you know?"

"I am a history major. Not that I know much about battles and wars, but it sounds like Leo may have been in the Battle of the Bulge in southern Belgium." His eyebrows rose, and revealed that he was either impressed or confused, so she added, "You know, the Battle of the Bulge? The allies marching on toward Germany. The eventual fall of Nazi control of Europe." She stopped because she could tell that he really wasn't familiar with the facts that she poured forth, and she was beginning to sound like a teacher questioning a student who hadn't studied for an exam.

"Oh, I've heard of the Battle of the Bulge," he said, "but I have to confess that I am shamefully ignorant as to the details. What do you expect from an economics major?"

"Don't worry, I know little more than you." She was hoping that she hadn't bruised his ego with her command of the subject and encouraged him to go on with his story about Leo.

"Good, back to Leo. Well, there they were, freezing in this deserted barn but contented to have time and shelter for a rest. He was about to doze off, he said, when all hell broke loose. Explosions all around them. Leo opened his eyes just in time to see his two best friends, one on either side of him, blown to bits. He tried to help them out, but there was nothing he could do for them. He heard the German troops storming the barn from the rear entrance, and he realized that he was about to be taken prisoner. He quickly removed the dog tags he was wearing around his neck and replaced them with a spare set that he carried in his pocket to be used in the event of his capture. Pretty clever, huh?"

"Why would he do that? I must've missed something."

"Leo's Jewish. I just assumed you knew, I guess. Anyway, they all knew what was happening to the Jews over there, so he didn't want to take any chances. Being a prisoner of war in a German camp was no vacation, but it was a helluva lot better than Auschwitz."

Elise suddenly felt a wave of queasiness roll through her stomach. Although their food had not yet arrived at the table, she had lost her appetite. "Imagine that" she said, "actually feeling relieved at being sent to a prison camp by barbarians who hate you less for being an American than they would for being Jewish. I can't even comprehend that situation. Can you?"

"Let's just say that I can't comprehend it the way Leo can, but probably a little better than you can."

Elise was not in the mood to investigate the meaning of his statement any further, because she knew it would lead to his discussion that was more like his personal mini seminar titled, "I'm Jewish, You're Not." She was not in the mood to hear him dwell on their differences this evening. Not while he seemed so willing to talk about a topic that just a few months ago seemed taboo in her presence. She hoped that this was a sign of his protective wall coming down, so she conscientiously kept their dialogue focused on Leo. "Was Leo ever wounded in the war?"

"Believe it or not, he was wounded in that same attack, but he said that everything happened so quickly, he didn't realize it until his legs collapsed beneath him in his attempt to escape. He fell to the ground, briefly losing consciousness. When he came to, moments later, the Germans were rounding up the American soldiers. Any soldier who refused to cooperate was put against the wall and shot with machine guns. Leo realized that in his unconscious state he was likely taken for dead, so he tried to move cautiously back into the position he was in while unconscious, hoping to be left for dead. But one man's keen sense of hearing resulted in a rifle being nudged in his lower back. He got up, followed the orders being spewed out in German and broken English, and realized, at that point that his left leg felt partially numb. Luckily, he was able to walk. He doesn't remember how long it took for them to reach the camp, but he had enough presence of mind, as they marched on, to draw a sketchy map that could be used in the event of an escape."

"Apparently, he didn't get to use it."

"No. He was encamped for about two months, trying with limited supplies and expertise to doctor his leg back to health. But an infection set in. And he was afraid to let any of the guards find out about his problem, so every day—now remember this was in the dead of winter— he and his fellow prisoners would work from sunup to sundown repairing railroad tracks that had been targeted by guerilla forces in the area. Then, at night, he would return to his squalid barracks in so much pain that he could barely eat. They were fed in the morning and at night—always a bowl of potato soup, which was really boiled water and chunks of raw potatoes."

"How did he get out of there? Did he escape or…" Elise barely had a chance to finish her thought, as Brad eagerly continued to recount Leo's saga, with a passion that contradicted his usual stoic nature, a clue, she thought, to how closely he held to his heart this story and this man named Leo.

"No, no. One morning he was awakened by voices outside the barracks. There were no windows in the quarters, so they couldn't see what was going on, and no one wanted to open the door to find out. Then someone pointed out that sunlight was coming in through the cracks in the door. During their entire imprisonment, they had never been awakened after sunrise—always in the darkness. So, they knew something had gone awry. And then, as the rabble got closer to their door, they realized that they could understand the shouting. The men outside were speaking English, and they knew their long battle was over. Those who were able stormed out of the barracks, but Leo said he couldn't move. Fever raged through his body, and his leg throbbed unbearably. He doesn't remember being lifted out of his bunk that day, and he has no memory of the days that passed between the liberation of the camp and his waking up in the clean, friendly surroundings of an Army hospital in England. He made it through, though. He still has a limp, but he was very lucky not to lose his leg—or his life for that matter."

Brad eventually told Elise everything there was to know about Leo. But he did so at moments of his own choosing, and Elise never asked for more than Brad's prudent nature would allow him to disclose in one sitting. She did, however, find herself captivated by the story of Leo's life, and as time went on and his story unfolded, she was able to understand the strong connection between Brad and Leo. More importantly, she found that it was only through becoming acquainted with the life of the older man that she could become sensitive to and comprehend the personality of the younger man, who was so different than any man she had ever known.

Elise knelt next to the big Rubbermaid container in the damp, humid attic and thought about the year that she and Brad started dating. As LaLa would say, "A lotta water passed under the bridge since that time." She and Brad had both changed in so many ways, yet the box she held in her hands looked the same as it did the day, she first saw it upon the shelf in Brad's apartment. She set the box in her lap and struggled to lift the lid on the container, which she hoped would keep her treasures safe in the event of any hurricane damage to her home. She removed the lid and was about to place the box in its new secure quarters when she decided to open the box and once again touch and see the items that Leo had saved throughout his life—the items that left such a mark on his life that he kept them and protected them as somewhat of an autobiography to be passed on to the person whom his life might influence most---to be passed on to Brad.

Elise considered the absence of any childhood memorabilia as the first profound statement of Leo's collection. After all, there was another container in that same attic filled with artwork, report cards, photo albums, clothing, and special toys that were saved by Peggy Anne from Elise's early years on Bayou Chouteau. But Leo's box skipped over his youth and began marking his life, instead, during his service in World War II. She found his two dog tags amongst several German coins, which lay loosely on the bottom of the box. There was a postage stamp depicting Adolf Hitler, which Leo had tucked away in a small envelope with the map he had scribbled on his road to captivity. And, of course, the Purple Heart medal that he was awarded for being wounded in the line of duty.

There were two wallet-sized pictures from the war years—one of a young handsome Leo, in his uniform, and the other of a pretty young woman wearing a stylish outfit from the '40s. This was Mary Jo Murphy, whom Leo married after the war. A small handwritten wedding invitation was kept beneath the two small pictures. There was another picture in the box, which never failed to twist Elise's heart. It was a black-and- white snapshot taken a few years after Leo and Mary Jo's marriage. The couple stood in front of their small house, snow on the ground, snuggled closely together and smiling at their newborn baby boy, Hank, whom Mary Jo was holding in her arms.

But the box also held two obituary notices and two prayer cards from the funerals of Mary Jo and Hank. One could say that the accident that claimed the lives of Leo's wife and child was the singular event of his past that defined the Leo whom Elise eventually met, admired, and longed to have as an integral part of her family life. It was the one singular event that she thought of when she looked into his nebulous, pale-blue eyes, wondering what he was really looking at as he stared past the life going on right in front of him to a reality of his own—somewhere out in a world beyond.

Leo never forgave himself for not being home that night—the night his pregnant wife discovered that their three-year-old son was running a high fever. She was a nurse and usually felt capable of taking care of the minor injuries and occasional illnesses that occur in homes with small children. But something made her panic on this particular night. Leo had stayed late at school to attend a lecture with a colleague. Since he had ridden with this friend to school that morning, his own car was parked in the carport connected to the house. As Hank's fever rose, the weather outside worsened. Mary Jo could not contact Leo and decided to drive the child to a nearby hospital. No one knows exactly what happened. Mary Jo was a good driver, even though she didn't drive very often. The roads were slick with ice and freshly fallen snow. And Leo had no doubt that his wife was probably extremely nervous, worrying about the driving conditions and most importantly, about her sick child lying on the back seat.

According to the police report, Mary Jo drove through a stoplight and was broadsided by a truck traveling full speed ahead. The truck driver escaped serious injury but was taken to the hospital to be treated for shock once he was told that the impact of his truck had just killed a pregnant woman and her three-year old son. Brad told Elise that Leo actually went to the hospital to visit the man and to reassure him that the accident was not his fault. But then how could Leo blame the truck driver when he placed all blame upon himself? No one could or would ever convince him otherwise.

Even after years of friendship, Leo never spoke to Elise about that night. He spoke quite often about the lives of his Mary Jo and Hank but never about the accident or their deaths. And while a part of her wished that he would talk to her about this painful time in his life so that she could help him to heal, a selfish part of her was glad that he chose not to. For in helping him deal with his guilt and pain, she would have to deal with the reality that such a tragic event can occur in anyone's life. Which meant, of course, that it could occur in her own life. For Leo was a good husband and a loving father. Why him? Why not her? She didn't like to think of tragedy and happiness in terms of random occurrences. She wanted to feel that she was more responsible for and in control of her family's destiny.

Elise was beginning to regret her decision to revisit Leo's "life in a box," when she noticed the yellowing envelope sticking out from underneath the box that contained his medal of honor. She knew exactly what she'd find inside the envelope, which was addressed to Leo, but conspicuously lacked a return address. It contained a tiny article that had been cut out of a St. Louis newspaper. The article was headlined, "Professor's Wife and Child Killed in Accident." The newspaper clipping was accompanied by a short, poignant note, written on a white note card that was personalized in practically illegible gold, gothic initials. It was obviously her mother-in-law's handwriting on the card, and Elise could almost imagine Phyllis Steiner sitting at her desk writing the sympathy note to her brother, addressing and sealing the envelope, and putting a check next to his name on her "to do" list.

Dear Leo,

I was quite saddened by the news of your wife and son's deaths. It is so unfortunate that your choices have made it necessary for you to bear your heavy grief alone. Under different circumstances, I would have been at your side the minute I heard of your loss. But I have to think of my own family life. I know that you respect my feelings. You always have.

Sincerely, Phyllis

P.S. I would appreciate your keeping this correspondence confidential.

PHYLLIS MEYER STEINER
1940s

It was the morning of her thirteenth birthday. But instead of waking up to the smell of her mother's special birthday blintzes, Phyllis was aroused by the smell of coffee, murmuring voices, an occasional shuffle of a chair and the delicate rattling of cups and saucers. It was seven in the morning, but these sounds and smells congregating at the top of the stairs, just outside her bedroom door, were the same ones that she had fallen asleep to just four hours ago.

"Well, at least it's going to be a sunny day," Phyllis thought, as she reached over and raised the window shade, just above her nightstand. She didn't see any neighbors out and about yet, but she was quite sure that for everyone else on West Carlton Street this would be a rather typical day. It wasn't supposed to be a typical day for Phyllis, though. In fact, it was supposed to be a very special day for her and her friends, as well. There was supposed to be a big party at her house that very evening, at six o'clock—her first boy-girl party. And how she and her friends had looked forward to it! Although she was not allowed to include all of her classmates from school, she did invite her entire Sunday school class, which gave her a perfect reason to invite Mel Steiner. She loved Melvin Steiner; she just knew that she did. Her friends knew it, too. And this bothered her, because she had never told them about her feelings for him, and if it were so obvious to them, then it must be obvious to him. She felt her face flushing as she thought of this possibility. Why did

God curse her with a flushing face, she wondered. If he did come to her birthday party, she would never be able to talk to him without revealing her deeply held secret. With this in mind, a very small part of her was glad that the party would likely be canceled.

She felt sure that there would still be the traditional family birthday rituals—like the birthday blintzes, a new party dress and new shoes from Mama and Papa, and perhaps a book to go along with a box of sweets from her grandmother. Not just the ordinary sweets one could find in the local grocery store. Grandmother would give unusual sweets, like chocolate-covered fruit or chewy fruitcake cookies, which were shaped like little balls rolled in different colors of crystallized sugar. Each year she wrapped her old-world delicacies in a pretty box, held together by a perfectly tied bow of satin ribbon. And each year she would tell Phyllis how, in her country, children did not receive extravagant birthday gifts like they did in America. But they did enjoy the wonderful sweets that were given to them by family members and friends. "Here, in America," she would say, "children say 'I want,' birthday comes, and they get."

Grandmother always complained about how spoiled American children were. She told the same story over and over about how she and her sister, Reba, had to work for neighbors every day for two years in order to earn enough money to buy their bicycles. Washing and ironing clothes, that's how she did it, she would say. And then she would always finish the story with her humorous note of irony. "Dats why Reba teases me in every letter dat she writes to me. 'How can you marry a man who works in laundry?' And I tell her, when I write back, 'Reba, you forget, my husband "owns" the laundry, heh!' " Phyllis's grandfather started a laundry service as a teenager and had built it up to be one of the largest laundry businesses in the city. Upon his death, the family business was left to his wife, Sylvia, and was run by their two sons, Phyllis's father, Stanley, and her Uncle Sam.

Grandmother had not heard from Reba for a long time. Ever since those news reports reached America, telling about what the Germans had done to the people in Poland. In fact, she hadn't heard from anyone in her family since then. Grandmother had moved to America when she was just a girl of fourteen with a wealthy family who employed her as their nanny. Her father had died just months before, and her mother was not able to keep the house in order and feed four children at the same time. The eldest son, Leo, took his father's place in the family leather shop. And Sylvia, being the oldest daughter, moved to America, leaving her mother, Leo, Reba, who was merely a year younger than she, and little Max, everybody's baby, back in Poland.

Grandmother never saw any of her family again. Her mother had since died, her siblings had married, had children and grandchildren, and her only connection was through their letters which crossed the ocean religiously, to be anticipated and answered with equal fervor and delight. She would have everyone gather in the parlor to hear the news from the old country, and for many years, Phyllis enjoyed these occasions. She would imagine this far-away mysterious country and picture her great aunt and great uncles going about their days in what Grandmother described as absolute happiness and simple pleasure.

Then, it seemed that Phyllis grew tired of her grandmother's idyllic memories of her childhood home, and she often wondered, as the old lady rambled on and on, if Poland were so wonderful, why did Grandmother stay in America? Grandmother never said one good thing about America. She just criticized Americans and their frivolous, irresponsible habits. And it often annoyed Phyllis, whose own youthful patriotism had been aroused in recent years by the war news and propaganda. "How can she talk that way, when my only brother and his friends are over there fighting for her precious homeland?" she would ask her mother, whose trying tolerance of her mother-in-law was derived from ingrained notions of family loyalty rather than a genuine love for the older lady. "Oh, she's old. Just ignore what she says. I do." That was her mother. Straight. To the point. Matter of fact.

Maxine Meyer, Phyllis's mother, was a very practical woman, who kept her emotions in check. Emotions interfered with the order of the household and the routine of the very structured family, for which she,

Maxine, was ultimately responsible. Phyllis always understood that although Mama appeared to answer to Grandmother and Papa, she was the person who held everything together. She made and enforced the rules of the house, all the while working in the guise of the submissive wife and daughter-in-law.

One of the rules, which Mama had taught her children and strictly enforced at early ages, was to wash up and dress for the day before descending the stairs to the kitchen. But on this birthday morning, Phyllis decided to tempt fate. After all, her elders would hardly be concentrating on proper morning attire this morning. She rolled out of bed, stepped into her big fluffy slippers, and tied her robe tightly around her newly developed waistline, giving a moment's thought to how much her body had changed— or matured as she preferred to put it—over the last year. She had been so afraid that it would never happen. Her friends had all changed at least a year before she did, and the ongoing discussions about their "cycles and cramps" always made her feel left out. Countless nights she'd gone to bed and been unable to sleep, wondering if something was wrong with her body. She didn't dare ask her mother or grandmother. It would hardly be considered an appropriate subject in her home.

So often she'd wish that she had a big sister to discuss girly things. But she just had her big brother, Leo, and after yesterday's news, she feared that she may be faced with being the only child in a reticent world of very conventional adults. She couldn't allow herself to think that way, though. Not today. Not on her special day. Anyway, the letter from the war department stated that he was wounded, not killed. And although it didn't go into specifics, it did inform the family that he was sent to an Army hospital for special treatment. And she hung on to the line in the letter, which informed the family that if all went well with his treatment, Leo would be sent home as soon as possible.

Trusting in the power of positive thinking, Phyllis held fast to the idea of Leo coming home and tried to think of yesterday's letter as good news rather than foreboding news. Leo was coming home, and there would be a bright spot in her home life again. For he was responsible for any amount of joy she ever experienced in that house. He was her source of happiness, her only connection with that notion of family love—the one she'd read about in novels, seen at the movies, and felt vicariously through her friends while visiting in their homes. Oh, she was sure her parents and grandmother loved her. But their love failed to touch her heart. It fed her stomach. It kept her clothed. It educated her. It kept her safe. But it failed to touch her heart.

Leo was different. Probably because he could sense this emptiness in his little sister's heart. Probably because he, too, needed the kind of love Phyllis longed for. She missed his playful ways, the way he teased her about the boys in her class, the way he would imitate Papa's reactions to certain problematic situations, and she especially missed the way that he included her in his outings in spite of their eight years age difference. Phyllis often wondered what his first eight years of life was like, being the only child in the house. Back then, their grandfather was still alive, so Leo had to deal with even more "loving" authority than she had to deal with. Maybe that was why he paid so much attention to her. Perhaps she was his diversion from the status quo.

Whatever the reason, she enjoyed it, and in all honesty, took advantage of it. Just before leaving her perfectly kept bedroom to go downstairs to the kitchen, she glanced at the picture she had stuck inside the frame of the mirror above her vanity. It was of Leo in his Army uniform. She loved the picture. He looked so handsome. He had sent four pictures. One to his parents, one to his grandmother, one to his girlfriend, Sandy, and the last one to her, which he autographed like a movie star—"To my favorite and most beautiful fan, always with love, Leo." She touched the eight-by-ten glossy and wondered what part of his body had been wounded. She knew that it had to be serious if it was already decided that he would be sent home. But she wouldn't think about that today. He wouldn't want her to. Not on her special day. He wouldn't want her first boy-girl party to be canceled, either. But she knew it would be. She was sure of it.

The aroma of coffee grew stronger and stronger as she descended the stairs to the kitchen, and it was a reminder to Phyllis that she was the only one in the house who had gotten any sleep. "Good morning," she said, rather cheerfully, trying to pick up the mood that in spite of yesterday's news seemed no different than any other morning, except that Papa was not reading the newspaper. He was just staring into space with a bewildered look in his sad, dark eyes. But Papa's eyes were always sad, she thought, and briefly wondered why. Mama's eyes seemed red and swollen from crying or lack of sleep, probably a little of both. And Grandmother—well, she seemed the least affected, speaking in her short, abrupt statements while the other two held silent, either consciously ignoring her or just plain too tired to deal with her typically bitter comments.

Grandmother looked up from her crocheting, as her best acknowledgement of Phyllis's greeting, then returned her attention to her task at hand. There was no "good morning," much less "happy birthday" sent her way. But then, Phyllis knew better than to expect anything more than a good breakfast on the table. She was determined, however, not to let them spoil her day. She would spend it as though her big brother were there, making funny faces and hand gestures behind their backs while she struggled not to laugh—finding humor in their otherwise stoic atmosphere.

Her brother amazed her, because she had never actually heard him complain about their strict parents and grandparents. He had developed a sense of humor, which he used as his wall of defense, and found, or rather, invented a bright spot in all aspects of their daily lives. Phyllis envied this characteristic of Leo's personality and wished she were able to be just like him. But something stood in her way. Something that she could only describe as respect. Respect for her elders. Honor thy father and mother. Heavy guilt. And yet, Leo never appeared disrespectful in his jocularity. Only funny.

And somehow, he was never in trouble. Somehow, she, who always tried to do the right thing, she was always in trouble. It didn't bother

her so much when Leo was around, because he could always lighten her load, but since he was gone, it had been harder to handle. That look of disappointment or disapproval, followed by that feeling of frustration over never living up to family expectations. "We expect you to do this," and "We expect that you will never do that." And for the most part, Phyllis did do this and didn't do that. But it was never enough—never enough for her to earn—to earn what? What was it that she wanted— no, needed?

"So, Maxine, it seems your daughter has forgotten that it is indecent to be in nightclothes in the kitchen, hmm? I always say that a person should only stay in nightclothes if she is sick, and then she should stay in bed, heh?"

"Phyllis, go upstairs and get dressed for the day," her mother said, not even turning to see her, much less acknowledge her greeting.

Phyllis didn't move. She didn't say a word in response to either woman's remarks. Normally, she would have turned right around and gone back upstairs to change her clothes, making sure to apologize, at some point, for her lapse in discretion. But this time she couldn't. She simply couldn't move. Her eyes set in a frozen stare at the old woman sitting at the table before her. "How dare you?" she thought in silent defiance. "How dare you dwell on your simple, ridiculous rules and regulations on this day—when none of you know if my only brother will live or die? On my thirteenth birthday, when I was supposed to celebrate the beginning of my life as a young woman."

It was as though Phyllis could feel her blood turning cold as it flowed through her limbs, and she wondered if hatred made one's blood run cold, for she was certain that she hated her grandmother at that moment. And then the wizened one added, "So. You heard your mother. Go upstairs and get dressed."

Phyllis broke her stare and looked at her father who now quickly and conveniently found refuge from the conflict in the morning newspaper, which had been neatly folded before him. Then she looked up at her mother who moved from the kitchen sink to the stove to the icebox then back to the kitchen sink to the stove to the icebox, on and on, like a wind-up toy, needing no thought or purpose to make her next move. Just as Phyllis imagined. There would be no rescue or support from them. "Yes, I heard my mother. And I am going upstairs right now. But I won't be changing my clothes, because I won't be coming back down."

Phyllis spun around in her fluffy slippers, but not so quickly that she didn't notice the three heads turn simultaneously in her direction within a split second of her declaration of intentions. She stormed upstairs, not in fear of being reprimanded but rather in her desire to be alone, away from them. Her heart was racing as fast as her feet. She reached the top of the stairs and turned left, going into Leo's room instead of right, toward her own corner of the world.

The second floor was her sanctuary. Two small, but adequate attic bedrooms were separated by a small, but adequate bathroom that the brother and sister shared. It was their safety zone. She slammed the door and threw her long, thin frame, face-down on the plaid bedcover neatly placed on the single bed, whose mate was in her own room covered in pink chenille. She lay there, her head beginning to pound, and she knew that she could expect one of those miserable headaches that usually announced the beginning of her menstrual period. Not now, she thought, knowing that these headaches could linger for a couple of days, sometimes making her nauseated, distorting her vision, and making her want only to lie in darkness with her pillow pulled tightly over her head.

The headaches had started about a year before, and Maxine had taken Phyllis to the eye doctor, convinced that her daughter needed glasses. But Dr. Appelbaum assured both of them that Phyllis's vision was twenty-twenty. "It could be her age," he said, ever so cautiously, as though he suspected how the mother would react to his venturing into somewhat of a different area of expertise. "Have you started your menstrual cycle yet?" He directed the question toward Phyllis, but

Maxine was quick with her snippy response, "What does that have to do with whether or not she needs glasses?"

Dr. Appelbaum turned his attention to Maxine, but before he could explain his reason for the question, Phyllis got the conversation back on track, thus alleviating some of the tension that was building between her mother and the hesitant physician. "No, Dr. Appelbaum, I haven't started yet. Do you think this means I'll be starting soon? My friends have all started." She didn't know why she had added that last bit of information. Maxine seemed shocked that her young daughter seemed so willing to discuss such matters with an eye doctor. The doctor, on the other hand, was relieved to be speaking to a cooperative patient rather than an argumentative mother and nodded his head in understanding. "Yes, Phyllis. I think that the headaches are a sign of the hormonal changes in your body."

With regained confidence, he turned back to Maxine, in order to bring her back into the conversation, but kept his comments directed toward his patient. Dr. Appelbaum was the first doctor to do this, and he made Phyllis feel so grown up. She liked this feeling, but she could see her mother shifting positions in her seat and knew that Maxine was far from pleased. Everything that Dr. Appelbaum told them about the headaches and the hormones made a lot of sense to Phyllis but was completely lost on Maxine's unwillingness to understand. After assuring Phyllis that he felt certain that this was her problem, he then said that this was only one possibility, and that there were tests which could be performed in order to rule out other possibilities. Of course, the tests would have to be ordered and administered by a different doctor, whom he would be happy to contact. At the end of the visit, he suggested to Maxine that an appointment with the family doctor may be in order.

If there was one thing that ruffled Maxine's feathers more than her being wrong about a certain topic, it was the thought of something being wrong with one of her children. Bad eyesight was one thing, but what if one of these tests that Dr. Applebaum proposed, found something wrong with her daughter. Well, it was just all nonsense anyway, she thought to herself, and proceeded to voice her opinion as she and Phyllis walked to the bus stop. "I think Stanley Appelbaum has simply gone mad," she said. And that was her only comment to Phyllis about the entire visit.

Phyllis was then taken to Dr. Schein and then two other doctors across town, all of whom confirmed the first diagnosis of twenty-twenty vision. In the meantime, the headaches continued to make their monthly visits just as Dr. Appelbaum predicted... Grandmother suggested that Phyllis used these headaches as an excuse to stay home from school, which she rarely did, or to get out of chores.

In the end though, Maxine had the final say. She took Phyllis downtown to see Ben Schott, who made eyeglasses in a little shop, which he shared with his brother, who was in the shoe-repair business. She had gotten his name and high recommendations from Selma Glassman at the beauty shop. The Schotts were Selma's first cousins and didn't they come from a good, "observing" family. Yes, Papa had agreed. Yes, the old wise one agreed.

So, there it was, in a little dusty shop that smelled of leather and shoe polish that Maxine's diagnosis was confirmed. A short, bald man wearing a smudged white apron with pockets filled with lenses of various shapes, sizes, and thickness, looked into Phyllis's eyes with his own spectacled eyes, asked her to read an eye chart hanging next to the front door, and informed her that she indeed needed glasses to see things at a distance.

"Jou vear dem to school, and jour headaches, dey go avay, heh," and he led her to a glass case located at the back of his narrow portion of the store.

Of course, the three most fashionable frames, which quickly caught her eye, were unavailable, so Mr. Schott disappeared behind a curtained doorway that separated his workshop and stockroom from the rest of the shop and returned with three frames which he said he had in stock and could readily be made available to her. And on top of that, they were part of the special he was running for the next two days. Upon Maxine's urging and Phyllis's willingness to please, the young, supposedly nearsighted girl selected a style of frames that would enhance her beauty about as much as the lenses would enhance her vision.

Phyllis knew that her eyes were really fine, mainly because she couldn't see clearly with her new glasses. So, although she took the glasses to school each day in the little case, which she had received "compliments of Schott's Opticals" (it said so right on the case), she never actually wore the glasses. She would take them out and place them on her desk, but never ever used them. So now, whenever the headaches took control of her body, she wouldn't tell her mother, because she knew that she would only be told that it was her own fault for not wearing the glasses.

On this particular day, she especially wanted to keep her ailment from her elders. Then they would think that she was in bed in her pajamas because she was sick, giving credence to her grandmother's conditions for doing so. On this day, she didn't want to appease anyone, especially Grandmother. She just wanted to be alone, by herself, with her own thoughts. And then it occurred to her that she didn't really have many thoughts of her own. All of her thoughts were governed by the tribunal downstairs.

The sound of heavy footsteps ascending the stairs came from outside of Leo's bedroom door. Closer, closer, they came. Then the light tapping on the door. "Phyllis? It's your Papa." Silence, as she wondered sarcastically why he felt the need to identify himself considering he was the only man in the house. "Phyllis, this is enough. Now open the door. You've upset your mother and grandmother, and I don't need this now." Silence. In fact, there was silence that entire day, in spite of a few more petitions made at the door by both parents.

At one point during her escape, Phyllis tore a couple of sheets of paper from one of Leo's college notebooks, which still sat on his small desk, a desk probably more suitable for a student of her own age rather than a grown man seriously involved in the study of history. That's

141

what Leo had majored in at the university. He wanted to be a college professor; he had told her. But he also piddled in the field of psychology, and she often enjoyed listening to him go on and on as he pretended to psychoanalyze some famous person or world leader long gone. She started writing, pouring her heart out to her sensitive, understanding brother, who would understand the disappointment, the fears, and the heartbreak of her thirteenth birthday. Surely, she could mail the letter through the war department or whoever was responsible for delivering the letter to her family yesterday. When she finished her letter, she folded it and let it fall next to her body as she once again resumed a somewhat fetal position in the warmth and comfort of her brother's bed.

It was nearly four in the afternoon when a nearly bursting bladder claimed victory over Phyllis's youthful anger and pride and forced her to unlock the door and venture out into the hallway. She intended to relieve herself as quickly and quietly as possible, ignore the hunger pangs which she knew were only making her headache worse, and slip back into the cocoon she had created with her brother's linens and bed coverings. "If I could only relieve this aching head so easily," she thought in a murmur, hoping the heavens were open for the suggestion. She sat on the toilet and felt the pain in her stomach dissipate as she folded her arms across her lap and leaned forward as though she were helping to force the urine out of her body. She felt a bit dizzy as she walked back to Leo's room, making a conscious effort to avoid making any noise, which would draw attention from below.

There were no sounds coming from the kitchen, so Phyllis assumed that her family had either gathered in the parlor or retreated to their own respective bedrooms to catch up on their lost night of sleep. With her eyes on the floor, watching each deliberate step, she noticed three beautifully wrapped boxes on the floor near the bedroom door. She wondered how she had missed seeing them on her way to the bathroom. How differently this birthday had turned out from all of the wonderful plans she had made.

The party was supposed to start at six. More than likely, she would have been getting ready by now, allowing plenty time to help her mama set up the food and decorations.

She would have secretly been thinking about talking to Mel, whom her best friend Joni had confirmed really, really liked her, although her mama and papa had no idea she thought of boys so much.

Phyllis reached over, picked up the packages and withdrew once again to her safe haven. She placed them on the bed in front of her and pondered whether or not she should indulge herself in material goods from the people she despised most in the world at that moment. And after a few moments of considering doing without birthday gifts on her special day, she gave in to what a more mature person would consider hypocrisy and considered it as most adolescents would—as something she had earned, something she deserved, something that parents and grandparents owed their offspring by virtue of the fact that it was their choice or actions that were responsible for the child being in the world and enduring the long hours of agony living in the household orchestrated by parents who have no insight into the heart and soul of their own child. So, with unfettered enthusiasm, she opened the first box, which she knew from size and scent to be the sweets from Grandmother. Once again, chocolate-covered dried fruit was the choice. She was quite hungry, so she set the opened box beside her and sampled the fruit while she continued to unwrap her treasures.

Phyllis expected to find a book in the next box and was pleasantly surprised to find instead, beautiful white, silky gloves and a shiny, satin hair ribbon which apparently were meant to accessorize the new frock her parents had already bought and given to her so that she might wear it for her party. She slipped her long, thin fingers into the fingers of the soft, smooth gloves and fell back in the bed, lifting her hands in the air to admire the elegant metamorphosis from nail-bitten, little-girl hands to the hands of a movie star. And then she remembered that there had been another box, an unexpected one.

Since the same wrapping was used for all the gifts, Phyllis couldn't determine from whom the gift was given. It was a tiny box wrapped tightly with lots of tape—not her mother's frugal style at all. But what would Grandmother be giving her? Under the wrapping, she discovered an old, yellowed box that had apparently come from the old country. The name of the shop, which was printed on the top of the box was not easily pronounced and certainly not the name of a store that she recognized.

With soaring curiosity, Phyllis carefully lifted the lid of the box, which was joined to the bottom of the box by an old, loosely held hinge. Inside the antique packaging, she found a gold pendant sitting on a little piece of dark blue velvet. She lifted the chain from which the pendant hung and let the pendant fall in the palm of her gloved hand. She recognized it at once. It was the chai that her grandmother had worn around her neck for as long as she could remember. This Jewish letter was a symbol of life, and Phyllis knew that it was, without doubt, Grandmother's most precious possession. She sat in bed, staring at the tiny pendant, which she had always admired but was soon distracted by an apparent note on pink paper, folded and stuck on the inside lid of the box.

Phyllis removed the paper from its tiny hold, unfolded it, and began to read the squiggly scrawl, which had been written by her grandmother's aging, shaking hands. "My dear Phyllis, when you wear this, I will live on through you, as my mother and grandmother have lived on through me. You must never forget the past. You must never forget your people." Words of advice, words of hope, from a knowing, suffering soul. It was Grandmother's way of acknowledging that her granddaughter was not a child anymore, that she did, in fact, understand the responsibilities of being a woman in a Jewish family. So often, she had heard it said that the woman of the family was the one who carries on the faith and the traditions of the past.

Phyllis had been very young when Leo was bar mitzvahed. His religious rite of passage had been witnessed and celebrated by the entire congregation at the synagogue as well as at home with a huge dinner for family and friends. She vaguely remembered seeing him dressed uncomfortably in his new stiff suit, nervously reading the Torah from the pulpit, as his parents looked on and hung on to every word as though God himself were speaking to them. But this—this tiny little pendant—was her religious rite of passage. And the nervous tingling she felt throughout her body made her realize that she was now a part of a long line of tradition, one small part of a culture that people like her own mother and grandmother had kept alive for thousands of years. The very seriousness of the matter did not touch her, however, as much as the fact that her grandmother was ready and willing to trust her with its future.

A sudden wave of nausea rippled through her stomach, but this time it was not due to her headache, which was now more like a numbness making her feel as though her head were filled with cotton. No, this time she was sickened by the way she had been acting toward her parents and grandmother the entire day. She went from feeling like a poor, suffering victim to feeling like an ungrateful, selfish brat. After all, weren't they doing their very best to hold things together at home, for her sake most of all. Shouldn't she have done her part to help her family through this rough time as well, rather than give them one more pain in their hearts?

"And poor Grandmother. Poor, poor Grandmother," Phyllis thought. "After losing her family in Poland, she hears about her only grandson, and just because she shows a little strength in dealing with her sorrow, I have to be rude to her? An old woman who is not very long for this world—an old woman who holds so much respect for me. How on earth can I ever face them again? How can I apologize or make it up to them?" She had felt so justified in her earlier actions and reactions, and now her feelings had turned a hundred and eighty degrees. She was now embarrassed, and in a strange way felt hurt by the way she had hurt them. Well, she had to apologize and do it soon, because she felt that she couldn't live another minute feeling so horribly guilty about her actions.

Without taking off her gloves, Phyllis slipped the long chain over her tousled hair and jumped out of bed with an uncharacteristic eagerness to confront the victims of her self-righteous attitude. She ran downstairs, through the immaculate kitchen that smelled more of cleansers than food and into the parlor where her sudden entrance startled the three silent occupants. "I...I...I just wanted to thank you for my birthday gifts. Especially you, Grandmother." She held the chain in her hand to show her grandmother exactly what she was grateful for and continued in her cracking voice, "And I also want to apologize for the way I've acted. I don't know why I..."

She so wanted to continue in order to lift the heavy burden from her chest, but her grandmother interrupted. "Why, what on earth are you talking about child? We know you had one of your headaches today and thought it best to leave you be. So. You feel better now, eh?"

Phyllis looked at her mother and father who nodded rather than vocalize their agreement with what was said, and she understood exactly what was going on. It was easier for them to create an illusion, rather than to recognize and deal with a burst of rebellion. Rebellion was uncharted waters in this family—a course never before taken. She let it go with Grandmother's scenario. There was nothing more to be gained by pouring her heart out to them in a full-fledged confession. "Yes, I'm feeling much better now, thank-you," she said, and moved from one to the other, delivering to each a hug and a kiss on the cheek. Then, back to his businesslike fashion, her father proceeded to tell her of his contacting Rabbi Rubin, who through his wisdom and lifelong list of important and influential friends, was at this very moment trying to get more information about Leo's condition and whereabouts. And while Phyllis and her mother responded with acclamations of hope, Grandmother could only reiterate a prediction she had made on the day of her grandson's bris: "Bad luck, I tell you. He will always have bad luck if you name him for a living relative. You name him Leo, the name of my brother who is alive and well in Poland. It's not right. Bad luck." It never mattered to Grandmother on that day or ever after that Maxine had named her son after her own father, who had passed away just two weeks before her son was born. But then, it wasn't Grandmother's nature to give much thought to Maxine's family at all. This comment would have enraged Phyllis earlier in the day, but her newborn maturity and sheer emotional exhaustion allowed her to overlook it. And that was a good accomplishment.

That night, when Phyllis went upstairs for bed, she went into Leo's room to make his bed as she had found it in the morning. As she straightened the sheets, she found the letter she had written to him in the midst of her anger and emotional turmoil, and without allowing herself any further thoughts on the matter, she tore the sheets of paper into little bits and dropped them into the waste can next to his desk. After brushing her teeth and washing her face, she walked back to her own room, gently touched the picture of her brother, and crawled into bed, feeling physically and emotionally wrenched. She hadn't long to think about how she would make better use of a new day before she ended her thirteenth birthday by drifting off to sleep.

Two years later, on Phyllis's fifteenth birthday, the war was over, and Leo was home. And nothing delighted her more than having her big brother in the house again. This, however, was not because things had returned to pre-war normality in their home. She felt that something was missing between the two of them—that magical connection was no longer there. One of them or maybe both of them had changed. When the news had reached the Meyer home that Leo was on his way home, Phyllis imagined their lives returning to the way they were before he left for the war. But that was four years ago. She was only eleven years old, and he was a college student, whose real-life experiences had not yet involved the fear or the tragedy of war.

He treated her differently, she thought, realizing that now she was a young woman, not just a kid sister. And he was so quiet, so reserved. When he smiled or laughed—a rare occurrence anymore—it seemed empty, like the motion itself lacked the emotion behind it. He never talked about the war, about his friends, about the places he'd been. And he particularly avoided talking about the event that led to the permanent limp he came home with. Shrapnel, he said—but that was all.

Even though Phyllis knew that it bothered him to talk of his past four years, she longed to hear the stories of Leo's heroic adventures. She knew that he had done something heroic, because he was given a medal called the Purple Heart, and Papa told her that to get one of those, a man had to be wounded in battle. Tragic and romantic—just like the movies, she thought. A real, live hero in her own home. She wanted to ask him so many questions, but Mama and Papa had both told her to leave him be. They told her that he needed time to heal and that eventually he would be his old self.

Mama pampered him in any way that he would allow. Even Grandmother seemed to soften up for his sake. Every now and then, Phyllis would find her mother with tears in her eyes, and she knew that her tears were being shed over her son who didn't come home complete. Something was gone. Something was missing. Something was left behind in the Old World, which was now as broken as those who had fought for her. Papa predicted that Sandy, Leo's girlfriend, would be the one to bring him back. But she too only grew more and more frustrated as she visited every day, looking like a picture out of a magazine in her pretty, fashionable outfits, not a hair out of place, perfectly manicured, and bearing little gifts and treats that she hoped would spark a flicker of interest and hope. But from Leo's response, one could've thought she was his favorite cousin. Phyllis knew that Sandy wanted to get married as soon as Leo returned. She had said so. She was so sure that he would feel the same way after his harrowing experiences. But nothing seemed further from Leo's mind now. And this was obvious to everyone, especially his impatient high-school sweetheart.

Sandy was at the Meyers' home on the evening of Phyllis's small family birthday celebration, and although there was that uncomfortable, superficial appearance of complete bliss and satisfaction that everyone had learned to wear in spite of the fact that they knew something was wrong, Phyllis was determined to focus on the positive. Leo was home. And this fact alone was something to celebrate.

After the candles were all blown out, the cake and ice cream eaten, and the presents opened and admired, Leo stood up, with an air of ceremonious flair, and announced to Sandy that he would like very much to walk her home. Sandy's eyes shot a hopeful glance from one family member to the other. After all, Leo had hardly taken a step outside of his home since his return. Papa thought he might be a little self-conscious about his limp, but Phyllis didn't think such a thing would bother her brother. This little outing was a sign that, perhaps, he was coming out of his shell. Earlier, he had asked Mama if he could borrow some money, which he would return to her at the end of the week. She hadn't asked what he needed it for, but now she assumed that he was taking Sandy out for a late-night date. The expression on Sandy's face when she agreed to the walk could not have been more radiant if she had been a bride saying, "I do." Leo, too, had a more complacent, if not cheerful, look on his face, and everyone sitting around the dining room table silently sighed in relief, thinking, "He's back, he's come home."

It is true that Leo's complacent look had come from a long spell of deep reflection on his past and his future. It is true that he had finally decided to come out of his shell and begin his life again. And it was also true that Leo was ready to move forward in his romantic life, but the idea that Leo had finally come home couldn't have been further from the truth. That night, Leo left a very tearful, dejected girl at her doorstep and walked to the bus station, where he caught the 10:30 bus to Little Rock, Arkansas.

Two weeks went by, and there was no word from Leo. Phyllis and her family knew that he was OK though, because they had had a visit from Sandy the morning after his disappearance. At that point, no one had even realized that Leo had not come home from Sandy's. They just thought that he had been out late and was still in bed. After all, they had gotten used to his seeking solitude in his room. Needless to say, the poor girl was extremely distraught as she delivered the news to the bewildered family. In fact, all Phyllis could think of was how she had never seen someone go from being so beautiful to so haggard in such a short time. Phyllis was never really crazy about Sandy, but she did feel a bit sorry for her right now. And even though she normally refused to listen to anything negative about her brother, Phyllis could not help being a little angry at him herself. In between spasmodic sobs, Sandy managed to relate to her once-imagined-in-laws that Leo had told her that he had changed, that he was not the same person he was when he left four years ago. He had told her that it had been his intention to return to his home, his old life, and pick up where he had left off, and that he had really hoped that he could, because that would make his life easier. But it didn't take him long, he said, to realize that he no longer fit in his old world. He told her that he had made some very difficult decisions, and he was prepared to act on them. He would never be happy in this world if he didn't.

"What did all of this mean," wondered Phyllis, "this talk of his 'old world' and his 'not fitting in?' How could he not fit in his own home? With his own family? With his own sister?" Phyllis silently gave much more thought to these questions than to the feelings of the pathetic, jilted woman, sitting before her, who seemed to be attracting sufficient pity from the parents of her perpetrator. Their hopes that this good Jewish girl would be the answer to their prayers had been shattered. Phyllis was not very disappointed about that particular part of the scenario, for she was too involved with dealing with her own feelings of being deeply hurt and extremely curious. She wanted some answers from Leo, so that she could understand for herself what was going on in his life. Didn't he realize how deeply she cared for him—how very important he was in her life?

The answers to Phyllis' questions came two weeks later. They came not in a letter or a phone call or a message from a friend. They came with a knock on the door, in the form of a pretty, red-haired, freckle-faced, Irish Catholic woman named Mary Jo Murphy. With Leo at her side, his arm wrapped casually around her shoulder, she extended her soft but cool, clammy hand in greeting to Phyllis, who had happened to answer the door. Just thrilled to see her brother standing before her, Phyllis returned the greeting and handshake to the stranger and threw her arms around her brother, tearfully telling him how worried she had been that she'd never see him again, and how she couldn't sleep at night wondering if she had said or done something to make him want to leave.   On and on she rambled, spilling out two weeks of fear and anguish until Leo stroked her hair, and said in his old, comforting tone, "Slow down, Phyl. Let us come in and get settled a bit, and I'll explain everything. Are the folks around?"

"Oh, sure," she said, gaining a little composure, enough to be a little embarrassed by her reaction at seeing him standing in the doorway. "They're in the kitchen—big surprise, right? I heard the knocking from my room upstairs. I was reading and—why did you knock at the front door like a salesman?" She heard her words spilling out of her mouth in a jerky, tentative manner, the way they sometimes do when a person offers superficial gibber jabber in order to be a part of a conversation while being extremely careful not to reveal the real thoughts and questions going through the mind. She backed up into the foyer, allowing her brother and his guest entry into the quiet house.

"I don't know. I guess I wasn't sure how the folks were taking my unexplained disappearance."

"Just as you might expect. They're acting like nothing abnormal is going on, while they walk around in silence. Except for Grandmother, who keeps saying that you've gone completely mad, because God is still angry about your being named after a living relative."

"What does that mean?" the red-headed, freckle-faced woman asked, with her smile that seemed to turn on lights in her eyes. Phyllis had heard about people whose smiles light up their faces, but she'd never actually seen it and doubted the existence of such a phenomenon. But there, right before her eyes, was living proof, and the woman's question reminded her that someone else was in the room besides herself and Leo.

"Oh, never mind that," said Leo. "You'll understand when you meet the infamous Sylvia Meyer. She's a real character. And by the way, I haven't formally introduced you to this real character," he said, putting his free arm around Phyllis's shoulder. "Mary Jo Murphy, meet my favorite sister, Phyllis Marian Meyer. Phyllis, Mary Jo."

"You're so funny, Leo, considering I'm your only sister. And anyway, that joke is too old to hold any humor anymore." They both laughed at her remark, especially Leo, and Phyllis could not believe the change that had come over her brother since the last time he had stood in their home. He was laughing and teasing her again, and although this made her happy, she couldn't get rid of a foreboding feeling in the pit of her stomach. And the foreboding feeling was caused by this pretty companion, who quite obviously from the body language indications, was much more than a casual friend. And more importantly, who quite obviously did not belong to the nearest synagogue.

After a couple of minutes of casual chatter, the three of them entered the kitchen, with Phyllis walking just ahead of the hand-holding duo. Da-da-da-daaah. A trumpet playing the first notes of Beethoven's Fifth couldn't have aroused more attention then their sudden appearance before the obviously surprised and shaken parents and grandmother.

There was a very loud silence as the parents and grandmother looked from each other to Leo to Mary Jo, but never at Phyllis, as though each was waiting for another to be the first to speak in order to give some direction as to the route the conversation should take. Phyllis wished that she could do or say something to break the tension in the room, especially for the sake of Leo's guest. Leo, also eager to clear the air, held up a hand, as though he were stopping an oncoming truck. "Before you say anything, I'm sorry. I am truly sorry for leaving with no explanation, and I hope I haven't caused you to worry. I know that Sandy had to come by—I know she was really upset when I last saw her. I didn't mean to hurt her—or you, for that matter."

Remarkably silent and ever attentive, his audience looked on with expectations of the explanation they so well deserved. Phyllis was so nervous for Leo and herself that she bit her thumbnail until it bled, causing a sharp twinge of pain to travel through her thumb and up her forearm in a split second. But she, too, remained silent and in her place, waiting. Leo went through a very awkward session of introductions and invited Mary Jo to a seat at the family table, although he chose to stand behind her chair.

"As you know, when I was wounded, in battle, I was sent to an Army hospital in London. I can't begin to describe my state of mind during that whole experience. All I know is that I didn't care if I lived or died. I didn't. I was beyond feeling pain, hunger, thirst. I didn't care to take another breath, perhaps, for fear of what this ugly world held in store for me. Because, believe me, I had seen such an ugly world." He swallowed hard and tears filled the pale blue eyes that had seen so much. The sight of tears in her precious brother's eyes brought and instant sickening feeling to his sister who had never before seen him cry.

He paused for a moment, passed his hand over his mouth and chin in order to regain the composure that seemed to be slipping away with each passing second. And although each of his family members could obviously see the difficulty, he had recalled the darkest days of his life, not one of them made any effort to reach out or say anything to console him. Their eyes still moved from Leo, to each other, to Mary Jo, back to Leo, in silence. And then, Phyllis noticed Mary Jo's small right hand reach up to her right shoulder where Leo's hand rested, and she slipped her hand into his. He looked down at her and squeezed the hand, which Phyllis remembered as cold and clammy, and he seemed to find his inner strength to continue.

"And then, I met Mary Jo. She was a nurse at the hospital and in charge of all of the patients in my ward, mostly guys from my squadron—guys who felt the same way that I did. Just didn't want to go on." He squeezed her hand again, as he cleared his throat, perhaps giving his listeners an opportunity to jump into the conversation with questions, remarks, anything to break that thick wall of silence that his hurtful words had to penetrate. But no one responded with anything more than their blank yet somehow accusing stares. So, he continued.

"I don't think I would've made it home, if it hadn't been for Mary Jo. She didn't just help to heal my wounds. She brought me back to life, and life back to me." Another pause. Another silence. Another squeeze of the hand. And then, just when Leo was about to embark on the next segment of his confession, his mother narrowed her eyes in a glare at Leo and then Mary Jo, and asked in a sharp, acrid tone, "And what about Sandy? What was she, chopped liver?"

"Mother." Leo was unable to interrupt, though.

"The poor girl waited for you, she wrote to you, she missed you, and she was faithful to you, Leo Meyer. What about that poor girl?"

"Mother, I loved Sandy, but it's not the same…" And again, he was unable to finish his response.

"Oh? And what exactly does that mean? 'It's not the same.' You say you loved her, then that's that. You owed her loyalty and respect. Just like she had for you. That's what love is, it's not as selfishly simple and convenient as choosing the prettiest face that happens to be around when you're lonely."

In all of this, Mary Jo Murphy sat quietly, in awe, expecting Leo's family to be surprised but not this upset. Leo took advantage of his mother's need for a breath of air and shot back a desperate attempt to defend his actions, "Is that what you think this is about, Mother? You think this is about a selfish, convenient choice? This is about one of the most difficult decisions I've ever made in my short life. I've given this a lot of thought. I feel quite badly about Sandy. I tried so hard to make things feel right with Sandy ever since I returned home. I wanted so much to feel for Sandy the way I do for Mary Jo, but it didn't work. It just didn't work. And it never will, because this is the woman, I want to spend the rest of my life with. This is the woman I'm going to marry. And I know that if you just give yourselves a chance to get to know her, you'll understand why I love her as much as I do. And you'll love her, too."

Suddenly, and quite uncharacteristically, Stanley Meyer shoved his chair away from the table and stood up. His face was reddened with rage, his lips tightly closed, forming a tight, straight line across the lower portion of his face, and when he slammed his hand down upon the tabletop, the resulting resonance caused everyone in the room to gasp, as though they were frightened by an unexpected specter. Phyllis, with her thumb throbbing, folded her arms across her breasts, hugging herself and protecting herself from the scene that was about to transpire.

"I've heard enough!" he shouted, this meek, sheepish man who rarely spoke in their home, with the exception of answering questions or responding to greetings. "For months and months, you have moped around this house, and we all tried to have patience. 'Wait,' we thought, 'he'll come around.' Your poor mother has barely slept at night for worrying about you, as well your grandmother. Not to mention that poor girl down the street. Just waiting. Not dating anyone else because of you. How many years of her life have you wasted? Did you think about that? Then, you leave my house with your mother's money in your pocket to go off on some vacation with this woman, and not even one word to tell us if you're dead or alive. All we know is this cockamamy story you told Sandy when you dumped her like an old shoe. And now you come walking back in my house—my house where I have raised my children with proper morals, values, and tradition. Now you walk back into my house, with this woman and tell us this…this song and dance, and you tell us you're going to marry her. Just like that."

Phyllis heard a quiet whimpering coming from Mary Jo's direction, and she could see that the woman's shoulders were trembling in spite of the tight supportive grip of Leo's hands. This disappointed Phyllis, who was hoping that Mary Jo would be the courageous type, the type of woman who would speak up to her father's verbal attack. She also wished that she had it within herself to defend her brother and his unsuspecting fiancée, but she, too, was crying and trembling. Leo had

155

never been in this position, and one could easily see that he was not equipped with an argumentative temperament.

"Please Papa," his passive words pathetically pleading his case, "You have to understand. I love her. Please give yourself a chance to get to know her. Just…"

"OK, son, you're right. Let me get to know her a little better." But the words were sarcastic, caustic. "Tell me, Miss Murphy, which synagogue do you attend?" And though he directed the question to Mary Jo, he stared angrily and in disbelief at his son, sending knives, it seemed, through his breaking heart.

Poor Mary Jo, understanding completely that the question, itself, was really meant to be a statement of contention, still tried to answer in her most polite, Southern accent, "Well actually, sir, I was raised Roman Catholic, but Leo and I have talked at length about religion, especially when he was recuperating in the hospital. And somehow, oh, I don't know, the war made us see things in a different way." She was pleased with her answer, and so was Phyllis. Not that it mattered to anyone else, but she liked this, Mary Jo Murphy. But Stanley Meyer was obviously not impressed and almost seemed insulted by the woman's attempt to explain her feelings.

"The war, huh. Well, I'm sorry Miss Murphy, and I hope you won't take any of my feelings personally. My disappointment lies solely with my son. My son who knows, because he has been taught, that for thousands of years our people have struggled for survival. Through many of your wars. And just look at this last one. How many of our people had to die brutal, demoralizing deaths, because of that very struggle to live their lives as Jews. You and Leo and your newfangled notions come from the war. Well in this house, they come from that struggle. You understand? That struggle for survival. And that struggle is inside of every Jew. It is in me, my wife, my mother, my daughter, and believe it or not it is in my son. But it will never, it can never be a part of you. It is what defines us, it is who we are, and it is the reason that my son will marry a Jew."

Mary Jo listened to him, watched him, and sat in a silent stillness that made her look like a porcelain doll, whose facial expression gave away no secrets about the feelings within. What could she possibly say in response to that soliloquy? Phyllis wondered. How could she possibly have a comeback? She suddenly felt anger building inside toward Leo, for putting his family and this nice woman through this scene from hell. What could he possibly have been thinking? Her father started walking out of the room, when Leo spoke, strongly holding his ground, "I'm sorry you feel that way Papa, but Mary Jo will be my wife."

"You are a man now, and you will do what you must," replied Stanley Meyer. "And so am I. And you know what I will do if you marry outside of your faith." With that said, he simply walked out. Maxine, in an absurd notion of doing the right thing, offered Leo and Mary Jo some coffee.

"I don't think so, Mother," Leo replied. "I think we have to be leaving."

"Well, when will you be back?" she asked in a controlled but distraught manner.

"That will be up to Papa," he answered, and he touched Mary Jo lightly on her shoulder. She is standing up, smoothing her skirt, and expressing her pleasure in meeting everyone, adding her apologies for causing such discontent among the family. As they walked out of the kitchen toward the front door, Leo leaned his lanky body over and kissed his little sister on her cheek. "I'm sorry, kid. I didn't mean to do this." He squeezed her shoulders as he had squeezed Mary Jo's just moments before. Phyllis was speechless. In awe. Her world was falling apart. Walking out of the door. She wanted to run to him, drag him back, tell him that she didn't care whom he married. She wanted to, but she didn't. Her gaze moved from the exiting couple to her mother and grandmother, back and forth, waiting for someone to make a move to stop the madness. But her brother's steps just took him farther and farther away from her, until finally the front door closed, and she was left once again with the silence, broken only by Grandmother's only comment throughout the whole ordeal, "Bad luck, I tell you. No one listens to an old woman, heh. Bad luck."

In the days that followed the family debacle, Phyllis saw very little of her father and spoke very little with the others. About a week after Leo announced to the family that he intended to marry Mary Jo Murphy, they received a handwritten invitation from the couple, requesting their presence at the wedding ceremony, which would be held at a small chapel in Northbridge, Arkansas. A letter from Leo was also enclosed, explaining his feelings, stating that he loved them very much and wanted them to be a part of his life. Wouldn't they please be a part of his marriage? Wouldn't they please reconsider? Everything could be worked out.

The letter was passed from Mama, to Papa, to Grandmother. Phyllis watched intently and unnoticed from the kitchen stairway. She didn't speak, waiting to see their reaction. Her hopes were lifted briefly when her father asked her mother to mark the date and time on the calendar. Strangely, however, while Maxine hunted for a pen in the kitchen desk drawer, Stanley Meyer lit the flame on one of the gas burners of the stove. He placed the small handwritten invitation, as well as his son's heartfelt letter on the grate of the burner and watched them both quickly become inflamed and burn to tiny little bits. His facial expression was a mixture of anger and pain, giving Phyllis the conflicting desire to feel sorry for this man whom she could hardly stand to look upon. And still, she said nothing.

The day of the wedding arrived, and the Meyers went about their business as usual. No one mentioned the event, no one mentioned Leo's name. The immeasurable pain that Phyllis felt was tearing her up inside. She had no appetite; she couldn't sleep; she was physically ill. And just as she had done on her thirteenth birthday, she spent her day in Leo's room, which had changed only slightly since his return from the war. She needed to talk to someone, but there was no one. She was forbidden to talk about the "humiliating" problem to any of her friends, and there was no way that her parents would listen to her plea to forgive Leo and accept the woman whose smile lit up her face. She did mention it to Melvin Steiner, though. But he was no comfort, because he agreed with her father. "Phyllis, how hard can it be to find a nice Jewish girl to marry, considering it's probably the only thing your parents' have ever asked of your brother?" he contended. And this led Phyllis to wonder if she really cared for him as much as she thought.

The wedding was to take place at one o'clock that afternoon, and just about that time, she heard her father's deep voice calling for her mother, then her grandmother, and then she heard him calling from the foot of the kitchen stairs for her to come downstairs. "Now what?" she thought bitterly, as she pulled her tired body out of her brother's bed, attempting to straighten her tousled, wavy hair with her fingertips. Even though she didn't know what to expect when she reached the kitchen, she was a little surprised to find her father in his black suit and yarmulke. He was standing at the table, where his daily prayer book rested in front of him, straightening his tie. When he noticed her standing there, staring at him in wonder, his facial muscles became noticeably tensed. His very thin lips became non-existent as he tightened them into a determined frown, an expression that gave the impression that he was attempting to hold back either a flood of tears or an outburst of anger.

She became frightened as she had never before seen this look on her father's face. His lips parted only to say, "It's one o'clock. Come into the parlor so we can begin."

"Begin what, Papa? What's going on?" But she knew. Her intuition was right. For there in the parlor sat the women of the house. There in the room shared only on special occasions and high holidays. There they were, gathered as a family, to mourn the death of her brother, Leo. To mourn the death of the elder child and only son of Stanley and Maxine Meyer. To mourn the death of a grandson, who was cursed from the day of his naming. Her mother and grandmother stood up from their seated positions on the sofa and dutifully faced Stanley. Maxine reached out and took Phyllis' trembling, perspiring hand and pulled her nearly lifeless body toward the tiny gathering.

"Nooooooo!" she screamed as the rite of Keriah began, with her father ripping the right lapel of his suit. "You can't do this," she continued to scream as he tore the collar of his mother's housedress and did the same to his wife's white blouse. "Don't touch me! Get your hands off of me!" she struggled, but to no avail, as her mother held her and her father ripped her thin, cotton shirt. And as she doubled over in agony, sobbing, falling to the sofa, crying out, "How can you do this to him?" But what she really meant was, "How can you do this to me?"

Stanley Meyer began to recite the Kaddish, the Jewish prayer of mourning. She hardly noticed the expressions on her mother's or grandmother's face. She couldn't even look at them. She was afraid this would happen, although her father had never actually spoken of it. But thinking back to the day that Leo and Mary Jo left the house, she realized that her brother knew. And in spite of these horrific consequences, he married Mary Jo. His love for her was stronger than his love for his family. And because this realization only served to bring her more pain, she allowed herself to listen to her father's deep, monotone voice, reciting the Hebrew prayer, a prayer created in a time so far from the present, in a language unknown to the women of the family—this traditional, yet meaningless prayer to Phyllis, marking the death of her brother, whose only desire was to be with the woman he loved, the woman who brought him back to life, who made him want to experience life again. And then she remembered how Leo had acted at home after returning from the war. And she realized that Leo had chosen life over his family, not just a pretty face.

For thirty days, the Meyer home was a home of mourning. The mirror on Phyllis' vanity, which once held Leo's picture, was turned around, as were all of the mirrors in the house. When she asked why this had to be done, her mother said that she wasn't sure, but that she thought that it had to do with eliminating vain thoughts during Sheloshim. Her father wasn't speaking to anyone. And her grandmother said it was to avoid seeing the ghost of the dead person in your reflection and having the deceased person rip out your soul. "Leo is not dead," she stated defiantly. "Mmm, hmmm," was the grandmother's answer, "In this family, he is. And it is best you accept it, heh?" Didn't they realize that her heart had already been ripped out, so why worry about her soul?

Word of the Meyer family's sad state of affairs spread like a wildfire through the cohesive, "well meaning" community. "A mark on the family," some said. A shame. A disgrace. A disappointment. An embarrassment. And Phyllis reluctantly had to hear Mel's sentiments echoed in the consensus of the congregation. "All he had to do was marry in his faith, a simple thing for good parents to ask." These words were meant to console her—to make her see that her brother was ungrateful for all that his parents had done for him in his life. He had been disloyal to his parents, his ancestors, and to all of the Jews who had died at the hands of the Nazis.

By the end of Sheloshim, the mirrors were turned back to their correct positions, and in the vanity mirror, which once held the eight-by-ten photo of Leo, Phyllis looked at her own reflection. She was no longer a child, for in this mirror she had watched her face and body change through the years. There were so many changes, and yet the world around her remained steadfast in its traditions and ideas. But Leo's world had changed with the war, with Mary Jo. His experiences had taken him beyond the boundaries of his childhood community and placed him in a world of "others." Other people, other cultures, other beliefs, other traditions. Phyllis knew that she would forever miss Leo. But she also knew that she could never live in Leo's new world. The old world was not perfect, but it was what she knew. It was what she was taught, and what she was prepared for. It was the world in which she would raise her own children, and her children's children.

Phyllis lifted the tiny gold Chai that hung from the chain around her neck, and with her other hand, she touched the place on her mirror where Leo's picture once hung, and she prayed that as she grew older in her own world that she would also come to understand and believe in

161

the duty and conviction that would drive a father and mother to mourn the death of their only living, loving son.

SUNDAY

E lise sat on the back porch swing, enjoying a moment of peace, watching Casey as he diligently played on the floor with what seemed to be a million Styrofoam building pieces. The television blared from the downstairs playroom—the same dinosaur video that J. P. played over and over again. As tired as she was of hearing this video, interrupted only by the Disney Channel, throughout every waking hour of her day, it was a relief to hear something other than the Weather Channel. There's nothing like an impending disaster to make you long for the daily, boring routine of housekeeping, or "homemaking," as some of her cohorts insisted on referring to their stay-at-home careers.

After all, "housekeepers" are the paid help who come to the house during the week to help clean. "Homemakers" are those special, talented, highly intelligent, nurturing souls, who give up professions or careers in order to dedicate their bodies and brains to the physical and emotional well-being of those individuals comprising the social unit referred to as the immediate family. That's what should be next to the word homemaker in the dictionary. Oh yes, and pets. Somewhere in the definition, it should be noted that some veterinary experience may be needed to fill the requirements of this highly skilled position.

She found herself giggling quietly to herself as her thoughts momentarily took her back to the year that Lilah was born. A few of her friends were pregnant at the same time, and they, too, were planning on switching from working outside the home to being stay- at-home moms. But somehow, in the early '90s, women found it hard to admit that they were going to quit their jobs because they were sick of working, and because their husbands made enough money to moderately support the family without an additional income. They couldn't admit that they would rather stay home and enjoy their homes and play with their children. Only the laziest, most unaccomplished woman would leave the working world—that world of challenge and productivity—to stay home and be a maid and day-care service.

So, in order to justify their decisions to stay home and be homemakers, these highly educated women of the '90s had to turn the image of staying at home from a cop-out to the ultimate professional challenge of a lifetime. And they did. They read the new "professional" journals that were popping up ad nauseam with titles such as Modern Mom, The Happy Healthy Home, and Parent and Child. They read quasi-scientific articles on topics such as "The Best Music to Play in the Home if You Want Your Child to Earn a Scholarship to Julliard," "The Most Popular First Names of the Wealthiest People in America," "Cloth or Disposable—How to Save the Environment," "The Best Childhood Stories for the Non-Violent Child." Elise started to laugh out loud as she created possible titles for the popular genre of reading material that cluttered the check-out stands at the grocery stores back then and provided interesting conversations at neighborhood playgroups. All of this for a job that their own mothers, grandmothers, and great-great-great-grandmothers had accomplished with no help from college degrees or child-rearing classes and articles.

Casey looked up at her, thinking that the smile on her face was for him, in praise and admiration of the creative ability it took to stick a Styrofoam "Toobers&Zots" into the mouth of the plastic white alligator he had just gotten at the Audubon Zoo. "So, what's the big alligator eating?" she asked. In response, he transformed his sweet little boy voice into the most ferocious growl, "He's eating Lilah!!!"

"Oh well," she thought, "I guess I should have read more articles." She took another long sip of mint tea and lifted her head slightly to catch the breeze from the oscillating fan in the corner of the screened in porch. "I've got to get this ceiling fan fixed," she said, as if her three-year-old were in the least bothered by the thick, humid air. She thought about calling on Monday and then realized that even if they were home on Monday, they probably wouldn't have phone service. And surely no one would be coming out to fix the fan. Then she said a quick prayer that they would even have a home on Monday. She heard the phone ring, then stop— "M-o-m! Telephone!"

"Who is it?" she yelled back, realizing she had just committed one of her own pet peeves, yelling like savages across the house. "It's Ms. Talia," replied the savage voice from the living room, where a rare moment of piano practicing was under way. Elise reached over and picked up the phone, which she had close by just in case a moment such as this would arise, and eagerly greeted her caller with a playful, "Hello, hello!"

"Buon Giorno!"

"Well, you sound like you're in a chipper mood."

"Yes, yes, yes. And do you know why?"

"Let me guess. You've heard from your father?"

"You are so smart!"

"And let me guess again. He's not coming for a visit?"

"Right again, my friend!"

"That's great, Talia. Now you and the boys can stay with us. The kids will be so excited."

"It's such a relief, I tell you. I don't know how I could have handled seeing my father with that slug. And my mother was such a saint."

"Slug, Talia?

"Yes, yes, slug—putanna. Isn't that the word you use for putanna?"

"Americans have many words for putanna, Talia, but the one I think you're referring to is slut. A slug is one of those slimy, wormy creatures that stick to your house and look like snails without a shell."

"Slut. Yes, well, slug, slut, putanna…however you say it, that's what she is. And my mother was a saint."

"Come on, Talia. I know that you don't like your father's new wife, and I know that your mother was a good woman, a wonderful mother, but a saint? It's pretty hard to be a saint."

"Yes, yes, yes, Elise. Just like your grandmother you talk so much about."

"Who? LaLa? LaLa was not saint. She was a good person, and a wonderful grandmother, but she was not a saint. And LaLa would have been the first person to admit that she fell short of qualifying for sainthood."

"You make her sound so perfect."

"Of course, I do. But that's because she loved me so much, and I loved her so much. But believe me, LaLa had a couple of very unsaintly characteristics. In fact, there was one thing—I'm actually ashamed to tell you this. Maybe, I shouldn't…"

"What? What? Tell me."

"Well, LaLa hated Italians."

"N-o-o-o. How could she hate Italians? We are so lovable, huh?"

"With a passion, that's how."

"But why?"

"Actually, it's kind of humorous. I'm not sure if I've ever mentioned that my father was sent to Italy during World War II. Unfortunately, he was injured while he was there, and he came home with his right hand partially paralyzed. Eventually, he was able to regain use of it as though nothing had ever happened, but my grandmother always blamed the Italians for his temporary disability."

"Well, I am a mother, too, and I can understand how she might have felt. I know that if one of my boys…"

"No, no, no, Talia. You don't understand. My father was injured in a jeep accident with a couple of his army buddies while they were out on some sort of weekend pass. And if you ask me, the only Italians involved were probably a few bottles of Chianti. I never would say that to my grandmother or anyone else in my family, for that matter. Who am I to discredit an American hero, and that's what my father was, in his mother's eyes."

"That is so sad, Elise, because your grandmother, she probably didn't even know any Italians. Everybody you grew up with was French, right?"

"Just about. But there was one Italian family who moved to Bayou Chouteau when I was about eight years old. Yes. I was in the third grade at the time. Anthony and Anna Barreca. They had one daughter, their only child, and she happened to be in my class. Rosalie was her name. I always thought that her name was so beautiful. It sounded like a song to me when I would hear Mrs. Barreca call out to her. Rosalie and I became very close friends. When she was not at my house, I was at hers. My father really liked Mr. Barreca. They weren't close friends, but they respected each other. I could tell. He owned a little restaurant, one of the first in Bayou Chouteau. They sold mostly sandwiches and hot lunches and had quite a business, actually. Rosalie's mother made the best lasagna. And as you can imagine, lasagna was not one of the staple meals on the bayou. I guess that's one reason I liked it so much. It was such a diversion from gumbo, jambalaya, and étouffée. Anyway, LaLa would always make these little comments to my mother, under her breath but just loud enough for me to hear, of course. Apparently, she had this idea that just because Mr. Barreca was a native Sicilian, he had to be involved in the mob. No one could convince her otherwise. Not my mother, not my father, and certainly not me. Mr. Barreca was so kind. I can still remember him, cooking in the kitchen, singing Italian songs at the top of his lungs. He had quite a nice voice, too."

"Does this Barreca family still live nearby?"

"Oh, no. My friendship with Rosalie, unfortunately, was very short-lived."

"Did your grandmother end it?"

"No, no. A lady a lot stronger than my grandmother ended it. Her name was Bertha."

"Bertha? Who is this, Bertha?"

"Hurricane Bertha. I was ten years old when she practically wiped Bayou Chouteaux off of the map. She left very few homes standing in her path. They think a tidal wave just rolled right on through. It was awful."

"So, this Rosalie, what happened to her?"

"Well, Bertha was predicted to be a killer storm. Even the old-timers who never left their homes and boats for previous storms were convinced to evacuate with their families. Bayou Chouteaux was deserted when the hurricane made landfall, thank God. We couldn't even get back to our homes for at least a week. And then what we returned to was complete devastation. Some people actually found their homes sitting in the middle of the marsh, miles away. The flood water just lifted them up and carried them off. In some cases, all of the furniture and belongings—pictures, dishes, and what-not—were found perfectly intact inside a house that had been carried away. The odor, the absolute stench that filled the air that September made us all sick. We longed for the familiar smell of seafood from the docks. To this day, when I smell pine oil I am taken back to that time, because that's what the Red Cross handed out with the cleaning supplies, and it seemed that everyone's house smelled like pine oil for years later."

"You still didn't tell me about Rosalie."

"I'm sorry. I guess I am rambling."

"Yes, you are. Now what happened to your friend?"

"Well, as I said, we all left our homes—evacuated to shelters, hotels, homes of relatives and friends in safer areas. So, Rosalie and her family left, too. Everything was so chaotic that I never found out where she went. I just assumed they were in a local shelter. When we all started coming back after the hurricane, I waited each day for the Barrecas to return, especially since their house and restaurant were still standing and just needed major cleaning. But they never did. About a week after we were back home, there was a fire, in the middle of the night. The fire station had been destroyed, and we still didn't have running water. The Barrecas' house and restaurant burned to the ground. Nothing was left. My father said that it was probably an electrical fire, due to the wet and exposed wires. But LaLa disagreed. She was convinced that it was the work of the mob. Insurance money was the motive, she claimed. She always suspected that Mr. Barreca's business was just a front for drug trafficking from the gulf. "He probably needed the money to pay off those slugs," she said.

"This is very interesting. Your grandmother referred to Italians as slimy, wormy creatures that stick to your house?"

Elise was taken aback for a few seconds and then realized that her ever-cheerful friend had just cleverly prevented her from turning a perfectly upbeat conversation into a depressing memory that would more than likely destroy her mood for the rest of the day. She didn't need that to happen. She laughed at Talia's question, while she silently reprimanded herself for allowing her thoughts to go back to that episode in her life. That could be detrimental to her peace of mind. Focus on happy times, she reminded herself. Focus on the positive.

"Talia, you are so funny. That's why I need a friend like you. You're always there to make me laugh."

"That's why everybody needs an Italian friend, right?"

"You are right about that. Now don't worry about food or any emergency supplies. Between my mother's cooking and Brad's shopping spree at the hardware store, I think we are well covered."

"That's another reason I am calling, Elise. I also got a call from Nicky today. He is very much worried about the storm, and he wants me to take the boys to a hotel. Of course, I would rather stay with you at your house. I think I would feel safe. But, of course, he is so far away and does not feel comfortable with us staying. He made arrangements for us to go to the Palace Hotel, and of course, you know you can come with us."

"Oh, Talia, that's sweet of you to offer, but there are five of us, plus my parents. I think it would be very hard for us all to weather the storm in one room. Besides, we don't know how long we'll have to be away. When are you leaving?"

"The boys are packing up now. Probably around four o'clock. Are you sure you don't want to join us?"

"I'm sure. We'll be fine. I wish we could be together. The kids will be disappointed, too. But I certainly understand Nicky's concern. Just please be careful and try to keep in touch."

"Don't worry. This Italian friend is coming home after the storm. Now you take care of yourself and don't take any chances. Promise me."

"I promise. Love you."

"I love you, too. Ciao!"

So, Talia was leaving, too. Elise suddenly felt like the protagonist in a horror movie. And the click of the phone at the other end was the sound of a key being turned by the evil housekeeper, locking her away, trapped and all alone, in a gothic, candlelit room of a haunted mansion. The image in her mind made her shiver for a second, bringing her back to the present. Why should she feel all alone, anyway? Her whole family would be with her throughout the next few days. She'd hardly be alone. But sadly, she could not shake the unease that Talia's conversation had planted in her mind.

Brad seemed to be getting weirder by the second, walking around with an empty gaze, not speaking to anyone except to give one- or two-word responses to her questions and comments. Her father, who had been her rock of strength and security as a little girl, seemed so tired of life itself that he long ago stopped dreading the end of his earthly life. Then there was her mother, Peggy Anne, who was willingly becoming more and more dependent on Elise for the most simple domestic decisions, such as, "How many onions do you chop for a pot of red beans?" much less the more critical decisions, such as, "Do you think your house is strong enough to withstand a hurricane?" And then, of course, there were the kids, the three innocent children, whom she and Brad brought into the world. They only felt safe and secure when she felt safe and secure, and she knew that fact from her own childhood.

She had evacuated many times with her mother for the numerous storms that threatened Bayou Chouteau during her childhood. And many of those evacuations turned out to be some of her happiest memories. Spending time with friends who lived in the city, waiting several days for the water to subside before returning home to just enough water in the yard to allow for a couple of days of paddling pirogues with her friends in their besieged yards. But that all changed with Bertha. She would never in her life forget the look of fear, pure fear, on her mother's face as they listened to the howling winds and torrential rains attack the home of a distant cousin who had opened her home to the Charlevilles. For hours during the night, she and her mother sat huddled in the corner, atop a twin bed, in a dark room, filled only by the sounds of Bertha.

Elise remembered the moment that she felt her mother trembling, and that was the very moment that terror crept into her body. She had been fine until she realized her mother was frightened. She never wanted her own children to feel what she felt that night. And what worried her most was that forecasters were predicting that Georgette would be a lingering storm. Moving at its present speed, the storm could take days to complete its barrage. So, given the supporting cast that she would be surrounded by Elise felt very much alone and trapped in a situation over which she had absolutely no control. God, she wished Talia would be staying with her.

Peggy Anne and Joseph Charleville arrived at their daughter's home around four o'clock that afternoon, laden with the food and mood one would associate more with a holiday than a disaster. But that was typical of the older generation on the bayou. This was nothing new. It wasn't their first evacuation, and it wouldn't be their last. It was an inevitable event on the bayou, and though you never learned to like it, you certainly learned to accept it and make the best of it. And you did this with food. Food was the secret to healing in the households Elise had grown up in. Peggy Anne and her contemporaries found comfort in their kitchens and shared comfort with the meals they prepared in them. This was as true for hurricane evacuations, as well as the gatherings after funerals, which the lady's auxiliary could put together on a moment's notice for a bereaved family of St. Michael's Church.

As Peggy Anne unloaded one of her two ice chests of food items into the freezer, she told Elise what was in each container and added little anecdotes about things that she did differently or things that happened during the preparation of each dish. "I hope your friend is going to bring some food, too. I'm sure those boys have big appetites."

"Talia and the boys are not staying with us," Elise informed her mother as matter-of-factly as she could, not wanting to reveal her disappointment.

"Well, I'm kinda glad she's not staying. I thought it took a lot of nerve for her to take advantage of your hospitality like that. And it would've been uncomfortable for me and your daddy to have strangers around while we're locked up and maybe stranded for goodness knows how long. And those kids of hers would've made your daddy nervous. I didn't want to say anything, of course, 'cause it's your house, and I would never want to interfere. But, if you ask me, it's the best for all of us."

Elise didn't say a word, not because she was speechless, but because she didn't want to start an argument. But her thoughts were racing at the speed of sound. "Best for all of us? What about me? What about me? Did you ever stop to think that I can't depend on my family members for strength? That I might just need my best friend at such a time. Of course not. Because you have me. Therefore, you can't imagine a stranger being important to me. To me. Hello, did you ever think that I might need someone to turn to, too?" None of these words were spoken. It would've been to no avail, she thought. Her mother would never understand, and she wouldn't even try to. She would just look at her with that pitiful look of a scared puppy—that look that was sure to induce several months' worth of guilt in just seconds—and then tell Elise to calm down and stop overreacting. What if the kids heard her outburst? It would frighten them, for sure, she'd say. So, Elise kept her anger tucked away.

She busied herself, purposely, alone in her bedroom until five o'clock, when she descended the kitchen stairs and beheld her mother and Brad sitting at the kitchen table in a comfortable, compatible silence. Elise broke the silence with inquiries about dinner. "Oh, honey, we have so much food here," her mother replied. "We have meatballs and spaghetti, turkey and gravy, shrimp and eggplant, we can make some po-boys…"

Elise interrupted her mother before the older woman proceeded to name every possible dinner with the food on hand. "No, no, no. We will probably be eating that food for days, and I am exhausted. I don't feel like cleaning up a messy kitchen tonight. I think we all need a nice relaxing evening. Let's go out. It'll be good to get away and pretend it's a normal evening."

"Do you really think we can find a restaurant open tonight, Lissy?" Brad asked.

"I didn't think about that," she admitted disappointedly but not yet ready to give up on her idea. "Let's take out the phone book and start calling around." After ten minutes of calling, Elise announced their dining choices. "OK. Here's the deal. There's Alberghetti's, Italian of course, Uncle Jo-Jo's Seafood Buffet, and China Grove, which is closed only for the Chinese New Year. Their words exactly." The prospect of going out had put Elise in a playful mood, and because her spirits were uplifted for the moment, she expected everyone else to be equally enthusiastic. She didn't care which restaurant they chose, she just wanted to get away for a while.

"Daddy and I had Chinese yesterday," Peggy Anne said. "And you know I don't like for him to eat that stuff too often. The sodium is bad for his pressure. Edna tells me that there's a lot of sodium in Chinese food. So, I don't know. But you kids just decide for yourselves. Don't worry about us."

"No, mom. We want you and Daddy to come, too, so let's just go where we'll all be happy. How about Alberghetti's?" Brad mumbled his approval at his wife's suggestion, and Elise turned to her mother, expecting a similar response.

"Well, you know I love Italian food, but Elise, you know how tomato sauce gives your daddy heartburn."

"No, actually, I didn't know that." Her patience level was slowly diminishing. "He loves my lasagna. In fact, he always seems pleased when I fix it for him."

"Well, honey, your daddy would never say anything to you about that. He would never want to hurt your feelings by not eating your food. But, trust me, that man suffers when he eats tomato sauce. Keeps him awake all night. Tossing and turning."

"Mom, why on earth didn't you tell me, then?"

"As if! He would be so upset with me if I said anything to hurt your feelings!"

The very thought of her daddy suffering through just one night because he wanted to spare her feelings just broke her heart. The blanket of guilt slowly fell upon her. She began to feel it wrapping itself around her shoulders. She was sinking, sinking, sinking.

"I suppose that leaves us with Uncle Jo-Jo's, then," Brad's abrupt words brought her back to the impending decision. "I could eat a few boiled shrimps," he said with a spark of enthusiasm Elise had not seen in days.

She made eye contact with him and realized that he had seen her sinking and had just thrown a rope to her. She knowingly nodded to him, in her playful mood once again. "Yeah, I'll share a few pounds with you, and I might even have a beer or two."

"Oooo, Mama," he answered, with a wink, which she returned in thanks for the rescue. But the joviality was stopped short by the third party.

"Y'all go ahead," Peggy Anne said, and Elise noticed a surrendering note in her tone. "Daddy and I will stay home. I'm not much for buffets. I always worry about how long that food has been sitting out. I'm so used to fresh. I read an article the other day that said that buffets are the cause of more cases of food poisoning than raw meat. You believe that?"

Elise got up from the table, ignoring her mother's question completely. Oddly enough, she knew that her mother was not expecting an answer anyway. "I'm going to freshen up, Brad. Rally the troops. They're all in the playroom upstairs. I'll be down in about twenty minutes."

Uncle Jo-Jo's turned out to be the perfect choice. The Steiners were the only patrons dining in the restaurant at six o'clock that Sunday evening. There was only a slight drizzle sprinkling the big storefront window next to their table, where a bright, colorful neon sign flashed alternately, "HOT BOILED CRABS" and "HOT BOILED SHRIMP." Because Jo-Jo Trosclair knew that he would be out of business for at least a few days, he decided to include his boiled seafood selections in his "all-you-can-eat" fare.

"No sense wasting good food. I'd rather give it away than throw it away!" Jo-Jo said, with his deep, guttural voice that always ended each sentence with a chuckle. "I tell you what, kids. I set up all 'em games in the back so y'all don't need to put in any coins. Jus' go and play all y'all want." The three kids jumped up from the table as though they had been freed from detention, called out a thanks halfway toward the arcade, and left their parents behind to enjoy a dinner for two. Or so

Elise thought, until Jo-Jo sat down next to her and joined in the feast he had prepared.

Elise had always liked Jo-Jo Trosclair. He was one of those Bayou Chouteau boys that Brad always referred to when they got into arguments. Jo-Jo had been in her class at St. Michael's for a couple of years, and every time their paths crossed, he would tell whomever they were with how he used to sit behind Elise Charleville and cheat off of her papers. He would tell how he always had such a crush on her, but Elise was too classy to like someone like him. She would always laugh and remind him that he and his wife Charlaine had been sweethearts since they were three, and that it was her, Elise, who wouldn't have had a chance with Jo-Jo. The same vignette came up every time they met.

Jo-Jo had done well without a high school diploma. He knew early on that he would stay in the seafood business, like his dad, but he would take it a step further. His boats worked for and supplied his restaurant, which he started only five years after quitting high school. Jo-Jo was more like the men in their grandfathers' generation than his own contemporaries. He was an entrepreneur, ready to take a risk, while the others struggled year after year with their dying industry, because they just didn't want to change with the times.

"Jo-Jo, Elise tells me that you designed and built all of your boats." Brad had been astonished when he saw the Trosclair fleet docked on the bayou. "Where did you learn how to do that? That's amazing!"

"I'll tell you where he learned," Elise jumped in, giggling after two beers. "When the rest of us were diagramming sentences in English class, he was drawing boats, and when the rest of us were drawing Venn diagrams in math class, he was drawing boats. And when the rest of us were drawing and labeling parts of the cell in science class, guess what he was doing." To this, they all chimed in, "Drawing boats!" It was a good time. But eventually the inevitable topic came up. Georgette.

"Don't tell me you gonna stay, 'Lise," Jo-Jo said, in a sudden, concerned tone.

Elise took a quick swig of beer, leaned over, and looked him right in the eyes, as though she were ready to take him on in a scrap "Yeah, you're staying, aren't you?"

"Hell no! Got my truck all packed up. My ol' lady's already in Baton Rouge with her mama and daddy. You know my youngest girl, Cherie, is at LSU, and me and Charlaine got her a little place up there. Cheaper than renting, you know. So, we gonna stay there. Even got the two dogs and three cats there. Only reason I stayed open here was 'cause I had to tie up a few loose ends and figured I might as well stay open if I had to be here anyway."

It was seven thirty when the Steiners left Jo-Jo's, and Elise was as eager to get home as she had been to get away just a couple of hours earlier.

The sun set and darkness settled in. An ominous silence enveloped the house, and it seemed to grow thicker and more impenetrable as the minutes ticked away. Every window and door were boarded, and the emergency supplies had been purchased and placed where they would be needed. The food was prepared, and the perishable items placed in the freezer, which would stay cold enough for a couple of days, even after the electricity was lost. There was plenty of drinking water and extra supplies set aside for flushing the toilets. Flashlights with new batteries and candles were placed in strategic locations throughout the house. Given Georgette's latest speed, forecasters were predicting that her eye would not make landfall until eight or nine the following morning. There was nothing more to do. The waiting period had begun.

For the first time in days, Elise settled down with Brad and the kids in their family room. Brad and her dad were watching the end of the Sunday night football game, which happened to be an out-of-town game for the New Orleans Saints. Lilah and J. P. were playing Battleship, and Peggy Anne was reading a new dinosaur book to Casey, whose eyes were betraying his desperate attempt to stay awake with the big kids. No one mentioned the eerie appearance of this normally cozy room, and a surprisingly peaceful mood prevailed, interrupted only occasionally by

Brad and Joseph's shouts of celebration or despair as they watched their home team move up and down the field in their attempt to win a game for their anxious and unsettled fans back home in the Big Easy. But in the end, a failed attempt at a last-second field goal allowed the Atlanta Falcons to hold on to their lead, so that even the sportscast on the ten o'clock news would be disaster coverage.

"I knew it," Joseph proclaimed assuredly. "He choked." The old man painstakingly stood up, waved his hand to everyone, said good-night, and turned in early, as if it were any ordinary Sunday night, leaving vigilance to the younger generation. He did this as though there were no boards on the windows, and as though the next morning would bring only the sunrise and not the accompanying hurricane force winds and torrential rains. Even Georgette failed to spark excitement in her daddy's life, Elise thought sadly. Is it total peace, she wondered, or just total apathy? She hoped it wasn't the latter, but she had her sincere doubts. She watched sympathetically, as her father walked toward the hallway, leading to the guest bedroom, wishing she could lift him up so that he could move as quickly and steadily as he did when she was a little girl. But the opening music of the ten o'clock news, with its sharp staccatos and crescendos, abruptly pulled her attention to the widescreen TV that Brad had just bought a month ago, after researching the different manufacturers for a year. Just one more of his personal treasures to be lost. She hoped he was not thinking the same thoughts she was at that moment.

The serious, forlorn faces of the recently married John and Wendy Davis, anchor-couple of the local news, filled the five feet of viewing screen. And as they began their hurricane "hot line" coverage, as they referred to their broadcast, Elise was reminded, once again, of why she rarely watched the news, before going to bed each night. In fact, she realized that, up to that moment, she had gotten all of her hurricane reporting from the Weather Channel.

"Now we're going to find out what's really going on," Peggy Anne asserted with an adamant air of confidence. "Frank Cable is the best weatherman on this planet when it comes to hurricanes." Oh, my word, Elise thought, as her mother began. "They say that even those big shots on that Weather Channel rely on Frank Cable's old-fashioned methods. I heard that he was the very first person to come up with ways of predicting hurricanes. They say that during the war, he flew his planes right into the eye of a hurricane to study how they grow and all. Those other guys only tell us they are using those fancy, newfangled radars. That's because they know that young people have more faith in machines than they do in people. But the truth is they all rely on Frank Cable." Elise could have predicted her mother's spontaneous and impromptu discourse on the unspoiled value of human endeavor and capability versus the evil of science and technology. Peggy Anne Charleville considered science and technology to be a subtitle under sorcery and, as every God-fearing person knew, sorcery was not to be tolerated by the creator or his worshippers. Knowing how her mother felt, Elise was not about to enter into a defense of the Weather Channel, because, in the end, she would just be called a "little heathen," which is how her mother ended all of their philosophic discussions, and of course, Elise knew that she would not succeed in budging her mother's opinion one iota. But much to Peggy Anne's chagrin, Frank Cable's appearance and latest assessment of the weather situation, would have to wait for the Davises' lengthy coverage of the special news items concerning the city's evacuation and hurricane preparations.

"Hurricane Georgette is expected to drop more than thirty-two inches of rain over the city of New Orleans," John Davis reported. "Samuel Clark, a spokesman for the Corps of Engineers, spoke at the mayor's emergency meeting this afternoon and warned that the one hundred and thirty miles of protection levees, which are swollen already from recent thunderstorms, may not be strong enough to prevent Lake Maurapas and Lake Pontchartrain from pouring into the city and its suburbs."

The next report showed live footage of Interstates 10, 12, 55, and 59, where traffic was bumper-to-bumper with cars, trucks, and trailers heading out of the city. A stout, administrative woman with a little, squeaky soprano voice that hardly suited her physical stature told reporters that the emergency shelters in Louisiana were expecting up to forty thousand evacuees by nightfall.

Wendy Davis confirmed that New Orleans International Airport had been closed to all flights. "Tourists who have not left the city by now," she continued, "may soon be able to experience a hurricane even stronger than the popular French Quarter drink." Her husband laughed on cue, and then the short-lived levity quickly turned to a more sober demeanor, more appropriate for the moment. John Davis turned to Jim Hallsley, a meteorologist from the National Hurricane Center, who was seated at the anchor desk to his left.

"Look at this," Peggy Anne sighed disgustedly. "Why don't they put on Frank Cable? We don't want to hear this man's opinion."

"Uh, actually I do want to hear his opinion, Peggy Anne," Brad responded. And Peggy Anne was silenced by the uncharacteristic, authoritative tone that was fired in her direction, from the mouth of her ever composed and patient son-in-law.

Seated next to the well-dressed and professionally groomed John Davis, Jim Hallsley had the look of the nutty professor. Tall and thin with a very bad haircut and thick glasses, his appearance added credibility to the long list of credentials recited in his introduction. His unkempt attire led the viewer to imagine that he was so absorbed in the details and tracking of the hurricane that he had very little time or attention to give to his television appearance. He didn't crack a smile. In fact, he looked as if he were incapable of doing so, which added conviction to his grave detailed information.

At the completion of Hallsley's segment, the camera turned to Wendy Davis, who flashed a perfect portfolio smile, as she announced, "We'll be going live to a press conference with Mayor Troy Hunter when we return from this commercial break," and she pointed at the camera as though her fingertip activated the five minutes of advertising that followed. Elise usually hated the interruption of commercials, but she was growing tired of the depressing news and welcomed the break.

A handsome, middle-aged couple sipped aromatic coffee at the break of day at a picturesque mountain retreat. A minute later, the scene shifted to another, more youthful couple speeding along California's rocky coastline in their brand-new red convertible, without a care in the world. The commercial that followed prompted laughter, as they watched a little boy spill a twenty-pound bag of dog food all over the floor of a pristine kitchen in an attempt to feed his St. Bernard, who licked his face profusely throughout the scene. Then there was a group of men enjoying a televised sporting event in a local bar, surrounded by their favorite brew and lots of cleavage. And last but not least, a young, beautiful housewife was shown taking a frozen dinner out of the oven and fooling her mother-in-law by making her think that she'd been cooking all day.

For a moment, the sixty-second vignettes reminded Elise that life was, in fact, normal in most of the country, and this thought initially soothed her. But then, an instant later, that same realization made her feel more alone than ever before, in the face of danger. It made her feel that no one else knew or cared about what was happening to the Steiner family and all of the others who were sitting in fear in their homes or in shelters. Just as she reminded herself that self-pity helped no one, Wendy Davis was back, but her portfolio smile was gone. "Welcome back to Hurricane Hot Line, and for you viewers who are just joining us, we're going to go live now to City Hall, where Mayor Troy Hunter will address the citizens of New Orleans and the metropolitan area.

Mayor Troy Hunter stood behind a podium bearing the city crest. He was an up- and-coming politician, already making history as the youngest man to be elected mayor in the entire South. Known for his ease in handling the press and his charismatic appeal to audiences of every race, creed, and gender, he handled all situations with two of his most powerful assets—his great timing in telling a joke and his impeccable style in dressing for the occasion. But on this particular Sunday night, even Mayor Hunter could find no good time for a joke, and because he had been standing in the rain all day examining locks and levees so that the press could report that he was, in fact, doing his duty, he was soaked from head to toe. He had a shocked and puzzled look on his face as he addressed the public, as if he didn't realize that he was actually responsible for the city in a time of crisis. As though he wanted to say, "Hey, I took this job thinking it would only involve black-tie soirees, riverboat christenings, and kick-ass fund-raisers. Isn't someone going to help me out here?" Brad also noticed Hunter's bewildered countenance.

"Look, Lissy. Just look at our fearless leader. Don't you feel safe, now? He's going to keep us safe. We have nothing to worry about." They both laughed as they watched the mayor's arrogance melt before their eyes. The truth is that the man looked so out of character that neither of them listened to what he had to say. And by now they had heard so many officials give their views and warnings about the hurricane that they really didn't think the mayor could tell them anything new or enlightening.

Lilah left the Battleship game, against J. P.'s wishes, and climbed up on Elise's lap, asking her mom to scratch her back. It was the one thing that the three children had in common—their love of Elise's back scratches. They allowed no one else to perform the service, vowing that their mom was the best backscratcher in the world. So maybe I'll never win a Nobel Prize, Elise conceded facetiously to herself, but I can always say that I am the best at something. She rubbed the tips of her fingernails in a circular motion, up and down Lilah's spine, and the little girl curled up close to her mom and rested her head on Elise's shoulder and buried her face in Elise's neck. Although this had been one of Lilah's favorite positions as a younger child, she had not snuggled up to Elise like this in quite some time, and Elise was quite content to have the opportunity to hold her little girl again.

"My sweet, sweet girl," she tenderly murmured in Lilah's ear as she stroked the soft skin of her back. "You must be very sleepy to climb up on my lap like this, huh?" But Lilah didn't answer. Elise didn't ask her question again, thinking the little girl was drifting off to sleep. She was already planning on letting her sleep the rest of the night on the couch, because she and Brad would probably be awake all night anyway, when she suddenly became aware of the tiny, jerking movements in Lilah's back. "Am I tickling you? Are you in a giddy mood?" she asked in a mushy, juvenile voice that usually made Lilah cringe. Again, no answer. It was the dampness on her neck that made Elise realize the child was crying. She had climbed up on Elise's lap so no one would see her crying.

"Lilah, what's wrong? What's wrong, Lilah, are you feeling sick? What's wrong, baby?" Elise was already getting frantic at the thought of someone getting sick and there not being a doctor around to help.

"I'm scared, Mama. I'm so scared."

"Oh baby, we're going to be OK. I'm not going to let anything happen to you." But deep-down Elise knew that she could never convince this perceptive child to feel safe and secure, if she couldn't first convince herself.

"But Mama, didn't you hear what the mayor just said? He said he's closing all the roads out of town. He said we're going to be stranded. Trapped. Didn't you hear him say we were going to be trapped with no way out?"

By this time J. P., who hadn't paid any attention to the mayor's address but heard every word of Lilah's recount of it, started to cry out, "I don't wanna be trapped. I don't wanna be trapped!" And he ran to Brad, crying so hysterically that Elise was afraid he would hyperventilate. Luckily, Casey was sound asleep. Otherwise, he would have joined in, and it would have sounded like ten-thirty mass at St. Michael's.

Within an hour, the car was packed. The night sky was dark purple—at once unsettling, yet enchanting. A steady, light rain came down on unprotected heads as the kids and their grandparents piled into the Brad's SUV, silently and obediently, following Elise's instructions without any complaint or delay. Brad and Elise both went back inside the house to do a final check, making sure all appliances were unplugged, placing any valuables that couldn't be taken in a more secure place. They also checked to make sure the kids didn't forget any stuffed animals or traveling toys that would be needed to make the evacuation more bearable. But really, for each of them, secretly, it was a chance to say good-bye to their home in case it was, in fact, good-bye.

Elise stood in the living room, her favorite room in the house, and switched on the museum light, which Brad had specifically requested during the designing of the house. The light shone above the fireplace on an oil portrait of Lilah at four years of age. The portrait actually glistened, with the total darkness feeding the brilliance of its muted hues. Elise remembered, like it was yesterday, the day that she and Brad walked into the artist's studio to see the portrait for the first time. She remembered how he cried when he saw it—like he did the day their baby girl was born. Now, it was she who was crying. All of the emotions of the last week were built up inside of her, held back. Fear, helplessness, anger, confusion, and, of course, guilt. Why did she always feel like everything was her fault? She felt Brad's arms wrap around her shoulders from behind. He gently turned her body around to face him and held her body close to his. They didn't say a word to each other. They didn't have to. She just cried, and he just held her.

It was about eleven thirty and the interstate was going to be closed at 2 AM. If they didn't run into heavy traffic, they could reach Casa Victoria in an hour and a half. They had called ahead, and Jacqui said she'd be waiting up for them, with chilled bottle in hand. Just like her dad, Elise thought. Brad turned on the radio, just in time to catch the latest bulletin. "Georgette is still expected to sweep directly over the city of New Orleans. By three o'clock in the morning, hurricane winds of 75 to100 mph will be reaching the area. Because the storm is moving at such a slow pace, it is possible that the city might feel the full force of the hurricane for up to thirty hours. Even if the storm decides to turn toward the Mississippi Gulf Coast, the heavy rains and flooding will still be life- threatening for anyone staying behind in the city. A storm surge of up to eighteen feet is expected when Georgette lands in the city famous for its below-sea-level elevations."

Although the news bulletin confirmed her decision to evacuate, Elise didn't want to hear another minute of forecasts, preparations, and predictions. Brad searched until he found a nice easy-listening channel and drove through the rain on surprisingly deserted roads. Apparently, the rest of the city heeded the warnings long before the Steiners. This was better, Elise thought, trying to look on the bright side of things. As the car ventured through the quiet stillness of the calm before the storm, the children slept, while their parents and grandparents sat in silence, looking out at the Louisiana wetlands bordering the interstate highway.

At one point in their lonely journey, a caravan of paramedic units and ambulances passed them, in the left lane. Lights were on in the rear compartments of each vehicle, and the medical personnel could be seen tending to their patients being transported from New Orleans hospitals to health-care facilities between Baton Rouge and Lafayette. Elise felt her flesh creep as she watched these people go by, imagining how frightened they must be, dealing not only with the pain and uncertainty of an illness, but also with their reliance on total strangers to find a safe haven for them during the storm. She thanked God that everyone in her family was well, and that they could all be together. Each of those patients was someone's mother or father, grandparent or sibling, or, worse yet, someone's child. "Thank you, God," she whispered again and turned around to look at each member of her family as though she had to make sure everyone was still there with her.

The little wooden sign, hanging from two chains on a rustic post, marked the entrance to the oak-lined drive that led to La Casa de Victoria. That was the official name for the ranch house and horse farm that Adam had acquired in a divorce case he handled for a well-known, rather flamboyant public figure, with renowned wealth and infamous scruples. The property was only partial payment for a job well done, Adam had told them when all the papers had been signed and finalized.

185

Victoria was an exquisite home, spacious and sprawling under a canopy of Louisiana live oaks, which gave the old place a setting typically seen in landscape portraits of the Old South. Once a working plantation, Casa Victoria sat on the banks of the Mississippi River, just north of Baton Rouge, a location that afforded easy access to the busy port city to the south. Elise loved to visit Victoria. It was so relaxing, and the kids loved the amenities Adam had added. There was a pool, Jacuzzi, tennis courts, a game room with a pool table, air hockey table, ping pong—the kids were never idle or bored during their visits to Victoria. But Brad never really liked the place. He never admitted it, in so many words, but Elise could tell. He always came up with the lamest excuses for not attending the weekend parties Adam threw throughout the year. She wondered why Adam kept including them on his invitation list, after being rejected so many times.

In her own amateur psychoanalysis, she had decided that Brad and Adam were more like brothers than college friends. They shared a mutual love and loyalty for each other that could never be questioned or threatened. In the professional arena, their partnership was a perfect balance for the successful practice they were building together. But there was a sharp contrast between the two men, in mannerism, attitude, and lifestyle. And nowhere else on the planet did this contrast become more apparent than at La Casa de Victoria.

Although Adam hated the sport of hunting, he was known for planning the best hunting expeditions. The parties and revelry that accompanied his sometimes weeklong, not to mention tax-deductible, outings were notorious amongst his friends and his friends' friends. They drank the best there was to drink and ate the best there was to eat. And Adam was not too modest to share with his guests how much these "bests" had cost him. Just to let them know, of course, how much his friends were worth to him. And if the lavish hospitality found at Victoria endeared Adam to his large circle of friends who stayed there, it had just the opposite effect on Brad, who had met Adam while he was working his way through college. They were different back then. Things were different back then. They were both single; both free to do as they pleased, more or less. Now Brad had Elise and the kids, and Adam had Victoria. Adam was still free.

Elise knew that Adam would always be free. She just hoped that Jacqui would be able to accept the inevitable when she realized that their relationship would not lead to marriage and kids. No doubt, Jacqui enjoyed Adam's lifestyle as much as he did, and Adam was definitely a kind and generous man. But Elise worried that her cousin was setting herself up for yet another heartbreak, and this one would be really awkward, since she was dating Brad's best friend and law partner. This arrangement made Elise feel personally involved, and she knew that even though she had nothing to do with the match, she would somehow feel partially responsible if Jacqui walked away with a broken heart.

As Casa Victoria came into view, Elise saw that the screened-in porch, which encircled the entire first floor, was lit up as though there were a party going on. And there was Jacqui, sitting on the front steps. When she saw the car coming up the drive, she stood up and waved a bottle of wine in one hand and two glasses in the other. Brad moaned, "Look at her. She's waiting for you, Lissy."

"I know. I'm glad we came."

"Tell you what—wake up your parents, and let's get the kids to bed. Then I'll unload the car and hit the sack. I'm beat."

"So am I. But maybe I'll have a glass of wine with her. After all, she's waited up for us, and she's probably bored stiff and suffering from cabin fever after being up here with Aunt Kitty for her only companionship." They both had to laugh at the thought of those two characters keeping each other company, all alone in the middle of nowhere.

It took only a half hour for the Steiners to unload the car and get settled in Casa Victoria. The house seemed so much bigger than it had in the past, yet so much cozier. But then, this was the first time Elise and Brad had been to Victoria when there wasn't a huge party going on. Brad seemed content, satisfied with their shelter. Elise tucked in, kissed, and blessed the three kids, and went outside to join Jacqui, who was patiently waiting for her on the front steps. She could tell that her cousin had been drinking long before her arrival. And although Elise was already feeling better with the safety and security that Victoria offered, she soon realized that the surroundings had an opposite effect on her companion.

"What's wrong, Jack? You and Adam have an argument or something? Or is this about your mom?" Elise knew she wanted to talk about something in particular and just needed a little prodding.

"Nope. It's not about Adam. I don't give a shit about Adam. Do you see him here with me? Of course not. And it's not about Kitty. It's about Marsh."

"What about him? Has something happened?"

"No, Elise. Why is it you always think something bad has happened?"

"I didn't say 'bad,' did I?"

"No, but I know how you think. And you're thinking 'bad.' "

"OK, stop. This is not about me, anyway. So, what about Marsh?" There was a long pause, then Jacqui closed her eyes for just a moment and shook her head, as though she were thinking of some place far away or some time long ago. Then she spoke the words that Elise had known to be true, yet dreaded hearing for years.

"I know that everyone thinks that I should be over him, after all this time, Elise, and sometimes, I can almost convince myself that I am. But the truth is I'm not. I'm nowhere near over him. And it scares me to think that I may never be over him. That I'll have to live my whole life with this pain. Actually, it's not pain anymore; it's more like this hollow pit in the center of my body that I'm only vaguely aware of, when I'm busy, preoccupied, or drunk. But then, on days when I'm alone with little to do, the hollow pit grows, and it spreads to every nook and cranny of my body. It's hard to describe. It makes me feel weak. Like hunger, only food doesn't make it go away. Like thirst, only drinking doesn't make it go away. Nothing makes it go away. It takes control of me—body and mind. Then I can't get Marsh out of my head. I think of everything about him, about us. When we were in the fifth grade, and we were both too shy to admit that we liked each other, so we hardly talked to each other for a whole year. I think of when we were in high school, and I remember the first time we held hands. His fingertips first, softly touching, exploring the palm of my hand, until my fingers interlocked with his, giving him the OK to go ahead and hold the rest of my hand. That was always his approach with every step we took together—gentle, sensitive of my feelings. Like the first time we made love—um." She tightened her lips in order to stop their trembling, and turned her big blue eyes, now glistening with the welling of tears, away from Elise, and focused momentarily on the dark woods beyond the house. The she took a big breath, and exhaled a sighing, "Oh Lord. When we made love…" She teasingly, slapped Elise's thigh and wet her lips with the tiny bit of red wine that was left in her goblet. She refilled her own glass and topped off her cousin's, emptying the bottle at hand. "Elise, I know you don't like to discuss sex, or do you still refer to it as the 's word'?"

"Ha, ha, ha," Elise laughed sarcastically, wondering why Jacqui never failed to slip some kind of criticism in the conversation. She was about to say, "At least I have three children to show for 'the s word,' which is more than you have," but she never would have said that to her little cousin, even if her thoughts hadn't been interrupted by Jacqui's voice adding, "I have to say, Lissy, his body and mine—they were made for each other. His for mine, and mine for his." Her spirits seemed lifted for a second. She even smiled rather sensuously, as she obviously thought of her intimate relationship with Marsh. As if suddenly awakened from a trance, she remarked, "No one else could ever feel that perfect next to me, and no one ever has. And now someone else is next to his body, and I know it can't feel right to him, you know what I mean. I just know that he has to feel the way I do—that what he has settled for may be good, but it's only second best. I just know in my heart that he has to feel that way."

Elise didn't respond at that point, not because she wanted to avoid talking about "the s word,' but rather that she found herself thinking of her body and Brad's together, intertwined, and how she knew exactly what Jacqui meant, because she had felt the same way. And she wondered if that feeling of being the "perfect fit" for each other was a sign of being with your perfect mate. A sign of reassurance that you did, in fact, find the person that God intended for you to live your life with. And how sad, if this were true, that Jacqui might never have this feeling again. These thoughts, mingling with the effects of the wine, caused tears to well in her own eyes and aroused both sentiment and passion to stir inside of her. She looked forward to crawling in bed next to Brad and feeling his body next to hers. But her longing had to be subdued with patience, because Jacqui was still talking, and Elise knew that she couldn't abandon her in the middle of her emotional conversation.

"Sometimes, Elise, I'll be thinking about Marsh, and my feelings, they'll be so strong that if I close my eyes, I can almost feel him close to me. And I think that if my feelings are so strong that surely, it's because he's thinking of me, right at that very moment. And that our thoughts are connected, like mental telepathy or something like that. Do you believe in that stuff, Lissy?" Elise may have nodded or shook her head in some type of response, but it didn't matter, because Jacqui really didn't skip a breath to hear her opinion, one way or the other.

"I think there's something to that kind of thing, being there's so little we know about the brain and all. So, then I start thinking really hard—please call me, please call me—just hoping and praying that he'll pick up the phone and call me and say, 'Hey Jack, I need to see you. I miss you.' All those things that I feel, Elise." There was only a short pause, a short, desperately pitiful pause, before she admitted, "But he never calls. And I'm left to wonder why all over again, and the pain is fresh again, like the day he called to end it all, and I'm left to pretend for the rest of my life. To pretend that I've moved on, to pretend that I'm happy, to pretend that I love some man whose body will never feel perfect next to mine. It's awful, Lissy. It's like he took this huge chunk of my heart with him, and although I may have it in me to care for another man, I will never be able to love someone else completely, the way I loved him—with my whole heart. I know you think I'm crazy. Join the crowd. Hell, I even think I've gone crazy, sometimes. After all, he's just one person in this whole wide world, and yet he is my world. He's part of who I am."

"Jacqui, I wish to God that I could make your pain go away. I wish I could just take you in my arms and hold you until all of the tears just wash away the memories. I feel so helpless. There's nothing I can say or do. I know that I could tell you, like everyone else does, to move on. But I don't know that I would be any stronger if Brad would just pick up and leave me, with no warning, no explanation. Especially, now, with the kids..."

"I should have had his baby, Elise. Then, at least I would have had a part of him with me. A part of him that would love me always." Elise immediately knew that she had made a selfish mistake by bringing up the subject of children, because Jacqui's sad, pathetic tone quickly took on a more bitter and resentful sound. "Now someone else will have his babies. Someone else will share those special moments with him, cry with him over the joy of their newborn children. And his children will never have my eyes or nose mixed with his features, or my personality—we used to talk about things like that, even when we were in high school, knowing for certain that we would one day be married and have children." She lowered her head and rested her forehead on the palm of her hand and then rubbed her crying eyes with her fingertips, as though she knew that her mind was taking her down an old, familiar path that would only lead her to a place of self-pity, self-destruction. And she didn't want to go there—not again. Yet how could she avoid it? "I've got to know what happened, Elise. I've got to find out, once and for all, what happened, what I did wrong. And I've got to do it before he gets married, or I'll regret it for the rest of my life."

"You know, Jacqui, that's the most sensible thing I've heard you say in a long time. I would never have encouraged you to call Marsh or try to find him, because I guess I've always wanted you to make a clean break and move on. But I don't think I've ever understood how you've really felt, until tonight. You've made me appreciate some of the little things I've probably taken for granted, too. I'm so sorry that I haven't really been there for you…"

"Oh, Elise, you've listened to my sob stories more than anyone else. In fact, I can't believe that you still let me go on and on like this."

"I know I've listened, Jacqui, but I never really understood how deeply you've been hurt, and I have to confess, I haven't been much better than everyone else who's tried to urge you to get on with your life. You've got to talk to him, Jacqui. For your own sake, you have to hear the truth from him—whether it's on the phone or in person. And you've got to make him tell you everything. He owes you that much, Jacqui. And the Marsh that I knew would want to do anything he could to help you move on. He loved you Jacqui, and no one will ever convince me otherwise. So, you do it, girl. You contact him. And if you need me in any way, I'll be there for you. You know that don't you?"

"Yeah, yeah, I know that. Like sisters, right?"

"Come here," said Elise. And they giggled and cried like little girls until Brad called out from inside, informing Elise that Casey was awake and needed his mommy. She could tell by the look on her husband's face that he was angry, so she quickly ran inside and followed the sound of Casey's crying all the way to the bedroom that she and Brad had chosen for themselves. The little one had apparently woken up, didn't recognize the unfamiliar surroundings, and resorted to an uncontrollable meltdown. To make matters worse, her mother had gone into Brad's bedroom to take care of her grandson.

"What were you doing out there, Elise?" Peggy Anne asked in an accusing tone. "Couldn't you hear the baby crying? Poor little darling."

"First of all, Mama, he's not a baby, and second of all, his father is here. Now, thanks for your concern, but please go back to your room. I think we can handle this on our own." Elise wasn't sorry that she had come to her own defense, but she hated that she had to pay the "guilt" price after watching her mother walk away looking as though she had slapped her. She put Casey in the middle of the bed, where he snuggled instinctively between her and Brad's bodies. She rubbed his back and hummed his favorite bedtime lullaby— "Hush Little Baby"—and he drifted off to sleep in no time. She carried him back to his bunk bed and returned to her own room, where she hoped to find Brad in a better mood. No such luck.

"My goodness, Brad, I can't believe you're so upset, because I didn't hear Casey crying. I came in as soon as you called me."

"Forgive me, Elise, if I can't be in a party mood with you and Jacqui tonight, OK."

"A party mood? It was hardly a…"

"Look, all I know is that I was finally getting some sleep after the craziest day of my life, and the next thing I know Casey's screaming at the foot of my bed, and I look up to see your mother standing in my room. For Christ's sake, Elise, I'm in my underwear! Does she have to have that much freedom in my life?"

"Look, it's been a long day for everybody. Everyone's on edge. Let's just try to get some sleep and pray that we're spared in the morning." She thought that her calm voice and message would soothe him, but instead he continued, as though she hadn't spoken at all.

"This whole ordeal is so damn unbelievable. I still can't believe this crap is happening to us. I'm sleeping somewhere in the woods in the middle of Louisiana, with my mother-in-law walking into my bedroom, unannounced, with me in my underwear, wondering if a frickin' hurricane is going to destroy my new home and everything in it." He was ranting out of control, and before she had a chance to respond, he changed the subject matter. "Where in the hell is Adam? Does anyone know where he is? I thought he was supposed to be here." She felt like a witness during one of his interrogations. After all, he knew more about Adam's life than she did.

"Jacqui told me that at the last minute he decided to stay in New Orleans. He was helping out one of his friends or something. She didn't know all the details."

"Oh, right! The Good Samaritan that he is. The 'friend' he's helping is Angela, his new law clerk. Your cousin is really blind if she doesn't see what's going on. But then again, she's as twisted as he is."

"Calm down, Brad. There's no use in getting mad at everyone in your life. We're all upset by this situation. Let's just try to make the best of it. At least we're safe."

"Sorry. Look, I'm just tired and aggravated. And now, I'm wide awake and can't get to sleep."

"Look Brad, I think I know what this is about. I know that you're upset because we haven't heard from your folks. But you know how they are. They're probably sitting there thinking that it's your place to call them. So, if you feel like you need to talk to them, just pick up the phone and call them. You know that it would not upset me if you did—your relationship with your parents does not have to involve me. You can…"

"Damn it, Elise! Why can't you let that go? You dwell on that shit all the time. What is it with you? What more do I have to do to prove to you that I don't want anything to do with them? What? Please tell me so that we can end this discussion once and for all!"

"I don't know what you can do! I wish I did! Maybe, though, you could start by just talking to me about your feelings. God knows I'd like to talk about mine. I mean, you and I can talk about anything and everything. We're best friends. And yet we can't talk about the one problem that will haunt us for as long as we live."

"No, Elise. Haunts you, not us. You're the only one who will not let this die. For Christ sake, we moved away. We don't have to deal with them ever again. And yet anytime I'm in a bad mood—which is only human, you know—you have to bring all of that crap back into the picture. You have to start psychoanalyzing me—'Brad, if you feel like you need to see your family, you really should go for a visit,' or, 'Brad, don't let my feelings stand between you and your family.' Why do you keep bringing it up Elise?"

"I don't know. I'm sorry. It's just that I can't even imagine being estranged from my family, and I never, in a million years, would have thought that I would be in a situation like this one. Let's face it, Brad, I know you had problems with them before I came into the picture, but it wasn't until I came into the picture that you confronted those problems. I feel like the wedge that severed the ties between you and your family. So, I guess I feel like I have to back away, if only for a moment, in order for you to have a family."

"I have a family, Elise! I have you and the kids, and…"

"You have me! That's just it. I am one person, Brad. One person. And I'm supposed to be your wife, your friend, and the mother of your children. I can do that. God knows that I love being all of those things for you. And I think that I am very good in those roles, but I am not so good that I can make up for the loss of your parents. I mean, as hard as I try to make you happy, I can't be worth losing your parents or your past over. I'm just one person. And I sometimes feel like I have to be three people for you. I feel like, no matter how hard I try, I will never be able to make up for your losses. No matter how hard I try, Brad, I could never mend that hole in your heart or fill that huge void in your life."

"Lissy, Lissy, don't you understand, after all these years, after all we've been through? When you met me, I already had that hole in my heart and that huge void in my life. And it could be that I never really wanted to admit to myself how painful and empty my life had been up to that time. But then you came along, and you mended that hole in my heart. And then the kids came along, and what can I say? The four of

195

you have filled that void in my life. So please don't feel like you have to be any more to me than my wife, and my friend, and the mother of my children. I am happy. I love my life. I love my children, and I love you.

She let the weight of her body fall into his arms, and she felt the heaviness of the burdens of the last days, weeks, months, and years just melt away, as he held her and gently kissed her face. "God, I needed to hear that," she said, as soon as she caught her breath.

"Not as much as I needed to say it," he answered.

That night would be the night that Elise and Brad would always recall as their most perfect moment together. More perfect than even their first night together. More perfect than their romantic nights in Paris, Venice, or Barcelona. They would never have to remind each other of the night on the horse farm, in the woods, somewhere in the middle of Louisiana. After fifteen years of marriage, the walls between them had come down. There were no more secrets, and the space between them, where neither ever dared to venture alone, was now a place where they could stand together. It was their perfect moment.

MONDAY

Elise rolled over on her side and opened her eyes just as Brad was walking into the room, obviously showered, shaved, and dressed for the day, holding two mugs of hot coffee in his hands. "Hey, sleepy head—decided to wake up today?" He handed her one of the steamy mugs and went to the windows to open the plantation shutters, which had done a very good job of keeping out a beautiful mid-morning sunlight. Elise covered her eyes for a few seconds to shield the glare, and in the confusion of those first moments of waking up in a strange bedroom, she mumbled a thanks. "What time is it?" she asked. "Where are the kids? What's going on?"

"Well, it's about 10:45…"

"Oh, my God, I have to get up. The kids need breakfast." She couldn't believe she had overslept with all that was going on. "Why didn't you wake me up, Brad?"

"Hold on. The kids have had breakfast. I am still the egg-sandwich specialist in our family, according to the kids, by the way. And in answer to your question about what is going on, you will be happy to know that Georgette missed us completely."

"What? You aren't kidding me are you? Because if this is some kind of joke, I will be furious, so…"

"Of course not, Lissy. Do you really think I'd joke about that?"

"No, but I just can't believe it. All of those experts were so sure that she was heading straight for us. What happened?"

"Well, I don't really understand the whole meteorological reason behind the change in path, but as soon as you fell asleep last night, I got up and went into the den to watch the updates. I also turned on the radio to hear the New Orleans stations, and I couldn't believe what I was hearing. The reporters were shocked, too. Apparently, when the outer wall was just south of Grand Isle, this Category 3 hurricane just stopped, and instead of building up strength, which they usually do when they stop, it started to weaken. One reporter said that she was like a runner, racing at full throttle and tiring out just before reaching the finish line. Anyway, she also changed direction and ended up going to the Mississippi coast."

"Thank you, God, thank you God." Elise sighed, and then remembered that there were others who were waking up to a different scenario. "I do feel terrible for those poor people who get the storm, but I'm so grateful that it wasn't us."

"According to the weather reports, I don't think it will be any worse than a bad thunderstorm. It's just that it's still moving slowly, and there may be some flash flooding, because of all the rain."

"Well, that's good to hear. Mama and Daddy must be thrilled. No mess to go home to. I'll bet they'll open the highways by this afternoon, and we can all head on home. Let me go see what they have in mind." But just before she reached the door, an expression on Brad's face told her to stop, so she did, and she sat back down on the bed. She knew there was something more that he wanted to tell her.

"So who are you? The 'good news, bad news' guy. What is it that you haven't told me?"

"I just wanted to warn you about your Aunt Kitty."

"Aunt Kitty? What about Aunt Kitty? Is she sick or something? What?"

"No, she's not sick, but she's as mad as a rabid dog. And she's mad at you."

"Me? I haven't even seen Aunt Kitty since we've been here. Why is she mad at me? Is Jacqui awake yet?"

"That's just it. Jacqui's gone."

"Gone?"

"Yeah, it seems she left, right after your conversation last night. She left a note, saying that she was going to the nearest airport, flying to Connecticut, and going to see her old boyfriend. She said that you encouraged her to find out the answers to all the questions she's had since he left."

"I guess I did sort of encourage her. I really just agreed with her. But why would that make Kitty so angry. Did she take the car, so that now she can't get back to town? What's the deal?"

"Oh no. I love this part. Jacqui left her car for Kitty to drive home. Instead, she took one of Adam's classic coupes from his car barn out back. He's going to be livid. Imagine, taking one of his prized possessions in order to dump him. Poor guy." The smirk on his face betrayed the sincerity in his sympathetic remarks.

Elise thought for a minute, in order to get all the facts straight, and then went in to face her family. She found both of her parents and Kitty in the kitchen. Peggy Anne and Joseph were having coffee, while Kitty was having her breakfast on the rocks. She held a cigarette in one hand and a sheet of paper in the other. Elise could only assume that it was Jacqui's letter. As soon as Kitty's eyes fell upon Elise, the screaming began.

"Just calm down, Aunt Kitty. Let's discuss this whole thing in a rational manner. Why are you so upset? Jacqui's a woman. She has a right to make her own decisions. Why does it bother you that she wants to talk to Marsh before he gets married? Jacqui needs some closure here."

"Listen to you. Closure. What in the hell is that supposed to mean? I'm sure you filled her head with all sorts of big psychology words last night, not thinking about how much hurt you could cause."

"How can she be hurt any more than she already has? Maybe she'll finally get the answers to the questions she's been asking all these years."

"Answers? You think the answers are going to change her life for the better?"

"I think that knowing the truth will give her a start on getting over Marsh, once and for all. Guessing at all the different scenarios only allows her to keep hoping that he'll change his mind—and come back someday."

"You know as well as I do that his mind has nothing to do with it." Kitty took a lengthy drag on her long, slender cigarette that she held between her wrinkled lips.

"You're wrong about that, because I don't know anything about Marsh's reasons for leaving. For years, I've wondered what made him leave so suddenly. So, if I've wondered, how do you think Jacqui's felt? Nothing is real to Jacqui anymore. Nothing. She will never allow herself to really love someone else, until she knows what happened. Do you realize that Jacqui has lost the two men that she's loved most in this world—and none of it has ever made sense to her. First, Uncle Billy…"

"Oh, that's right. Her precious daddy. Ha! Billy Charleville is the reason she lives in her fairy-tale world, thinking that her little Prince Marsh will come back for her and carry her off to his kingdom, where they'll live happily ever after. Billy was the one who filled her head with that kind of nonsense, and that's all he ever did for her besides spoil her rotten. So rotten that I couldn't do a thing for her. She never listened to me. And it only got worse after he died."

"Now, Kitty," Peggy Anne calmly interjected, "I wouldn't start blamin' Billy…"

"Just shut up, Peggy Anne. You wouldn't see the truth if it slapped you on your simple face. Or you wouldn't admit it, anyway, since the truth might upset the precious Charleville name."

"Aunt Kitty, you apologize to my mama, right now!"

"It's OK, Elise. She can't hurt me. She can't hurt anyone but Jacqui. Nothing she can say to me can equal the hurt she's laid on that child."

"What are you talking about, Mama?"

"Tell her now, Kitty. You tell her, or I will."

"Like she doesn't know, already? Like you and that witch of a mother-in-law haven't already let her in on the little family secret? You think I'm stupid? You think I don't know that the little miss here hasn't known the truth all along?"

"Known what truth, known what?"

"Oh, look at you. You're not bad. Not bad at all. That puzzled, innocent look. Yeah, you're real good."

"Would you just stop it and tell me what's going on here. Mama, what is she talking about?"

"If you really cared about Jacqueline, the way you say you do, you would've stopped her. Nothing good will come of it if Marsh tells her why he left."

"Why do you keep saying that, as though I know the reason myself?"

Kitty turned to look at Peggy Anne, with a questioning, but unbelieving glare. Elise's mother shook her head. "Why, I'll be damned. You really don't know, do you?"

"Know what?"

KITTY PIERCE CHARLEVILLE
1960s

"Just another Monday," Kitty thought, looking at the date stamped on the bus ticket she held in her hand. Her mama had left River Bend, Mississippi, on a Monday—just disappeared. Left husband, home, and her six-year-old daughter for a "new life," she said. And no one ever heard from her again. And it was just a week ago, last Monday, she thought, when Freddie checked out. Left for that eternal life that church people talked about. But Kitty couldn't be sure where her father would spend his "eternal life." Didn't even know the options. And she was sure no one else really did either. Everyone who claimed that they knew about that eternal life only hoped that they knew. They couldn't really be sure. That's what her daddy used to say, anyway. And, as in most cases, she agreed with Freddie.

This thought was of very little comfort to Kitty Pierce, as she boarded the bus, that would take her away from River Bend, her small hometown outside of Jackson, Mississippi. The big engine of the bus rumbled and caused the vinyl, bench-style seat to vibrate, just enough to tickle her rear end. Kitty hoped this would not annoy her all the way to Baton Rouge, which for the time being was her chosen destination—the place where she could start her new life. She would start all over in Baton Rouge, Louisiana, where she could escape the Pierce legacy of self-destruction, denial, and dead-end streets. She left behind everything, and everybody associated with her past—everything, that is, except her

202

career. Kitty had just completed all of her training at the beauty college, the very same one that her mama and her Aunt Dee had attended. And that was the one part of her life that she loved. Aunt Dee had begged her to stay on in River Bend and go into business with her—sort of take her mama's place that had been left vacant so long ago. But Kitty knew that it had always been just a matter of time before she left that town for good. She never could have left her daddy behind—but now that he was gone forever, so was she. "Aunt Dee will get over it," Kitty thought. "It's not as though Baton Rouge is across the world." And anyway, Dee had promised to visit Kitty every now and then. Especially since she had that cousin of hers living in Baton Rouge.

Dee's cousin, Dottie, had a beauty shop, too. In fact, Dee had arranged for Kitty to work in Dottie's shop until she could get "good and settled." Kitty would be a manicurist to start. Dottie said that after a couple of months, she would work in a few hair styling appointments here and there, in order to ease the novice into the business. Kitty didn't mind the limited responsibilities. She didn't mind that she would be watched under the scrupulous eyes of her new employer, who sounded like the complete opposite of Aunt Dee, who seemed to run her shop for the mere pleasure of visiting and talking to her clients rather than for the prosperous business opportunity which it presented. But that was OK, too, because Kitty wanted to work with someone who could teach her the business side of her career—how to run the shop, as well as how to satisfy the customers. She expected to be on her own for a long time, and she wanted more from her life than Aunt Dee ever wanted or expected from hers.

Kitty loved Aunt Dee but hardly wanted to be like her. Dee knew it, too. She laughed about it occasionally, saying, "You may look like your daddy, girl, but you are your mama to the bone!" Comments like this were so unnerving to Kitty, but she never admitted this to Dee or anyone else who offered similar sentiments.

Kitty wanted to look like her mama and be like her daddy. Then, in her opinion, she would be perfect. She had heard tell that her daddy was once a handsome man. That he was a real "looker." But she didn't think so. He looked so old to her, when he really wasn't. He was tall and skinny, and his thinning hair was so blond that it looked prematurely white. His face was haggard and red. When Kitty was younger, she used to wonder how her daddy's face got so sunburned, spending all of his spare time sitting in his recliner in the darkness of their tiny living room, where all of the shades were pulled down in order to keep out any bright sunshine, which tended to give Freddie migraine headaches. He suffered so much with those headaches. So much that Kitty would lie awake at night worrying that she might lose her daddy, too. It wasn't until she was twelve or so that Aunt Dee explained to her that Freddie had a drinking problem—had one ever since her mama left. So, from then on Kitty didn't worry about his headaches, and she realized that the sunburn wasn't sunburn after all.

Freddie had also become a chain smoker, a habit that left telltale signs on his once-handsome face, marked prematurely with the deep wrinkles one would expect to see on a grandfather rather than a father. But Kitty looked past her daddy's weaknesses into his kind heart, which never allowed him to speak harshly to her and always prompted him to treat her with a gentle spirit. She accepted the fact that he would never again be the same strong man he was before her mama left them, and, without complaint or hesitation, she appointed herself as his sole protector in the world.

Kitty liked feeling needed by her daddy. It made her feel important in a way that she never could when her mama was around. Even though she knew that her daddy loved her, she also knew that he worshiped her mama. She never thought about this before her mama left them. She remembered crying for a solid week after her mama walked out—cried all day long, cried herself to sleep, and woke up with tears in her eyes. And then, one day she just stopped. She just couldn't cry anymore. She was worn out. She wondered if maybe her eyes had just plum run out of tears. All that she knew was that something had happened to her; she felt different. She felt older and more grown-up, while her daddy just looked more and more pathetic each day. From that day on, she referred to her daddy as Freddie and her mama as "she" or "her," whichever the case might be.

Freddie never mentioned the name "Donna" in the house again, either. He and Kitty had made an unspoken pact. They would take care of each other, and they didn't need anyone else in their lives. And that was that. With the exception of Aunt Dee, of course, who had always been like a second mama to Kitty since the day Donna and Freddie brought their baby girl home from the hospital.

Of course, Dee needed some support, too, because losing Donna was like losing a part of herself. But she had the beauty shop to keep her busy. Kitty had school. And Freddie had his full-service gas station right in the center of town. Freddie was proud of the business he had built from the ground up. He always knew that he would have to be successful to keep Donna happy, and things seemed to be going their way. He had been dedicated to his business, proud of the services he provided. But after "she" left, the business slowly began to fall apart. His headaches would prevent him from going in to work, he'd say. And well-intentioned friends would fill in for him until they, too, realized the root of Freddie's illness.

When Freddie died, the business wasn't clearing enough to pay the household bills. In fact, Kitty had to borrow money from Dee to settle up past due accounts, in order for her to move on. She'd pay her back, though, every penny plus a little more for her kindness. "Poor Freddie," she thought, as the bus seemed to soar down the narrow, two- lane roads of rural Mississippi. "I didn't even cry at your funeral. I spent all my tears on her."

And then the tragic thought occurred to her that she couldn't cry for Freddie, because she was so happy for Freddie. On the day of his funeral, she sat in a chair by the side of his open coffin. Aunt Dee thought she was crazy for paying Kramer's Funeral Home for the whole morning, knowing that hardly a soul would be coming by, since Freddie had basically dropped out of River Bend society so long ago. She even left early, telling Kitty that there was nothing she could do for Freddie anymore but take care of his little girl, and she had every intention of doing so. But she was not going to sit in an empty funeral home all day because it gave her the heebie-jeebies. So, for the most part, Kitty sat alone with Freddie's body all day, and in those still, silent moments, she realized that for the first time since "she" left, Freddie's face no longer revealed an agonizing existence. The lines of pain were gone, and his face reflected, instead, the presence of peace and sheer contentment. So, she couldn't be sad for this man, even though his life had ended at a relatively young age. She couldn't be sad, for his suffering days had come to an end. And she couldn't cry. She was glad that there were so few visitors that day, because she and Freddie could be alone in the end, just as they had lived their lives. And she didn't have to feel ashamed that she couldn't cry.

But a week later, on her bus trip out of town, she began to think about the fact that she would never see her daddy's face again. She would never again feel his arms wrap around her to reassure her that she wasn't alone in the world. She rested her head against the bus window, feeling the cold glass next to her warm cheek. A light rain began to fall, and tiny raindrops streaked the windowpane, leaving diagonal stripes in their paths. In the past, Kitty refused to think of her home life as being painful. She preferred to think of how successful she was in keeping some semblance of family life in their tiny broken household. But now that Freddie was gone, and she was sitting alone in a cold bus amongst strangers, she could only remember the painful existence behind her pretense of contentment. And for the first time since she was six years old, Kitty felt a tear rolling gently down her cheek. She was so glad that she was not sharing the seat with another passenger, because she didn't have to worry about attracting unwanted attention. It felt so good to cry, and Kitty wondered why she had allowed herself to keep so many years of pain locked up in her bruised and broken heart.

When Kitty stepped down from the bus with her small carrying case onto the curb of the bus station in Baton Rouge, she felt her body innervated with the thrill and excitement of starting a new life in the unfamiliar surroundings. She spotted a pay phone along the outside cinder-block wall of the train station, opened her rather unfashionable handbag, and reached for the colorful slip of notepaper on which Aunt Dee had scribbled Dorothy Dobson's phone number and address. She walked over to the phone and dialed the number with a bit of trepidation, unsure as she was of the woman whom she expected to answer her call. As she waited for someone to pick up the phone, she used her right foot to slide her two bags closer to where she was standing. After all, they contained her only earthly possessions. She wasn't nearly as worried about the clothing in the larger canvas duffle as she was about the little square cosmetic case that Aunt Dee had given her as a going-away gift. She had filled it with every female necessity from cotton balls to curlers.

Kitty heard a click on the line, followed by a sugar-coated drawl, "The French Twist, this is Dottie. How can I help you?"

Kitty smiled when she heard the name of the beauty shop. She liked it. She had a momentary picture of Aunt Dee's sign outside her tiny, two-room shop—a little wooden sign, hanging from a post, hand-painted red, white, and blue by her husband, Darryl—"D&D Beauty Shop"—Donna and Dee, of course. But Dee never changed the name after "she" disappeared.

"Hello. Anybody there?" Dottie's inquiring voice picked up in volume as if she wanted to wake up her caller.

"Oh. Yes, I'm sorry. Um, my name is Kitty. Kitty Pierce from River Bend, Mississippi. My Aunt Dee contacted you a couple of days ago."

"Yes, yes, she did. Are you in town, Kitty?"

"Yes ma'am. I'm at the bus station right now. I wanted to call first before going to your shop to make sure you had time to see me. I don't want to inconvenience you."

"No, no, not at all. Why, you get in a cab and come right over here. You have my address, right?"

"Yes ma'am, I do. But I was wondering if your shop might be walking distance from here, since I'm not quite sure I can afford a cab. To be quite honest, I've never ridden in a cab before, so I have no idea how much it would be."

"Now don't you worry about that, honey. I'll take care of it for you. As a matter of fact, one of my clients is a cab driver. His name is Rusty Lee. I'm gonna give him a call right now. Now you just sit tight over there and wait for Rusty. He'll be there real soon."

"You're so kind. I really do appreciate it. I have to admit I wasn't looking forward to carrying my bags down the road after that long bus ride."

"Don't you mention it. Now, what time is it? Let me see. OK, it's 2 o'clock. Get over here. I'll get you a bite to eat, and if you're ready, I can put you to work today!"

"Great! I'm ready. I'm definitely ready." A few more cordialities passed back and forth, and the conversation ended. Kitty picked up her two bags and found a seat on an empty bench near the entrance to the lobby of the station. Her stomach growled, and Kitty was glad that Dottie had mentioned feeding her. Aunt Dee would have thought about food, too. She laughed to herself thinking about the loud, slightly rotund beautician back in River Bend. She wondered if Dottie would be like Dee. She doubted so, but this consideration gave her food for thought while she waited for Rusty Lee's cab to come around for her.

Dee was the plain, homely girl whose excitement in life came from being the sidekick of the small-town beauty queen—the true and loyal friend of a girl who placed more importance on matching her lipstick with her nail color than on returning the friendship.

Dee coached Donna through cheerleader tryouts and prayed for her to be chosen prom queen, although Dee herself didn't even have a date to the prom. And the night that Donna was crowned Miss Cotton Blossom of River Bend, Mississippi, Dee wept with joy, as if she had just won the honor herself.

Dee was sure that Donna was headed for something big. She knew her very best friend in the world would be famous someday. That's what she told Kitty, anyway. She told Kitty that she was plum shocked when Donna told her, a few days after high school graduation, that she had decided to marry Freddie Pierce. She was deeply disappointed, she told Kitty, even though Freddie was the catch of their graduating class at RHS. Dee's attitude quickly changed, however, when Donna asked her to be maid-of-honor, and their planning began for what they referred to as River bend's wedding of the century. It was finally an opportunity for Dee to shine, standing right alongside of the local star. The parties, the clothes—why, it was elaborate, even in Jackson terms.

"But after the wedding, things changed," Dee told Kitty. "Oh, she loved your daddy, and Lord knows he loved her, still does, for that matter. But Donna needed to shine, like the rest of us need to breathe. We both went to beauty school, and for me nothing could've been better than opening the beauty shop with your mama. But it wasn't enough for her. I always knew she'd fly away. Too caged up in this little town. You'll fly one day, baby. And that's OK. You gonna break your Aunt Dee's heart again—just like your mama did—but that's OK. As long as you remember me and drop a line now and then. That's what breaks my heart most about your mama. It's like she forgot me. Like I was never a part of life."

Kitty remembered well the day that Aunt Dee spoke those words to her. Kitty remembered how badly Dee felt when she realized that she hadn't heard from her mother, either, and Dee couldn't imagine how much worse it must be for a little girl to feel forgotten. "I'm sorry, baby. Aunt Dee just rattles on and on, don't she?" And then she pulled Kitty onto her lap, which seemed to be getting smaller and smaller as the rest of her body grew rounder each year. "I bet your mama is thinking about the two of us right now. She's probably starring in some play or something in New York or maybe even Hollywood, and she's thinking about the two of us back here. One day, maybe we'll be sitting in the front row of some fancy theater watching your beautiful mama starring in a romantic love story. Now won't that be exciting, huh? We just have to give your mama a little more time to get settled and get famous, that's all." And she gave Kitty one of her big squeezes and kissed the little girl's forehead. But none of the words and hugs and kisses could ever erase that agonizing feeling of being forgotten.

Well, those days are over, Kitty sighed, as her thoughts returned to her present surroundings in the Baton Rouge bus station. A freshly waxed, white cab speeded up to the curb, nearly screeching to a halt when the driver spotted Kitty, sitting alone with her bags, and that self-conscious look of a newcomer. He saw that look all the time in his business, especially at the bus station and especially with women traveling alone. They look around the unfamiliar surroundings, he thought, trying their best not to appear lost and uncomfortable around so many strangers. Kitty was a little startled by the car's sudden approach, and the driver's abrupt but courteous greeting.

"Howdy do, ma'am. You the lady headin' for Miz Dottie's place?" he asked politely, while proceeding to pick up her bags and place them in the trunk of his car, before she was able to return an affirmative reply.

"Yes, I am. Thank you for coming so soon. I was prepared for a longer wait." As she spoke, she checked out the door of the cab, which pictured what appeared to be a blue capitol building, surrounded by a circle of red stars, and right below it, the name "Russell E. Lee." He slammed the trunk shut.

"I never let Miz Dottie's patrons wait," he said, walking back toward his charge and extending his right hand to her, "Rusty Lee, at your service, ma'am."

Kitty shook his big hand and felt remiss in not giving her name in return, standing temporarily speechless in his presence. "Nice to meet you," was all she could manage to say, before she climbed into the back seat of Lee's car.

In an instant, Kitty was taken aback by the interior of Rusty Lee's cab. She felt as though she were sitting in a traveling Confederate

Museum. Both seats were draped with Confederate flags. The dashboard was bedecked with a collection of miniature figurines, apparently Confederate soldiers, kept in place by their magnetic bases. Hanging from the rearview mirror was a tiny framed, black-and-white portrait of a man in military garb.

Although she really had no intention of striking up a conversation with this man whom she assumed she'd only see this one brief episode in her life, she couldn't suppress her curiosity, and asked, "So, are you a Civil War buff?"

"I guess you could say that. Fact is, you lookin' at a direct descendent of the most famous and honorable general himself—General Robert E. Lee. So, I see it as my family duty to keep the Confederate spirit alive." Perhaps it was the way he spoke with such pride and sincerity, or maybe it was just being with someone who was proud of his ancestry and upbringing that sparked her interest in this unusual character, who for the moment seemed very entertaining. So, she decided to stretch the truth a little, if not outright lie in order to keep the conversation going.

"I've always had an interest in the Civil War myself, bein' from the South and all."

"Is that right?" Lee asked skeptically, looking in his rearview mirror to see if the pretty lady's facial expression could help in determining her sincerity. "What parts are you from?"

"Jackson. Actually, a little town outside of Jackson."

"Jackson, huh? Why you should know all about my other ancestor, Stephen Dill Lee, who settled down near your neck of the woods after the war."

She was suddenly feeling uncomfortable in the little web she was weaving but continued the conversation. "Well, I have heard the name before, but I can't say that I know much about him."

He was quick to answer in her defense. "Most people haven't. But they should, because he was the very man to start the firing on Fort Sumter, which in turn started the whole war."

He could see from his vantage point that this Mississippi lady had no clue as to what he was talking about. "Course, I don't 'spect ladies to know much about the war, anyway. All's they know about now is Scarlett O'Hara and Rhett Butler." He laughed in a confident, authoritative manner. "But ol' Stephen Dill, he was an important man."

Kitty wasn't sure why, but she couldn't take her eyes off of the man. She should've been looking around as he drove her through the streets of her new hometown, but she was surprisingly captivated by his willingness to share the wealth of his knowledge. She was actually sorry to see the brief ride come to an end when he pulled up to the door of "Miz Dottie's place."

Russell E. Lee jumped out and opened the door for his attentive passenger, then quickly retrieved her bags from the trunk of his rolling Confederate Museum. Kitty was thoroughly mesmerized, not so much by this man's eccentric character, but more by his own comfort with himself. Here was a cab driver in Baton Rouge, Louisiana, making his living by moving people from one venue to another, who saw himself instead as a noble, aristocratic Southerner, responsible in his duty to preserve the memory of and respect for his Confederate ancestors. He was handsome, too, Kitty thought, and she found herself imagining this man garbed in the gray uniform of those brave, but ill-fated Southern soldiers.

Russell opened the door to the beauty shop and promptly announced the arrival of the "pretty little Jacksonian." And though Kitty would've normally despised such an indulgent, sweet talker, she kind of liked the fact that he noticed her. Dottie was the first to come forward—first of all to greet her newest employee, and second, to pay Russell E. Lee for delivering her to the doorstep. There were lots of "heys" and "nice ta meetchas" exchanged in the first five minutes of Kitty's arrival, but nothing really soaked in until the eccentric cab driver left the shop. As he left, he looked in her direction, pointed an index finger, winked, and said, "Now you call me if you ever need a ride, ya hear?" Then, he slipped a card in her hand and left, pulling the door shut and causing the little bell at the top of the door to jingle. Kitty liked him. She didn't know why, but she liked him. She didn't want to, but she did. She slipped the card in the side pocket of her purse, with the intention of giving it her full attention later on that evening.

The scent of fingernail polish and hairspray awakened her senses, and she realized that she had been standing, staring at the door in silence for a little too long, when Dottie's loud, twangy voice asked, "You got second thoughts about staying, suga'?"

"Oh no. Not at all. I'm just a little tired, I guess. And I really wish you would've let me pay for the cab. I didn't expect you to pay. After all, I'm just grateful for the opportunity to work here."

"Aw, now, don't get too indebted on your first day, honey. You may be wishin' you'd stayed in River Bend with Dee by next week." Kitty's puzzled look was her only reply and prompted Dottie's comforting comeback, "Just a little joke, sweety. You gonna love it here. Right girls? We're like a family. One of us has a problem, we all have a problem. One of us has a reason to celebrate, we all celebrate. So you go in the back room, putcha things there, grab a nice, cold Coke and some fried chicken outta the fridge, and then come back out—I'm gonna introduce you to everybody and get you started right here at the manicure station. And, by the way," Dottie added, as Kitty obediently proceeded to follow her first command, "lighten up. We joke a lot around here. Just for fun, though. Nothin' hurtful."

"OK," Kitty smiled. "I think I can do that." But she had to wonder if she could ever lighten up, because she had been wound up tight as a spring ever since the day her mama walked out on her and Freddie.

There were three other "girls" working for Dottie, all with the same bubbly, vivacious personality. "Honeys" and "sugas" spilled out of their mouths every other second. "Aunt Dee would fit right in here," Kitty thought. In fact, Judy Ann sort of looked like Dee. About the same age, round, pink face, pinkish, blond hair, pink nails, pink lips, talk, talk, talk. Lorraine was just the opposite in appearance and older, too. She was probably in her sixties, Kitty surmised. She was skinny as a rail, with her clothes falling so loosely around her body that one had to wonder what was holding them on. While she worked, she smoked one cigarette after another, and she kept a Coke within reach at all times. She'd stop in the middle of her cutting or styling, take a long, deep drag off of her cigarette, take a sip of coke, and continue to work, all the while, keeping up with the lively conversation that never ended as long as there was a warm body in her station.

Faye was the third employee at The French Twist. She had been hired just a year before Kitty and was about the same age as the newcomer. Unlike the others, Faye was single and lived on her own, in a small apartment above Justin's Jewelry Shop, just two blocks from the beauty shop. Dottie had wisely arranged for Kitty to stay with Faye until she could afford a place of her own. Kitty suspected that Dot was giving Faye a little bonus money for the favor, but Faye never let on. All she requested of Kitty was to split the utility bills. Everything seemed to be set in place for Kitty's new life to begin.

Dottie had a booming business, with a very well-to-do clientele. The shop was strategically located near the capitol, and Dottie had a wonderful reputation amongst the secretaries, wives, and, of course, the mistresses of the astute statesmen of Louisiana. Therefore, Dottie had a strict rule about keeping the secrets of the capitol confidential. "They come here as much because we're trustworthy as they do for our services, honey," she'd say. She was impeccable when it came to scheduling and no one but Dottie was allowed to schedule appointments. After all, it would be absolutely disastrous to have a wife and a mistress in the shop at the same time. Just about every patron, as she referred to her clients, had a designated day and time each week to come in for their coiffures and manicures. Weekends were reserved for emergencies—like broken nails and unexpected hair problems, which would be an absolute crisis if left untreated. Because even though the politicians living in Baton Rouge during the legislative sessions found reasons to congregate in the best Baton Rouge restaurants every night of the week, weekends were reserved for the biggest and best parties. And God forbid any of Dottie's patrons having to attend one of those soirees with a broken nail or a hair out of place. Yes, Dottie knew how to handle these women in a way that they never realized they were being "handled." The wives marched in with their haughty airs, and each of Dottie's employees would pamper them and indulge them, admiring the new diamond or sapphire they just so happened to be wearing, all the while knowing that the mistress was in just the day before, showing off a bigger diamond or sapphire. It was all part of a day's work at The French Twist.

It wasn't very hard for Kitty to live by Dottie's rules of confidentiality, because she spent most of her time listening and not speaking—smiling and being friendly but not partaking in the spicy conversations that became a part of her job. This was partly because in order for her to start her life anew, she would have to let her past go. Therefore, she really didn't have any basis from which to draw experiential opinions.

But, she listened, and she watched, and she learned. Kitty had waited a few days before asking Dottie if she was a good friend of Russell E. Lee. "Oh, yeah, suga'," Dottie returned. "Rusty and I go back a long way." And then her usual loud, passionate voice lowered to a compassionate tone. "Poor thing. He kinda lost it when he went in the Army during WWII. I actually used to date Rusty back in high school—only occasionally, of course. He was handsome enough, let me tell you. Still is, if you ask me." And then she turned two suspicious eyes on Kitty, "Why you wanta know about Rusty?"

"Oh, just interested, that's all. He seemed so intelligent, telling me all about the Civil War, and all. I was wondering what he's doing driving a cab. Seems he should be teaching or something. Is he married?"

"Heck no! Probably never will be, 'cause everybody 'round here knows that he's not right."

"He sure didn't seem crazy to me the other day."

"Oh, I don't say he's crazy—he's just not right, honey." Kitty didn't really understand the distinction between being crazy and just not right, and Dottie could see the look of confusion on her face. "Let me explain. You see, Rusty Lemoine—that's his real name, you know—he was born and raised right here in Baton Rouge. He was adopted, though, by his aunt and uncle, because his own parents just plum couldn't afford a tenth child. The aunt and uncle couldn't have no kids of they own, so it seemed a good thing to do. Everybody's happy, right? That's what we all thought, anyway, because Rusty was better off than any of his brothers and sisters, and shoot, he never seemed to mind. The aunt and uncle had big plans for Rusty. Gonna send him to LSU so's he could get a degree—and Rusty was all for it. But the war lasted longer than he thought. He was graduating from high school at the tail end of it, and he wanted to go. Wanted to do his part. So, he went—against the wishes of the aunt and uncle.

He was fine when he left. Then six months later we all hear he's in some big Army hospital. We all thought he had some kinda war injury, but come to find out, he was in a mental hospital. Seems old Rusty was never even in battle—spent his time in the states. Seems he did a lot of readin' up on wars and somehow got stuck on the Civil War. He was so involved with the stuff, that he started tellin' everybody that his name was Russell E. Lee, and that he was the great-great-grandson of the famous general, himself."

"Well, maybe he is. Maybe he did some researching of his family tree. Some people do that…"

"Honey, Rusty is no more the great-great-grandson of Robert E. Lee than I am the real Lana Turner." Kitty and Dottie both had a laugh at that thought. "Nah. Them Lemoines are Cajuns. No Virginians in that stock."

"So why did they let him out of the hospital, if he obviously wasn't cured of his delusions?"

"I guess them doctors figured he was harmless, and the government had so many other more serious medical problems to deal with, they just let him come home. His aunt and uncle sure couldn't afford the kinda treatment he needed, so we just all let him believe he's a Lee. Whatcha gonna do? He's a good, kind man. Don't hurt nobody. Happy. And still a looker, if ya ask me. I give him a lot of business here, since a lot of my patrons don't drive."

"Does he ever go out with anyone?"

"What are you thinkin' about, Kitty? Don't tell me you're interested in Rusty Lemoine."

"Oh no. Just interested in his story, that's all." But that wasn't all. She was now even more intrigued with this man who called himself Russell E. Lee. This man who decided to change his identity, change his past, in order to create a new life. Even when they thought he was "not right," he stuck to his story. Russell E. Lee was not crazy. He just didn't like Rusty Lemoine's life anymore, so he created another one. One that he liked and admired. One that he could be proud of. The whole idea excited her. After all, wasn't she trying to start a new life? And the most difficult part of starting her new life was dragging her past along with her.

That evening, when the shop closed, Kitty told Faye that she had a few things to buy at the drug store, and that she wouldn't be home for a while. She did, in fact, go to Peltier's Drug Store, ordered a cup of coffee and felt in the pocket of her purse for the little card Russell had handed her at Dot's. It was still there. It was a business card. "Imagine that" she thought. "How many cab drivers have their own business cards?" It was a white card with his name, written in red, surrounded by blue stars. Just like the door of the cab, she remembered. Only the card did not have Capitol Cab on it. Just his name and phone number.

Kitty used the pay phone right outside the entrance to the drug store and dialed the number. When his familiar voice answered, she realized she must have dialed his home, not a cab station. He answered,

217

"Hello," instead of "Capitol Cabs." This rattled her thoughts for a few seconds, and he said "hello" a second time. "Hello," she said, "is this Russell E. Lee with Capitol Cabs?" She knew that it was.

"Speakin'," he replied.

Kitty quickly continued, afraid that she would lose her nerve and hang up. "Hi, Mr. Lee. This is Kitty Pierce. You gave me a ride from the bus station to The French Twist a while back." For a few seconds, she didn't think that he remembered her and was relieved when she heard his voice lighten.

"Well, I'll be! Don't tell me Dottie's been so tough on you that you need a ride back to the bus station, now?" He laughed as the words flowed so casually across the wires.

"No, no. It's nothing like that. Miss Dottie's been wonderful. In fact, everyone has. I was just wondering if you could swing by Peltier's Drug Store and give me a ride to a restaurant, nearby."

"Why sure, honey. I'll be by in a few minutes. Which restaurant might you be talking about?"

"Oh, I'm really not sure. I thought you might have some suggestions." Strangely enough, that's how Kitty's relationship with Russell E. Lee began, and to be sure, the relationship proceeded and ended quite strangely enough.

Kitty couldn't call it a clandestine relationship, because that might lead one to imagine a much more exciting, amorous, maybe even erotic affair. And that couldn't be further from the truth. It was, however, a secret friendship in the sense that Kitty told no one about it. But she might have, if anyone had asked. The truth is no one ever did. She and Russell were two loners, who purposely kept to themselves and purposely avoided any contact or conversation with anyone who could get to the real truths about their lives—their pasts. Kitty knew that Russell would spend the rest of his life as a loner, because he knew that most of the people in his town knew too much about his real life and thought he was "not right."

And Kitty knew that this particular place and time was merely a temporary stop in her own life. She felt no need to develop any long-term friendships or business connections. And she especially did not feel the need to settle down with a man. What she needed was time to figure out what she wanted to do with her life, where she wanted to go, how she would go about making it happen. It was a lot to think about. It would take some time and space. And the last thing she needed was a commitment of any type.

The whole time she was with Dottie and the others at work, they talked on and on about men. They bragged about them, complained about them, wished to be with them, and couldn't wait to leave them. All day, every day, they talked about men. Their men, available men, other women's men, and the famous men pictured in their Hollywood magazines. "Ooooh, the things I could do for him," Dottie would say, as she pored over a picture of a good-looking actor, while thumbing through the shop periodicals.

"And what about Jimbo? What would you do with that man of yours?" one of the others would ask, teasingly.

And Dottie would answer, "Oh Cher, I'd give him to you. You would like that, huh?"

The response would fly back, "No way, Dottie. I don't want your man. He's too demanding—wants everything when and how he wants it. Unh, unh, he's not for me."

And then Dottie would defend her Jimbo. "Well, baby, it's only demanding if you don't like things the way he likes it." Then you'd hear all of the giggling from everyone in the shop, except maybe Faye, who didn't catch the sexual connotations in Dottie's last remark. Too personal for Kitty. She wasn't ready or willing to partake in such conversations. She actually had nothing to add to such conversations. So, she just listened and smiled at the appropriate times. Whenever she heard the "ooooh" chorus, she knew that a smile would be applicable.

Kitty enjoyed and looked forward to her evening rides with Russell E. Lee. That was, in fact, what their relationship consisted of—evening rides. They would drive through the streets of Baton Rouge between six and seven o'clock every evening. Faye thought that Kitty was attending a Bible class somewhere and never ever questioned her about it, because Faye was a devout Catholic and wanted nothing to do with some "tea-totaling protestant religion."

Russell always made it a point to stop working at six o'clock each day, taking no fares while he spent his hour with Kitty. They would just talk and talk, until seven or so, when he'd drop her off at any of the little diners located in the vicinity of the apartment. She would have her dinner alone, then walk back to Faye's place, take a nice, hot bath, and turn in for the night. On one such occasion, Kitty asked Russell why he could only be with her until seven, and he simply explained to her that he had things to do. He told her that he was a man of habit, and he didn't like to stray from his normal routine. "I guess that's the soldier in your blood," she replied, seriously, as though Dottie had never told her the Rusty Lemoine story. "Yup, I assume so. All us Lees are the same way." Kitty was mesmerized by this man, who never, no matter how much he was coaxed, ever stepped out of his chosen role. Could she do it so well? she wondered. What if a person had to be "not right" to be so confident and convincing as an entirely different character in life?

Kitty was continually amazed with Russell's self-taught history education. She imagined him going home after dropping her off and reading all night before starting his day shift for Capitol Cab. "And he probably reads between his fares. He would have to," she thought, "in order to be so knowledgeable." Sometimes, though, she realized that he could be making up his facts, creating his own Civil War history, and she would never know the difference. She could hardly remember studying about that war in school, but then it wasn't exactly a war that native Mississippi teachers wanted to spend much time on. It wasn't until she was about eleven years old that she realized the South had actually lost the war, and that was only because of a student teacher, who was from Ohio. Raymond Peabody, the smartest boy in her fifth-grade class, thought he'd impress the young educator with information he had obtained from the library book he had just completed. He stated that he was proud to live in a country that had never lost a war. Half of the class snickered, and the other half moaned, but the new teacher from Ohio stood, stone-faced in front of the class and robotically replied, "Well, that's not exactly correct, Mr. Peabody, because technically, as a Mississippian, your country lost the War Between the States." With that response, Raymond adjusted his glasses, pulled up his pants by tugging on his belt, and sat back down in his seat. Kitty remembered that her reaction, upon hearing this startling bit of information, was to dismiss any word that escaped the mouth of that carpetbagger. That day was probably the last time she gave any serious thought to the fate of the Confederate States of America.

But Russell E. Lee captivated her interest with his simple country charm. He had the kind of face that would never grow old. She could tell that he'd look like a big kid for the rest of his life. She liked that. Her daddy seemed to have grown old overnight. So, it was refreshing to be in the presence of this youthful, middle-aged man. Russell appreciated his one-person audience, as well. Everyone else in town would seem interested, at first, but then make a big joke of him behind his back. But this lady from Jackson was different. He wasn't sure why. He really couldn't figure her out, but it didn't matter, because, for whatever reason, she was the only person in Baton Rouge who took him seriously. She made him feel important. So, he was determined to return the favor for this lonely woman. He was going to do his best to make her feel important, too.

Kitty had been in Baton Rouge for about six months, spending most of her days in the same manner, going to work from eight to five, walking to Peltier's Drug Store for a cup of coffee, riding with Russell until seven, eating dinner, then going home for the night. She was beginning to get a little impatient with herself, for she was nowhere near making any decisions about her future, which meant that her past was still looming around her like a thick fog on the river. Then, one night, as Russell walked around the back of the car to open the door for her, he stopped to get a couple of packages out of the trunk. He handed them to her when she stepped onto the sidewalk in front of Capt. Mike's Seafood, the restaurant Russell had chosen for her that evening. "What's this, Russell?" she asked, holding the D. H. Holmes bags in her hand.

"It's just a little something for you to wear tomorrow night. We're gonna do things a little different, OK?"

"Different?" Oh Lord, she thought, he's asking me out. She was silently chastising herself for allowing this seemingly platonic relationship to get to this point. She should have realized it would happen. "How are things going to be different, Russell?" She was surprised to hear her own voice, sounding so excited, eager to hear the plans. And she wasn't pretending.

"Well, let's just say that tomorrow night will be a night you'll never forget, Miss Kitty from Jackson, Mississippi. I'll pick you up at the usual spot at eight o'clock."

"Eight o'clock? Isn't that kind of late for your schedule?"

"You just be ready, OK?"

"Won't you at least tell me where we're going?"

"You, my sweet lady, are goin' to New Orleans."

Her mouth opened to speak, but nothing came out. He walked back to the car, watching her, and smiling at her with a devilish look on his baby face. And, for the first time in her life, she felt her heart racing. He winked at her before he hopped into his shiny, white Capitol Cab and drove off to the secretive world of Russell E. Lee. Kitty stood on the sidewalk, watching the car drive away, still in shock from the driver's sudden step toward a more involved relationship. Her feelings of apprehension, just moments earlier, were transformed into feelings of excitement. She started toward the front door of the restaurant, then glanced down at the bags full of boxes that Lee had just given to her and decided that her hunger was not as peaked as her curiosity. So, she headed back to Faye's apartment like a little girl running home from school to open birthday presents.

Kitty couldn't remember the last time she was bestowed with surprise gifts, such as the ones she was holding in her hand. The type of gifts that come for no other reason but that someone holds another person "special." Aunt Dee would give her little goodies occasionally, always trying to fill at least a small part of the emptiness in her heart, left there when her mama walked out. She remembered, in particular, the little bags of tiny sample lipsticks that Aunt Dee would give her every few months. In addition to her hairdressing business, Aunt Dee sold cosmetics in her shop. And whenever the cosmetic company sent her samples of the new seasonal shades of lipsticks, she'd give the old ones to Kitty. The tiny, little white tubes of beautiful bright shades of pink, orange, and red were bright spots in her dull, uneventful childhood that appeared to her in shades of black, brown, and gray.

She would take her little bag of lipsticks into her bedroom and organize them by each respective shade. She loved the names—they seemed so exotic—names like "Romance and Roses," "Moonlight Melon," "Passion Pink," "Mauve Melody." With a box of tissue at hand, Kitty would sit in front of her mirror and apply each exotic color to her perfectly contoured lips. Sometimes her hair would be pulled back and, with a black pen, she'd draw a beauty mark on her cheek. She would look at her image in the mirror, purse her thickly coated lips and raise her right eyebrow, the way her mama did when she was in an angry or coquettish mood. That was the only feature that her mama had passed on to her—raising her eyebrow. Aunt Dee told her that a gesture like that was sexy and effective when trying to get a lady's point across. So she practiced raising her eyebrow regularly, especially when she tried on her new lipsticks, and she learned how to control the brow movement completely.

No matter which shade of lipstick she tried, however, the face in the mirror was never as beautiful as her mama's. And each time she came to this conclusion, her makeover would end. With the help of her Pond's Cold Cream and tissues, she'd wipe away all evidence of her makeup session, because her daddy forbade her to wear makeup. "No more beauty queens in his house," he'd say. And he'd always add, "You're pretty 'nuff without that stuff, anyhow."

With her big D.H. Holmes bags in hand, Kitty ran up the steps behind the jewelry store, which led to the apartment. Faye was not home. She religiously went to her parents' home every Thursday for dinner and wouldn't come home until after she watched Johnny Carson with her mama. She never missed a Thursday, no matter how tired she was, even if she were invited to a grander, more exciting evening. On Sunday mornings, Faye always went back to her parents' house at nine thirty, so that the whole Jeansonne family could attend ten thirty mass together. Then they'd all go back to the family home to eat "dinner" at twelve noon, sharp. And every Sunday, they'd eat chicken and andouille gumbo, pot-roasted chicken, mashed potatoes, peas, homemade bread, and bread pudding with whiskey sauce.

Kitty had spent her first Sunday in Baton Rouge with Faye and her family. There were Faye's four siblings, each with a spouse or significant other. Two of them had babies, which were passed from arm to arm. And in the middle of all these people were two Chihuahuas that barked incessantly. Kitty enjoyed it at first. Faye's family was a close, loving family. They laughed a lot. Talked nonstop. Hugged and kissed each other as though they hadn't been together in years. They congregated in the kitchen, talking loudly, in a state of constant motion—busily preparing the meal, setting the table, washing, drying, and "saving" the dishes. Then dessert and coffee, doing the dishes again, going from one stage of the visit to the next. Everyone knew his or her role from years of experience, because no one ever missed going to Mama and Daddy's on Sunday, sparing a birth or death in the family. Then they'd gather, instead, at the hospital or funeral home. Kitty enjoyed her day at the Jeansonnes' and hated to see it come to an end. But she never went back, although Faye never failed to invite her. The perfectly delightful, loving family was the antithesis of her own family and being with them only made her own family life seem bleaker, if that were possible.

Kitty always wondered what it would be like to have a family like the Jeansonnes'. How different her life would've been. And more importantly, how different she would've been. Oh, there was love in her home, between her and Freddie, but there was no real happiness. No matter how hard she tried, she could never spark that family magic that she read about and saw in the movies. And then to see the Jeansonnes together, with this magic flowing so effortlessly, so naturally in their little unpretentious home—it was more than she could handle. It depressed her and made her feel like she missed a whole chunk of life that every human being deserved. It made her feel alone, like an orphan. She had to talk to Russell E. Lee about those feelings, because she remembered that Dottie had told her that he was somewhat of an orphan. She had been careful, however, not to let him know that she was aware of his real past. He let her talk on and on about it, and then he spoke. He told her that he knew a lot of girls like Faye. "Umbilical cord 'as never cut." He said it was common for Louisiana girls to be that way. "Never growin' up," he said. And then he added, "That's what I like about you. You can put yo'self-first, do whatcha want. All 'ese women put their mamas and daddies first. Never break away. Never explore other possibilities in their lives. One thing's fo' certain—they'd never move to another town to make a life the way that you did. Hell no! Excuse my French, suga'." Russell E. Lee's simple, profound way of thinking and talking made her feel better about herself, as she absorbed yet another chapter of the cab driver's philosophy on life. And from then on, she viewed Faye's routine visits with her family as an unhealthy desire to prolong her childhood. She never went back to the Jeansonnes' home.

As she struggled to unlock the door on that particular Thursday evening, however, she was glad that Faye was away. Kitty slept on the couch and had no bedroom of her own, and she didn't want Faye to see her new things, because she was supposed to be at a Bible study. And this way she could pose in front of the mirror in any fashion or form,

225

with no fear of being seen—just like the days when she got a new bag of lipsticks. Faye wouldn't be home for another three-and-a half hours. Kitty made herself a drink with the stash she hid under the sofa—Faye thought she was a tea-totaling Baptist. Then she took the packages out of the bags, laid them out on Faye's bed, and tore off the lids of the boxes.

"Oh, my heavens," she exclaimed, when she removed the neatly placed tissue to uncover the most stunning red satin she had ever seen in her life. She lifted the bodice of the dress by its full, off-the-shoulder shawl collar and let the skirt of the dress fall, pressing the dress up against her body to get a better idea of the fit and just to experience the fabulous fabric and radiant color against her body. The dresser mirror, in Faye's room, only allowed her to see from her waist up, so, barefooted, she jumped up on the bed and slipped into the dress, zipped it up, and swayed from side to side to see the full skirt flow gracefully with every step. She was talking to herself, all the while—girly comments, like those that filled the air at The French Twist, such as, "ooooh girl," and "look at you, girl." She had never known such a moment in her life. And her excitement was intoxicating.

Kitty carefully got down off of the bed, careful not to rip the hem, and looked at herself, waist up, in the mirror. She lifted her auburn hair and pinned it up off of her shoulders, and stood, in amazement. For the first time in her life, she saw her mother's face looking back at her. For the first time in her life, she felt beautiful, sexy even. And for the first time in her life, she not only wanted to look like her mother; she wanted to be like her mother. She was tired of looking into the mirror and seeing an image that reflected a little girl shut up in a run-down house, taking care of an alcoholic father, who had given up on his life. Her father was gone now. And wanting to look like her mother was no longer considered being disloyal to the pitiful, pathetic victim of her mother's selfish whims.

Kitty eagerly opened the smaller box, which she guessed contained jewelry. She was right. The sparkling rhinestone necklace, which fell just above the neckline of the dress, drew attention to the soft, sensuous curvature of her bare neck and shoulders. And with the addition of the matching earrings, only a crown could've made her feel more like a queen.

The last two boxes held the finishing touches—a red satin wrap and the sexiest, slinky, stringed, black-sequined sandals Kitty had ever laid her eyes upon. She glanced quickly at the clock and figured that her fitting session had only taken up about an hour of her free time. She wished that she could've had the rest of the night to herself, but she would just have to settle for another two-and-a-half hours. Kitty turned on the radio, raising the volume a few notches, and made herself another drink—this time a little bigger and a little stronger. And when that one was gone, she made another and another.

With her eyes closed and her free arm wrapped around her waist, Kitty moved around the tiny living room, her body absorbing the beat of the rhythm-and-blues, which she eventually turned up to a blaring level. Bourbon went to her head, and the music went to her hips, and together they created a harmony that Kitty had never before experienced. It was as though someone else had entered her body, moving her flesh and bones and red satin dress back and forth across the floor. And although Kitty had, on occasion, given in to the temptation of her sexual desires back in River Bend, Mississippi, she had never before felt as sexy and erotic as she did on this evening—or as beautiful. But there was something else that she had never before felt. Something else empowering a stranger within. Something else driving these unfamiliar emotions to the surface. It was her unleashed sense of freedom.

For the first time in her life, Kitty felt free—free to do whatever she pleased, free to go wherever she wished, free to be whomever she wanted to be. Her desire to start over as a new person, re-creating her past in order to move on to an exciting future could finally be a reality. There was nothing to hold her back now—nothing to be ashamed of, nothing to cause guilt. She was on her own now and the possibilities were unlimited. Who could stand in her way but the old Kitty? And she was buried, with her past. She found herself thinking of Russell E. Lee. He was a "looker," just as Dottie said. And he definitely had good taste. As far as finances, well, he did pretty well to afford the new outfit she was wearing. Since she was hardly thinking about settling down anyway, Russell E. Lee would be a good man to start with.

Kitty lost track of the number of drinks she had imbibed, lost track of the song she had been belting out while she celebrated her new beginning, and had very definitely lost track of the time, because just as a slow, sultry melody wooed her to the couch for a bit of a rest, she heard the keys jiggling in the door. She quickly placed her glass down on the coffee table within her reach and closed her eyes, pretending to be asleep. Angry with herself for not watching the time and too dizzy to think about an explanation, she let herself fall into a very peaceful slumber. She barely heard Faye's voice speaking to her, and she didn't hear her roommate stepping quietly around the couch to turn off the music and clear the table of the half-filled glass and nearly empty bottle of bourbon.

In the morning, however, Kitty heard everything as though every sound in the apartment had been raised to the highest volume, as the music had been the night before. Noises reverberated through her head, and she could have sworn that even if she held her head completely still, her brain would continue to vibrate. She opened her eyes to the slightly spinning ceiling and remembered the previous evening, which was responsible for her ailing head, and then she smiled, because in spite of a very wicked hangover, she was ready for anything this day and especially this night had to offer.

And then she realized that she was lying on the couch in her new dress, wrap, new shoes, and jewelry. What would she tell Faye? Kitty hadn't much time to think about her dilemma, because, in what seemed like two seconds later, Faye was standing over her with a glass of juice and two aspirins. "Wake up, Kitty. Come on, honey. I thought you could use this, if you're going to work today." Kitty sat up slowly, feeling every millimeter of movement like an earthquake.

"Thank you, Faye. I truly appreciate it." She sipped the juice, and swallowed the pills, realizing Faye had not moved, and was staring at her, waiting patiently for the details of the little soiree that had apparently taken place in her absence. Not that she felt that she was owed an explanation; she was just downright curious.

"I guess you're wondering why I'm dressed like this, huh?"

"Well, yeah. But I have to say, you look absolutely gorgeous! What's all this getup about, anyway? Did you have a man over last night? I wouldn't mind, you know. I've never mentioned it to you, only because you never ever seemed interested. But honey, I know one thing for sure—you ain't been to no Bible study last night."

Kitty thought fast. "Well, actually, I did go to my Bible study last night, Faye. And to answer your question, no, I did not have a man over here. I promise you; I would not have assumed your approval of such a thing without asking first."

"Then what's going on?" Faye asked, with her curiosity peaked.

Kitty just opened her mouth to start speaking and hoped that the right words would come and, luck being with her, they did. "Faye, I hadn't told you anything, because I didn't want you to get the feeling that I didn't like it here in Baton Rouge—everyone has been so good to me and all. Dottie and you girls at the shop have been like family to me, and then you letting me stay here—well, what more could a girl ask of a friend? But, still, I get awful homesick from time to time, and I happened to mention it in a letter to one of my aunts back in Jackson. Well, don't you know, that she and a bunch of my kin pooled together to send me these beautiful things just to cheer me up. I was so touched. I just had to try everything on. But before I did, I ran down to the corner and bought a little booze, thinking that it would help me to think I was back home with my old friends at the Jubilee Jazz Room. That was where we'd all go to listen to music on weekends. Anyway, it's been so long since I had a drink, all's it did was knock me out. I'm so sorry if I made a mess or anything, Faye." The last line came out in such a whimpering voice that Kitty was inclined to believe the lies that had just spewed from her mouth. And her lies had accomplished their purpose, because Faye reached out and hugged Kitty, just like a good Jeansonne would in such a case.

"Oh, Kitty, baby, I am so sorry that I've been too selfish to notice how sad you must have been. Can you ever forgive me, sweetie?"

"Don't be silly, Faye, your being here right now and listening to my sniveling complaints mean the world to me. Just don't mention this to Dottie and the girls, OK? I wouldn't want them to think I'm ungrateful or anything."

"My lips are sealed. Now you have to promise me that from now on, you have to talk to me when you're feeling low, all right?"

"I promise," Kitty said, hugging Faye, wondering to herself, "Is she so gullible, or am I so convincing?" She rolled her eyes in relief and hoped it was the latter case.

Then Faye sympathetically touched her roommate's cheek and added, "Now you take your time and pull yourself together. I'll tell Dottie you're a little under the weather. She's pretty good about that as long as you don't try it too often. Take a nice long, hot bath, drink some coffee, have a nice breakfast…" Then, looking out of the little window trimmed in yellow gingham above the kitchen sink, she changed the subject. "Oh, my goodness, looks like a mean old storm coming. I better take my umbrella and get going so I can beat the rain." Another quick embrace and off she went, leaving a very smug Kitty, lying on the sofa in her red satin dress.

"Whew," she sighed. "If I had to listen to that simpering, maternal voice a minute longer, I would have screamed." Then, realizing that Faye had provided her with a free day off, she slipped off her clothes and lay naked on the couch, with her eyes shut, thinking about how she would spend the rest of her day, preparing for her evening with the mysterious Russell E. Lee. The dark clouds began to shed their steady stream of raindrops, and the still, quiet room darkened as though the curtain had fallen on a stage performance, and all the actors on stage were waiting for it to rise again before they'd come to life.

Kitty remembered how it rained the day she took her bus ride from River Bend to Baton Rouge. "It's fitting," she surmised. "Wash away the old and start anew." Although she was not very spiritual or philosophical and didn't like to be in the company of those who were, she would, for the rest of her life, view rainy days as times to make changes in her life, no matter how subtle or how monumental.

If it hadn't been for the lightning causing static on the radio, Kitty probably would have slept for hours. But her head would not allow another minute of the scratchy, irritating noise blaring across the tiny room. She reluctantly got up, turned off the radio, and shuffled into the kitchen to fix a cup of coffee. It was already cold, but she didn't feel like making a fresh pot, so she searched in the cabinet for the right size pot to warm some milk with her coffee. Standing in front of the stove she realized this was the first time in her life that she had stood in a kitchen completely naked. She liked the way it made her feel—totally free. It was an amazing feeling. She wondered if Russell E. Lee ever thought about her body. Did he wonder what she would look like standing in front of the stove naked? She giggled—not the playful giggle of an innocent girl—but rather the devilish, mischievous giggle of a woman able to envision the successful result of her charm and enchantment. She liked being naked and thinking about Russell E. Lee.

Kitty poured the simmering café au lait into a cup and broke off a piece of stale French bread from the paper bag on the counter and returned to the sofa, where she once again nestled in peace and quiet. She had to think of a plan. How would she leave the apartment at eight o'clock at night, decked out for a night in New Orleans, and not arouse Faye's suspicion? Ever since Faye broke up with her last beau, as she referred to her boyfriends, she never left the apartment on Friday nights.

As Kitty sipped her last drop of scalded coffee, lightning struck, and the loud, roaring, thunder that followed assured her that the bolt of electricity had found its target nearby. The lights in the apartment blinked until they died altogether. It was so dark outside that it appeared to be late evening rather than early morning. She remembered her mama telling her when she was a little girl that the safest place to be during a thunderstorm was in bed. She was not aware of any scientific data to support her mama's theory, but she was certain that she would feel more comfort under the bedcovers than she would anywhere else in the tiny apartment. So, she went into Faye's bedroom, which was cooler and darker than the other rooms, giving her the feeling of taking refuge in a cave.

Just before crawling under the blankets, Kitty noticed a little stack of magazines that she had not noticed the night before. Dottie always gave "her girls" past issues of the magazines she offered her clients in the shop, but these looked brand new and sparked her interest. There was a how-to magazine about sewing and two pattern magazines featuring all of the latest available fashions for the "thrifty seamstress." Kitty laughed, as she thought about her new red satin dress, and looking at the woman on the cover, she promised herself, "No homemade clothes for this girl!" And as she tossed the magazines back on the chair, a bright yellow sheet of paper fell to the floor. She picked it up and in the dim light read the black, bold print announcing: "BINGO at St. Rita's Church Hall— sponsored by the Knights of Columbus—All proceeds go to Victims of Hurricane Agnes in Lafourche Parish." Faye's daddy was in charge of the Knights of Columbus, so Faye would feel obligated to attend. "Bingo!" Kitty shouted. "Thank you, Jesus!" The storm broke shortly thereafter, and the sun shone through the windows so brightly it was as if it were saying it would never let it storm again. "There will be no more storms," Kitty felt. At least, that's how it seemed to her for the moment and for the rest of the day, for that matter.

Everything went along as planned, even better than planned, because Faye came home that evening only for as long as it took her to step into her bedroom, grab her Bingo clothes and cosmetic case, and head out the door to her mama and daddy's. She was "eatin' supper" there and would just get ready at their house, too. "In fact," she said, "don't be surprised if I don't come back tonight, 'cause I may jus' sleep at my mama's. You sure you don't wanna come? It might be just what you need to pull yo'self outta that slump you're in."

"No, no, Faye. Thanks, anyway. I wouldn't want my mood to bring down anyone else's."

"Well, I'm sure that wouldn't happen, but I understand how you feel."

"Tell the family I said 'hello.' "

"I sure will, honey." Faye gave Kitty one of those kissy, kissy hugs that flow through the Jeansonne clan at Sunday arrivals and departures. And Kitty quickly shook off the first trace of sentiment that tried to settle in that empty space in her heart—the space that had once been reserved for emotional attachments. If ever she had put up fences around that empty space, her transformation that occurred the night before had locked the gate and thrown away the key. She kindly coaxed Faye out of the door, anxious to step into her new dress, her new shoes, and her new life.

She hoped that Russell E. Lee would be just as excited about the evening. While she was dressing, she thought about how strange it was that she could be going to New Orleans with a man who didn't even know where she lived. Then, she thought about calling a cab to pick her up at Faye's and drive her to Peltier's for eight o'clock. That way she wouldn't arouse any suspicion walking down the street, alone, all dolled up in a red satin dress and three-inch heels. People could get the wrong idea, she thought. And it would be awful if someone's dog chased her or if it started raining again. All sorts of hypothetical situations popped in and out of her mind to support her decision to hire one cab driver to deliver her to another.

Everything went smoothly, and at 8:05 her hired car pulled up in front of Peltier's, right behind the biggest, black Cadillac she had ever laid her eyes on. She was not thrilled about the other car being there, because there was no room for Russell E. Lee to pull up to the curb, and she wanted to sit in her car until he arrived. The windows of the big car were tinted, so she couldn't see if there were any people inside. After a few moments, the door on the driver's side opened, and the familiar quick step and little-boy grin of Russell E. Lee soon caught her eye as he headed toward her car. A dropped jaw and wrinkled forehead greeted Russell when he opened her door, and she was rather speechless. He was wearing a short-sleeved, plaid shirt, blue jeans, and cowboy boots. "Hey girl," he said, smiling and gazing down at her in the cab. "You gonna get out and let me have a look at you?" He reached for her hand to assist her out of the car and leaned over to pay the driver, who turned out to be one of his good buddies. "Man, man, man," he exclaimed, as his buddy drove away, "you're even prettier than I expected."

"Why thank-you, Russell," she finally said, gaining composure after the initial shock. "Is this your car?"

"Why, yes, it is," he answered , very matter-of-factly, as though he didn't expect this bit of information to surprise her.

She stood, hesitantly, on the sidewalk, purposely not venturing toward the Cadillac. The thought of going to New Orleans in this car should've excited her, but something was not right. She looked at the way her date had dressed for the evening. Very casual. Nice, but very casual. "Russell, I feel a little overdressed next to you. I mean, you look real nice and all, but I'm so…so…"

"Beautiful. That's what you are. And a beautiful lady like you deserves a real special night, with a real special man. Not somebody like me, suga'. You weren't meant for a cab driver."

The tentative smile left Kitty's face, and she turned her attention to the black Cadillac and then back to Russell's smiling, green eyes. She felt a burning in her cheeks, as though her face were on fire. "What on earth are you talking about? What are you suggesting?" And though she asked the questions directly, she gave him no time to answer. "Is there another man in that car? Are you running some kind of escort service? You're some kind of pimp?"

Russell was trying to put his hands on her shaking shoulders to calm her down. He was trying to talk to her, too, but her angry questions kept coming. "You think I'm some prostitute, some whore you can lend a friend? Is that what you think? You bastard! You insulting, conniving bastard!" She turned to walk away but realized she had no place to go. The car was gone. And she didn't want to go back to Faye's apartment anyway. Not after the plans, the excitement, the anticipation. That apartment was another world, another life. She was so angry, she couldn't even cry. But the tears were there, she could feel her eyes swelling, waiting for the proper moment, waiting for her tense body to relax in order to unlock the floodgates. Her stomach ached. She wanted to vomit. Russell's dumbfounded look exasperated her even more, and when he tried again to console her, she snapped back, "Shut up! Just shut up! I never want to speak to you again. Now, leave. Just leave! Take your buddy to New Orleans without me and find some other woman for hire. Isn't that French Quarter full of them?"

"Yes. As a matter of fact, it is. But that's just my point. The senator is not looking to share his evening with one of them kinda women. He's looking for a nice respectable female companion to share a nice respectable evening in town with. Is that too much to ask for? These poor men spend all week in meeting after meeting, session after session, through all hours of the night. The man's lookin' for a little relaxin' meal at a good restaurant and maybe some good jazz at a couple a clubs."

"As if he can't find his own women!"

"Kitty, these men can't take just any woman they know on a night on the town. It'd attract all kinda attention. So I told the senator I knew a perfectly lovely lady for him to take to New Orleans. I promise you I didn't think you'd take it so wrong. I guess I shoulda realized you're not accustomed to this type of situation, being's you not real familiar with living in a city like Baton Rouge and all."

His cool, calm drawl was calming her down and cooling her off a little, but she was not quite ready to bite. "Who is this senator?" she asked. "Where is he from?"

"Senator Lamar Delacroix. He's from the Moss Point-Bayou Chouteau area."

"Well, that means nothing to me. I assume he's not married. I won't do that type of thing."

"He's separated, I think. I don't think the divorce is settled. You know these things take some time in Louisiana. We got that Napoleonic Code going on down here. That's another reason Lamar can't go skipping around town with just any local Jane. You see what I mean? These things can be complicated, suga'. And look here, I'll be driving you all night— you think I'd let anything happen to you?"

She looked at him and once again saw a baby face with kind eyes, and she remembered how she had thought about being with him, romantically, less than an hour before. And she confessed as she motioned toward the jewelry and the dress, "I thought all of this was because you were attracted to me."

"Hell, Kitty, you know I'm attracted to you. But I'm not stupid. And I'm not selfish. You'll never find happiness in my way of life or even Dottie's. You need to set yo' sights higher. And tonight's yo' first step up. You gotta know that—deep down"

She wondered if Freddie had ever felt that way about Donna but went ahead and married her anyway. Damn Freddie. He could've saved her a lot of grief if he had forced her mother to set her sights higher right from the beginning. And damn Donna. She should've been strong enough to take her steps toward her higher sights before she had a child to leave behind. "Let's go," she told Russell E. Lee. "I got myself a senator to meet."

"That's my girl."

The senator did not get out of the car to greet Kitty, which didn't seem very proper to her, but Russell E. Lee explained to her that gossip spread like wildfire through the capital city, and that a man like Senator Delacroix could lose his political career if the wrong wagging tongue got the least bit of information to talk about. She was fairly satisfied by his explanation. The good senator was handsome enough, Kitty thought. Tall. That was good, because she herself was about five feet eight inches tall and with those three-inch heels, she needed a man at least six feet tall. She sensed that his dark brown eyes were pleased with what they saw in her, too. At first, she thought he was wearing a tuxedo, but on closer inspection she determined it was a black suit—one of those custom-made suits, she decided, because even though he wasn't standing she could see that it was made for his body—his tall, well-built body. She could see that he was well-built by the way his suspenders accentuated his pectoral muscles, which would rise and fall slightly with every breath he took. "Yes," she thought, "this is a man you'd like to see the town with." Was it magnetism or charisma or perhaps simply political savvy? Whatever it was, she was glad to be sitting next to him in that big black Cadillac going to the city that care forgot.

Kitty would always remember that night as the most magical night of her life, and so often she wished it had never ended. Dinner at Antoine's, dancing at the Blue Room, drinks at the Sazerac, and a suite fit for a princess at the Roosevelt Hotel. And when the senator looked down at her with his sweet brown eyes, as their bodies lay between those fresh-smelling hotel sheets, and said, "You are one gorgeous woman, Miss Kitty Pierce," she knew she'd follow that man anywhere he'd lead her. And she did.

Kitty never saw Russell E. Lee again. She never went back to Baton Rouge that night or any other night. She stayed in that hotel suite for two weeks, while Delacroix made arrangements for her to live in a nice, quaint, rather secluded apartment in the French Quarter, which was owned by Delilah Charleville, a constituent of his from Bayou Chouteau. To her delight, he managed to land a job for her at the most chic salon in the Vieux Carre. Things were definitely looking up for the hairstylist from River Bend, Mississippi. For the first time in a very long time, Kitty didn't have to think or worry about her future. She didn't have to plan. Someone else was taking care of her. And she loved it. She spent her week working, shopping, and getting herself ready for the weekend. And only the good Lord knew where those weekends would take her. Sometimes they went to the Gulf Coast, a couple times to Las Vegas, and sometimes they just stayed at her place in the Quarter.

There were many little trips to Lamar's weekend home in Grand Isle. He liked to call it his camp. But Kitty had never been in such a spacious, luxurious home in her life. He sometimes invited a few gentleman friends for a few days' visit, and this always disappointed Kitty. On these occasions, the senator would be occupied with fishing during the day and poker at night, all the while consuming nearly toxic amounts of booze—beer while the sun was shining and Chivas Regal by the light of the moon. The male guests rarely brought women and never their wives.

Kitty didn't care for most of Lamar's friends. Except for one—Billy Charleville. Billy was the only living soul she knew who was actually from the senator's hometown of Bayou Chouteau. He and Lamar were boyhood friends. They had gone to school together, attended the same church and played high school football together. In fact, anytime someone new graced their presence, the two men would inevitably banter, "Yeah, I had to count on Lamar's slippery fingers to catch my passes." To which the senator would add, "That's right Billy Boy, and I did, too." And then, Billy would jokingly counter with, "Not all of my passes, Lamar. You used to watch the cheerleaders too much." And then the two men would laugh and wink at each other as though it were the first time they had brought up the topic. Kitty would sit back, knowing word for word what would come out of their mouths. But she enjoyed hearing stories, even tall tales about Lamar's past, especially since he rarely spoke of it in their own private conversations.

Lamar had told Kitty about his back-home buddy, Billy Charleville—how he was the class "stud" and that every guy in school both envied and admired Billy, including himself. He would often say that if he had to choose one man in the world to trust his life to, it would be "Billy C." Kitty liked him, too. He had trusting eyes. Kind eyes. And she could tell that he liked to laugh and have a good time. In fact, having a good time was his first priority in life. He had said so.

It was from Billy Charleville that Kitty found out that the senator and his wife, Felicia, were not separated as she had been told by Russell E. Lee. This occurred the weekend after Thanksgiving, when Kitty saw Billy on a hunting trip in Lake Charles. Lamar had fallen asleep just after lunch, and with all of the brandy he had been drinking to stay warm in the duck blind, it was sure to be a long, hard nap. Kitty was sitting on the front porch of the hunting camp, perusing the latest issue of a hair-do magazine, when Billy came out and sat down in the Adirondack chair next to hers and started talking as though she had just insisted that he join her.

"So how was your holiday, Kitty? Did you spend it with your family?"

"No. It was quiet. I just stayed at home and enjoyed a little time off. I'm not much for holiday hoopla and all. How about you?"

"Oh, I was with my mama, and my brother, and his family. My mama would never forgive me if I ever missed a holiday meal with them. But it was good. Always is. Good food. Good people." She was beginning to feel like she was talking to Faye and was about to make up an excuse to go back inside, when he said something to arouse her attention. "After dinner though, I went over to the club to meet some of the boys for a little drink and a little booray. While I was there, I saw Lamar and Felicia. I couldn't help but wonder how you were spending your holiday. I just want you to know that you don't have to be alone, you know. I mean, I know the score and everything. But I like you, Kitty. I like you a lot. So next time, say for Christmas, I could take you home with me. It might not be what you really want, but, hell, it'd be better than being all alone. Lamar said he wouldn't mind."

Kitty had waited Thanksgiving Day—all morning—all afternoon—all evening—until she fell asleep waiting that night. Waiting for the phone call from Lamar, telling her he was on his way to pick her up. But the phone never rang one time that day. He had told her that he had the flu. He told her he was in bed, medicated, sleeping away his illness. He was ever-so-sorry and would the one-carat diamond earrings make up for her disappointment? "Of course," she assured him, as she admired the gorgeous, sparkling gems and thought how lucky she was to have found such a man. And she just had to ask, "Are you feeling better now, baby? I'm so sorry I was thinking such bad thoughts about you while you were so sick."

Now, as Billy Charleville spoke, Kitty tugged on one of the one-carat diamond earrings and wondered how many other lies she had been told during her romantic involvement with Senator Delacroix. Her stare moved from the ground to Billy's inquiring eyes, and she was brought back to their interesting conversation. "Christmas? Oh, Billy, that is such a sweet offer, but I do have plans for Christmas. I'll most likely go back to Jackson for Christmas, to be with my aunt."

But Kitty was not going back to Jackson at all. Kitty was making other holiday plans. Plans that started to unfold that very afternoon when the senator woke up and found her lovely, willing body next to his. By Christmas, Kitty knew, without the official diagnosis from her doctor, that she was carrying the senator's child. She saw very little of Lamar during the month of December. He told her that he was busy wrapping things up in Baton Rouge before the holiday break. But she knew that he was really busy going to holiday parties with Felicia, because she had taken up Billy's offer of companionship during her lonely hours. Billy was under the impression that he was doing a favor for Lamar while enjoying the company of his good friend's lady. During Billy's visits, Kitty was able to ask questions that she was always hesitant to ask Lamar.

Billy told Kitty all about Felicia Galvez, the woman Lamar had married just after he graduated from law school. She was from an old, aristocratic Baton Rouge family, with roots that went back to the time when Louisiana was a Spanish colony. She was a very proud woman, who was never too shy to inform anyone of her membership in the Daughters of the American Revolution, the Daughters of the Confederacy, the Junior League, and so on. She complained to Lamar constantly about living in Bayou Chouteau, even though she loved her social position amongst the ladies on the bayou. She didn't really like to travel, at least not too far from home, because at home she was important. Everyone noticed, recognized, and respected her. But out of town, she was a nobody. And if she felt that she was important in Baton Rouge, she could feel that she was of monumental importance in Bayou Chouteau and Moss Point. Billy knew from his close friendship with Lamar that Felicia's biggest heartbreak was that she was unable, thus far in her marriage, to have a child. She knew how much Lamar wanted a son. Kitty listened to these words, masking her secret jubilation with a look of empathetic concern for the other woman in Lamar's life. And all the while her heart was filled with anticipation for the day, she could break her news to the senator.

That day finally came—two days after the loneliest Christmas Kitty had ever spent in her life. Lamar came bearing gifts, of course—a diamond pendant and bracelet to match her Thanksgiving earrings. And he came bearing excuses for why she didn't see him or hear from him on Christmas Day.

"Let me guess," she said sarcastically. "You had pneumonia and were entirely too weak to pick up your phone and dial my number."

Her remark caught him by surprise, but his immediate expectation of an ugly, angry discussion was soon alleviated by her massaging hands on his shoulders and the back of his neck. He closed his eyes and sat in perfect silence for a few moments, until the fingers on his shoulders moved ever-so-gently down his arms, sending a tantalizing tingle down his spine. "Mmm, Kit, you sure know how to make me relax. I think this is the only place in the world where I feel no pressure, only pleasure."

"Is that right, Senator?" she asked flirtatiously.

"Mmm hmmm," he replied, as though he were being lulled to sleep, but instead he reached for her and pulled her body close to his.

241

As he started to unzip her black velvet dress, she said in the voice of a whining little girl pleading with her daddy, "Aren't you going to let me give you your present now?"

"Sure, baby, if that's what you want to do. I just didn't see a gift anywhere, and, hell, you don't have to be buying me anything. I want you to spend your money on yourself. The more you pamper yourself, the prettier you look for me." They both giggled, his eager hands wanting badly to get back to work on that zipper.

"Well, you don't have to worry about me spending too much money on you, because this is what you might call a homemade gift."

"Is that right? I guess I never thought of you as being one of them arts and crafts kind."

"I'm not. I'm all thumbs with that sort of stuff. But I guess you might say I had a little help on this project."

"Is that right? Well, now you've got my suspicions rising, so, bring it on out, sugar."

"OK, OK. Now, close your eyes." She passed her fingers over his eyes. "Shut tight, now."

"Aw right, aw right, come on now."

She finished unzipping her dress and let the black velvet fall to the floor around her ankles. "Keep your eyes shut now."

"Kitty, what in the world…" She took his soft, white hands with their perfectly manicured fingers and placed them on her stomach just below her waist. He opened his eyes at the touch of her soft, silky skin and saw her standing before him, in her bra and bikini underpants, her eyes filled with tears. He waited for her to speak, to give him some other clue as to what he should say or do.

"My gift to you, Lamar, is your child. I'm going to have your baby." He removed his hands from her body at once, looking at his palms as though he expected to see the impression of the baby. She could see that he was stunned, but she expected that reaction initially, and gave him a few minutes for the news to soak in. He sat down on the sofa, leaned forward, with his elbows on his knees and his face in his hands. She sat down next to him and put an arm around him. But he pulled away from her touch.

He stood up and glared at her. "How could you let this happen? How could you possibly let this happen?" He started pacing back and forth, passing his hands across his cheeks and mouth as though he were wiping dirt off of his face.

Kitty quickly got up and slipped on the black velvet dress, suddenly feeling ashamed of the naked body this man had seen and touched so many times before. But he was definitely seeing her in a different light now. She could see it in his eyes. "Lamar, I thought you'd be happy for us. I know your wife can't…"

"Leave my wife out of this. I have never discussed my wife or my marriage with you, and I don't intend to now."

"Oh, I see. The sacred marriage, right? The good little protected woman back home. Uh-huh. Well then, what part am I playing in this life of yours, Lamar? At this point, I think you should tell me if there is any future for me and you and now our baby."

Delacroix broke out in a roaring laughter, a sarcastic, uncontrollable laughter. And then he put a hand on his chest, as though his laughter were causing pain, and it was. But it was Kitty who ached, through and through every fiber of her very being. But the real pain commenced when he stopped laughing and started speaking.

"Did I ever give you any reason to believe I would leave my wife for you? Did I ever complain about my wife to you? Kitty, I love my wife."

"You love your wife? Fifteen minutes ago, you were trying to undress me for sexual pleasure, and you tell me that you love your wife!"

"I didn't say that my wife excites me sexually, the way that you do. I'd be lying if I said that. But sex is only one part of a marriage, Kitty. My wife and I got married when we were kids outta college. Started my practice with her by my side. Took my oath as a judge with her by my side. And then as a senator. And through all the campaigning, nights and weeks that she's home alone. And she never complains. Her whole adult life has been about doing her part to help me succeed, to reach my goals. About being there when I need her. And I love her for that. I would never leave her for the sake of exciting sex."

"I hope you're not expecting me to respect you for this touching little tribute to your lovely little wife. Because I've done a little research of my own, and I happen to know that she supplies a little more than moral support to your political endeavors. Her family is loaded and provides most of your financial support as well, right Senator?"

"Look, I don't have to justify my feelings for my wife to you or anybody else. The point is, she needs me now, and I will be there for her just as she's been for me."

"What are you talking about? Is she ill?"

"It just so happens, Kitty, that you are not the only woman carrying my child. Felicia is pregnant. I've known since Thanksgiving. I've wanted to end things with you, but I wanted to wait until after the holidays. That's why I haven't been around so much lately." Silence filled the space between their two bodies, and then he spoke again, in a gentler tone. "So, what are we going to do about this situation?" He pointed his finger and nodded his head in the direction of her stomach.

"This situation? Is that what you think this baby is? A situation? I'll tell you what I'm going to do with this situation. I'm going to have this child. And I am going to be a mother to this child. And now I'll tell you what you're going to do about this situation. You're going to support this child. And you're going to give this child every advantage and opportunity that you're going to give Felicia's child. 'Cause if you don't, you'll never have to take another oath for political office again, with or without your devoted lady by your side."

"And exactly how am I supposed to do that?"

"You'll be hearing from me, Senator. Now get your self-righteous ass out of here."

Four days later, Kitty's new plan was in action. Billy Charleville was taking her out on New Year's Eve. She told him it was over between her and Lamar. She was tired of spending holidays alone, playing second fiddle to a wife he'd never leave. She told Billy that she should've come to her senses long ago. And then a few drinks later, she told Billy that she had always been attracted to him but never wanted to cause trouble between the two good friends. And when they kissed at midnight, she told Billy that she had wanted him to kiss her for so long, and that the new year would bring a bright new future for both of them. And a few hours later, back in her apartment, Kitty set her trap. A month later, she told Billy that she was pregnant with his child. Two weeks later, they were married, and she was living in Bayou Chouteau, a half a mile down the road from Lamar and Felicia Delacroix.

Marshall Lamar Delacroix was born that summer on July 12. And exactly one month later Jacqueline Elizabeth Charleville entered the world, slightly prematurely, according to her mother. Every month thereafter Kitty received a check from Jackson, Mississippi, which she claimed was being sent by her aunt, who had been left in control of the enormous inheritance she was entitled to after the untimely deaths of her wealthy parents, who were killed in a summer boating accident when she was just a child. She boastfully explained to everyone in Bayou Chouteau that her father had made his fortune in real estate. Not just in Mississippi, of course, but all over the world. She was only nine when they died and was sent to live with her mother's sister, who had three children of her own. She swore that her aunt had spent half of the inheritance on those three brat cousins of hers, and that it really didn't bother her until she had a child of her own. The only thing she could do, she insisted, was to threaten her aunt that she would sue for the entire amount of money that was rightfully hers, and her aunt wisely agreed to send monthly payments in order to keep the family at peace. No one in Kitty's circle of attentive listeners ever suspected that the monthly check really came from an account in a small, family-owned bank in Baton Rouge, sent to Aunt Dee in River Bend, and then mailed to Kitty. It was, after all, Kitty's solution to handling the "situation."

Kitty was less than convincing, however, in playing her role as Billy Charleville's loving wife. It was a role for which she had very little preparation, much less desire. She was well aware that most of the women in Bayou Chouteau would give anything to be married to her husband. Handsome, fun-loving, and fairly well-to-do according to Bayou Chouteau standards. Why, the Charlevilles practically owned the bayou town, and what they didn't own, they had their hands in. They were founding members of the country club at The Manors, founding members and leading contributors of St. Michael's Catholic Church and School, and they were the economic heartbeat of the entire community, since they owned the only seafood market and general store on the bayou. So, marrying a Charleville of Bayou Chouteau could've given Kitty that sense of stability and security that she longed for as a child. But it didn't, because Kitty had already pictured herself entering the grand ballroom of an elegant hotel on the arm of her senator. Now, nothing else would ever add up. Nothing and nobody. And the fact that Billy took her little game of charades so seriously only made her more bitter and more cynical. For years, she watched him dote over the child who wasn't his and parade her around like his very own princess, all the while throwing little scraps of attention and affection her way. Each day of her life brought more and more anger.

In the beginning, Kitty found pleasure in the control she covertly wielded in the senator's political and domestic life. But it was of small significance when she realized that it came to her at the price of the short-lived freedom she had discovered and enjoyed in her own life just months before. There was no time when she felt this loss more than when she had to spend time with the whole Charleville family, whether it was for a holiday, a family member's birthday, or just ordinary Sunday dinners in that old kitchen of Delilah Charleville. It drove her crazy.

"I will never understand why your mother found it so hard to accept me, Billy, when she treated your white-trash sister-in-law like some princess that graced the family with her presence." It was a Monday morning when she started nagging Billy with this subject that never failed to arise several times a week, especially on days following a Charleville family gathering. The day before was Easter Sunday, and as usual, it was celebrated in style—Bayou Chouteau style, that is. A close family friend had volunteered to captain one of the family fishing boats out into the lake. Joseph and Billy brought all of the necessities for a barbecue on the water. Peggy Anne had baked a beautiful Black Forest cake, which everyone knew had been Delilah Charleville's traditional contribution to the community celebration in the past. And Jacqui and Elise were raring and ready to jump in the water the minute the boat arrived at its destination.

When the boat approached the girls' favorite swimming spot, they noticed at least ten other boats anchored in a circle. And their boat was anchored right in the center of them all. The whole fleet was out to celebrate. And celebrate they did! Loud country music filled the air, as everyone prepared their grills and spread boiled seafood over tables covered with newspaper. Kids and grown-ups alike were swinging out over the lake on the thick ropes tied to the boats' tall masts. Then they'd drop into the water that provided the livelihoods for all who were present. It turned out to be a perfect day for everyone. Everyone, except Kitty, that is. Everything that happened that day seemed to remind her that she didn't belong. And she had reached a point where hiding her feelings became impossible.

So, Billy wasn't surprised the next day when his wife confronted him with her old reliable, resentful attacks. He had heard the whining so many times that he didn't bother to answer her with comforting, reassuring comments. So, instead, the only reply she heard was the pop-top on his third can of beer for that afternoon.

"You know, I do believe I married an alcoholic. Do you realize it's only two thirty in the afternoon, and God knows how many empty cans of beer you've thrown into that garbage can already?"

"Do you realize it's only two thirty in the afternoon, and I'm already tired of hearing your same old complaints, Kitty. Get over it, would you?" And he walked up to her and put his hands on her waist. "Come on baby, there's a little squall brewing outside, Jacqui's at school, whataya say we make the most of this time alone, huh? It's been a long time since we've had a little time to ourselves, huh?"

It was over that day. The whole charade was over. Why this morning, this moment, she didn't know. She just knew that it was over. Billy Charleville repulsed her—his strong beer breath, his hands on her waist, the thought of pretending one more time in bed that he was the love of her life, it all repulsed her. She pushed him away.

"Get your hands off of me, you fool. All these years, that's all you've been is a fool."

"What the hell's wrong with you? What'd I say?"

"Nothing. You never said nothing. You never do. You just walk around here and Bayou Chouteau like you have it all. Like you and your family have it all. Your good looks, your money, and your precious little girl. Your spoiled rotten, precious little girl. Well, guess what, honey. I could burst your little bubble in a second. I could make your whole life a sham." Billy started laughing, sipping his beer and laughing, which made her mad. "What have you got to laugh about?"

"Nothing, Kitty. Just calm down before you get all heated up and say something you really don't mean to say, that's all."

"Oh, I mean to say something, all right. I just wish your mama would be living and standing right here to listen to what I have to say. That's what I wish. And I wish your big brother and his perfect little wife could be here, too, so they could listen along with her. That's what I wish."

Billy picked up the phone and teased her, "Come on, Miss Kitty, call them up. I'll dial the number for you. Come on. What would you like to tell Joseph and Peggy Anne, huh? That Jacqui ain't their niece? That Jacqui ain't really my daughter."

Kitty's face paled in an instant. She dropped into the chair behind her. Her mouth was parched. These were her lies. He was supposed to be the one shocked and hurt. And yet, she was. She couldn't speak. In fact, she could hardly swallow. So, Billy continued in his same boyish manner. "You must've really thought I was stupid, Kitty. The fact is, I did love you. I knew you were carrying Lamar's baby when you told me you were pregnant, but I loved you. And call me crazy, but I still do. And I love my little girl. She will always be my little girl. No matter what you say, Kitty. She's mine."

"How on earth did you know?" she managed to ask. A sly smile crossed his face.

"'Cause I've known since I was a boy that I was sterile."

"What?" she shrieked.

"That's right, babe. Shootin' blanks!"

"You lying son of a bitch! Don't you think you should've told me something like that? Don't you think I had a right to know?"

"Well, hell, Kitty, I might've owed this bit of info to some other woman, but I figured you weren't exactly being straight with me. You know what I mean, baby? Now. Our secrets are out on the table. Let's try to go on from here and make the best of our lives. None of us is perfect. So, what. I love you. That should matter a little, huh, Kitty Cat?"

"What matters is that all of this—all of this has been a lie. Lie upon lie upon lie. And now I don't know where the lies end and the truth begins. And you just tell me who else knows about our little secret. And don't tell me that your sweet, simpleton of a sister-in-law has been in on this."

"Well, honey, my whole family knows, including Peggy Anne. But I promise you, they'd never do or say anything to spoil our lives, especially for Jacqui's sake."

"Stop calling her Jacqui. Her name is Jacqueline. And if you think for one minute that a principled woman such as myself could go on one more minute playing out this little drama in front of the pretentious, judgmental clan you call our family, then you have no understanding of what kind of person I am."

Billy squeezed his empty beer can and tossed it toward the overflowing garbage can, where it bounced off and fell to the floor. "Principled woman, huh? Well now, I have to admit Kitty, I have admired certain characteristics of yours, but these principles you're talking about—why don't you enlighten me—exactly what principles do you live by?"

"As if you'd ever understand! You're just like your backwoods brood."

Billy had had enough of her remarks about his family, and the smile disappeared from his face. "Exactly what is it that you're so angry about, Kitty? The fact that I didn't tell you that I knew your secret all along? Or is it merely that you were actually proud of your little scheme, proud of the fact that you could outsmart the bayou boy, while you blackmailed your wealthy senator? Is all this rage over me or your pride?"

"Get out of here, Billy Charleville. Just get out of here. I never want to lay my eyes on the sight of you again!" She started throwing things at him. Anything and everything. And he just laughed as he dodged her flying weapons. "Get out of here, and never come back!"

"Oh, I'm leavin' all right. For now. But I'll be back. I promise you that. If not for you, for my baby girl." And just to add a little fuel to the fire, he laughed and added, "Don't forget, my mama left me this house! It's all mine, darlin'!" He packed a few of his belongings in his biking bag while she continued yelling in a rage from the kitchen. Then he left on his motorcycle and headed for St. Michael's School, where he knew that he'd find his daughter seated outside the school with the other children waiting to board the bus for their trip back home.

It started raining, just as he reached Jacqui amongst the screaming crowd of children, eager to get home after sitting quietly in their classrooms all day. She was so happy to see Billy, and thought, perhaps, that this would be one of those special days when Billy would pull out the kid-sized helmet, place it on her head, prop her up on the big, black-leather seat, and ride her right out of the school parking lot. She was the envy of every St. Michael's student on those special days. Her daddy knew that, and that's why he did it. He loved making his little girl feel special.

But this was not a special day. He had gone to St. Michael's to tell Jacqui that he had to go away for a few days. He had a business meeting somewhere in another city. But he'd be sure to buy her something real special while he was there. Jacqui cried but knew she had to get on the bus and go home, in the same monotonous way that everyone else did. The rain began to come down harder as the bus moved slowly down the narrow, winding bayou road. Elise and Jacqui were sitting together in one of the front seats, and they kept their eyes on Billy who happened to be right in front of the bus.

Neither child could ever remember the sequence of the events that changed their world that day. Everything happened so quickly. Billy's motorcycle went out of control when he hit a pothole filled with rainwater. The motorcycle went down and slid, while Billy held on, trying to gain control. Mr. Martin, the bus driver, slammed on the brakes of the old school bus, and the girls ears were deafened by the combination of the screeching tires and the screaming voices of the frightened bus driver and children. Then there was the loud bang, which would echo in their ears, years later.

Mr. Martin ran out in the rain, crying and screaming for help. He never would drive the bus again, not because he had his license taken away or because he had to serve any time for reckless driving. It was because every time that man got behind the wheel of any vehicle, he remembered the day he killed Billy Charleville.

AFTERMATH

It was a beautiful morning to drive back home, Elise thought. God had answered her prayers once again, and for that she was grateful. Their lives had been spared. Her home and her parents' home had been spared. Less than two days ago, an outcome such as this would have seemed nothing short of miraculous. The car should have been filled with laughter, excitement, and sheer jubilation. But it wasn't. It simply couldn't be. Because something more valuable than a house had been destroyed, and unlike a house, it could never be put back together again. It could not be fixed or repaired by a flood insurance settlement or rebuilt with bigger and better materials. It was destroyed, crushed—gone forever.

Elise begged Brad to let her drive home, hoping that the concentration she'd need for the drive would prevent her from thinking about the events of the day before. He didn't argue, and she knew why. He and Peggy Anne had been so worried about her they had taken turns sitting up with her during the night. Her mom even gave her one of her "nerve pills" to help her settle down. And although she was feeling a little better this morning, she still couldn't escape the harsh realities and memories of her encounter with Kitty, just twenty-four hours ago. Her mind kept playing the drama over and over.

"He's her brother," Kitty had said, just as matter-of-factly as if she were telling her that he didn't like broccoli.

"Wha…What are you telling me?"

"I'm telling you that Jacqueline and Marsh have the same father. Jacqueline is really a Delacroix."

Elise felt the room spin, and her stomach turned upside down. She couldn't speak. She put her hand over her mouth and ran into the bathroom. Bent over the toilet, her body wretched and trembled as she tried to vomit, tried to rid her body of the sick, sick feeling that consumed it. Finally, her attempt was reduced to an uncontrollable, mournful sobbing. Her mother knelt next to her on the cold bathroom floor and gently rubbed her back, as she did when Elise was a child. Only this time, she wasn't consoling a child, whose pain ran only as deep as the scrape on her skinned knee. This time she was consoling a grown woman, whose pain now reached down into the depths of her heart. She knew that it was a pain that would never go away, because the wound would never heal.

"Aw, come on now. There's no sense in getting yourself in a tizzy, Elise. That won't help anybody, especially Jacqueline." Elise and Peggy Anne looked up to see Kitty, standing casually in the doorway. Perhaps it was the casual tone, or maybe it was the fact that her aunt was trying to console her, albeit in a lame fashion; but more than likely, it only took looking into her aunt's lying eyes to turn all of the pain into anger: a very passionate anger.

"You knew this all along? You knew this and never said anything to Jacqui? Why? How could you watch her fall helplessly into a pit and not help her out of it? All these years, you've just watched her."

"I did it for her own good." It was Kitty's simple statement of self-exoneration, but it didn't satisfy her niece, who pulled away from her mother's grasp, stood up, and walked the short distance that allowed her to stand face-to-face with her aunt.

"You did it for your own good, you selfish bitch!" And along with these words, Elise delivered a sharp slap across Kitty's face.

"Elise!" She heard her mother's shaky voice attempt to bring her to her senses, and she knew that she was probably struggling to get to her feet in order to come to her rescue. But this time she would not be stopped by her mother's compromising efforts to protect family harmony.

"How dare you slap me! I am still your aunt, and you will show me respect!"

"Get out of my way. I am going to pack our things and get my family out of this place. I can't bear to look at you."

"Oh really. Well, consider this. I am still Jacqueline's mother. I carried her, fed her, clothed her, and gave her a decent home her whole life. I had the right to choose whether to tell her or not."

"Yes, you are Jacqui's mother. The mother who watched her play with Marsh as a child, then date him, fall in love with him, plan a future with him. And the abortion—so that was the real reason. Oh my God, it's all making sense. It's all making disgusting sense. And you think you had the right? You think being her mother gave you the right to destroy her life? Is that what being a mother means to you? Obviously, when you had your little fling with lamar Delacroix, it was your choice. When you had his baby, it was your choice. And when it came to telling your daughter the truth, again, it was your choice. Jacqui's life has been under your control for thirty-five years. And just look at the wonderful life you've created for her!"

"Would you stop being so self-righteous. The perfect little mother, huh? Oh, it's easy when they're young, like yours. But we'll just see if you're so perfect when they're grown." Elise totally ignored her aunt's warning and spoke as though she had never been interrupted.

"When she finds out the truth, and she will someday, even if Marsh doesn't confess—your lies will have taken away the two most important men in her life. She worshipped Uncle Billy, and she'll have to deal with the fact that he wasn't even her father. And after he died, she worshipped Marsh, and…" she swallowed hard to make the lump in her throat go away, but it didn't, especially when it dawned on her that she and Jacqui, as close as they were, had never been related, at all. In the back of her mind, LaLa's words came to light, "Look out for Jacqui, Elise. She's not like you and me. More like her mama." Elise turned to Peggy Anne, her body racked with disgust and pain, and although she felt as though she couldn't take a step forward without passing out, she faintly addressed Peggy Anne, "Mama, can you help me get everything packed up. I have to leave. If I stay here any longer, I'm going to be sick."

"Don't bother packing, Pollyanna, I'm leaving," Kitty said, in an amazingly unaffected manner. "I was never a part of this family, and I curse the day I ever thought I could be." Kitty left without any of her belongings. She walked out to the car with nothing over her head to protect her from the rain that Georgette's outer feeder bands were dropping over Casa Victoria. She got into Jacqui's BMW, without looking back to acknowledge the two women on the screened-in porch. With the windshield wipers set at high speed, she sped away, probably wondering where that rainy day would take her.

Once Kitty was out of her sight, Elise was able to catch her breath and stop trembling, calming down to a moderate level of aftershock. Peggy Anne found some chamomile tea in the kitchen cupboard, probably left behind by one of Adam's sweeties, because she could hardly imagine Adam sipping tea during one of his outrageous weekends. Elise was not concerned with its source of origin, though, because she seemed to feel a little stronger with each sip. She was amazed at how composed her mother was in dealing with the revolting revelation, and then it dawned on her that her mother had known the truth all along. She was a witness to the lies and destruction of Jacqui's world.

"Mama, did you know that Jacqui and Marsh were siblings?" She wanted so badly for her mother to answer 'no, of course not,' but she knew that that was not the case.

"We knew. We all knew—me, your daddy, and your grandmother. That's what made it so hard."

"How did you find out? When did you find out?"

"Well, as you know, I went to school with your Uncle Billy. And he and I became real good friends during out last couple of years at St. Michael's. I know you heard all about that—I worked for Delilah, at the general store and all. Billy and I were together a lot back then, and we really helped each other out in a lot of ways. In the process, we became real close to each other, real special. Nothing romantic, just special, in a way that I could never describe to myself, much less anybody else. Billy and I could talk for hours on end in that old store—about everything from my problems at home to his problems on the football field. Before I really got to know Billy, I couldn't imagine that he would ever have problems. Heck, he led a charmed life for a boy on the bayou. But Billy wrestled with his own demons, and one by one, I got to know each of them. I know he never talked about those things with his friends, because Billy liked his image at school. He was what you kids call the Big Man on Campus. But those people only saw the shell of Billy Charleville. They knew him on the surface. I knew the part of Billy that stayed within that shell, the part that never ventured out. And it's funny, because that's the part of Billy that I grew to love. Respectfully—you know how I mean. And Elise, one of those demons that your uncle struggled most with was the fact that he would never be able to have children of his own. He was sterile. It seems that he had had a bad, bad case of the measles when he was a child—about seven years old, if I remember correctly. Delilah never ever talked about it. They say she nearly lost her mind, because he was around the same age as her baby brother who died in her arms when she was just fifteen years old. But your daddy remembered it well. He said she just sat next to Billy's bed for two days while the fever raged in his small body. Wouldn't even talk to anybody, he said. That's why he never complained about the way Delilah babied Billy so. He said that he knew that Billy would always hold a special part of his mother's heart because of his scrape with death. Anyway, he pulled through, thank the good Lord, but the doctor told Delilah that when boys hold on to high fevers for a long time, the way that Billy did, they become sterile. And Billy trusted me enough to tell me about his predicament, and I promised I would never tell a soul, and

I never did until today. And I'm trusting you now to respect his trust in me, Elise.

"Mama, you know I will."

"You have to promise me that you won't tell a soul what I've told you today."

"Mama, I promise I won't say a word. But tell me, did Aunt Kitty know this?"

"I don't know. And as far as I'm concerned, I don't need to know."

"Jacqui thinks that she's an only child because her parents didn't love each other enough to have any more children. She thinks her mama trapped her dad into marrying her because she was carrying an illegitimate Charleville."

"Well, there's no doubt that she trapped him. Why, I'll never forget that Sunday night when we gathered in the kitchen at Delilah's house. You know how we always ate supper at your grandmother's. You were about four years old then, and I remember you sitting at the counter coloring in one of those big thick coloring books you used to love. We had finished eating supper, and Delilah was about to bring out her angel-food cake and coffee, when Billy goes into the store and comes back with a bottle of chilled champagne. 'What on earth is that for, Billy?' I can still here your grandmother's surprised expression. 'It's for a little celebration, Mama. I wanted you and Joseph and Peggy Anne to be the first to know.' And then he proceeded to tell us he was going to marry Kitty Pierce. And that they were going to have a baby. Just like that. Like none of us knew about his being sterile and all. Well, I thought I was going to suffocate, holding in my feelings, and your daddy just sat there in shock. All's he could say was, 'What did you say? You're gonna do what?' But Delilah, bless her soul, just let loose on him. I swear, I don't think I ever saw your grandmother so upset. I thought she was going to have a stroke that night. It got so bad your daddy made me take you home, 'cause you started crying for fear in all of the commotion. I'm surprised you don't remember that night, with that good memory of yours."

She shook her head, while trying to dig deep in her mind for a glimpse of that evening, but surprisingly, she couldn't remember a thing. "He obviously ignored any advice he may have heard from his mother and brother that evening."

"Sure did. I told your daddy that night that Billy was only doing it for the baby. He knew he couldn't have one of his own, and if this woman thought she was carrying his child, well, that would be the next best thing to having his own. He told me once that he could never marry a girl like me, because he couldn't live with himself if he couldn't make babies for the woman he loved. And oh, how he loved children. I think being the baby in his own family made him want children even more, because he never had the opportunity to live with little ones in his own home."

"Is that why you and Daddy chose Uncle Billy to be my godfather?"

"Shoot, we didn't have a choice. Your Uncle Billy volunteered! And I don't have to tell you how much he loved you." She started laughing and shaking her head. "I know I told you about the party he threw at the hospital the night you were born. Those doctors and nurses in that hospital didn't know what to do when he walked in that waiting room with his ice chest filled with beer and started passing them out to all of the people sitting there waiting for news of their own newborn babies. They tried to stop him, but you know Billy. Charmed his way out of every situation. Convinced everybody in charge that there was no harm in celebrating at a time like that. Everybody who had received one of his beers agreed, and in the end those in charge just gave in to him."

"I can just see him doing that," Elise said, happy to be thinking about a cheerful event in her family history once again. "He was one of a kind, wasn't he Mama?"

"He sure was. Your daddy and I used to get the biggest kick out of Billy. Course, your daddy never let him know that he found him amusing. He could drive your daddy crazy with his shenanigans. How he used to strut around—the Casanova of Bayou Chouteau. Delilah Charleville's playboy son. Everybody talked about him, but everybody loved him. But when he married Kitty, Billy's life and luck started to change. She was so different from any of the Bayou Chouteau women we thought he might end up with. I can't explain it, but she just never fit in."

Elise and her passengers were stopped in traffic on the I-10 crossing at the Bonne Carre Spillway. It seemed that everyone in the city had chosen this morning to return home. She didn't mind, though. Everyone was napping in the car, except her daddy, who was surprisingly awake in the passenger seat. He had not spoken one word about the debacle that his brother had helped to create, and Elise didn't want to force him to talk about it, either.

"Daddy, why haven't you ever told me that my lasagna gives you heartburn?"

"What are you talking about? I love your lasagna."

"It's all right, Daddy, you can tell me. Mama told me the other night, before we left home."

He chuckled, "She told you that, did she?"

"Yes, she did. And I wish you had told me yourself, because I would never want to give you anything to make you sick."

"I will never understand that woman," he sighed. "She's the one who can't eat your lasagna. Every time she eats it, she stays up all night with diarrhea. It's not just your lasagna, though, Lissy, it's all Italian food."

"Well, Daddy, why on earth didn't she tell me the truth?" his exasperated daughter asked.

"Just didn't want to hurt your feelings, I guess."

Elise didn't bother to respond. She just shook her head in disbelief. There would always be a storm in her life, she thought. There would be storms from which she could escape, and others that would wreak total havoc in her life. But there would always be a storm. After all, the climate and conditions for a storm were always present in the atmosphere.

CPSIA information can be obtained
at www.ICGtesting.com
Printed in the USA
BVHW040831080223
658081BV00001B/3